The Shattered Drum

A FIVE DIRECTIONS PRESS BOOK

The Shattered Drum

A NOVEL

C. P. LESLEY

LEGENDS OF THE FIVE DIRECTIONS 5: CENTER

ISBN-13 978-1947044142
ISBN-10 1947044141

Published in the United States of America.

A Five Directions Press book

Cover photographs: Horsemen riding at sunset © dtopal/Shutterstock; yew trees via Pixabay (no attribution required). Drum on title page © Stepan Popov/Photos.com. Map adapted from "Map of the Volga River System," © Karl Musser (reused under Creative Commons Attribution-Share Alike 2.5 Generic license).

Book and cover design by Five Directions Press
Five Directions Press logo designed by Colleen Kelley

FIVE DIRECTIONS PRESS

CONTENTS

MORE BY C. P. LESLEY

The Not Exactly Scarlet Pimpernel

Legends of the Five Directions
The Golden Lynx (1: West)
The Winged Horse (2: East)
The Swan Princess (3: North)
The Vermilion Bird (4: South)
The Shattered Drum (5: Center)

Tarkei Chronicles
Desert Flower
Kingdom of the Shades

Cast of Characters

(in alphabetical order by first name)

FICTIONAL CHARACTERS

Alexei Bulatovich: Formerly Tulpar Sultan; Bulat's eldest son, cast out at the age of sixteen by his father, reinstated after his marriage to Maria; father of Timur and Alexander. (In Tatar usage, sultan means "son of a khan," not "supreme ruler," as among the Ottomans; the Russian equivalent is tsarevich.)

Anna Semyonovna Kolycheva: daughter of Solomonida; Lyuba Koshkina's best friend.

Azamat Bey: The young leader of the horde located closest to Ogodai's summer grazing lands, who allies with Ogodai against their joint enemy Sheikh-Mamai.

Bulat Khan: Tatar khan in Russian service; fictional older half-brother of the historical Shah-Ali Khan, ruler of the semi-independent Russian principality of Kasimov; father of Alexei, Nasan, and Ogodai; husband of Sumbeka.

Daniil Nikolaevich Kolychev: Bulat's son-in-law, a Russian nobleman; husband of Nasan; sworn brother of Ogodai.

Firuza: Ogodai's wife and Nasan's sister-in-law; mother of the twins Irek and Altan-Alia; twin sister to Jahangir Bey.

Fyodor Mikhailovich Koshkin: Maria's father; an enemy of the Kolychev clan since his plans for an alliance with them failed to yield the desired results.

Grusha: Nursemaid to Firuza's children, formerly a slave of the Kolychev household.

Guzel: Mother of Timur and former lover of Alexei, furious with him because of his abandonment of her and her son several years before; member of Ogodai's horde.

Ilya Petrovich Shuisky: Junior member of a princely clan; fictional nephew of the historical Prince Vasily Shuisky.

Jahangir Bey: Twin brother to Firuza; leader of the Mangyt tribe and Ogodai's righthand man.

Father Job: The Kolychevs' chaplain. Married, like all Orthodox priests (except monastic priests), and father of a large family.

Juliana (Roxelana): Estranged wife of Fyodor Koshkin and Alexei's former concubine.

Kazbek Argyn Bey: Leader of the Argyn tribe, one of the four lineages that traditionally ruled as khan's advisers in the Tatar lands.

Lyuba Fyodorovna Koshkina: Maria's seven-year-old sister.

Malik Shirin Bey: Leader of the Shirin tribe, the senior of the four lineages that traditionally ruled as khan's advisers in the Tatar lands; sworn brother of Alexei.

Maria Fyodorovna Koshkina: Widow of Daniil's older brother, Boris Kolychev; wife to Alexei Bulatovich and sister-in-law to Nasan; mother of Alexander. Her marriage to Alexei gives her the title of tsarevna (khan's daughter or daughter-in-law). In addition to Lyuba and Mikhail, who appear in this novel, Maria has a married sister, Varvara, and three brothers—Foma, Timofei, and David, all of whom currently live with Varvara.

Mikhail Fyodorovich Koshkin: The eldest of Maria's four brothers.

Nadezhda Shuiskaya: Wife of Prince Ilya Shuisky.

Nasan (Irina Bulatovna) Kolycheva: Daughter of Bulat Khan, sister of Ogodai and Alexei, and wife of Daniil Kolychev; mother of Boris Daniilovich (Borya to the family); once known as the Golden Lynx, a legendary hero who aided the poor.

Natalya Vasilyevna Kolycheva: Daniil's mother and Nasan's mother-in-law; died October 1537, before this story begins.

Nikolai Borisovich Kolychev: Daniil's father and Nasan's father-in-law; a high-ranking Russian nobleman (boyar).

Ogodai Khan: Son of Bulat, older brother of Nasan, half-brother of Alexei, sworn brother of Daniil; married to Firuza and leader of her deceased father's horde; father of Firuza's twins, Irek and Altan-Alia.

Rafik Argyn: Son of Kazbek, Ogodai's good friend, and next in line to succeed his father as leader of the Argyn family/tribe.

Ruslan: Alexei's close friend and ally; another sultan from Crimea.

Solomonida Sheremeteva: Daughter of the Kolychevs' next-door neighbor and related to them through her marriage, now ended, to Daniil's cousin Semyon; mother of Anna, Lyuba's best friend.

Father Spiridon: Fyodor Koshkin's chaplain.

Sumbeka: Bulat's chief wife, mother of Nasan and Ogodai, stepmother who raised Alexei from the time of his mother's death until the conflict that alienated him from Bulat.

Timur: Alexei's son by a previous nonmarital relationship with Guzel.

Wali: Leader of a group of merchants who take refuge with Ogodai's horde.

Yusuf Bey: Jahangir's successor as head of the Mangyt tribe, despite his youth and excessive self-confidence.

Zahid: The youngest merchant, who aids Ogodai's scouts in identifying the location of Sheikh-Mamai's camp.

HISTORICAL CHARACTERS

As often happens with medieval and early modern people, we have limited information about Russians and Tatars, even royalty, who lived in the sixteenth century. To the extent possible, I have ensured that details about real people included in the Legends novels match the historical record, but often these details do not extend much beyond dates of marriages, deaths, and sometimes births. Therefore, these characters' appearances, personalities, words, and motivations are just as much my invention as those of their fictional counterparts.

Andrei Ivanovich of Staritsa: Youngest brother of Vasily III, uncle to Ivan IV; incarcerated by his sister-in-law Elena in June 1537 after an unsuccessful and perhaps unwanted campaign against her.

    Elena Glinskaya: Grand princess and regent of Russia; mother of Ivan IV, known to posterity as Ivan the Terrible, and his younger brother, Yuri Vasilyevich; widow of Grand Prince Vasily III, whose death in 1533 led to much uncertainty and aggression at home and abroad.

    Islam-Girei of Crimea: Nephew, rival, and heir of Sahib-Girei and his predecessor; Alexei's chosen overlord from his exile in 1524 to the fall of 1536, when he entered Russian service. Islam-Girei was assassinated in August 1537 after more than a decade of intermittent rebellions against his uncle. The Girei dynasty ruled Crimea for centuries; the name is often spelled Giray.

    Ivan Fyodorovich Ovchina Telepnev Obolensky: Boyar, prince, military commander; favorite of Elena Glinskaya and a prominent court figure during her regency.

    Ivan IV Vasilyevich: Grand Prince of Russia (1530–1584, r. 1533–1584); crowned tsar 1547.

Safa-Girei Khan: Ruler of Kazan 1524–1531, 1535–1546, and 1546–1549 (a brief coup interrupted his rule in 1546); nephew to Sahib-Girei Khan of Crimea; an enemy of Bulat's family and of the Russians, against whom he launched frequent raids.

Sahib-Girei Khan: Ruler of Crimea, 1532–1551.

Sheikh-Mamai Bey: The ruler of one group of Nogai Tatars who refused to join the coalition organized by Said-Ahmed Bey in 1537 and raided the area to the west of the Volga and as far north as the Meshchera (Kasimov region) much as described here, but without encountering defeat at the hands of my fictional characters or even significant opposition.

Vasily III Ivanovich: Grand Prince of Russia (r. 1505–1533), father of Ivan IV and Yuri Vasilyevich.

Vasily Vasilyevich Shuisky: Boyar, prince, leader of the Shuisky clan; a prominent member of the government, especially in foreign affairs, until his death in November 1538.

Yuri Ivanovich: Younger brother of Vasily III, uncle to Ivan IV, prince of Dmitrov; died in captivity 3 August 1536.

Yuri Vasilyevich: Younger brother of Ivan IV.

The Journey of Ogodai's Horde

All routes are approximate. ✣ indicates the location of the final battle.

Spinner of Tales

THOSE WHO HAVE FOLLOWED MY CHRONICLE FROM WEST TO east and north to south have witnessed the Russian government spinning into a cyclone of greed and ambition, fear and fury, driven by the urge for vengeance, status, and power. Accompany me now into the center of the vortex, where the sins of the past collide with the demands of the present, destroying the fragile peace established at home and abroad.

Among my husband's people, the Tatars of the steppe, a shaman handles such crises by beating a rhythm on her drum that opens a pathway to the realms above, permitting communication with eternal spirits that offer guidance and wisdom. Heeding the advice of these immortal powers restores order to the universe. But if the emotional energies become too strong, the drum shatters, and the horde wanders in darkness until the shaman can reestablish a connection to the hidden lands beyond our own.

It is the same with kingdoms. If those who should rule follow their selfish desires—rejecting the constraints of morality and good sense, ignoring the messages sent by their ancestors and their gods—their actions shatter the balance between those who govern and those who serve. Then only time and great effort can restore the broken nation. How that once happened in Russia has been the thread that ties my tales together.

As my mother used to say when I was small, "Sit. Let me tell you a story."

Chapter 1

NASAN BLEW AIR ACROSS HER BABY'S TUMMY AND GIGGLED as he waved both chubby hands in response. Boris, known as Borya within the family, had reached the ripe age of seven months. With his father's honey brown eyes and her dark hair he looked fit to become a sturdy and handsome boy, but she didn't share that opinion out loud lest she attract the notice of dangerous spirits. In case even the thought could draw unwanted attention, she murmured a short prayer in her son's ear. His baby scent, floral soap mixed with a hint of milk, filled her nostrils.

But as she released him to sit on the rug, his face crumpled. He grabbed his right cheek with one hand and batted her away with the other. Concerned, she touched his forehead and found it warm and damp. "What's wrong with him?" she asked his wet nurse, Zhenya. Since birth Borya had been a placid child, not given even to such small outbursts as this.

"He's teething, Tsarevna." Zhenya crossed the room and crouched next to the baby. "He didn't sleep well last night or feed well this morning. No doubt his gums hurt."

"But he feels hot," Nasan argued. "He shouldn't feel hot, even if he's teething. Suppose it's something else?"

Zhenya patted the baby's cheek, and he pushed her hand away as well. His outraged howls rose in volume.

A man's voice cut across the child's cries. "Time to go, wife of mine," Daniil said. "It won't do to arrive late for a royal funeral—especially this one, which will harbor more serpents than chickens. Let's not offer ourselves as prey."

Alerted by the edge in his voice, Nasan turned to study him. Resplendent in robes that matched her own, black velvet trimmed in gold, the snow-laden sky of late afternoon behind his head no match for his tawny good looks, he never failed to provoke a shiver of desire.

But her child needed her. She pressed her hand against Borya's forehead once more. "He's ill," she said. "I should stay with him."

"He's teething, Tsarevna," Zhenya repeated. "He will be right as rain by the morning, I promise. Or if not then, as soon as the tooth breaks through."

"You don't know that," Nasan snapped. "Babies get sick even when they're teething."

"Besides," Daniil interjected. "I'm sorry, but we *must* go. The funeral procession will start within the hour. Unless one of us dies before then, we have no acceptable excuse for staying away. Whether Zhenya's wrong or right, you'll be back with Borya soon. Bad enough that we must return after dark and risk assault by villains and robbers. Let us travel there by daylight, at least. Come."

Nasan bit back the retort that hovered on her tongue and studied her baby.

Was Zhenya right? Nasan had seen plenty of babies in her father's harem, and teething did show itself in various signs, including a slight fever. Borya had reached the age when teeth should begin to appear. Her medical books insisted that no harm came from it. Her touch revealed an uncharacteristic warmth, not a child burning up; he might recover even before she returned.

But she had also seen slight fevers escalate at terrifying speed. And this was her *baby*, her precious son, not a child in a medical book. She didn't want to move so much as a step until she felt certain nothing more ailed him than his first tooth.

Yet she couldn't stay. As Daniil had pointed out, the highest families in the land must attend any burial service for a royal prince—even one callously murdered by his sister-in-law, who seemed set on covering up that inconvenient reality, known to the entire court. Some duties a khan's daughter could neither skip nor postpone, no matter how little she welcomed them.

"*Ana* will be back soon, Borya," she told him in Tatar. He was still too young to respond or even understand, but she wanted him to learn the languages of both his parents. With one last snuggle she handed him to Zhenya. "Send for me at once if he seems sicker," she said before crossing the room to join Daniil.

"It's teething," Zhenya said once more. "He will do fine. But of course we will send a message if there is need."

As if it mattered, Nasan thought bitterly. She could not depart in the middle of this wretched ceremony even if Borya stood at death's door.

Yet the assurance comforted her enough that she refrained from snapping at her husband when he caught her round the waist. "What happened to my warrior princess?" he asked. "Tell me she's not wholly submerged in Mama!"

"Don't tease," she said. "If he's only teething, I won't worry. But infants sicken so fast."

"Make no mistake." He kissed her. "I too worry about our son. I'll bring you home as soon as possible. Agreed?"

"Yes." She allowed herself a small sigh of relief that he had abandoned his question about the warrior princess, which she no longer knew how to answer. How to explain the conflicting demands that tugged at her heart? Without her archery and her riding and her swordsmanship, she would become like any other Russian lady of the house. Daniil, too, deserved as much attention as she could give him before war and government duties again called him away. Yet Borya changed and grew with each passing day, and she hated the thought of missing his first smile, his first word, his first attempt to sit or crawl or stand. She loved them both beyond bounds, her husband and her son. She could never choose one over the other.

God willing, I will never have to.

In a perfect world the three of them would live together in her brother's horde on the steppe, where Borya could learn firsthand the skills his ancestors knew as well as the many things his Russian father could teach him. But that was a fantasy she shared with no one. Since her mother-in-law's death two months ago any possibility of leaving Moscow seemed ever more an idle dream.

"Come, wife of mine," Daniil said. "The carriage awaits, and the poor horses will freeze in this wind if we don't get them moving. Given that the grand princess and her favorite starved poor Prince Andrei to death, couldn't they have had the decency to keep him alive until spring?"

Nasan took her husband's hand and let him lead her down the stairs to the covered sleigh waiting below. The December air bit at her cheeks. To her the frigid temperature matched too well the callousness with which Grand Princess Elena had treated her brother-in-law Andrei in the last year of his life. How much more vicious to bring him to the brink of spring, only to dash the hopes raised by warm air and honeyed scents!

Then again, perhaps that second choice *would* have been more in character.

But Daniil thought of the mourners, no doubt, and the brutal wind swirling around the noblemen carrying the casket from the old grand princely palace near the Cathedral of St. John the Baptist's Nativity—the chamber where Andrei had been brought to die, his manacles removed at last—past the entire length of the Riverside Palace that had held him in captivity, to the Cathedral of the Archangel Michael. There, interred among his male ancestors, he might find peace at last.

Tsarevich Alexei Bulatovich stood with his friend Ruslan at his father's right shoulder and surveyed the swarm of nobles in black with a jaundiced eye. After more than a year in Moscow he recognized many of them by sight, although his half-sister Nasan and her husband had yet to make an appearance. His stepmother Sumbeka had joined the horde of women without delay; he could see only the gold tip of her pointed headdress among the crowd.

The wind howled as if they stood on the open steppe. For a moment Alexei allowed memory to sweep him back to the grasslands. He yearned for that vast sense of space, of possibility—the air cold but clean, unlike this fetid palace fortress with its enclosing walls and wood-covered streets mired in ice and mud. "Those clouds will drop a blizzard on us before sunrise," he said to his father. "I'm glad Maria didn't insist on attending."

Not that his wife had a choice. Seven days after childbirth she couldn't enter a church even if she wished to, but in any case he would have hesitated to expose a new mother to so biting a wind, especially for a meaningless ceremony like this one. Better that she stay snug at home with the baby. After a long and difficult labor she had presented him with a fine son, and he cherished them both.

"Have you decided what to name him?" Bulat asked. "The ceremony is tomorrow, is it not?"

"Tomorrow, yes." Alexei rubbed his upper arms. Velvet and sable could not keep out the winter gale. "Midmorning. We've settled on Alexander. You and *Ana* will attend, will you not? It's at the house, not a church." The Russian Church did not welcome his Muslim father and stepmother to its houses of worship. Even their participation in today's funeral would not extend to the burial service itself. "Nasan's chaplain has agreed to perform the rite. You know him, I think."

"Alexander Alexeyevich Bulatov." Bulat sounded the name out, then blessed it with a curt nod. "After the Great Iskandar. A good name for a descendant of Genghis. My chief wife and I will be there to wish my latest grandson well."

Ruslan leaned forward and waved a hand at the swarm of nobles. "Something's happening. Good. I'm fit to perish in this cold."

"And there's my sister." Alexei raised a hand to Nasan, emerging from a sleigh with her husband. She ran across the courtyard to embrace them, then in response to a word from Alexei dashed to join her mother. The two gold-tipped hats briefly touched, gleaming in the last rays of the setting sun, then established themselves side by side near the front of the heaving crowd of women.

Daniil followed at a more sedate pace, bowed in greeting to Bulat and clasped Alexei's hand, then Ruslan's, before choosing to stand with them rather than press his way into the mob. "This should be fun," he said.

From the dryness in his tone Alexei deduced that Daniil meant the exact opposite. "How so?" he asked.

"Don't you see how they're milling about?" Daniil did not quite point at the noblemen standing near the palace door, who increasingly resembled an anthill stirred up by a stick with every moment that passed, but the jerk of his head indicated the group he had in mind. "They should be in order of precedence. Simple thing: khans and sultans at the front"—he nodded at Bulat, Alexei, and Ruslan, all three of whom belonged in that category—"and everyone else following by rank. Usually you just get into position and hope that someone of greater standing isn't fuming behind you, ready to punch you in the gut for your lack of respect."

Alexei studied the noble anthill writhing about Prince Andrei's polished oak casket. Although still rather hazy on the details of Russian precedence customs—never mind royal funerals, which he had not attended before—he knew enough after sixteen months to grasp what Daniil meant. "You're right. It's as if they're scuffling." Indeed, he could see several pushing matches that would turn into brawls if not stopped. Fortunately, stopping them was not his responsibility. "But are they fighting to get closer or to move farther away?"

"Good question," Daniil said. "I could make a case for either one. Prince Ilya Shuisky, for example, has managed to put three large uncles between himself and the coffin." With a quick twist of his hand he motioned at a short, round man with light brown hair, pale blue eyes, and an unmistakable air of self-satisfaction that often aroused Alexei's basest urges to violence. "I'm guessing he wants to take no chance of anyone associating him with Prince Andrei. Some of those who secretly sympathized with Andrei's cause, in contrast, may wish to support him on this last journey."

"Or not." Alexei scanned the crowd once more. Personally he regarded Prince Andrei as a nuisance whose inability either to keep the peace with his sister-in-law or to mount a credible campaign against her had led to the Muscovite forces wasting four precious weeks in pursuit of a victory that the rawest recruit could have predicted from the outset they would attain.

But he recognized that certain members of the Moscow court, including Daniil to some extent, felt otherwise. "I wouldn't put it past those in power to take notes on who goes where and does what, for later use in their deliberations on whom they can and can't trust."

"True." Daniil shivered. "Either way, I wish they'd get on with it. I can no longer feel my toes. Can you imagine what icicles we'll have become in an hour?"

Whether the realities of winter triumphed over political calculation or some additional factor came into play, Alexei could not tell. But after another round or two of dodging and shoving the noblemen managed to organize themselves into something that Alexei, if he felt charitable instead of frozen, might dignify with the name "procession." Led by a group of priests and deacons, they set off across the open courtyard, the casket bobbing at shoulder level as if borne on a restless sea.

"I hope they don't tip the deceased out on his head," Alexei said to Daniil, who acknowledged this sally with the suppressed laughter it deserved. As the procession approached, Bulat and his entourage, including the two of them and Ruslan, took their places near the front. The women surged behind the men, weeping and keening. To all appearances the court grieved at losing its beloved prince. Impressive, given that everyone present knew that the truth was quite different.

From his present vantage point Alexei could not see how the nobles had resolved their disagreement. He was aware of Prince Vasily Shuisky, a massive man aged sixty or thereabouts whose gray hair only enhanced his powerful frame. As the man in charge of foreign affairs and the highest-ranking among the princes, Vasily Shuisky strode near the front, almost level with the khans and sultans. A brother and a cousin flanked him, and his deplorable nephew Ilya trailed behind, still using the uncles as a shield. On Alexei's left Prince Dmitry Belsky elbowed his way forward, keeping pace with every step taken by Vasily Shuisky. Everyone else, from Alexei's perspective, was hidden from view.

With the Riverside Palace on their left, the fortress wall on their right, and the wind behind them, the air warmed the slightest degree. Ahead of them the golden cupolas of the Annunciation Cathedral became visible, then the scalloped limestone niches that topped the towering walls of their destination.

Waiting near the cathedral doorway was the chilliest sight that Alexei had seen so far, even on this classic December day. The sky had darkened to twilight during the procession, and a forest of candles cast an unearthly, flickering glow on both the marchers and those who awaited them. Grand Princess Elena, a Lithuanian blonde of statuesque proportions and icy blue eyes, stood dressed in full court finery next to her favorite, Prince Ivan Telepnev—the man who at her command had convinced Andrei to surrender to the Muscovite forces, promising a safe conduct that Elena had abrogated within two days of Andrei's arrival in Moscow. Between them the seven-year-old grand prince who was the nominal ruler of Russia held a hand of each adult, staring with a set face at the advancing procession. Behind the threesome a portly noblewoman dressed in black velvet and a sable cloak held a smaller boy—the royal nanny, Agrafena Cheliadnina, and the five-year-old Prince Yuri Vasilyevich, Elena's younger son.

Not one of them so much as blinked away a tear.

Standing in the front line of the assembled noblewomen, Nasan clasped her hands and stared at the royal doors separating the worshippers from the altar. Although she had long since made her peace with the Russian tendency to adorn every interior surface of a church with painted frescoes of saints and angels, she found her first experience of the royal mausoleum more than a little creepy. Alternately revealed and concealed in the flickering candlelight, the crumbling tombs combined with the odor of decay to provide constant reminders that she prayed amid a sepulcher of bones. The haloed saints on the walls, indistinguishable one from the other with their upturned hands and flattened gloomy faces, made her shiver. If they waited at the gates of Heaven, they gave no signs of anticipating eternal bliss. The torments of Hell, rather.

Or perhaps her shiver came from the temperature in the church. The assembled bodies of the noblemen and noblewomen who packed the cathedral could not offset the chill December air. The candles supplied no heat and little light, and the tombs that lined the south, north, and west walls of the cathedral made their own dank contribution to the cold. Memorials to dead princes pressed up against the iconostasis, leaving only the royal doors entirely clear.

The large number of noblemen in attendance had pushed most of the women far away from the eastern end of the cathedral, where the priests and the royal family prayed. With a line of stone tombs at her back and the memorial that encased Tsarevich Peter, a former sultan of Kazan who had died when she was seven, within reach of her right hand, Nasan could not help but think of other funerals she had attended. Her younger brother's in Kasimov almost four years ago was the most painful, but the more recent event threatening to send tears down her cheeks was the burial of her mother-in-law, Natalya, two months before.

Although long expected, Natalya's death when her failing heart at last abandoned its attempts to beat still grieved Nasan and, even more, Daniil. Natalya's husband of thirty years, Nikolai, had yet to recover a shell of his former self. And the memory remained fresh, because the forty-day memorial for Natalya lay less than two weeks in the past. It seemed cruel that events outside their control should force them to relive that terrible moment of farewell so soon after they had begun to put it behind them. Every prayer, every hymn, led Nasan to stretch out her hand to seek comfort from her husband, only to recall that he stood not beside her but far ahead with his father, a few rows behind her half-brother.

From instinct she reached for her mother, only to recall that her parents remained in the vestibule of the cathedral with Ruslan Sultan. When the prayers ended, they would rejoin the cortege.

Nasan understood that the rules of the Church meant her parents had taken the only path open to them, but she nonetheless wished that *Ana* stood beside her. Such a relief that her mother lived in Moscow, not weeks away in Kasimov as she had during the first three years of Nasan's marriage. Yet if *Ana* were here in the church, she would recognize the creepiness, the sadness. Nasan would know someone shared her reaction to this cold and unwelcoming place.

And more important, Nasan could whisper her fears about Borya. Did he cry out for her? Had his fever worsened? Would Zhenya take good care of him? *Ana* would not mind that she had already issued more than one reassurance; she understood a mother's anxiety.

Unlike Daniil, who would no doubt remind her she would see the baby soon.

Nasan sighed. It was unfair to blame her husband for not fully sharing her concerns. He loved Borya as much as she did, played with him, took pride in him. In a few years he would assume full responsibility for teaching his son what a noble heir needed to learn, just as Nikolai had once taught Daniil and his older brother, Borya's namesake. But infants lived in a world of women. Nasan saw every shift of expression, marked every tiny achievement, as Daniil did not—yet.

Perhaps *Ana* would return to the house with them. If she viewed Borya's discomfort herself and ascribed it to teething, Nasan would believe her.

Then she remembered that Papa-in-law had asked to speak with his son and daughter-in-law after the funeral. He had not said why. Tomorrow then. They would see *Ana* tomorrow at the naming ceremony for Maria and Alexei's new son.

It was no use trying to pray amid such turmoil and strangeness, so Nasan surveyed the cathedral, attempting to gauge the mood of the court. Although most of the noblewomen were arrayed in rows behind her, that order of precedence did not include Grand Princess Elena and her inner circle, who occupied a place at the very front, closer to the altar than even Alexei and the other Christian tsareviches. Amid Grand Princess Elena's clustered ladies, she saw the black satin and elaborate headdress of Solomonida Sheremeteva, her neighbor and friend. At Solomonida's right, next to the grand princess, stood Nadezhda, the unfortunate wife of Prince Ilya Shuisky. Those two were still in favor then.

On the grand princess's right, next to her young sons, Prince Ivan Telepnev hovered. In view of the entire court the favorite could not openly express his feelings, whatever they were, but his stance vis-à-vis the grand prince and his mother struck Nasan as distinctly fatherly, not to say proprietary. For years— even before the death of Grand Princess Elena's husband— rumor had branded Telepnev as Elena's lover. Some people insisted that he had sired Elena's two sons. Nasan had always dismissed such tales as vicious gossip aimed at undermining a woman who in the eyes of many noblemen exceeded her natural authority. But watching them now, she wondered. The four of them certainly looked like a family. The presence at

Telepnev's right of his sister, who served as the princes' nanny, heightened the sense of a protected inner circle.

Her wandering eye caught sight of the cathedral's newest tomb, on her left, directly opposite Tsarevich Peter's memorial. It faced the corner where, according to what Daniil had told her, Prince Andrei was destined to lie. The tomb of Prince Yuri Ivanovich of Dmitrov, Andrei's older brother, also starved to death in captivity on the orders of his sister-in-law Elena and her favorite.

Nasan and Daniil had both been away from Moscow, although in separate locations, when Yuri Ivanovich died. Enduring today's travesty of a memorial made her glad she had escaped *that* funeral, where tensions among the mourners must have equaled or exceeded the grimness she sensed among today's crowd.

Nasan had not met either prince, although her husband had more than once expressed his respect for Andrei (not to mention his suspicions of Yuri). And as a descendant of Genghis she had heard plenty of grim tales about assassination and treachery, even within her own extended family. Her uncle Jan-Ali, although no more than nineteen years old, had died under an assassin's blade in Kazan two years ago. Despite that history, the deliberate brutality needed to starve a relative to death over the course of months or years, combined with the macabre ceremony designed to portray this most recent death as natural, implied a steely nerve that even Jan-Ali's murderers could not match.

Sickened, Nasan again looked front. The metropolitan of Moscow, magnificent in his ornately embroidered and jeweled robes, was singing Psalm 51: "O give me the comfort of Thy help again, and establish me with Thy free Spirit. Then shall I teach Thy ways unto the wicked, and sinners shall be converted unto Thee."

Grand Princess Elena and Telepnev bowed their heads, as did the noblemen and their wives, mothers, sisters, and daughters. Nasan did the same, but she could not escape the thought that rose to taunt her.

What if the sinners rule the land and will stop at nothing, even the murder of their own kinsfolk, to stay in power?

※

Prince Andrei's funeral ended at last. The metropolitan completed the service, blessed the memorial dish—boiled grain mixed with fruit—and distributed it to the mourners. In December the rock-hard ground did not yield to a shovel, so Prince Andrei's casket lay in the section where the north and west walls joined, awaiting burial when that became possible. One day he would receive a stone memorial like his brother, Nasan assumed. Bearing the twisted wax candles handed out as gifts to those who took part in the procession and the funeral, she joined her male relatives, Ruslan, and her mother at the cathedral door.

"Will you come with us to greet your nephew and your sister-in-law?" Alexei asked when they had squeezed through the crowd in the porch.

"Tomorrow," Nasan said. "Papa-in-law has something he wants to tell Daniil and me. He asked us to come straight home after the funeral, and he grieves so for Mama-in-law that we don't want to delay. And I must check on Borya, too, in case something more than teething ails him. But give Maria and the baby a hug for me and tell her that we will get there in the morning, long before the ceremony starts." In response to his assurances she embraced him, then her parents and Ruslan. Daniil took her elbow as he said his farewells, and together they walked through the lantern-lit courtyard, searching for their sleigh among the many lined up awaiting their owners.

As if released from the weight of the funeral, the lowering skies had cleared enough that a few stars shone among the clouds, although Nasan still expected snow before dawn. The temperature had risen a bit, but she knew from experience that only made the appearance of snow more likely. She took time to gather her scattered thoughts, then grasped the opportunity to compare notes with her husband. Despite the difference in their vantage points, they had drawn the same conclusions. But then, they usually did.

The one thing she did not ask him was what his father planned to say. If Daniil knew, he would tell her. And Nikolai's decision to travel alone to and from the funeral worried her. Over the three and a half years of their acquaintance her father-in-law had occupied his position as head of the household as if it were a second skin. What did it mean that today he left his son and daughter-in-law to fend for themselves?

Chapter 2

FYODOR KOSHKIN PASSED THROUGH YET ANOTHER SET OF double wooden doors, noting the brightly colored tiles that decorated the center of each panel. Anticipation spurred him forward as he followed his benefactor, Jan Radziwill, into a whitewashed airy room with similar tiles embedded in the ceiling. Months of disappointment as he dragged himself from failure to failure in Russia, in Livonia, and through one Lithuanian town after another had left a heavy burden on Koshkin's shoulders. But today—today!—his fortunes had turned. Jan, mindful of past kindnesses during ambassadorial visits to Moscow, had promised to present him to Sigismund Augustus, co-ruling with his father as grand duke of Lithuania and king of Poland, as well as to Sigismund's mother the queen, the Italian witch Bona Sforza.

In truth, Koshkin could have dispensed with the latter introduction. Making the acquaintance of a lady known to dispatch anyone who displeased her with strange and exotic poisons carried a certain risk. But a queen was a queen, and he would conduct himself with as much aplomb as he could muster.

Besides, Jan, vigorous in his late thirties and Koshkin's counterpart in age, did not readily allow demurrals to pierce his enthusiasm. Brown hair, trim beard, and ruddy cheeks signaled the élan of a much younger man, and Jan's short stature gave him the appearance of a lively rooster. But Koshkin, although priding himself on his own dapper elegance (somewhat marred by his current straitened circumstances), much preferred a man whose head reached his chin to the usual towering Russian boyar.

"You'll meet the grand duke's latest mistress too," Jan promised as they came through the door. "A luscious flower if I ever saw one. The body of a khan's concubine, scented and painted, has the exquisite Juliana. Wasted on a boy of seventeen, royal or not. I wish I had access to her charms."

A khan's concubine. Koshkin permitted himself a sigh of remembered regret. Only last spring *he* had enjoyed such a body, but Divine Will had intervened—Divine Will abetted by the machinations of Prince Ilya Shuisky and Koshkin's fears that his wife still yearned for the lover she had deserted for marriage. Koshkin and Roxelana had perforce parted ways, but he ached at the memory of those few months of bliss.

Unlike the sparsely furnished chambers he had traversed so far, the one into which Jan ushered him next rang with music and voices. Men and women intermingled, laughing and flirting—a sight that shocked Koshkin, since Russian custom permitted such mixing of the sexes only at weddings. Among the men, everyone but the rare elderly courtier bared his lower limbs to the world, and the women showed their waists and their breasts with an effrontery reserved in Moscow for strumpets.

Koshkin had never considered himself a prude, but long exposure—he chose the word with care—to these foreign women might well change his mind.

"There he is." The jerk of Jan's chin drew Koshkin's attention to the center of the gathering. "Indeed, there *they* are. I'll present you, shall I?"

On a carpeted dais three people stood chatting: a young man who from the jeweled cap, the full-sleeved and embroidered silk doublet, and the chain of office must be Grand Duke Sigismund Augustus himself; a fading blonde of perhaps forty who at least had the modesty to conceal her aging chest with a fichu; and a young woman in her early twenties wearing a gown of rich cobalt silk banded with black. Her velvet sleeves, also black, were slashed to reveal the white silk lining. The lovely Juliana—for who else could she be?—had her lace-trimmed neckline cut so low that it barely concealed her cleavage, further emphasized by the magnificent pearls dangling from her ears and clasped about her neck. The necklace ended in a small gold cross. Her elaborately dressed dark brown hair, cascading over her right shoulder and topped with a small velvet cap embroidered in gold, only highlighted her creamy brown skin, flushed with pink from excitement or perhaps the heat of the room. More gold bound her narrow waist and dangled to her knees. She exhibited such astonishing beauty that Koshkin could do little more than blink at her, wondering where he had seen her before. He had never met a woman named Juliana—never mind one dressed like that—yet something about her struck him as familiar.

The grand duke had his arm around her waist, and as Koshkin watched, Sigismund placed his free hand under her chin, turned her face toward his, and kissed her. The sinuous way she pressed herself against the grand duke's body struck a chord, and Koshkin's eager anticipation crashed to the soles of his boots. *Now* he recognized her.

How dare she? How could she? Devil take her cheating soul, how did she even get here?

Koshkin shoved his clenched fists into the long sleeves of the one shabby court robe he still possessed after his eight months on the road. Assaulting the ruler of a foreign power would give inconceivable offense, but oh, how he wanted to knock the grand duke to kingdom come, grab the Lady *Juliana* by the arm, and hustle her out.

"An angel, isn't she?" Jan sighed in passion. "Arrived six months ago from Moscow, and one snap of her fingers had Sigismund panting after her. Rest of us didn't stand a chance, especially after it came out that she has a husband somewhere. Even the queen—she's the one next to the beauteous Juliana—didn't object after that. If Sigismund can't run off to the altar with her, let him have his bit of fun is Queen Bona's view. Too bad for the rest of us, though. I would give everything I own for a night in those arms."

"Well, you can forget about that." Koshkin bit each word off as if it were bread. Could he get away with assaulting Jan? Alas, probably not. The Radziwill lineage came right after the grand duke's in terms of authority, and to make matters worse, Jan was hosting Koshkin in his house. "And stop calling her Juliana. Her name is Roxelana."

Jan stared at him, his mouth gaping like a fish hauled to shore. "What makes you say that? In fact, how do you know anything about her? I thought Russians didn't let their women out in public. Is she a relative of yours?"

"In a manner of speaking." Koshkin glared over the heads of the heedless crowd to where the grand duke murmured in the young woman's ear. "May the bitch burn for eternity. She's my wife."

"*You're* the missing husband?" Jan's clear, carrying bass stopped the babble in the chamber cold. The young man on the dais ceased murmuring to Roxelana and turned to stare. The older blonde craned her neck—trying to determine the source of the commotion, Koshkin assumed. Roxelana conferred her sultriest smile on the grand duke, then regarded her husband with an imperious air that boded ill for any prospects of a reunion.

"I am." Koshkin took Jan by the elbow. "And if you will fulfill your promise to present me to your grand duke, I will respond in kind by introducing you to my wife. I'm sure she will appreciate the competition for her favors."

The bitterness in his own voice made him wince. Less than a year ago he had considered himself the happiest man alive.

Nikolai was ensconced in his study when Nasan and Daniil reached the house. A quick check of the nursery revealed no change in Borya, so Nasan managed to greet her father-in-law with at least the appearance of equanimity. He still wore his black robes, and the expression in his clear blue eyes struck Nasan as troubled. When they entered the room and huddled near the tiled furnace, blissful at escaping the outside chill after so long, he was stroking his bushy gray beard and staring at the icons in the far corner.

Nasan put her hands together and bowed to the painted saints, then took her seat on the bench facing her father-in-law. Whatever he wanted to say, she would allow Daniil to lead the way in responding. Nikolai had accepted the presence of a tempestuous daughter-in-law given her appeal to his son and her proven ability to produce an heir, but he still tended to expect silent obedience from women.

A chased goblet emitting the fragrant steam of heated wine sat next to a metal ewer covered in a linen towel at the center of Nikolai's desk. He pushed the ewer and a pair of goblets toward Daniil, who poured the spicy crimson liquid into them and handed one to Nasan. She sipped it, grateful for the warmth spreading through her cheeks and her hands. It did not escape her notice that Nikolai himself did not drink, although the first goblet was clearly intended for him.

Daniil sat beside her, balancing the goblet on his knees. "What is it, Papa? A problem at court? Today's funeral?" He sounded hopeful that the answer could be anything so predictable. His father's odd behavior must bother him too.

Nikolai did not answer at first, just stroked his beard and stared. Nasan and Daniil waited, not speaking, from time to time exchanging anxious glances. Each moment that passed tightened Nasan's nerves. She wished for the simple joys of playing with her baby, of practicing swordplay and archery with Daniil, of riding her mare, of conversing. But whatever worried her father-in-law clearly had enormous import; she had never known him so reluctant to speak.

At last he turned to face them. Resting his elbows on his desk, he steepled his fingers. "I wish to retire from the world," he said. His voice—flat, heavy—bore witness to the momentous nature of his decision. "If I could, I would live on our northern estate, but that would not exempt me from service as long as I remain in good health. So I have arranged to enter the Miracles Monastery in the Kremlin after the new year. Elder Gennady has agreed to accept me as his student while I discover whether the monastic life indeed offers the best path for me to follow."

Nasan gasped. Of the many possibilities that had raced through her brain since she heard that Nikolai wanted to see them, this one had not occurred to her. Yet the glisten of unshed tears in her father-in-law's eyes spoke louder than words. He had lost interest in the daily business of household and government since Natalya's death. Nasan had watched it happen but had expected him to recover in time. Would he yet do so? Would he come to regret his choice?

But as a student he could return if he wished. The objection died on her tongue.

"Because of Mama?" Daniil asked. "But what of the family?"

Nikolai sighed. He relaxed his arms, pulling back to lay his wrists against the edge of the desk. "You and your wife will lead the family. I have faith in you, son." He nodded at Nasan. "And you, daughter. You have learned much in the years since my wife fell ill, and you have a good housekeeper in Sonya. I know you will manage the estate and the outlying properties well."

Nasan's throat tightened, and she felt matching tears prick her eyes. Much as she had loved her mother-in-law, Natalya had seldom acknowledged, never mind praised, her daughter-in-law's efforts to keep the household running and Natalya herself alive. Even less had Nasan expected her father-in-law, who spent most of his time elsewhere, to notice the many hours she put in each day no matter the season.

"And yes, son, because of your mother," Nikolai went on. "But not only for that reason. Wherever I go and whatever I do from now on, I have no choice but to endure the rest of my life without her. But I cannot imagine remarrying, and it pains me to live *here*, where we were happy together."

There was no adequate response to that, and neither Nasan nor Daniil attempted one. After a short pause Nikolai continued. "And I will not be far away, if you need counsel. One reason I have hesitated to take this step is because the situation at court disturbs me. Elena should have stopped when she defeated her first brother-in-law, who posed an actual threat. The boyar clans did not band together to protect Prince Andrei, it's true, but his death within months of his arrest leads them to wonder whom Elena and her favorite will attack next. I thought I should set my own needs aside for the sake of the family and the land. But with this plan I will be right there in the Kremlin if things deteriorate. I don't intend to take my vows right away."

"If there is danger, should we not fight together to protect the grand prince and his brother?" Daniil, his face intent, gazed at his father. "What of our oath of allegiance, which you have so often quoted to me?"

"A good point," Nikolai admitted. "But you will defend the princes as I no longer can. I am four years older than my Natasha. How much time have I left? Whatever my allotted span is, I wish to spend it in prayer and in service to the Lord. You have a fine son, and God willing you will make many more, expanding our lineage. I leave our family in good hands."

"I lack your experience and your connections," Daniil argued, his voice hoarse with suppressed emotion. "I don't have your rank. I can *not* defend the princes as you can."

"You will have the rank before I go," Nikolai said. "I have spoken with Telepnev. He has promised to persuade the grand prince to name you a junior boyar, an *okolnichy*. From there it is just a matter of time. I am a boyar, and you are my only surviving son. You will inherit my position."

"I'd rather be an adjutant with a father," Daniil muttered under his breath, but only Nasan heard him.

He continued to argue and, when that did not work, to plead. After a while Nasan murmured her agreement with his points. But Nikolai remained adamant, and in the end they withdrew to their own chambers, not agreeing with him but accepting that he would not change his mind.

It required an inordinate amount of time for Koshkin to separate his errant wife from Grand Duke Sigismund and Queen Bona. The longer he stood at Jan's side, watching the debonair grand duke and his no less stylish mother, whose high-waisted gown with its enormous fur-trimmed sleeves bore evidence to her notorious extravagance even as its soft rose-colored silk gave her skin the glow of a much younger woman, the more aggravated Koshkin became. Roxelana studiously ignored him, flitting like a bee between her lover and his mother, until only a direct plea to the queen won him the favor of a private conversation.

Even then his wife's stormy expression provoked a protest from the grand duke. "After what he did to her, Mama? Surely you would not deliver Lady Juliana to a man who cares so little for her welfare?"

Queen Bona allowed her eyelids to droop, her rouged lips to tighten. She waved a careless hand. The tassels that hung from her ivory belt shimmied and jingled as she turned away. "Calm yourself, son. I didn't say he should run off with her. A husband has the right to talk with his wife, and Lady Juliana can no doubt explain for herself why she no longer wishes to share his bed."

"And if I did order her to come away with me," Koshkin said, "I would have that right too."

Only when the two royals stared at him haughtily did he consider that he might have done better to express himself with less heat. "I won't do that, of course," he added with haste, hoping they would not notice his gritted teeth. With a fierce yearning he longed to return to Russia, where people understood a husband's rights.

"Go, Juliana," Bona said with a well-directed shove to the small of Roxelana's back. Koshkin extended his elbow, in the manner these westerners seemed to prefer, and with obvious reluctance his wife placed her fingertips on his forearm. At last he was able to escort her to another room—separate from the company although no less oppressive with its wood ceilings inset with tiles, the tapestries and paintings that decorated its whitewashed walls, the chandelier that hung from the center, its heavy oak tables and upholstered armchairs.

They hadn't crossed the threshold before Roxelana dropped her hand from his arm. Koshkin grabbed her and spun her about. "How the hell did you get here? Are you bedding that boy? And what's this Juliana nonsense?"

She dragged herself free and stamped on his foot. While he cursed and rubbed his toes, she touched the gold cross that hung from her neck. "I have accepted the Catholic faith, and the queen conferred a new name on me. The rest ceased to be your business when you left me alone in Moscow. Did you think for as much as one moment about what would happen to me as a result of your treachery?"

"Nothing did, did it?" he snapped. "No doubt your precious Alexei Bulatovich took you back under his heathen wing. Then tired of you again? But that doesn't explain how you wound up in Vilnius."

In the fifteen months Koshkin had known his wife, he had never seen her lose her temper. Usually she coaxed and wooed, as she had earlier with Sigismund. Now she held hands crooked into claws before his face, forcing him to grip her wrists to keep her at a safe distance.

"You idiot!" she said. "Alexei did nothing of the sort. He's in love with your *daughter*, you dolt. And even without that, how could he sleep with me? You hadn't been gone a day when the government seized your property, arrested me, and confined me to the estate of that abominable Ilya Shuisky. And since you're so sure I have no morals, let me tell you that *he* didn't hesitate to force himself on me. That's why he persuaded you to flee, and like the fool you are, you let him do it!"

"W-w-what?" he stammered, feeling every bit the fool she called him. Alexei had rejected her … for *Maria*. Russia's villainous grand princess had arrested his wife and handed her over to Prince Ilya Shuisky, who had spurred Koshkin into flight solely to get his hands on Roxelana—and then had the gall to rape the wife of the man whose life he had destroyed. Koshkin didn't know where to start.

"But how did you get away?" he asked when he could speak.

She hauled her wrists free of his grip and slapped him hard across the face. "Why should you care? Didn't you hear what I said? He hooked you like a fish on the line. He'd have me in those grubby paws to this day if it weren't for Maria, who had the wits to figure out the hints I was dropping and the grace not to hold your insinuations against me, and Ilya's wife, who lost patience with his adultery and interceded with Grand Princess Elena for my freedom. Not to mention Tsaritsa Sumbeka, who sent women warriors to keep Prince Ilya away from me until his wife could act. The grand princess arranged for me to travel here. As for you, you can kiss my behind before I spend another moment in your company, never mind returning to your miserable, freezing country to live in a state worse than *slavery*—and I have lived as a slave most of my life, so I know what I'm talking about when I say that."

Koshkin stared at her, too dumbstruck to retaliate in kind to her blow or even to object to manhandling by his wife. Maria had saved her. Maria, his beloved daughter whose arrogant Tatar husband had not, it seemed, wanted Roxelana back in his bed. Maria and Tsaritsa Sumbeka and Prince Ilya's wife, with help from his archenemy Grand Princess Elena. And women warriors. The stars whirled in their courses, spinning him into a web of confusion.

"And who spared you from slavery?" he demanded, incensed as the import of her last sentence penetrated his fogged brain. "Don't you owe me something for that?"

"I owe you nothing," she retorted. "You took what you wanted, then abandoned me while you ran off to save yourself.

You're like every other man I've known—including Alexei, damn his uncaring hide."

"I meant to keep you safe," he said. "I couldn't drag you into a war. Ilya told me I'd be arrested if I stayed."

"You would have been." She turned away. "The troops arrived that very morning." Her admission sounded grudging at best, but she was no longer screaming at him.

"I thought they'd leave you alone. Or that Alexei would protect you if need be," he said. "Did you not seek him out?"

The excuse sounded lame even to his own ears, but Roxelana relaxed her hands to the point where he no longer feared she meant to claw out his eyes. She didn't look at him, and at first she didn't answer his question, but after a while she said, "Didn't you hear me? The troops took me with them when they left. I had no time to send for aid. I don't know who told Alexei—or when."

Past experience made him wary, but he decided not to challenge her. If she had sought out her former lover, he hadn't helped her. However casual her attachment to veracity, the statements she had flung at him in her rage had the ring of truth.

Desire for her, long suppressed, reared its inconvenient head. Remorse, a lingering suspicion that she might have seduced Ilya and claimed the opposite, more remorse at entertaining so vile a notion for even an instant, a yearning for her forgiveness, the urge to shake some sense into her and remind her that she had married him in the sight of God and man and had no right to spurn him, anger on her behalf, a weird joy at again being in her presence, however brief or troubled their reunion—these emotions and impressions wrestled with one another in his head like the trained bears who accompanied wandering minstrels and jugglers from one Russian town and village to the next.

But beneath, above, and around them a burning flame of hatred ignited: against the court that had betrayed him, the grand princess who headed it, the favorite who stood at her side and made her rule possible, and Prince Ilya Shuisky, whose perfidy had stripped Koshkin of his lands, his rank, and his wife's affection.

"I shall avenge your dishonor," he choked out. "Prince Ilya will pay for what he did to us both."

Her outburst over, Roxelana raised her chin. She attempted none of her usual seduction but with a chilly indifference not unlike that so recently adopted by Queen Bona said, "Suit yourself. Where you go and what you do does not concern me. I can't divorce you, but our marriage ended for me the day you left for Staritsa." And self-possessed as ever, she lifted her cobalt skirts in one graceful hand and swept from the room.

Only as Koshkin watched the door close behind her did he recall that she had never answered his question about where she stood in relation to Grand Duke Sigismund.

With a sigh he realized that the answer didn't matter. He had already lost her.

No, not lost. She was his wife. He could win her back. In time. But he clearly had a great deal of apologizing to do.

Chapter 3

NASAN DANCED AT THE OUTER DOOR, IMPATIENT TO PASS through. She ignored Daniil's amused gaze; she didn't need him to remind her of yesterday, when he'd pushed her to leave for Prince Andrei's funeral and she'd begged for more time with their son. Today was different, not least because Borya, wrapped against the cold, lay wriggling in Zhenya's arms, ready to accompany them. The tooth had poked through overnight, and although still fretful, Borya no longer showed signs of fever. Nasan need not fear that she might bring infection into her sister-in-law's house, and the baby's presence meant that she would not worry about what might happen to him while she attended his even younger cousin's naming ceremony.

Besides, this ceremonial promised to be a joyous family occasion, not a grim state obligation performed under duress and fraught with threats of surveillance and subversion. Today no one lurked in the shadows taking mental notes of who wept and who exhibited a stony forbearance. Today no strangers would attend. She expected to see her half-brother, long distant from her but becoming dearer by the day; her sister-in-law, once a foe but now a beloved friend; and her parents, whose decision to reside in Moscow reassured and delighted her.

Father Job, assigned to perform the ceremony, had also earned Nasan's affection and respect in the three and a half years since her marriage. Only the loss of her mother-in-law and the absence of her brother Ogodai and his family cast the smallest shadow on Nasan's joy. And the imminent withdrawal of her father-in-law's support, but Nikolai had agreed to travel with them today. She could hope that the presence of family might change his mind about leaving his children and grandchild for the life of denial embraced by the monks.

Although Nikolai was also the source of Nasan's impatience, since he had yet to appear despite the advancing hour. Father Job had gone ahead, as he needed time to assume his vestments after his passage through the frosty, muddy streets. The ceremony could not begin until Nasan and Daniil, the baby's future godparents, arrived—even though the actual baptism and Maria's churching would not take place for another five weeks. But impatient or not, Nasan hesitated to chivvy her father-in-law out of fear that he might stay home altogether rather than inconvenience them.

At last he appeared, dressed in the somber but rich hues he had worn since his wife's death—robes in a blue so dark that only when he stood in the thin winter sunshine could one be sure he did not wear black, embroidered in silk of a lighter tone. After a quick apology, which Nasan and Daniil brushed off, he led the way down the outer staircase and into the waiting sleigh. Nasan took the baby from his nurse's arms. The girl circled the sleigh to assume her place beside the driver. He clucked to the horses, and they were off.

That their journey, although shorter, at first followed the same path as yesterday's did not escape Nasan's notice.

Grandmothers, she prayed, *let it not be a bad omen.*

❦

Alexei bent to kiss his wife, arranged against the pillows of a sofa in the main reception area of their home. She wore a caftan of pale yellow brocade patterned with vermilion phoenixes, a perfect match for her creamy skin, brown eyes, and auburn hair—although every wisp of the hair remained tucked under her pearl-strewn headdress, as was proper for a married woman. Pearls also banded the sleeves of her tunic and formed a wide collar about her neck and upper chest.

It delighted him that she was here at all. The baby had not presented himself properly, prolonging his birth, and so many women died in childbirth even without that complication. But eight days after delivery she showed no signs of infection, and he would do whatever he could to help her rebuild her strength.

Rather than inflict his concerns on her yet again, he touched her cheek. "You look lovely."

She giggled. "Thank you, but will *Kaenana* agree?"

He laughed. It was an old joke between them. His stepmother Sumbeka had taken it upon herself a year ago to educate Maria according to her own idea of how a khan's wife and daughter-in-law should behave. Clothing formed a large part of Maria's transformation, but however hard she tried, she seldom received more than a nod of appreciation—"adequate" so far marked the height of Sumbeka's approbation.

"Let's hope her eyes are blinded by the light of her new grandson." He brushed his fingers across his son's head, a light caress designed not to wake the sleeping child. "You get along well otherwise, and she will have Nasan and Borya to deflect her attention, as well as this fine boy."

"She's an absolute darling," Maria said, still laughing. "And who can complain about fabulous clothes?"

The door burst open, and whatever she might have added was drowned in the turbulent arrival of the household's other children. Baby Alexander awoke with a yell, switching to howls as the noise went on. Maria rocked him, singing softly about birds and their nests, sunshine and flowers.

"What on earth?" Alexei demanded. "Don't you two know better than to pile into a room containing a sleeping baby while making such a to-do?"

"Sorry, *Ata*," the older culprit said. Timur, aged ten, had the grace to hang his head—although how, in what couldn't be more than the space of an hour, he had managed to reduce his ceremonial robes to something that resembled the offerings of the city ragmen required explanation.

Lyuba, in contrast, was neat as a pin except for the wild hair that ringed her head like a copper nimbus. Timur had been tugging at it when they tumbled through the door, and the effect gave her the air of a wood spirit surprised halfway through a midsummer orgy. Quite remarkable in a child of seven. "He pushed me!" she announced in a voice piercing enough to provoke another round of infant howls.

Alexei exchanged glances with his wife, whose soothing croon had been making headway against the disturbance introduced by his son and her sister until Lyuba started shouting.

"Right," Alexei told Lyuba. "Well, he should not do that." He glared at Timur, who looked more crestfallen than before. "But I suspect you pushed him back or pushed him first, because you usually do and you know he won't tattle." Lyuba blushed but admitted nothing. "And whoever's to blame, the pair of you look like you belong in the stables. Off with you before the guests arrive. Don't come back until you, Timur, have changed your clothes into something as fine as those robes were before you turned them into dust rags." He tapped the crown of Lyuba's head. "You get one of the maids to comb your hair. And I expect you both to apologize to Father Job and my parents if you keep them waiting."

They each produced a jerky bow and again dashed for the door. "And no pushing!" Alexei called after them.

The sound of their steps had barely faded when his half-sister Nasan—with her husband, father-in-law, infant, and nursemaid—walked into the room.

"Have you imported a herd of horses?" she asked when he went to welcome her. She stood on tiptoe and touched his nose with hers in the greeting to siblings. He took Borya from her arms and held him up, speaking to him in Tatar while she crossed the room to kiss Maria on both cheeks.

"Worse," Alexei said. "Lyuba and Timur, squabbling as usual. They'll be back once they look like something not guaranteed to send our parents into the nether realms. Before the ceremony begins, I hope."

He nestled Borya against his chest so he could shake Daniil's hand, tipped his head to Nikolai, then carried the baby to Maria's sofa and presented him.

"Your cousin," he told Alexander. "Look how big you'll be in six months." The baby, soothed once more, squeezed his eyes tight shut.

"He's not impressed." Nasan patted the newborn's tummy, then straightened and reached out her arms. "Too busy pondering his new name, I suppose."

Alexei grinned and handed Borya to her. "Too busy grabbing a nap while he can, more like. Those two imps woke him. I hope he'll sleep through the ceremony. Much better than having him wailing for milk the whole time."

"It's a short service. He'll do fine." Nasan pulled a hassock into place next to Maria and settled Borya on her lap. The two women fell into murmured conversation about babies, siblings, and various related topics.

"That's good," Alexei said before leaving them to it and going to join the men.

They were still discussing yesterday's funeral when a subdued Timur and Lyuba returned, clothes, hair, and behavior orderly enough to please the strictest general. Soon after that Bulat Khan and his chief wife, Sumbeka—Alexei's stepmother—arrived, followed closely by Father Job, who had almost certainly been monitoring for the appearance of these last and most prestigious guests.

"You look charming, *kilen*," Sumbeka said as she bent to press her powdered cheek against Maria's, then did the same to Nasan before admiring the babies. Across the room Alexei raised both eyebrows at his wife, who bit her lip as if suppressing a smile.

What a difference a child made, to be sure. Or was Sumbeka, too, delighted that her daughter-in-law had survived the birth?

It was also Sumbeka who deserved the most credit for that spectacular achievement. She had almost singlehandedly saved both Alexei's wife and his son. For that he owed her a debt he could never repay.

The brief ceremony ended, and Father Job departed with the family's thanks ringing in his ears (and more tangible rewards lining his pockets). Nikolai, pleading fatigue, went with him. Only when the servants arrived with food did Nasan realize that most likely both the priest and her father-in-law had left to avoid an awkward confrontation. Russians believed that one should not eat in the presence of an unchurched woman. She glanced at Daniil, but he seemed unconcerned. Not for the first time, she said a silent prayer of gratitude for his flexibility when it came to observing her customs.

Lyuba settled herself on the richly patterned scarlet rug next to Borya and cooed at him, playing with his fingers and toes, tickling his tummy. He opened his mouth wide, showing his brand-new tooth, and cooed back at her. Timur stood to one side, looking somewhat at a loss, until Sumbeka, with the air of a fairground magician, pulled an exquisite amber rattle from the bag at her feet and held it out to him. "It's for Alexander," she said, "but he's too young for it yet. Shake it for Borya."

"I want to!" Lyuba said at once.

"Later," Sumbeka told her. "If you're good." She held up a brightly colored book. "And Timur can read him a story when he gets tired." She held the book above her head as Lyuba reached for it, but a quiet word from Maria caused the child to drop her hand. "If you're good," Sumbeka reminded her.

The men had ignored this byplay, but now Bulat spoke. "I had a letter from your half-brother Ogodai this morning. He sends his best wishes to mother and child." He dipped his head toward Alexei in the austere gesture typical of him. "And congratulations to the father on his new son, of course."

"Thank you, *Ata*." The curve of Alexei's mouth suggested he appreciated what it cost their father to offer even this grudging acknowledgment of Alexei's place in the family. Although they fought side by side these days, the two of them had long approached each other with more acrimony than amity. "What news from the steppe?"

"Not good," Bulat said. "Something is changing along the Volga. Ogodai doesn't know what, and neither do I, but since the autumn he has had to beat back several raids by competing Nogai. The horde has lost about fifty sheep and goats, a dozen horses—some of which they recovered. So far, not many warriors. But if a rogue leader has decided to move in on their grazing lands, he won't stop unless challenged. I may need to send you to aid Ogodai in defending his horde."

Alexei's eyes widened in astonishment. "I can't imagine anyone whose help Ogodai wants less than mine. Besides, he has a perfectly competent commander in his brother-in-law. So long as Jahangir refrains from drink, that is."

"I'm not sending you yet." Bulat twirled his empty plate against the tabletop. "But if the raids get worse, be prepared. Moscow is a powder keg waiting for a spark. We serve the Russian grand prince as long as we can do some good, but I have no intention of giving up every hold we have on the steppe."

Nasan darted a glance at her husband, who sat watching the interaction with narrowed eyes. From the look of him he was recording every word in his mind.

"You think the situation here could deteriorate to the point where we decide to leave?" Alexei leaned back and crossed his arms over his chest. "I respect your judgment, and if it comes to that, I will follow you, not least to keep my family safe. But these raids by the Nogai have nothing to do with the Russians, so far as we know, and Ogodai is good at what he does. I see no reason to force my presence on him when I have a wife and three children in my care. He won't welcome my aid, I assure you."

"I hope the situation here will *not* deteriorate," Bulat said. "But you saw that funeral. Shuisky pushes himself forward. Belsky matches him step for step. Elena pretends a lack of concern she cannot feel. Telepnev hangs by the thread of her approval, and she's already shown that she won't hesitate to sacrifice him in pursuit of her goals. And the nobles are restless, wondering who will fall next." He glared at Daniil, who jerked as if startled, having done nothing to deserve the glare. "Seeing relatives who joined Prince Andrei hanged by the side of the road has more than a few of the grand princess's former supporters thinking that continuing to back her may not be the best way to ensure their own survival."

"The members of my clan agree," Daniil noted. "I lost more than one cousin in that fiasco. Papa and I swore to support the grand prince, and we will continue to do so, but we're not blind. I understand why Elena feared her brother-in-law, but I don't think she's improved her position one bit by treating him and his men the way she did."

Bulat harrumphed, but he did stop glaring. "In any event we need to prepare for the worst. You too, young man. You have a wife and son to protect as well." He waved a hand at Alexei. "And if that means defending your brother's horde, defend it we will."

Alexei opened his mouth—to agree, Nasan guessed, because nothing else would stop their father once he got into one of his states—but his newborn son cut him off, awakening with a wail and thrashing fists.

"He's hungry," Maria said.

Nasan watched with interest as her brother intercepted his wife's pleading glance. He responded at once. "Then let's move to another room so we can discuss strategy while my son feeds in peace. Come, Timur."

Bulat rose to his feet, Daniil and Alexei followed, and so it was settled.

As Alexei ushered his father, his son, and his brother-in-law out of the room, he turned and winked at Maria. "Enjoy your moment of quiet, love," he said, then the door closed behind him.

♪

With Timur gone, Lyuba lost no time in claiming the rattle, but Borya's eyes drooped from too much excitement. In response to a gesture from Maria Nasan called for Tanya, Maria's housekeeper, and asked her to direct Borya and his nursemaid to Baby Alexander's nursery. Lyuba jumped up, offering to show the way. When they left the room, Nasan again settled herself on the sofa, prepared to chat.

"He's very protective of you, my brother," she said over Alexander's wails, once the room had cleared. "It's good to see it."

"He recognizes the danger she was in, no doubt." Sumbeka reached out a hand and patted Maria's knee. "And rightly so. For a while I feared to lose you *and* your sweet Alexander. But God was merciful."

"And you were skilled." Maria clasped her mother-in-law's hand in turn. "I can't thank you enough. If you had not found a way to turn the child …" She left the sentence unfinished.

"But how are you?" Nasan asked. "No signs of fever? I brought my packets of herbs just in case."

"No signs." Maria unbuttoned her outer robe, lowered a placket she had designed for her tunic, and put the baby to her breast. He quieted at once. "And the child is as you see him."

Nasan nodded. Like Maria, she would not risk attracting the Evil Eye by praising an unbaptized infant (even one so recently commended to God's care), so instead she said, "How clever you are with your needle. Will you make me a tunic like that if I again find myself with child? It looks so much easier to manage than the usual robes!"

Maria laughed and agreed. The three of them chattered for a while, then Sumbeka said, "I should tell you that we received a second letter from the steppe. Your sister-in-law wrote to me. She too is quite concerned, and not only about you and about the raids. You are fortunate, *kilen*, that my stepson holds you in such high regard."

Maria blinked. "But Ogodai adores Firuza."

"Indeed," Nasan chimed in. "So I've always believed. What has he done, *Ana*, to convince her otherwise?"

Sumbeka pulled a rolled scroll from her bag and sighed. "Well, that's the problem, dear ones. I don't know that he's done anything." She pulled the red ribbon that tied the scroll, unrolled it, and held it out to Nasan, who perused it and handed it back.

"Firuza will need your needlework before I do," Nasan told Maria, who couldn't yet read the Tatar language with its Arabic script.

"She's with child again?" Maria asked. "I suppose it's not that strange, as the twins must be almost three by now, but poor Firuza—what a handful!"

"She has plenty of help in the harem," Sumbeka said. "But it's the harem that's troubling her now. You know her husband is not supposed to visit her in that way when she's with child. I'm sure she delayed telling him as long as possible, but one cannot conceal these things forever."

Maria blushed, as if she did know, although her husband had converted to Christianity before their marriage. Nasan decided not to pursue that angle. "Ogodai didn't stray the last time, did he?"

Privately she wondered. A khan with dozens of concubines—would a night here and there mean anything to her brother? Love had never stopped her father, although Bulat valued and respected Sumbeka above his many other women.

Sumbeka acknowledged the unspoken reality with a shrug. "Not often, I think. Not in terms of how he feels about her, for certain. But as you saw in the letter, now she fears something more specific: that the twins' nurse, that Russian girl you sent them, has been sneaking away from work to meet a lover. That your brother is the lover she goes to meet."

"Grusha?" Maria asked, astonishment in her voice. "Challenging Firuza for her husband? I don't believe it. She hasn't the gumption to do such a thing." She flushed. "Oh, how dreadful that sounds. Do forgive me."

Nasan threw up her hands. "Maria's right, *Ana*. Firuza has lost her mind—I do sympathize with her, but still. If Ogodai has ever looked twice at Grusha, you can roll me up in that rug and toss me out the window. Why, he usually refers to her as pasty-faced!"

Another eloquent shrug greeted this statement. "Apparently she stayed in his tent when they traveled to the camp from Moscow eighteen months ago. I suspect it was to keep the other men from bothering her, but Firuza's suspicions seem to have started there."

"Oh, but that's still nonsense." Nasan waved her hands once more. "Why, Firuza came north for Alexei and Maria's wedding, which was at least six months after Grusha left Moscow. I saw no evidence of strain then between Grusha and Firuza. It must be the pregnancy that has turned her thoughts in a different direction. I don't believe a word of it."

"I must say I find the whole thing quite incredible," Sumbeka said. "The girl's not ugly, but there are many more beautiful women in the harem. And I know for a fact that Ogodai never responded to Roxelana's lures, because Firuza told me so herself. If he could resist Roxelana, then surely a pasty-faced Russian would leave him cold whether he's seeking relief in the harem or not. But I can't swear to Firuza that she's traveling in the land of wind horses, can I?"

"No," Nasan admitted. "None of us knows for sure. And I suppose she hasn't told him what she fears."

"I assume not," Sumbeka said. "Would you?"

"Never," Maria and Nasan said at the same moment.

"If it were not for this business with the raiders, I would go to her." Sumbeka scanned the scroll once more, then rolled and tied it. "I'm sure she doesn't need this worry on top of caring for the children she has and growing another in her womb."

"And governing the horde," Nasan put in, to remind her mother that Firuza did more than raise children.

"And governing the horde," Sumbeka agreed. "Although if the horde is at war, I expect she leaves that part to her husband and brother. I hope so, in any event." In fact, she sounded more resigned than hopeful. She had known Firuza for years.

"We could invite her here," Maria said. "We have plenty of space for her and the children."

"But then she would leave her husband alone with the harem." Sumbeka tapped the tied scroll against the small hexagonal table that stood nearby. "No, I thought of that already. I would love to see her and the twins, but it won't serve." She dropped the scroll back into her bag and stood. "I'm afraid that as with the raiding we must wait and see. Perhaps Firuza will discover where Grusha goes and solve her problem that way."

She bent forward to press her cheek against Maria's, then curled her finger against the baby's neck. "But for now, *kilen*, I think we should leave you and the little one to rest. We want you well as soon as possible. That darling child needs you, and so do we."

Chapter 4

"HOW WAS YOUR SHIFT?" NASAN ASKED HER HUSBAND AS he came through the door to her sitting room, once her mother-in-law's. She ignored the pang that memory brought; one day, no doubt, she would take it for granted that she, not Natalya, ruled the Kolychev household. "Did the grand prince remember you?"

"Not in the least," Daniil said cheerfully as he bent to kiss her. "How could he? He wasn't more than three the last time he saw me close up. He asked after Papa, though. And his mother recognized me. As for the shift, I'd rather handle horses than dress and undress a pair of princes, but at least while I'm on duty I can keep an eye on them. And I'm paired with my cousin Roman as well as a few others I know from military assignments, so the company's congenial. Some of it, anyway. Prince Ilya Shuisky, alas, has also become a gentleman of the chamber."

She extended a hand, and he came to sit beside her. "Did Grand Prince Ivan understand why Papa-in-law wasn't there? It's not easy to lose a tutor."

"Especially when you're seven years old and lord of the universe," Daniil said. "I explained that Papa had gone to live in the monastery and had sent me to serve in his stead. I don't know that Grand Prince Ivan fully grasps why, but he's visited enough monasteries with his mother, young as he is, that I think he gets the general idea. It may help that Papa's in the Kremlin. Ivan can summon him if he feels so inclined."

He hesitated, then added in a soft voice, "Those rumors about his mother and Telepnev …"

He left the sentence unfinished. Nasan raised an interrogative eyebrow. His promotion to junior boyar and appointment as gentleman of the chamber meant that he spent days and nights in the royal apartments on a rotating shift, four men at a time. If anyone was in a position to confirm or deny the rumors, he was. No doubt the grand princess had picked him in part for his unswerving loyalty, but there were limits to discretion, and Nasan placed herself inside them.

"True?" she said, as quietly as he had.

He nodded. "And that's not all." He beckoned her closer, then spoke quietly in her ear. "While they're preoccupied with each other, the Shuisky clan makes mischief. I saw Prince Ilya sneaking about at night, spying on Elena and her lover. What good he thinks proof of their liaison will do him I can't begin to guess, but the sneaking worries me."

"Does he want to manipulate them into giving him a higher position? A better estate?" Nasan pondered this information. Her limited experience with Prince Ilya, who pawed women at weddings and had forced himself on Roxelana during her imprisonment, left her with no high opinion of his morals.

Daniil shrugged. "Possibly. Telepnev's an old hand at this game. I think he'd be as likely to send Ilya to a permanent punishment post on the White Sea as reward him, but Ilya may not have the wit to imagine that outcome."

"And the grand prince? Does he like Ilya?" It seemed hard to imagine that a seven-year-old boy, autocrat or no, would warm to so self-satisfied a pigeon as Ilya Shuisky, but if Ivan did, Daniil's task would become more difficult.

"I doubt it," Daniil said with a grin, returning his voice to a normal level. "Shuisky struts through the royal bedchamber as if he owns it, and young Ivan has a healthy sense of his own divinely appointed destiny. He scowled like a bear with a hangover, and Shuisky didn't pay him the slightest attention."

"And you?" Nasan said, laughing. She had no trouble picturing *that* scene.

"We talked about horses and hunting dogs, and I showed him how to hold a bow." Two years after a bullet wound wrecked his right shoulder, destroying his ability to wield the weapon he loved, Daniil had at last recovered the full use of his arm and his skill with an arrow, a source of great joy.

"Horses, dogs, and archery. What boy wouldn't like that?" Nasan clasped his hand and leaned forward to kiss him. "Welcome home, husband."

He cupped her ear with his hand and drew her closer. "I'm glad to be here. What did you and Borya get up to while I was gone?"

Nasan launched into a long story about their son's latest accomplishments, then guided him to the nursery to see for himself. When suppertime arrived, the two of them sat clustered on the floor babbling in two languages to the baby who, bolstered by pillows, clapped his hands and babbled happily back. Nasan, looking from one beloved face to the other, silently thanked the grandmothers for the gift of their presence. She would not say so aloud for fear of tempting fate, but in her heart she felt that life could not be more perfect.

ƒ

"Konstantin Kobylin! What brings you here?" Koshkin stopped halfway into the reception room where he had first seen Roxelana, whom he still refused to call Juliana whatever the Lithuanians might say. He had heard from Jan Radziwill of the approach of envoys from Moscow, but he had not expected to find one of his cousins among the group, especially this one. As a rule the Kobylins distinguished themselves, when they did distinguish themselves, in the military. Only Koshkin himself had early shown an affinity for such essential diplomatic skills as maneuvering with tact and according to protocol.

Kobylin, a typical large light-haired Russian, turned his ample bulk slowly. His robes swung in the still air, and Koshkin rejoiced at the familiar sight. In the last two months he had perforce adopted this land's fashion of wide sleeves, long hose, and tight-belted waists, but when he glanced in a mirror he still felt as if the image belonged to a stranger. He missed his loose trousers and boots, his floor-length caftan and outer robes.

"By the Mother of God," Kobylin cried. "Is that you, Fyodor? You look like a Lithuanian!" Without waiting for an answer, he wrapped both arms around his cousin in a Russian bear hug, lifting Koshkin half off his feet and smacking a kiss on both cheeks.

"What happened to you?" Kobylin asked as he let Koshkin go. "We heard terrible things in Moscow. That you'd deserted to Staritsa. That you narrowly escaped arrest. They imprisoned your wife and confiscated your estate, you know. Disgraced your daughter and demoted your older boys. Now I find you here. Astonishing. Were the rumors right for once, then? If not, why did you run?"

Koshkin winced. Roxelana hadn't mentioned that Maria, Mikhail, and Foma had also paid a price because of Ilya's machinations. "Varvara and her husband too?" he asked. If the wicked grand princess and her favorite would punish his eldest daughter and his two older sons, why not the second daughter as well?

"Not as of the time I left Russia. She rarely comes to Moscow, and her husband has powerful relatives. They seem safe enough. The younger boys as well, since they're living with her. And Bulat Khan vouched for his son and took Maria and Lyuba under his wing, so in the end no harm will come to them. But what of you?" Kobylin delivered a buffet to Koshkin's shoulder that set him reeling.

He clutched at a nearby chair. "Control yourself, Kostya. I ran because I learned of the planned arrest, not because I sympathized with Prince Andrei. Lord, did you ever see a more pathetic excuse for an uprising than that one? I left when it became clear he'd do nothing but dither and eventually made my way here. By then I couldn't go back." Sorrow tugged at his throat. He missed Russia. If he saw an opportunity, he would go home. But without a guarantee that the grand princess no longer sought his arrest, he feared to make the attempt.

The yearning nonetheless tugged at his heart. How sweet it would be to incapacitate Prince Ilya, to wreak his revenge! If Koshkin made the right moves at the right time, success would guarantee him a position of power.

For sure, no such boon awaited him here. What he'd failed to take into account when selecting Vilnius as his place of refuge was that Sigismund's court was already packed to bursting with highborn Russians. Many, captured during the war that had ended last year, refused to return for fear of being regarded as traitors. Others, like Koshkin himself, had fled the realm of a harsh and unyielding grand princess. All had their hands out looking for support and employment, a place at court and advancement. Finding himself under siege from constant demands, the grand duke preferred to treat the petitioners equally—that is, to offer no more than minimal support, regardless of qualifications or need. Few of the new arrivals had as much to offer as Koshkin, but his pleas for special consideration had so far fallen on deaf ears. As a result, his welcome from Jan Radziwill wore thin, and the Lithuanian lords squeezed him dry of information about their sometime adversary without producing either lands or position in return. Perhaps he *should* take a chance and go home.

"They'd kill you," Kobylin said, deflating Koshkin's burgeoning belief that with the right plan he might both survive and succeed. "As they did Prince Andrei and his supporters."

Perhaps, but was he not dying slowly here? Koshkin decided to ponder the pros and cons of his situation tonight, once he was alone. For the moment he should find out as much as he could from Kobylin about conditions in Moscow. "What's the nature of your mission?" he asked.

"Oh, that." Kobylin waved a hand. "Absurdity, really. The rest of them are going on to Hungary. To visit some king named Ferdinand. They need permission to travel through Vilnius to Cracow and beyond. My job is to report to the grand princess whether they get it."

"You're going back to Moscow?" Koshkin tucked a hand in his cousin's arm and led him from the room. "Let me show you what hospitality I can while you're here. And you can tell me more about what's going on at home."

Because I need all the information I can get if I'm to make the right decision.

Yes, one never knew. A swift return to Moscow seemed unlikely, but a conversation with his cousin might reveal an opportunity Koshkin had not foreseen.

He would welcome that chance. He'd offered the Lithuanians his best, and look where it had got him: he'd become no more than a beggar.

It was time to move on.

⌘

"Tulpar Sultan and Ruslan Sultan. What a surprise—and a pleasure."

Everything about the speaker was familiar: the dark hair and sparse beard; the small, neat frame of his body; the intricately tied turban and brilliant fabrics, trimmed with luxuriant furs. Since his arrival in Moscow Alexei had welcomed few sights as much as he did this one.

He laughed and dipped his head in the direction of Prince Bayim. "So good to see you, Bayim *mirza*. Is all well in Crimea? What brings you here?"

Because of their familiarity with Tatar customs and language he and Ruslan had been summoned to greet the embassy from Crimea's khan, Sahib-Girei, which had arrived not long after Christmas. The exchange of courtesies, the sound of his mother tongue—the whole experience made Alexei quite nostalgic for the land where he had spent almost half of his life.

"I bring declarations of friendship from Sahib-Girei Khan. It seems that both he and the grand princess have rid themselves of their inconvenient relatives, so it behooves them to ally with each other—or at least to declare their undying friendship—now that the Lithuanians no longer require our services against Moscow." Bayim produced an elaborate shrug that underlined the irony in his voice.

"Or Moscow against Lithuania," Alexei responded in kind. "You can raid them both until one decides to increase the reward for turning against the other. But what's this about Sahib-Girei? Has he defeated his nephew at last?"

A flash of regret—remorse, even—tore through him. He glanced at Ruslan, his friend and ally, and saw a similar expression cross his face. They had both served Sahib's nephew Islam-Girei for more than a decade.

"You haven't heard?" Bayim said. "It happened last summer. A pair of rogue Nogai stole into Islam-Girei's camp, killed him by treachery, then ran off with his herds and his women. Sahib-Girei's been like a cat on hot stones ever since. He doesn't want to punish the assassins because they did him a favor, but by letting them go, he fears he may be setting himself up as the next victim."

Something in their faces must have alerted him, because he added, "It wouldn't have helped if you two had stayed. You'd have died with him, if he didn't murder you first. Most of his supporters had already fled under threat of execution. But something must be done about the Nogai."

"Because of two rogue warriors?" Ruslan asked. He sounded incredulous, but Alexei's brows creased as he thought about the letter sent by his brother Ogodai. Rogue warriors attacking a camp in Crimea. Unknown raiders on the western bank of the Volga. The second lay much closer to the traditional Nogai grazing lands than the first.

"No," Bayim said. "They've banded together under Said-Ahmed Bey, appointed an heir apparent and a *beglerbey* who will be third in line if anything happens to the other two. The only holdout is Sheikh-Mamai, and he's causing trouble from the Caspian to the Meshchera, damn his uncooperative hide."

"May they rot in hell." Alexei gripped the hilt of the sword that hung from his belt. "My brother Ogodai reported encounters with raiders. My father's in a stew already. If it's warring Nogai, that's serious." He sent Ruslan a rueful grin. "I hope you and your men are ready to ride."

"Does the sun rise in the east?" Ruslan gestured to a set of chairs in one corner. "Sit, Bayim *mirza*, and tell us what other news you bring from Crimea."

They talked for a considerable time, until Prince Ilya Shuisky poked his head around the door. "Tsarevich Alexei Bulatovich," he said, bowing. Somehow he managed to perform even this standard gesture of respect with an air of pomposity. "My noble uncle sends me to inquire when your meeting might conclude. The grand prince sends his regrets that he cannot invite the noble ambassadors to dine with him, because he is too young and still eats with his mother. But my uncle would count it a great favor if the khan's envoys would honor his table with their presence."

Tempted to snap a retort that would cut Shuisky down to size, Alexei stopped when he saw Prince Bayim's expression. Only then did he realize that he had not spoken of his marriage, his conversion, or the name change that went with it. "It was necessary," he said in Tatar. "A matter of alliance, not conviction."

The shock on Bayim's face spoke louder than words. A barrier lay between them, a barrier Alexei had built. But there was nothing he could or would do about that. He had made his decision. So he stood, bowed once more, delivered Shuisky's invitation to dinner without missing a single lofty adjective, and did his best to ignore Prince Bayim's—and his own—discomfort.

Chapter 5

"ABSOLUTELY NOT." ROXELANA REGARDED KOSHKIN WITH the same chilly expression she had bestowed on him every time he tried to talk with her since he arrived in Vilnius. After numerous evasions she had at last agreed to meet him in the same room where they had spoken on the day he first attended court. "And you can't force me to go with you. I have spoken to the grand duke. He and his lady mother agree that I am welcome at their court—more welcome than you, may I note?"

The urge to grab her by those indecently exposed shoulders and shake her almost overwhelmed Koshkin's better nature. Only the certain knowledge that she would run to the grand duke with the tale kept him from acting on impulse.

That, and his mixed feelings at the sight of her. God help him, he *still* yearned for her, despite everything. How the styles of this western land offset her beauty! Today she wore a robe the color of ripe cherries, its low neckline lined with the finest lace, its puffed sleeves slashed to reveal a lining of the palest pink. The tight waist, lower than the cobalt silk creation she had worn during their last conversation, emphasized that gorgeous figure, once his for the taking, now at the service of the grand duke—or so he assumed. The entire court seemed to believe it in any event, so if Roxelana kept Sigismund dangling out of some previously unsuspected loyalty to her marriage, a concern for her reputation, or just the urge to prolong the chase for as long as possible, her efforts appeared, to her disgruntled husband, misplaced.

"Don't you want revenge on Prince Ilya, even Grand Princess Elena, for what they did to you?" he asked. "My cousin tells me that Prince Andrei has died in captivity—no surprise there—and that at least a few of the Moscow nobles have developed a backbone, or at least a sense of self-preservation. Also that Prince Ilya is rising high under protection from his uncle. I intend to bring him down if I can."

"Good for you." Roxelana lifted the brass pomander that hung from her waist and sniffed it. "You'll do it without me. Although ..." She stopped, a calculating look in her eyes that Koshkin could not recall seeing before.

Will she change her mind? That irrepressible adversary, hope, flooded him unawares, and he caught his breath, afraid to speak a word lest it sway her in the opposite direction. Was it possible that she cared for him after all?

The pomander had several segments besides the one containing the orange stuffed with cloves believed to protect against the plague, which she had sniffed just now. As Koshkin watched dumbfounded, his wife twisted one of them apart and produced a small glass vial containing a dark powder.

She held it out to him. "For Prince Ilya. If you can manage it. Put about half the vial in something he will eat or drink. Preferably drink, as you want him to consume the entire dose at one time. Otherwise it's just a cosmetic. It will widen his eyes and distort his vision but do him no serious harm. Consider it a gift from me. Or from Queen Bona, if you prefer."

"But what is it?" Koshkin took the vial and examined it from every angle.

For the first time since he had encountered her by chance in the grand duke's reception room, Roxelana smiled. It was not a pleasant smile, and her hazel eyes remained cold enough to send a shiver down Koshkin's spine. "Why, dearest," she said, as she used to do before they parted. "Don't you know Queen Bona's reputation? She is a relative of the Borgia family, and like them she dispatches her enemies with untraceable poisons. That one is dried belladonna root. Deadly nightshade. She gave it to me in case you proved intractable, but you won't, will you?"

At a loss for words, he shook his head. Who *was* this woman he had loved and married?

"Good," Roxelana said. "Then regard it as my contribution to your cause."

Again she swept from the room without waiting for a response. Which, Koshkin concluded, was just as well, since he could not have produced one if he tried.

Alexei and Ruslan met Daniil as he dismounted from his horse in the courtyard of Bulat Khan's estate. A groom led Daniil's black gelding away.

"What does your father want with us?" Daniil asked Alexei when the greetings ended. By then the three of them had entered the ground floor of the house and were making their way to what Alexei tended to think of as his father's lair. Unjust, he knew, but his relationship with his stern parent, although much improved, still at times left him feeling like a deer pursued by a particularly fierce and intransigent wolf.

"A letter from my brother," he said. "More disturbing news, I assume." He nodded at Ruslan. "What we learned from the Crimean ambassadors last month hinted at ongoing trouble on the steppe. I expect *Ata* wants to discuss strategy."

"And he's asking me?" Daniil sounded skeptical. An understandable response, given that Bulat's willingness to take advice from his juniors was distinguished primarily by its absence.

Alexei grinned. "He respects your judgment. Yes, I know, he hides it well." This in response to the shocked expression on Daniil's face. "And you have the right, as a family member and friend of Ogodai's, which last is more than I can say. I suspect he also wants a Russian perspective, but he hasn't admitted to that."

"You're head of your clan too," Ruslan put in. "As well as in personal service to the grand prince."

Daniil shuddered. "Don't remind me."

"Of which?" Alexei—although in no hurry to see his father pass away, however strained their interactions at times—had lived alone for long enough not to fear heading the clan. Indeed, since his father-in-law's flight last year he did head the Koshkin clan to all intents and purposes. Royal service, on the other hand …

"Both," Daniil said. "The clan isn't causing much trouble at present, but half of us are under a cloud for supporting Prince Andrei, and we have few friends at court as a result. The grand prince and his brother don't bother me—how could they, at their ages?—but watching the boyars scheming at council meetings when I could be on horseback in the open air doesn't make me want to leap out of bed in the morning."

They had reached Bulat's study. Alexei pushed the door open, then stood back to let the others enter first.

Once inside he looked around. Every time he came here, the room appeared more oriental, more familiar. Although a Russian building, it had housed Bulat and Sumbeka for more than a year, and over that time they had transformed it to reflect their own tastes. Other than the massive oak desk, which Alexei suspected his father kept because its imposing style reflected his own, the study bore little resemblance to the room he had first seen the day before his marriage to Maria in February 1537. Brass braziers on mammoth metal saucers and multi-legged tables inlaid with mother of pearl dotted red carpets patterned with geometric designs. Long padded sofas lined the walls, and light poured in through square-gridded windows of unusual clarity decorated with patterns formed from colored panes. Panels of Chinese silk hung between the windows, picking up the colors of the panes and carpets.

Behind the desk sat Bulat, clad in a heavy tan robe trimmed in dark fur and embroidered in gold medallions the size of Alexei's palm, an elaborate turban wound about his head, and impatience visible on his face. "Well, come in," he said as they lined up at the door to greet him. "Don't stand on ceremony. We have a problem on our hands."

Don't stand on ceremony? When you've demanded nothing less on every previous occasion?

Alexei let the thought lapse unspoken and found a seat on the closest sofa that faced the desk. Daniil joined him on the left and Ruslan to the right. Together the three of them stared at Bulat, waiting for him to disclose his news.

He delayed long enough for a servant to pour cups of koumiss before pulling a scroll from his desk drawer and unfolding it. "The Nogai raiders are still harassing your brother's horde," he said bluntly. "And although he has succeeded in keeping them at bay, has recaptured the animals they stole or taken replacements from their herds, has protected his people and defeated the enemy more than once, he suffered a major setback last month. They killed his brother-in-law Jahangir during one of the retaliatory raids. Ogodai writes that the next in line to replace Jahangir as Mangyt bey is an untried youth with—his words—more fire than wit. We can't allow that to go forward unchallenged."

"We can't stop it," Alexei said. "The Mangyts choose their own bey. Ogodai knows that."

And so should you, he added silently. Khans ruled at the consent of the tribes. Oppose the tribal elders, and support would vanish quickly. Vanish in the most literal sense: in the vastness of the steppe those who lost confidence in their ruler packed their tents and drove their herds to another destination.

"You knew Jahangir better than any of us." Daniil gestured to his right to indicate that he meant Alexei. "Was he much of a loss? That sounds horrible, I know, but last time I saw him, he could barely stand."

"Me too," Alexei said. "He'd been drinking for months, then someone stuck a knife in him, so he was in pretty bad shape for a while. Almost died, in fact. But from what Ogodai has said since, I believe Jahangir did reform. Too late to worry about that in any event. If Ogodai considers his death a loss, then it is."

Alexei paused as scattered thoughts—some pleasant, most not—about that time more than three years ago assailed him. His battle with Ogodai, his attempt to steal his brother's betrothed (in fairness, she had once been promised to him), his departure with Roxelana, and that short but blissful period in which passion had consumed him. He had not liked Jahangir or even respected him, but he had not disliked him either. And in the contest with Ogodai Jahangir had backed Alexei.

"He was only twenty-two," Alexei said. "I'm sure his sister is devastated. She always protected him, even when he deserved it not one bit."

"May God have mercy on his soul," Bulat said. They repeated the phrase, then sat in silence for a moment pondering the finality of death. As warriors they sensed its presence ever looming, but for that very reason they pushed the image into dark corners of the mind except at times like this. Otherwise they could not do what they had no choice but to do.

The moment passed. Bulat sipped koumiss. "In any case," he said. "I didn't mean that we should interfere in the Mangyts' choice of bey. They would simply flee to the side of the raiders, who may well be their kinsmen, and more ill than good would result. What other options have we?"

"You want to send someone to fill Jahangir's place as military leader," Ruslan said. It was not a question. "But has Ogodai Khan asked for that kind of help?" Bulat sent him an approving glance.

"Under normal circumstances I would go." Daniil stood and paced to the window, where he gazed into the courtyard for a few breaths before returning to the sofa. "Ogodai would welcome me, I'm sure. We are sworn brothers. But I can't leave Moscow at the moment. Papa called in more than a few favors to get me this appointment, and anyway the welfare of the grand prince comes first. As well as the lineage. I can't take off for the steppe and leave the entire clan without a representative at court." The glum expression on his face suggested that he might regret that, but no one could argue the truth of what he said.

"You want us to go," Alexei said, accepting the inevitable. He couldn't claim that his father had surprised him. Bulat had hinted as much two months ago. "Ruslan and myself. The prospect has a certain appeal, I admit. But like Daniil, I pledged my service to the grand prince. I too have a clan to protect, including a wife not long recovered from childbirth and three children in my care. And even though my conversion to Christianity means that I no longer pose a threat to Ogodai's control of his horde, you won't convince me that he will rejoice if I show up unannounced and unrequested, no matter how many warriors ride in my train. We put up with each other;

sharing a father does not make us brothers in the same sense as Ogodai and Daniil."

He stopped there. If anyone bore responsibility for the hostility between himself and his younger half-brother, Bulat did. A wound slowly healing and thus not worth stripping free of its scar tissue once more.

"Perhaps you can do better," Bulat said. For a wild moment Alexei thought he heard a wistful note in his father's voice, as if Bulat hoped for such an outcome. "I will take your wife and her sister and your sons—unless you wish to escort Timur to visit his mother—into my home as I did before. No harm will come to them or to her other siblings. I will see to that. And you need stay only a few months, until you and your brother beat these raiders back across the Volga, if that's where they come from. I will arrange for your absence. Sheikh-Mamai is causing trouble for the Russians too, threatening Kasimov and Ryazan. Who knows how much damage he will do if not stopped? And the generals have not yet assigned you your own command. Here you will have one."

Ruslan and Daniil sent him sympathetic glances. Alexei swore under his breath, but he saw no real alternative. His father had countered every one of his objections, including the one he had not bothered to raise: his desire for a command of his own. Bright memories—of Ogodai as a worshipful eight-year-old; as a youth eager to extend the hand of friendship; and most recently, if grudgingly, as the best man at Alexei's wedding, whose donation of a house had made it possible for Alexei and his wife to live apart from her father—danced at the back of his brain. He and his half-brother had not always seen each other as adversaries. Maybe their father had the right of it, and the time for peace had arrived.

And he wanted that. But oh lord, what was he supposed to tell Maria, especially if he accepted Bulat's suggestion that he take Timur to visit Guzel, whom he had never married but had loved, on and off, for seven years?

"When should we prepare to leave?" he asked.

"Within a couple of weeks," Bulat said. "The sooner, the better. If your brother has assessed the new Mangyt bey correctly—and I feel certain he has—we have no time to lose. Those raiders will follow up on their success at the first opportunity."

※

"Oh, poor Firuza!" Nasan handed the letter back to her mother and conveyed the gist of its news to Maria, who echoed her cry.

"I never met him," Maria continued. "When Ogodai and Firuza came here, the brother stayed behind. But I liked her. Were they close, she and her brother?"

"Very," Nasan said. "Twins. To be honest, I didn't know her brother well either. From what Ogodai told me, Jahangir gave her a lot of trouble until Ogodai arrived and forced Jahangir to sober up. But Ogodai and Jahangir had been friends as boys, and they worked well together once Ogodai married Firuza and became khan. Jahangir was a good warrior. He handled most of the military operations, defensive and offensive. Ogodai and Firuza focus on building the herds, horses especially, so their people have a means of support other than raiding. And they handle justice, administration, and so on. I'm sure they miss Jahangir. Ogodai's a good fighter too, but if he's taking care of that, it's hard to find time for administrative tasks."

"And my daughter-in-law must worry about her husband's safety as well." Sumbeka retied the scroll and placed it on the table, then picked up a steaming brass jug and offered to pour. They were meeting at Maria's house, not hers, but habit took precedence over protocol—or so Nasan concluded. Her mother often served tea at Nasan's house as well. And really, among family what difference did it make?

She accepted the delicate porcelain cup and placed it next to the scroll to cool. "You seem better, Maria. Have you fully recovered?"

"Completely." Maria picked up her embroidery. "Our little Alexander smiled today."

When they oohed and aahed, she went on, "And how is your Borya? Has he finished cutting teeth and driving you mad with anxiety each time?"

"Goodness, no. I wish he would, but he has only six so far." Nasan wrapped a linen cloth around the cup and lifted it to her mouth. Lemony steam swirled around her nostrils. "If only he did not develop a fever with each one. Not a high fever but enough to upset me. And it sounds mad, but he sleeps so well and has such a sunny disposition when he's not teething that when I hear him cry inconsolably as he does at those times, I inevitably think the worst. Zhenya loses patience with me, but I can't help it."

"All those medical books," Sumbeka said with a shake of her head. "And here you are, anxious as any mother who suffers in ignorance."

"I think the books just fuel my imagination," Nasan said. "I recall everything I've read and imagine it's happening to Borya. I'm glad I studied, but alas, one's own baby is different."

Sumbeka shook her head again, but her eyes were warm and she reached out to pat Nasan's hand. "Always," she said. "Meanwhile, what can we do for Firuza? We can't visit her, with the situation so unsettled and the two of you such new mothers, but we must find some way to show her that we're thinking about her."

"Is she still worried about Grusha?" Maria asked. "Of course you're right. We must send condolences and whatever help we can. Your couriers get through, obviously, or there would be no letters."

"She is still worried," Nasan said. "Not only about Grusha, I think, but of what Grusha represents: losing Ogodai to war or another woman. The first seems more likely than the second but is perhaps harder to bear."

"Yes, I agree." Sumbeka sipped tea from a cup held in her left hand while tapping the scroll with the fingers of her right. "And there's more. Firuza has lived in that camp her whole life, and these strangers threaten her people and her livelihood. They have killed her twin brother and placed the husband she loves at risk. We are far away, so who but she can defend her children? To imagine an affair, however silly and painful that may be, must hurt less than facing the real danger. If I could, I would go to her in a heartbeat, but I fear my husband would not permit it."

She glanced from daughter to daughter-in-law, her dark eyes alight with laughter. "You expected never to hear that from me, I'm sure, but even I hesitate to defy a direct command, if only so that I can call on him for help if needed."

"You are an example to us both, *Ana*," Nasan said, giggling. "I will keep that idea in mind for future use."

⚘

"*Bozhe moi*," Kobylin said. "You look like the veriest tramp. I want to hide my moneybag at the sight of you."

Koshkin grinned, delighted. He had aimed for exactly that response. How else could he hope to sneak back into Russia among the returning ambassadors? "So no one will recognize me, you think?"

"Not as the dapper Koshkin, for sure," his cousin confirmed. "They may wonder why I hired a rapscallion to hold my horses—or pick you up on general suspicion of ill intent. But no doubt I can adopt a lordly air and secure your freedom. Just don't go off on your own. If the bailiffs don't get you, your fellow criminals will probably slide a knife between your ribs before anyone can intervene to save you."

Examining his reflection in the large looking glass that adorned his bedchamber—one of the many amenities he would miss when he returned to Russia—Koshkin had to agree with his cousin. Eight months of flight followed by three of near-dependency on Jan Radziwill's generosity had left Koshkin longing for his wealthy and landed past. But even a shabby and worn-down noble robe or secondhand doublet and hose identified him as the aristocrat he was, albeit one fallen on hard times. His present outfit would shame a peasant: loose shirt tucked into homespun trousers, birchbark shoes, a sheepskin coat and rabbit-fur hat—both worn with the fur side in for warmth.

But that was the point, was it not? To wreak his revenge on Prince Ilya without attracting the attention of the grand princess's soldiers, Koshkin had to get back into the Russian lands undetected. The best way to travel was as his cousin's servant, at least until the ambassadorial party made its way past the border guards. Among the dozen or so envoys led by Kobylin—returning to Moscow to report on their success in securing free passage for those charged with continuing on to Hungary—none would recognize him by sight. Indeed, in his present garb he doubted his own mother could have called him by name.

Once past the border he could decide whether to remain with the envoys or head for Moscow on his own. Either way he'd go first to Maria's estate. He had always loved her best, and he could count on her being delighted to see him.

And her husband? Would he be as pleased at his father-in-law's return?

Koshkin banished that inconvenient question to the netherworld where it belonged. Alexei had not, it seemed, lusted after Roxelana as Koshkin once feared. Alexei had no other allies in Moscow, and his marriage to Maria meant that he and Koshkin stood or fell together, so what choice had he but to support his father-in-law? He was an arrogant son of a bitch, for sure, but a pragmatic one.

In a specially designed pouch attached to the inside of the sheepskin coat Koshkin carried the vial of deadly nightshade root that Roxelana had given him. What to do with it, he hadn't decided. Feed it to Prince Ilya as payback for his manipulation and deceit? Deliver it to Grand Princess Elena, the ultimate source of his troubles? Or could he, perhaps with Maria's help, do both—or even find a way to blame Prince Ilya for a murder that Koshkin himself committed?

He would have to wait and watch, see what opportunity presented itself. In the meantime, he was heading home.

Chapter 6

Moscow, March 1538

"WHEN WERE YOU PLANNING TO TELL ME?" AT THE SOUND of that furious feminine voice Alexei turned his head to see Maria standing in the doorway to his private sanctum, tapping her foot.

He set aside the book he had borrowed from his father, some Cathay general's treatise on military strategy, and rose to face her. He'd known he would pay a price for delaying the sharing of Bulat's plans, but he'd delayed anyway, telling himself tomorrow would do as well.

Alas, tomorrow had arrived with a bang, and his attempts to avoid confrontation had done nothing but stoke the flames. He'd rather face an entire army of charging Nogai than explain to his wife that he planned to leave her and the children for some indefinite time.

And you call yourself a warrior!

"You're wearing armor," Maria said in an accusing tone. "Please tell me you aren't planning to leave today."

"I'm not," he said. "I wear the mail shirt to accustom myself to the weight again before riding in it for weeks at a time. And of course I meant to tell you. What do you take me for?"

She looked as if she had to bite her tongue to avoid stating exactly what she took him for, and his quick temper rose to match hers.

He controlled it. He could silence her by shouting at her, but she did have a point, and he had learned from experience that cutting even an angry conversation short only delayed the resolution.

"How did you find out?" he asked instead.

"Timur." She pointed at the shirt. "He came to show me his brand-new mail. Very excited at riding on campaign with *Ata*. You promised me we would go together as a family, did you not? Even Lyuba, you said. And why did you withhold the news from me? I can't forbid you to go. I'm not your mother. I thought we were done with secrets!"

His mouth twitched. "Cowardice?" he suggested. "I knew you'd rip up at me, my adorable shrew."

His ploy worked. "Cowardice," she repeated, moderating her voice. "Seriously. You expect me to believe that?"

"I didn't want to disappoint you." He held out his hand, and after a moment's hesitation she came forward and took it. He resumed his seat and pulled her onto his lap. "I did promise, *kaderle*. And I had every intention of keeping the promise. But my father is desperate to resolve this situation with my brother's horde, and I can't take you and Alexander and Lyuba into a camp at war. God knows I'd love to leave Timur behind as well, but he hasn't seen his mother in more than a year. If we can't fix this, he may not have another chance. I don't plan to let him fight, but bringing him with me seems like the least I can do."

He refrained from adding, "I don't want my son to suffer the loss of his mother as I did," but Maria's face softened, and she patted his cheek. He knew she understood even before she replied. "You must take him, I agree. Guzel will want to see how he's grown, and he will much prefer to stay with you. What of us? Do we go to your parents' again?"

"Yes. *Ata* has promised to look after the three of you." Watching her, he narrowed his eyes. Something still troubled her. Guzel? Not wanting to create a problem where none existed, he said as a test, "I'll have my hands full with military matters. And I'll take your beautiful banner to remind me of home. I'll be back before you know I'm gone."

"It's not like the last campaign, though, is it?" She furrowed her brow. "There will be real fighting this time. I hope you can keep yourself and Timur safe."

She didn't doubt his fidelity; she feared for his life and his health. They had made progress, then. "Believe me, so do I. I will miss you and Alexander. Lyuba as well. I'll count each day until I return. And send frequent letters."

"Me too." Maria clasped his hand in both of hers, then pressed it against her face as if inhaling his scent. "When do you leave?"

The question he least wanted to answer. "In a few days," he said. "A week at the most. I'm waiting for word from *Ata*."

She dropped his hand and leaped to her feet, darting away from the arm he extended to catch her. "A few *days*? Alexei, you are impossible. I don't know why I put up with you!"

The door slammed behind her as she ran out. Alexei smacked his fist against the sofa cushion. The book he'd been reading when she stormed in fell to the floor, and he bent to pick it up. The title caught his eye.

The Art of War. He sighed. The art of marriage, more like.

⚘

Maria was still sniping at Alexei the next morning, although she had accepted him into her bed the night before. She claimed she'd consented only because he intended to desert her so soon, but Alexei knew better than to believe that. She enjoyed their nights of passion—so recently resumed after the long months of late pregnancy and recovery—every bit as much as he did. It was one of the things he loved about her.

Still, the combination of snappy retorts and glowering looks annoyed him enough that he took himself off as soon as he'd dressed. Yes, he should have told her sooner about the assignment from his father. Yes, she had responsibilities to fulfill caused by the change of plans. But on a list of spousal sins, postponing the delivery of unwelcome information lay a long way from the top. He'd apologized, hadn't he? More or less, anyway.

As a result, he greeted the news of a strange and disheveled visitor who insisted that he belonged to the family (despite looking as if he had never come closer than the family's rubbish heap, in the words of Tanya the housekeeper) with greater than usual impatience. When the door opened to reveal a ruffian dressed like a nomadic Tatar from one of the less hospitable desert regions, Alexei moved fast. The visitor's throat felt unexpectedly smooth in his iron grip, but the real surprise came when he knocked the disreputable rabbit-fur cap off the man's head and looked straight into his father-in-law's brown eyes.

"What in Hades?" Alexei released Koshkin, with difficulty resisting the urge to backhand his father-in-law across the room. "Where did you spring from, and how dare you show your face here after the damage you've done?"

"A pleasure to see you too." Koshkin rubbed his throat. "Ungrateful bastard. I came to visit my daughter, not that it's any business of yours."

"Stow it." Alexei snarled. "What affects my wife is very much my business. Do you have a clue what you put her through? She suffered for weeks fearing that the troops would catch you. She endured a public disgrace from Grand Princess Elena because of your disloyalty, then spent more weeks convinced that you'd died in some godforsaken hole. And now you're back to plague her again?"

"I want to see her. She's my dear, beloved child." Koshkin produced what might be intended as a pacific smile, raising Alexei's temperature further.

Alexei clenched his fist and held it right under his father-in-law's nose. "Forget it. I'm not letting you anywhere near her. But I will tell her she can stop worrying about your miserable hide. Now get out of my house before I throw you out."

"Papa?" Maria's voice sounded over his shoulder. "Alexei, what are you doing?"

He swore in Tatar, dropped his fist, and took three reluctant steps back. "Your father has stopped by to visit you," he said through his teeth. "To express his concern for your welfare. I was suggesting that he might better have considered the potential impact of his actions before he fled. The question is, beloved, do you wish to receive him? Personally I would prefer you do not."

She stopped in mid-rush, put a finger to her mouth, and thought. "You seem well, Papa. What do you want?" she said at last, her voice stiff as an overstarched shirt.

"To talk with you, kitten. To ensure that this brute has not abused you."

Maria doubled over laughing. "Abused me?" she asked when she could speak. "Papa, even from you that's the most ridiculous thing I ever heard. Alexei loves me, and I love him. You're the one who ran off and left us to deal with your mess. So I'll ask you again. What do you want from us?"

Alexei mentally applauded her. He'd expected her to offer a heartfelt welcome, but he saw now that he'd underestimated her intelligence. Koshkin's long absence without a word of reassurance contradicted any profession of concern. Maria was right: he wanted something from them, or he wouldn't have come to visit. The callous selfishness of that again clenched Alexei's hands into fists.

Maria sent him a warning glance, but he ignored her. However tempting the prospect, he had no intention of actually beating the truth out of his father-in-law. It might not hurt, though, if Koshkin believed he would.

"Yes, spit it out," he said. "What brings you here?"

Koshkin peeled off the deplorable sheepskin and dumped it in a corner. "Cursed thing itches," he said. "Besides, it's hot enough in here to roast a fowl."

"You probably have lice," Alexei said, not bothering to conceal his distaste. "You should burn it. And answer my question."

"Isn't it obvious?" Koshkin clasped his hands together like a penitent. "A change of clothing and a place to stay."

Alexei stepped forward. Fury rose within him, and only Maria's cry of distress stopped him from tossing his father-in-law out on his ear. He stopped less than a hand's breadth from Koshkin and said in biting tones, "Maria, order him a bath, a meal, and clothes appropriate to his station."

He shifted his attention to Koshkin. "For my wife's sake I will grant you that much. And once you're dressed, you may leave under your own power. But you will *not* live in my house, and if I catch you here again, I will throw you out the door myself."

✤

Cursing his son-in-law's ingratitude and announcing that he would stay with his second daughter, who appreciated him, Koshkin departed not long before the family's midday meal, which Alexei had pointedly not invited him to attend. After asking Ruslan to preside over the warriors' tables, Alexei joined Maria in her sewing room. As he approached, he heard her singing. He stopped near the doorway, standing to one side so the servants could bring in the food. Maria's gorgeous soprano never failed to delight him.

Or the baby, to judge from the ecstatic coos sounding from the cradle.

When the servants left, Alexei filled two bowls with mutton stew, placed them on a tray with a basket of bread and a pair of spoons, and carried the tray to where she sat. "Can we talk without yelling at each other?" he asked when she looked up.

"Of course," she said. "I'm sorry about losing my temper. Again. I don't want you to go. And I don't want you to hide yourself from me. But I do understand why you put off telling me. I might have done the same in your place."

"And I'm sorry, too. I should have told you as soon as I received the assignment from *Ata*." Alexei clasped her hand, acknowledging her apology. Although quick to anger, Maria had learned since their marriage to admit her faults when she calmed down.

And to be fair, he was quick to anger as well. "I didn't plan to attack your father, you know," he said. "Not after I realized who the visitor was. At first I took him for a thief or an assassin." He rubbed the hand with which he'd been threatening Koshkin when she walked in. "Although I can't blame you for thinking otherwise. I don't remember the last time I so wanted to throttle someone."

"He would have deserved it too, after what he did to us." The baby hiccuped, and Maria rocked the cradle more gently. "I can't help thinking I should have told him he has a grandson."

"Why? He hasn't earned the right to know. He'll give us enough trouble as it is. You especially: you're more vulnerable to his wiles." Alexei tasted the stew, then placed the other bowl in front of her. "Here, eat. It's delicious, and you need it." He touched the cradle. "And he needs you to regain your strength."

She took the bowl, still rocking the cradle with her foot, and they ate in silence for a while.

"What if he comes back after you're gone?" Maria asked as she set down her bowl.

"More?" Alexei offered. When she declined, he said, "I'll warn my parents. Receive him if you must, but not alone. Even he should think twice about trying to manipulate you in front of my stepmother."

"And if he doesn't, she will certainly set him straight." Maria laughed softly—at the thought of Sumbeka's reaction, he assumed—before becoming serious once more. "Yes, very well. Am I to conceal Alexander's birth, though? That could prove difficult if Papa arrives at the wrong time."

"No, what's the point? Varvara will tell him, unless she throws him out as well. But we needn't volunteer the information. I want your father to pay a price for what he's done—to understand that his own misdeeds have cut him off from the family, that we don't owe him forgiveness. Instead he owes us an apology. And until I see some evidence of remorse, never mind a desire to compensate for the damage he's caused, I want him to suffer and to know why he's suffering." He sighed. "I do wish *Ata* would not insist on my heading south right now. No doubt it's the right thing for him and for Ogodai, but for us these raiders could not have come at a worse time."

Her fingers, warm from the bowl, tangled in his. "I will miss you, my love. That's the real reason I'm so crotchety about this. I want you to stay."

He took her in his arms and kissed her, tasting the rich and complex spicing of the stew. "And I will miss you. So let's enjoy every moment we have together, shall we?"

⚓

Koshkin did not in fact approach his second daughter for aid. For one thing, she lived too far from Moscow, and his sketchy plans required him to remain close to the Kremlin. For another, Alexei's anger had shaken him. Suppose he traveled the whole way to Murom, only to encounter a similar reaction there? First he would try one of his older sons, Mikhail or Foma.

But were his boys here in town? Koshkin's cousin Kobylin had thought not, although he'd also insisted that Grand Princess Elena had disgraced Maria and demoted both of Koshkin's older sons. Now, having seen his daughter not only in good health and spirits but laughing as she defended her obnoxious husband—against her own father!—Koshkin had to wonder whether Kobylin had misunderstood the situation. Military assignments changed quickly, and a transfer need not indicate a demotion. Moreover, Kobylin had left Russia four months ago, including the month he'd spent in Vilnius. Perhaps Mikhail and Foma had already negotiated their return to Moscow. To find out, a tavern would serve Koshkin best. The kind that soldiers frequented.

It took some careful maneuvering to ask about his sons without revealing his own identity, but Koshkin prided himself on his skill at getting others to talk. After a few rounds of drinks he had the information he sought. Foma had gone to Murom with Varvara's husband not long after Koshkin himself fled Moscow, and in Murom Foma remained. Mikhail, however, had taken lodgings in the trading quarter outside the city walls—although he had lost his position as a palace guard and served in a punishment post manning the outer walls. So Kobylin might have had some grounds for his story, even if it seemed likely that Mikhail's own limited abilities had more to do with his current misfortunes than did

Ilya Shuisky's plotting. Either way, the boy would profit from his father's counsel.

Koshkin spared a moment to shake his head at his sons' foolishness. How he'd managed to sire such a pair of gawks never failed to amaze him. Without constant oversight and correction both of them would drive their careers into the ditch like overloaded wagons.

Never mind all that. Mikhail's humble lodgings and inferior situation suited Koshkin's present purposes excellently. After he restored his own wealth and status, he would repay Mikhail by seeing him elevated once more. In the meantime he had a place to hide.

Alas, when he at last discovered the correct house, Mikhail, too, failed to greet his father with the unbounded joy Koshkin felt he deserved. On the contrary: the boy seemed not much more welcoming than Alexei. But after a good deal more grumbling than Koshkin thought necessary, Mikhail stepped back and permitted him entry.

"Good, you've another bed." Koshkin surveyed the sparsely furnished apartment with disfavor. A single room under the eaves, it had a long way to go before it met the standards appropriate to a nobleman whose lineage had served the House of Moscow since the fourteenth century. A simple wooden table lined with benches, a pair of cots at opposite ends of the room where the ceiling sloped so low that even someone of Koshkin's height would risk hitting his head when he sat up in the morning, three or four round-topped wooden chests, a row of pegs along one wall bearing an assortment of robes and military equipment, and a small collection of icons arranged in a corner—these few items constituted the entire furnishings of the room. No wonder his son had fallen foul of the supercilious grand princess if this was his idea of how to live.

"You're not planning to stay, I hope," Mikhail said.

"Of course I'm planning to stay." Koshkin glared at his glum-faced son. Was there no limit to his family's ingratitude? "Where else would I go? I'm told that bitch Elena has grabbed our estate. Probably gave it to her lover."

"She gave it to Prince Ilya Shuisky," Mikhail said, his tone an offense. "As a reward for denouncing you."

"Shuisky!" Koshkin twisted with both hands the robe that his daughter and son-in-law had given him, imagining he had Ilya's neck in his grip. "That whoreson lied about me so he could get his paws on my wife, and Elena rewards him?"

"You didn't have to run." Mikhail still sounded grudging. "You did nothing but convince them that Ilya told the truth. And you can't stay here. They already kicked me out of the palace and stuck me in a post a dog would scorn. One more word in the wrong quarters, and I'll be lucky to get the job of emptying the royal chamberpots."

"Where else can I go?" Koshkin demanded. "You're my son, dammit. How dare you speak to me like that? You're supposed to honor your father, remember?"

"And you're supposed to care for your family," Mikhail said, manifestly unimpressed. "As for where, Maria has room. Bulat Khan looks out for her, too, so she's better protected than the rest of us." Mikhail swept his arm from wall to wall. "Look at this place. There's not space enough for two. We'll bump into each other forty times a day."

"Not my fault you choose to live in a dump," Koshkin retorted. "And I went to Maria first. That arrogant bastard she married showed me the door. Refused even to let me talk to her until she walked in on her own." He touched his borrowed robe. "Although they did give me this."

Mikhail put both hands on his hips and scowled. "It *is* your fault. What did you imagine would happen if you ran off like that? Elena and Telepnev went after the whole lot of us—

except Varvara, because Murom's under siege more often than not from the Tatars anyway. It's a punishment post at the best of times."

"Alexei and Maria still have their estate." The injustice of that rankled.

Mikhail groaned and swore under his breath. "I told you. That estate belongs to Bulat Khan's family, and he went straight to the grand princess to vouch for his son. The boyars didn't dare touch either of them after that. Otherwise Maria and Alexei would be as badly off as the rest of us. I got kicked out of the Kremlin and sent to Kolomna to fight Safa-Girei and his godless horde. I came back last week, assigned to a shit job on the outer wall. This is the best I can afford on the miserable wages they pay me, when they bother to pay me at all. I curse your name every night before I fall asleep."

"And Alexei wouldn't put you up either?" Koshkin ignored that last complaint. The lack of appreciation among his children defied belief.

"I didn't ask him. I have *some* pride. He didn't want to live in your house. Why should he want to host the whole clan at his?" Mikhail pulled off his boots and threw them against the wall.

"Well, he's an ingrate, and I'm going to make him pay. But I have a plan to restore our fortunes, and it requires me to stay in Moscow long enough to carry it out. Without getting arrested. So …" Koshkin mustered his most amiable smile. His son's temper tantrum would abate soon enough. "You won't throw your old father to the wolves, will you?"

Once more he assessed the pitiful room. Rage burned in his chest: against Elena and her brats, against the despicable Prince Ilya—now ensconced at Koshkin's estate!—even against his own son-in-law for withdrawing his support. They would pay. Every one of them would pay.

Mikhail threw himself on the far mattress and groaned. "Oh for God's sake, you can bunk on the other bed. But don't get too cozy. I expect you to move on first chance you get."

"Thank you, son," Koshkin said, relishing the irony as it dripped from his tongue. "I'll make it up to you soon. You won't regret it."

"I already do," said his thankless child.

Chapter 7

ALEXEI SUMMONED HIS TWO FASTEST RIDERS. "TAKE BULAT Khan's banner," he told them, "and head for my brother's camp. Quick as you can." He pointed east, where the unbroken forest looked fit to continue forever. "You can't tell from those trees, but we're almost within sight range. Let Ogodai know our troops are on the way. We don't want to get shot by the man we're trying to help."

The warriors acknowledged the order, collected Bulat's nine-horsetail standard, and moved into the woods. The rest of the force, flying Alexei's own winged horse, spread out to allow the animals to graze.

Ruslan rode up, the reins of Timur's pony held firmly in his left fist. "He's about to explode with excitement," Ruslan said by way of explanation as he reached Alexei's side. "We don't want him flying ahead and getting himself in trouble."

"I wouldn't," Timur protested. "I'm not a baby that needs his reins held."

"You were doing just that when I grabbed them, stripling, so don't try it." Ruslan held out the reins to Alexei, who accepted them. "Your turn."

"But we're so close. Can't I ride as far as the edge of the woods? *Ata*, please! I promise I'll stop there." Timur twisted his face into the king of pleading glances.

"No," Alexei told him. "Ruslan's right. Think, son. Your uncle's camp is at war. Five hundred armed men show up without warning on the horizon. How will they react?"

"Oh," Timur said. "Is that why you sent the scouts ahead?"

"Exactly. So they'll know we're friend, not foe. I brought you all this way so you could see your mother, and you've done beautifully. I can guess how anxious you are to get there. But she won't thank me for letting you show up dead at her door." Alexei bent, chucked the boy's chin, and added in a teasing tone, "I might miss you myself."

Timur's tense face broke into a smile, then a giggle crept out. He stopped dragging at the reins in his father's hand, and after eliciting a promise to behave, Alexei released them. "Won't be long now, son," he said.

The scouts soon returned, led by a surprised and, Alexei thought, not entirely pleased Ogodai. "Welcome," his half-brother said. "I wasn't expecting reinforcements, but I can use more men." Ogodai looked down the line, which stretched far into the woods, and his eyebrows rose. "*Ata* is generous."

"*Ata* is worried," Alexei said. "He doesn't like the rumblings of discontent he hears around Moscow. Dissatisfaction with the grand princess and her favorite, mostly. He wants to keep open the option of retreating to the steppe if need be." He produced a rueful grin. Whether he and Ogodai got along well or not, they both knew Bulat. "At least that's what he says. I think he might care just a bit for your continued good health."

"And would never admit it." Ogodai returned the smile, although it didn't reach his eyes. "Yes, I can believe that. Well, let's show your men the way to the camp. You have your own tents, I hope."

"A whole supply train," Alexei said. "I'm not a novice, you know." Timur pressed forward, eager to greet his uncle, and Alexei caught his reins again. "You remember this young man."

"You brought Timur? Why?"

Alexei released his son's horse, and the boy kneed the pony forward to hug Ogodai. "To see *Ana*," Timur said, his excitement bubbling once more. "And you and Auntie Firuza and the twins. I rode most of the way and even practiced shooting. I almost hit the target lots of times!"

"A slight exaggeration, stripling. Only if we consider the target to include the entire forest," Ruslan put in, his voice amused. He touched his hand to his heart. "Greetings, Khan. Your nephew is learning well, but the raiders can sleep snug in their beds for a while yet."

"And he did ride most of the way," Alexei said. "Not bad for a boy of ten."

"Indeed." Ogodai patted Timur's shoulder. "Let's go see your mother."

"Lead the way," Alexei said. And they set off.

❦

Nasan swept through the reception halls of Grand Princess Elena's Kremlin palace, greeting one noblewoman after another. After some thought and consultation with her mother and Maria, she had chosen her favorite crimson velvet robe, embroidered in gold, over a tunic of white silk. Her jeweled headdress with its pointed tip from which a white gauze veil floated underlined the point she wished to make: that she attended the court by right of birth, as a Tatar tsarevna, the daughter of Bulat Khan. She might lack the grand princess's height, but she yielded nothing to the royal family in terms of lineage. She would approach Elena as an equal, and she wanted every woman present to know that.

Maria, exquisite in a forest green robe and turquoise tunic edged in pearls at wrists and throat, walked at her side. With Alexander past his third month Sumbeka had declared his mother free to pursue other tasks, at least some of the time. Given that Maria's most important task in unsettled political circumstances like the present was to act as the family's eyes and ears at court, Sumbeka had wasted no time in petitioning the grand princess to revoke her edict of disgrace. Yesterday word of Sumbeka's success reached Bulat's estate in the form of a summons for Maria to present herself the next morning. So here she was, with Nasan at her side to support her in the often prickly and rejecting atmosphere of Elena's court. As the wife of a gentleman of the bedchamber as well as a khan's daughter, Nasan had no reason to doubt her own welcome.

"You do this as if you were born to it," Maria whispered as Nasan dipped her chin to yet another princess, greeted her by name, and inquired after her relatives.

Nasan shot a mischievous glance over her shoulder. "I was. You've seen Alexei at occasions like this. He doesn't misidentify a single person. It's a survival skill, a way of constantly monitoring who's loyal and who's not. *Ana* drilled me every day even before we left the steppe. I hated it, but it's good practice."

She drew Maria into a corner where they could observe the gathering. They had already paid their respects to the grand princess, who stood in the center of the room surrounded by her ladies. Solomonida Sheremeteva, Nasan's cousin by marriage, left the group of chattering attendants to join them. A lovely blue-eyed blonde in her mid-twenties, Solomonida was also the mother of Anna, the best friend of Maria's youngest sister.

"What a fabulous pair you make," Solomonida said as she approached. "The tsarevnas at court. I wish I had those gowns." She touched the tip of Nasan's headdress. "And the hat. I would commit a serious crime for that hat."

Nasan laughed and kissed her on both cheeks. "You look gorgeous, as always. And the hat wouldn't suit you. You're tall. You don't need to put a tower on your head so people will notice you."

Maria kissed Solomonida too, then held out her hand. "Is that Princess Nadezhda Shuiskaya?" She indicated a woman standing near the grand princess. "She doesn't look well."

"Because she's married to Prince Ilya, poor woman," Solomonida said. "I don't know what that bottom-pinching beast has done lately, but he's always up to something. I'm sure he wears her down."

"Maybe." Maria watched Nadezhda with narrowed eyes. "Something's bothering her, for sure."

Nasan chose not to respond. Solomonida was probably right, and she preferred to avoid thinking about Prince Ilya Shuisky as much as possible. The man was a menace, and any lady unfortunate enough to wind up as his princess deserved as much sympathy as Nasan could offer.

But Maria's comment had sparked a different train of thought. Nasan excused herself from the conversation and moved toward the group of ladies-in-waiting with the grand princess at its center.

Careful not to draw attention to herself, she circled the group, observing Elena and her ladies-in-waiting from every angle except straight ahead. Princess Nadezhda did appear tense, her face taut and drawn. She wasn't the only lady-in-waiting expressing concern, either. Solomonida showed no signs of concealing an unwanted secret, but Solomonida, the survivor of a difficult marriage to a brutal husband, knew well how to hide her feelings. She might tell Nasan the truth in private—but she might well not, if doing so meant betraying her ruler's confidence. Either way, it would be a waste of time to interrogate her here at court.

The stress so visible in Nadezhda, among others, only heightened the contrast between her and Elena, who glowed with happiness. The grand princess's face was softer than usual, her cheeks more rounded. Nasan recalled the sparkle in Elena's eyes, usually distinguished by their icy stare, when she and Maria made their bows earlier.

Curious.

Nasan moved into the crowd, even more anxious to escape notice as she pondered what she'd seen. If her dawning suspicions were correct, knowing the truth could be dangerous.

She stopped as soon as she reached a point where she would not attract attention and turned to survey the circle around Elena once more. Anxious ladies-in-waiting, a grand princess glowing with health. The loose caftans everyone wore made it impossible for Nasan to be sure, but a childhood in her father's harem, her own recent introduction to motherhood, her sister-in-law's pregnancy, and years of immersion in medical books made her almost certain of her diagnosis.

Grand Princess Elena, a widow since December 1533, was with child. And, Nasan guessed from the occasional glimpse she caught of the grand princess's curves as fine silks drew taut and swung free, the infant would arrive in no more than three to four months.

No wonder her ladies-in-waiting shivered in their elegant velvet slippers.

§

Timur burst into his mother's home, calling, "*Ana,* I'm here. Where are you?"

A gasp sounded from inside. Alexei, uncertain of his welcome, waited at the door. Ogodai had left after pointing them in the right direction, tossing over his shoulder a casual invitation to join him and his family for a meal when they finished. Alexei had yet to decide whether his half-brother appreciated the assistance from their father or resented it. He decided to accept the supper invitation, not least because it would give him a chance to find out.

Of course, he would command Bulat's troops and defend the camp whether his half-brother liked it or not. But he preferred to meet trouble head on.

Timur dashed back and grabbed his hand, and Alexei allowed his son to pull him into the tent where he had lived for years with Guzel, Timur's mother. The light from the hearth fire revealed a pair of toddlers whom Alexei recognized as his brother's twins, Irek and Altan-Alia. A third child, a stocky boy with light brown hair, played with them. He saw no one who might have charge of the children, and that puzzled him.

When had Guzel descended to the level of a nursemaid? In gratitude for Timur's birth Alexei had endowed the mother of his child with sufficient animals and goods to ensure her independence, even before he transferred his flocks and herds to her when he left the camp three and a half years ago. It seemed unlikely that she had squandered her property; he had never known her to be other than thrifty. Things must have changed more than he'd expected. Had the raiders who attacked his brother's camp destroyed her livelihood?

"Guzel," he said. "I trust I find you well."

She released their son and stepped back. "Did the slut throw you out?" She meant Roxelana, he assumed.

He blinked at the hostility in her face and voice, then decided for Timur's sake not to retaliate in kind. Instead he said mildly, "We discovered we didn't suit. She married a Russian nobleman more than a year ago." He hesitated before adding, "I married as well. My wife and I have a son."

"So I heard." Guzel shrugged, an elaborate gesture that conveyed extreme disinterest in anything to do with the man who had supported her for so long. So extreme that Alexei didn't believe it. "Then you can leave this one with me." She again pulled Timur close. "I let him go with your brother to Moscow. I didn't expect you to *keep* him."

"No," Alexei said. "I brought him here because I have no wish to separate the two of you permanently. But when I leave, he will return to Moscow with me. He's ten years old. He needs to live with men, train with men. In two years, if we stop the raiders and Ogodai agrees to foster him, he can come back for a while." He had worked out this plan during the journey. Ogodai would agree, he felt certain, out of love for Timur. But they must stop the raiders first.

Guzel looked as if she might argue, but Timur caught her arm and begged to show her how well he had learned to shoot. "Leave us, then," she said. "I don't want to waste a moment with him."

"You've no need to be rude." Alexei heard the snap in his own voice. "I brought our son to see you. I could have left him in Moscow." When Guzel bit her lip rather than responding, he said, "Perhaps I should have. He would be safer there."

She blushed, loosening her grip on their son, who tugged his hand free and dropped down, cross-legged, in front of the twins. Irek reached out a hand as if he remembered Timur, although that seemed unlikely. At least a year had passed since Ogodai brought his wife and children to Moscow for Alexei's wedding.

"Thank you," Guzel said, her reluctance audible. She gripped the skirt of her caftan as if his presence made her uncomfortable. "May I not spend time with him, in that case?"

"I'll go." Alexei gestured at the twins. "But before I do, are you in need? When did you start caring for the khan's children?"

In the dim confines of the tent he couldn't tell whether Guzel's blush deepened, but she shifted her feet in a way that indicated discomfort.

What's that about?

"It's temporary," she said. "Their nursemaid was called away. I expect her back soon."

Timur abandoned the twins and dashed across the tent to join them. "*Ana*, please, don't you want to see how well I can shoot?"

"Yes, darling." Guzel patted her son's head, sending Alexei a glance that he interpreted as pleading.

"Until later, then." He bowed and headed for the doorway, but he hadn't reached the threshold when the wooden door burst open and a young woman came in, looking disheveled.

At the sight of her Ogodai's twins let out yells of greeting, pushed themselves to their feet, and ran toward her as fast as their short legs permitted. Their playmate shouted, "Mama," and toddled after them.

Grusha bent to catch the children in her arms and spoke over her shoulder to Guzel. "I'm so sorry. Everything took longer than expected. The khan delayed me. Otherwise I'd have arrived before your visitors." She stood and bowed to Alexei. "Sultan, my apologies for not greeting you. I didn't realize at first that Guzel had company."

The familiar title, delivered with a Russian accent, both startled and reassured him. Alexei stared at the newcomer. Even in the fitful light cast by the smoke hole he recognized her, although he'd seen her only once or twice, caring for his niece and nephew during his wedding last year. The woman was Grusha, the Russian nursemaid whom, according to Maria, Ogodai's wife suspected of having an affair with her husband. And Grusha's disheveled state and hurried explanation suggested that Ogodai's wife might have reason to worry.

What had she been doing while delayed by the khan, and why had she left her charges in Guzel's care?

There was no accounting for tastes, of course, but Alexei, accustomed to Maria's fiery beauty, couldn't imagine falling for the bland prettiness Grusha displayed. Firuza demonstrated passion and personality; this washed-out girl had neither.

Ogodai's extramarital adventures were, however, not his older brother's concern. Alexei dismissed the question of Grusha's whereabouts for the moment and focused his attention on his former lover, now clutching Timur's hand and resisting the boy's attempts to drag her toward the outdoors.

"Timur, behave," he said. "I'm leaving for a while. If you need me, you'll find me in your uncle's tent. But no running off, understood? Listen to your mother."

Timur acknowledged this order with a nod. Guzel tightened her lips as if even this simple concession to her status as Timur's other parent irritated her, but she didn't speak.

"I'll go too," the Russian nursemaid said. "Come, Sultan, Khanim, Stenka." She gathered up the twins, who wriggled to get free. Her own son tugged at her skirts.

Alexei took the boy she held from her. "I'll carry him. You take your Stenka. Do you remember your uncle Alexei, Irek?"

"Alexei, not Tulpar?" Guzel asked. "Oh, that's right. Firuza told me you became a Christian. Married a *Russian*." Her words dripped bitterness. "And had a son with her. And here I thought you hated Russians as much as I do." She stopped and patted the nursemaid's arm. "Sorry, Grusha. I didn't mean you."

Her savage tone shocked Alexei anew. His sense of shifting emotional sands under his feet, initiated by his half-brother's less than cordial welcome, intensified.

What am I doing here when my family needs me in Moscow?

He had opened his mouth to respond when Timur interjected, "I like Auntie Maria. She's very nice to me." The boy seemed blissfully unaware that every word that left his mouth fueled his mother's anger. "She has a little sister who lives with us. Lyuba. I call her Goose because she can be a real pest, but when she's not a pest I like her too."

"What a charming happy family," Guzel said, her voice so biting that even Timur's mouth dropped open. "Please don't let me keep you, *Alexei.*"

Whew. And for the space of a few breaths there he thought he'd overcome her resentment.

Well, it was simpler this way. For Timur's sake Alexei again suppressed the many possible retorts that sprang to his tongue, dipped his chin to the mother of his child, and left. Irek jounced in his arms, apparently unaffected by the strife between the grownups. Grusha, bearing Altan-Alia on one hip and Stenka on the other, followed in his wake.

Outside the tent he turned. "Show me where to find my sister-in-law. I assume you're taking the children to her."

"This way, Sultan." Grusha walked in front of him along the row of tents, heading for a large one at the far end. Irek, perhaps in response to Alexei's firm grip and no nonsense style, ceased wriggling and clung to him—as Timur had once done, as Alexander would no doubt do in a year or so. A pang of longing filled Alexei's chest—for Maria, for the baby, for home.

Observing the sway of Grusha's hips, he concluded that she did have more appeal from the back. But he still couldn't imagine why Ogodai had picked her to entertain him during his wife's pregnancy. Surely his harem must contain more than a few beauties. Why settle on a pale, skinny mouse?

Chapter 8

KOSHKIN, ARMED WITH INFORMATION THAT HIS UNSATIS-factory son-in-law had left Moscow for an unknown destination and duration, decided to approach his eldest daughter once more. Surely he could talk some sense into her if he tried. Without Alexei on hand demanding that she choose her husband over her father, Maria would remember that she'd always been Papa's favorite. He'd never had trouble persuading her to help him before. Why, she'd even protested her husband's mistreatment of him! She'd take him in, and by the time Alexei had the opportunity to complain, the deed would be done. Let Alexei learn where his wife's true loyalties lay. It would do him good.

Although staying with his son Mikhail had its advantages— the news of Alexei's departure had come from him, for example—the combination of poverty and crowding ground Koshkin's nerves to a powder. Showing himself in the streets did pose a certain danger, but for his plans to succeed, it was a risk he had to take.

Apart from anything else, Koshkin could hardly walk into the Kremlin and hand his poisoned goods to the grand princess, could he? Whereas Maria, who according to Mikhail had won a reprieve from her disgrace, could not only help him but do so in a way that would pin the blame firmly where it belonged: on Prince Ilya Shuisky. Then Koshkin would enjoy the full fruits of his revenge at no cost to those close to him. With luck, he could, by manipulating the head of the Shuisky clan, restore his status at court. That triumph would bring his children to their senses, if nothing else did.

And if Vasily Shuisky somehow found the gall to refuse the bait—although the threat to expose his nephew's murderous plans should ensure that Vasily would not even attempt such a thing—Koshkin would return to Lithuania. By then, Roxelana might have forgotten her grievances enough to take her husband back.

His flush of happy anticipation crashed on the shoal of the remembered coldness in his wife's eyes and her casual mention of using the belladonna on him if he proved "intractable."

So be it. No Roxelana, then. Not yet, anyway. No penitent he to pant at the heels of a woman who had made no secret of her disdain. For now Koshkin would put all his efforts into restoring his position in Moscow. That was a better solution to his problems anyway. If he succeeded, his wife would realize that returning to him served her best interests. And his miserable descendants would rue the way they had treated him in his hour of need. It would serve them right if he cast them off. Let them petition *him* for favors for once.

Mikhail, in particular. Why, this very morning Koshkin's eldest son had launched another barbed suggestion that his father would be more welcome in Roxelana's bed in Vilnius than sprawled across Mikhail's pitiful excuse for a cot in Moscow!

Koshkin was still musing on his hopes for a glorious future when he encountered the first check to his plans. After a nerve-racking journey through the city streets, his rosy imaginings constantly interrupted by glances over his shoulder for pursuers or even suspicious bystanders, he slipped past the gateway of Maria's estate only to learn from her housekeeper that she and the baby—and why had no one mentioned that he had a grandson?—had moved to Bulat Khan's home until her husband returned.

Disappointing but not a huge setback, especially if it meant that Maria's house had no master. He would do nicely here, with or without Mikhail, and it would give the housekeeper something to occupy her time. But before moving in, he should attempt to speak to his daughter. Then, even if she refused to receive him, he could tell the housekeeper that he had approached Maria and had her approval to stay. So with that goal in mind and again keeping a wary eye out for anyone who might recognize him—more likely than ever in this part of town, which lay so close to his former home—Koshkin made his way to Bulat Khan's estate.

As Koshkin climbed the outer stairs, he half-expected Bulat, too, to show him the door. But the noble clothing provided by Maria worked its magic, and his request to speak with his daughter led him, in the wake of a young dark-haired steward, to an airy apartment furnished in the Tatar style. There he found Maria ensconced with her mother-in-law and her sister-in-law, the Kolychev girl. His youngest daughter, Lyuba, sat on a rug playing with two infants—one large enough to crawl, the other rolling back and forth within a circle of pillows. A servant, presumably the babies' nursemaid, crouched nearby, watching the three children.

Lyuba jumped to her feet and ran to hug him, calling, "Papa, Maria said you came back! See how good an *apa* I am!"

Maria set aside her stitching and rose, regarding him with a wary expression. The two Tatar women acknowledged his entrance with no more than a nod.

"Jamil," Sumbeka said to the steward. "Bring refreshments for our guest." The steward departed.

"Come and meet Alexander and Boris," Lyuba said. "Alexander is your grandson, Papa!"

"What is an *apa*?" Koshkin asked his youngest, who tugged at his hand as if eager to introduce him to the babies.

"Auntie," she said. "I can speak Tatar, Papa. Timur used to practice with me, but then he rode off with *his* papa. And we came here, where everyone speaks it, so I can practice whenever I want. I can read and write too. And do sums! I have learned lots and lots of things since you left—about people who lived ages ago and warriors and heroines. And how to look after babies. But I missed you. Why did you go away for so long?"

He patted her tangled hair. Of his seven children he knew her the least, but her heartfelt and voluble welcome stood in sharp contrast to the restraint exhibited by everyone else. And she was brighter than his sons, if she could pick up new skills so quickly. He experienced a flash of fatherly pride.

Lyuba was not, however, the reason for his visit. "Go back to what you were doing, kitten," he told her. "I'll meet Alexander and Boris later. Right now I need to talk to Maria." He crossed the room and kissed his eldest daughter's cheeks, ignored her wince, then greeted Sumbeka and her daughter. "Thank you for receiving me in your home, Tsaritsa. Greetings, Tsarevna. Will you grant me a few moments alone with my daughter? I have a request to make of her."

The distrust on Maria's face grew more pronounced. "I have no secrets from *Kaenana*," she said.

Another Tatar word. What is happening to my family?

Before he could protest, the servants arrived with trays of food and cups of a dark-red liquid that turned out to be cherry juice.

"Please be seated, Fyodor Mikhailovich." Sumbeka gestured to one of the covered benches that lined the walls. He saw no evidence that she planned to grant his request.

The Kolychev girl rose to her feet. "Come, Lyuba," she said. "Let's take the babies into the next room, shall we? I'll ask Jamil to bring us some of the sweets." Maria sent her what might be considered an anxious glance as she left with the larger infant and Lyuba, trailed by the nurse carrying the smallest child, but Koshkin appreciated the gesture. If he couldn't speak with Maria alone, then the fewer people who overheard him the better.

He *especially* didn't want to share his secrets with a seven-year-old prodigy who chattered like a magpie—and in two languages at that.

Perched on the strange covered bench, he focused his gaze on Maria, hoping through his intensity to sway her to his will. After a long round of chit-chat he moved toward his goal. "Your brother Mikhail is back from Kolomna, but he's in dire straits. Since you've decided to stay here, I came to ask you again if we may live at your house for a while until I can recover the property taken from us."

Despite doing his best to ignore Sumbeka in the hope that she would take the hint and leave—she did not—he couldn't miss the jerk of her fingers when he said that. Maria looked quickly to her left, as if taking instructions from her mother-in-law. "Impossible," she told Koshkin. "My husband has strictly forbidden it."

Her husband. Always her husband. As if she expected him to believe for a moment that she—his clever, fiery eldest daughter; his second self—had no more gumption than his pathetically meek and obedient wife, thankfully gone to join the saints these three years past.

"And you do whatever your husband tells you?" he said, his tone caustic. "I remember a time when you didn't want to marry him. Not so long ago, either."

Maria raised her chin. He saw anger in her tight lips and narrowed brown eyes, which was the effect he aimed for. Unsettle her, annoy her, implicitly deride her until she recalled where her true loyalties lay.

"I hadn't met him then." Maria clenched her hands on her sewing. "And is it not a wife's duty to obey her husband?"

Hearing scorn in her voice, Koshkin narrowed his own eyes in response. "She should obey her father first." Which wasn't true, but she might believe him. During her first marriage she had done his bidding readily enough.

"But you are speaking of property belonging to my *husband*'s lineage," Maria retorted. "It is not mine to dispose of, and if it were, I wouldn't allow you to stay there. You've done enough damage to the family through your scheming and your flight. Even receiving you here in this house puts the rest of us in danger. Solve your problems by yourself, without involving me and mine."

For a long moment he stared at her, at a loss for words.

Incredible. After his many efforts on her behalf *this* was his reward? But his daughter stared back as if carved from oak, and Sumbeka spoke in a voice that exceeded even Maria's in its chill.

"Make no mistake, Fyodor Mikhailovich," she said. "If my stepson and daughter-in-law did not forbid you to live on our estate, my husband would certainly intervene. So you see, that road is closed and will remain so." She drained a cup of juice, its dark red uncomfortably reminiscent of blood, and set it aside. "And should you feel tempted to evade our restrictions, rest assured that Maria's servants, who work for us, will report your presence."

Koshkin, blocked and furious, addressed his daughter. "And what of Mikhail? Have you no concern for him?"

Maria hesitated, then reached into the bag of embroidery supplies and drew out a gold case the size and shape of an apple. She twisted the two halves apart and tipped the bone needles the object contained onto the table next to her, then held it out to him. "Mikhail has suffered enough for your sins. This belongs to me, not to Alexei's family. Aunt Theodosia gave it to me the day before my wedding. You may sell it to feed and clothe yourselves."

He took the apple. It weighed heavy in his hand. Solid gold, he guessed. And inlaid with jewels. A valuable present indeed. "Thank you," he said, somewhat mollified by her concession. The bauble would fetch a good price, and the money, if husbanded, would keep him in better condition long enough for his schemes to work. But for that he needed another kind of assistance from her as well.

"I have a plan to restore our fortunes," he said, careful not to hint at what the plan entailed. "It includes presenting a gift to Grand Princess Elena. I can't enter the Kremlin myself. Nor can your brother. Mikhail tells me you have resumed your visits to court. Will you deliver it for me?"

Anger flashed in Maria's eyes. Sumbeka muttered an incomprehensible comment in what he assumed to be Tatar.

Koshkin held his breath, expecting another rebuff. But after a brief pause Maria said, "I make no promises, but bring me the item when you have it. When I see what it is, I will decide whether to help you."

Sumbeka sent her a warning glance, but Maria stared unflinching at Koshkin. Two bright circles of red adorned her cheeks. When he didn't respond, trying without success to read her stony expression, she said, "Is there anything else, Papa?"

He had half of what he'd sought, including the opportunity he needed most. Clearly he would get no farther today. Koshkin stood and bowed. "No, thank you. Tsaritsa, you have been most gracious. Daughter, I will see you again soon."

⸕

Nasan returned to find Maria pacing back and forth across the room, raging. "It's a good thing I sent the babies and Lyuba to the nursery," she said. "What did he want?"

"He's up to something." Maria smacked her palms together as if imagining her father's face between them. "He tells me he's planning to give Grand Princess Elena a present. As part of some scheme to restore his fortunes. He actually imagines that I'm foolish enough to believe he cares about winning her support! And he tried to talk me into letting him and my oldest brother stay at our house while I'm here. A request I would refuse even if your brother hadn't thrown him out and told him not to come back the last time Papa tried that. How could he even ask when he knows that would implicate us in his guilt?"

She picked up the longest of a set of needles that had not decorated the small table when Nasan left. "I could stab him and not shed a tear." She demonstrated, using a pincushion, then dropped both objects on the table again. "I gave him that monstrosity of a needle case that I got from Aunt Theodosia and told him to sell it."

"Why?" Nasan struggled to follow this tirade. "If you're angry with him, I mean. Won't that encourage him to come back?"

"He will come back," Sumbeka said. "*Kilen* told him to bring her the item for Elena. He asked her to deliver it for him."

Nasan dropped onto the sofa next to her mother. "I'm completely confused. You told your father he can't stay at your house. That I understand. But then you handed him that ugly but expensive needle case and told him you would deliver something to the grand princess for him? Why?"

Maria sighed, stopped her pacing, and came to join them. "I gave him the needle case because he's battened on my brother Mikhail, who already lost his prestigious position because of Papa. I don't know where they're living, but Mikhail can't have much money now that the government has confiscated our lands and assigned him to a horrid post on the outer walls. I don't want him to suffer any more than necessary. If *he* had come to us, Alexei and I would have taken him in, but Mikhail is too proud to beg for help. If nothing else, I can make sure my brother doesn't lack for food or clothing."

Nasan nodded her comprehension. "And the gift?"

"I don't trust Papa. He's crooked as a badly formed nail, but he's not stupid. He must know there's nothing he can offer Grand Princess Elena that would change her mind about him. To her he's a traitor. He abandoned her son and ran off to serve her brother-in-law in the midst of an uprising, and even though that's not the whole truth, Elena doesn't care about the details. Where did he hide this last year? Why did he return if he had a safe place to live? He has some nefarious plan up his sleeve. I can sense it. That's why I told him to bring the gift here. So I can make sure it never reaches her." She clutched her opposing elbows, as if raising a barrier against whatever harm Koshkin intended.

"Yes, I see." Nasan touched Maria's crossed arms. "We'll do whatever we can to help."

"Yes, we will." Sumbeka tapped a contemplative rhythm against her teeth. "But I think we must do more than wait." She walked to the door and called for Jamil. When the steward arrived, she stood at the window, an empress at her most imperious.

"Jamil," she said. "That man who came to visit my daughter-in-law this afternoon. Send one of my husband's warriors to discover where he lives, then have him kept under observation. We want to know where he goes, what he does, whom he contacts—every hour of the day from this moment until I tell you otherwise. Understood?"

"Understood, Khatun," he said, and departed to fulfill her orders.

As the door closed behind him, Nasan looked at her sister-in-law. "Your father has no idea how much trouble he's in."

"He never does," Maria said, the edge in her voice sharper than a dagger. "Nor how many problems he causes for the rest of us."

Firuza managed more warmth than Guzel as she took her son from Alexei's arms, although under the circumstances that meant cool courtesy and a hint of withdrawal that ensured he had no desire to linger beyond the delivery of his nephew. He accepted her thanks and responded with condolences on the loss of her twin brother and compliments on her appearance, which was blooming. He noticed that she kept a sharp eye on Grusha, but other than deciding to write down the whole story in his next letter to Maria, who would enjoy it, he made no comment. Instead he mentioned that Ogodai had invited him, with Ruslan and Timur, to join the family for supper. "But I think Guzel wants to keep Timur with her," he finished. "You will see him later."

Firuza nodded, as if she already knew more than he about Guzel's feelings (which he suspected she did). Back amid the rows of tents he looked about, considering what most needed his attention. His men, he decided, and headed off to find Ruslan and the warriors he had brought from Moscow.

The snap of tentpoles joining and the thud of felt thrown across the raised frames drew his gaze toward the outskirts of the camp. Someone had realized that so many additional horses must be corralled away from the center if they were to find sufficient fodder. From the arrangement of the circular trellises that defined the shape of the portable houses Alexei saw that his men had decided to form a large circle around the existing camp, far enough away that the horses could graze but close enough to protect the mobile village from raiders.

A good choice. If he hadn't yielded to Timur's entreaties but instead stayed to supervise, he would have recommended that very strategy.

He started toward the outer circle, looking for someone who could direct him to Ruslan and, depending on the distance, supply a horse. Before he reached the end of the row of tents, a voice hailed him. "Tulpar Sultan! Is it you indeed?"

Joy rushed through Alexei as he turned toward the voice. A man of his own age—shorter and stockier, with a barrel chest, powerful limbs, and the dark hair and eyes so common among the nomads—stood at the door of one tent, his arms spread wide.

"Malik Shirin!" Alexei embraced Malik, his sworn brother since the early days of his exile, when Malik's father had offered the only refuge from the cruel world Bulat had created for his oldest son. "An unexpected pleasure. Have you joined my brother, then? And how do you fare? It's been almost two years."

Malik returned the hug. "I do well enough. Growing into my father's shoes. And yes, we decided in the end to renew our oath to the khan. Many hordes out there, most not as well managed as this one. But what brings you here? I thought you didn't get along with your brother."

"Walk with me." Alexei pointed to the outer circle of tents. "I've a tale to tell. Much has changed since we last met. To answer your question, my father sent me with five hundred warriors to help fight off your raiders. I doubt my brother's delighted to see me, but he's stuck with me. And I with him, I suppose, but I'm no longer looking for a horde of my own. And I've discovered Ogodai's not such a bad sort. The situation is awkward, but I'll survive."

"Bulat Khan sent you? He's reinstated you, then? Despite Ogodai chasing you off our lands a couple of summers ago? Things really have changed." Malik clapped his hands and, when a servant responded, said, "Fetch two horses, and make it fast." When the servant ducked his head and ran off, Malik said, "Don't tell me you prefer to walk. The men will decide you've addled your brain in Moscow if you don't show up on horseback."

Alexei laughed. "I think my horse went with Ruslan and my men. I'll accept the loan of yours with pleasure."

"Ruslan's here too? That's good news. And we heard you married. A Christian. What do they call you now?"

Alexei hesitated, remembering the response of the Crimean envoys when he revealed his change of name.

But Malik's tone suggested no more than idle curiosity. "Alexei," he said. "And yes, *Ata* revoked his edict of banishment a week before the wedding. He didn't explain the change of heart, but I'm in no mood to complain. He's been a huge help the last year. And my wife's a good woman. She's already given me a son." He indicated the camp. "As a Christian, I can't act as khan, of course. But you've made your peace with Ogodai, you say, so you and the Shirins will do fine. And you know I'll always stand with you if you need me."

He sensed a subtle withdrawal in his sworn brother. Did Malik, too, consider him an outsider, merely because of a change in religion? After all they'd gone through together, that loss would cut deep.

Then the servant arrived with two saddled horses. Malik threw an arm around Alexei's shoulders. "Congratulations—

on making peace with your father and on your new son. Let's go check on your men."

❧

Alexei didn't expect to enjoy the evening meal with his family, but he also hadn't anticipated walking into a domestic war. As he stepped through the door, his eyes met those of his younger brother, whose frown and rigid posture suggested a man under siege. Between them stood Firuza and Grusha, almost nose to nose. The twins played in the background, but no one was watching them.

"Where *were* you, Grusha?" Firuza demanded. "I sent for you, and the servants couldn't find you anywhere. You weren't in the women's tent, obviously, since Alexei Sultan was carrying Irek when you returned. Why should I trust you with my children when you keep sneaking off?"

"I spent the afternoon with Guzel." Grusha twisted her hands in the rough homespun of her robe. Her apologetic stance and tone didn't eliminate a hint of frustration, and Alexei guessed she had produced this defense more than once.

Of course, he knew well that she had *not* been with Guzel when he arrived. He raised his eyebrows at his brother the khan, who had delayed her on some unknown errand by Grusha's own report, but kept his silence. Thankfully, the problems in Ogodai's family were not his older brother's business.

Then Firuza pounced. "*Was* she with Guzel, Sultan?" she asked.

Not even brother-in-law. Alexei swore to himself, wrestled with his conscience for the briefest moment, and said, "Yes. We left the tent together."

Grusha, who seemed incapable of acting in her own best interest, sent him a look of gratitude. Unfortunately for her,

Firuza intercepted it. "Aha," she said. "But you're both hiding something. Was she there the whole time?"

Alexei shrugged. So much for trying to deflect tension. "Not when I first walked in, no. But she arrived soon thereafter." He held out the gifts he'd brought, wrapped in silk. "Her whereabouts are really not my concern. Perhaps you could settle this later? If nothing else, Irek is about to fall into the fire."

A concerted gasp greeted this announcement, and both women rushed to grab the twins. Alexei took the opportunity to cross the room and hand his brother the present selected for him, an Ottoman dagger in a gilded sheath. "I'd planned to express my condolences on the loss of your bey," he said, "but it seems you have more immediate troubles."

"Too true." Ogodai echoed his brother's somewhat sardonic tone, then exclaimed over the beauty of the gift. "Thank you for the condolences." Lowering his voice, he murmured, "Where was she?"

"I've no idea," Alexei said. "Don't you know? She said the khan delayed her, or she would have returned before Timur and I arrived."

Ogodai's frown deepened. "I delayed her for a few moments, yes. After I left you, I talked with Ruslan Sultan regarding the disposal of your troops, then checked on the supplies our father sent. As I rode back, I saw her walking alone and stopped her to ask what she'd done with the children. She said someone was watching them. Guzel, I suppose."

One of them was lying. Alexei couldn't tell which, Grusha or his brother, although on the whole he tended to believe Ogodai, who had no reason to hide a liaison that no one would question. Even Firuza could only fume in private if her husband chose to satisfy himself elsewhere. Grusha, meanwhile, had certainly lied to Firuza.

In all candor, Alexei didn't much care who spoke the truth, except that the tension in the tent complicated an already uncomfortable family encounter. "They were with Guzel when I reached her tent. Timur ran in first, but no one else was there. It surprised me, because at first I thought Guzel had become their nursemaid, and I'd left her well provided for."

Firuza's return with Grusha, carrying the twins, interrupted this short exchange. "Take them straight to the women's tent," Firuza ordered, still sounding annoyed. "I won't warn you again. One more incident like today's, and I'll find another woman to care for them. See how you like being dependent on your lover to look after you and your son!"

"I don't have a lover, Khatun," Grusha said, although her blush undercut her statement. "I told you before. I took a short break to relieve myself."

Firuza produced a sound remarkably close to a growl. "I'd have sent you away already if I didn't know that the children love you. Think about that before you lie to me again." Grusha dipped her head without speaking and left.

Alexei let out a long breath of relief at seeing the confrontation end—or, rather, pause. Ogodai's sigh, replicating his own, drew his gaze in that direction before he again turned his attention to his sister-in-law, pacing back and forth across the tent. After a moment, she stopped and bowed. It didn't escape his notice that her dark eyes still flashed. "My apologies, husband's brother, for subjecting you to such a scene. Please forgive me."

"It's of no importance," Alexei said. He extended the remaining gift to her: a decorated bridle and reins, for Firuza owned the most beautiful Turkmen palomino he had ever seen. "We are family. I brought you this, for when you can ride Kubelek again."

She took the package from him, turned back the silk, and, for the first time since his arrival, smiled. "Oh, it's lovely. Thank you! I do miss being able to ride every day." She gestured at the platform in the center of the room, already covered with bowls, jugs, and other utensils. "Shall we eat? Your friend Ruslan won't be joining us, I gather."

"Not this evening," Alexei said. Good thing, too, given the scene he'd walked in on. "He wanted to supervise the raising of our camp. And Malik Shirin offered to stay and fill him in on what you have learned about the raiders."

The conversation turned to more general topics: news from Moscow, tales of Alexei's and Nasan's children, compliments on the health and charms of the twins, updates on the situation in the camp. Nothing military, nothing overly personal. Alexei took care to avoid even the appearance of interfering in his brother's household.

After a while, though, he decided it might be best to get one potential source of conflict out of the way. He raised a toast to his brother and sister-in-law, then said, "Tell me the truth, ené. Can we work together, or do you wish I had not come?" He permitted himself a rueful smile, thinking of their father's reaction. "Not that your answer will make any difference to *Ata*, but if necessary I'm sure we can find a way to coordinate without stepping on each other's toes."

Firuza gave a soft gasp, as if in protest, but Ogodai leaned forward, his gaze intent. "That depends," he said after a pause, "on your goals for this mission. You've challenged me in the past, and I wouldn't have asked for your help. But I don't want to turn away support if it's offered. Whoever is leading these raiders has a larger force and greater reserves than I expected. We should have beaten them back long since."

"I said as much to *Ata*," Alexei told him. "That you would prefer anyone's help to mine. And I did challenge you in the past, that's true. You've misunderstood me as well, at times."

Ogodai raised his eyebrows in an unspoken question.

"Two years ago, when you thought I'd broken my oath, I hadn't. My sworn brother asked for my help. Malik Shirin." Alexei added the name in response to his brother's expression of disbelief. Did Ogodai really believe him unworthy of friendship as well as incapable of keeping a promise? "Against some of his kinsmen who thought, after his father's death, that he should abandon you for another khan. I couldn't refuse."

Ogodai acknowledged this reality of steppe life with a curt nod. Alexei couldn't decide whether his brother believed him or not.

"But my situation has changed," he went on. "I have a wife I love and a son in Moscow. I want to finish this business as quickly as possible and return to them. With Timur, for the next two years, but then I would like you to tutor him for a while. It will do him good to establish himself on the steppe as well as in the city. Will you consider it?"

"Of course," Ogodai said without hesitation.

"Good." Alexei smiled and clasped his brother's hand. "Then we both have something to gain from defeating your enemy as soon as we can. And I have news about who that might be that you will find valuable, I think."

Chapter 9

KOSHKIN WAITED TWO WEEKS BEFORE HE RETURNED TO Maria's temporary home. When he reached Bulat Khan's estate, he again found her with her mother-in-law, not stitching this time but bent over a book. Had she learned to read like Lyuba, then, as well as to speak Tatar? One year away from his family, and so much he didn't know!

But no point in bemoaning the past. He had done the best he could under difficult circumstances, and God willing, he would have years to make up for lost time.

Lyuba and the babies were not present, and neither was the Kolychev girl. Once more he asked to speak to Maria alone, and for a second time she refused.

Irritating. He handed over the gift, an enameled box with a domed lid and a small padlock dangling from a pair of brass hasps, the key no longer than the top half of his thumb. Said to hail from distant Frankia, the box boasted exquisite inlays of flowers and birds never seen in nature—not in Russia, in any event. He had tied a horn spoon to the box with a string across the top. Maria examined it from every angle, twisting and raising it. When she moved to turn the key, he reached for her hand. "Don't."

"Why not? What's in it?" Maria treated him to the same stony non-smile she had bestowed on him the last time he visited.

"Cosmetics," he said. "A rare element from Lithuania that brightens a woman's eyes and imparts a special glow to her complexion. But you can't open it because it loses its power when exposed to fresh air and light. That's why I locked the box. Keep it locked to preserve the gift." *And my secret.*

"Really?" Maria sounded skeptical. "And what do you know of cosmetics? Or Lithuania, for that matter. You never traveled there as an envoy."

"Stop being so cold, daughter." He hardened his voice to remind her of his rights as a parent.

"You lost the right to rebuke me when you ran away and left me to face disgrace." Maria held a hand toward her mother-in-law. "My husband's family intervened to protect Lyuba and me, even Roxelana. You saved yourself. So answer my question. When did you develop an interest in cosmetics?"

"When I realized I needed a present for Grand Princess Elena, of course." He nodded at the box. "That came from Roxelana. I spent some time with her in Vilnius. She has become quite the center of court life there, and she asked not to accompany me to Moscow. But our marriage continues." Another half-truth, if not an out-and-out lie. But Maria had no need to know that.

"You ran to Lithuania," she said, her voice flat. "Unbelievable. And what sins have we committed that you chose not to stay there rather than return to pester us?"

"Will you deliver the box?" Koshkin asked, ignoring her pique, intent on his one hope of revenge. "Elena should consume a spoonful at a time." He touched the horn spoon so she could not mistake his meaning. "It works from the inside, and as I said, it doesn't maintain its power for long. If she wants to see the full effect, she should take it as soon as possible."

"And shall I tell her it comes from you?" Maria lowered her eyebrows, an expression that made Koshkin think of a witch, and for a moment he hesitated. Would she betray him? Surely not. Her own father!

"I doubt she will believe that you have her best interests at heart," Maria added. "Or is it my name you wish to associate with this gift of yours?"

Trust her? Don't trust her? For certain, he couldn't confide the whole to her. Bad enough that his only road to success lay along this indirect path.

But he saw no alternative. And she was his daughter, his favorite, his twisty, clever Maria. She would never betray him. A few moments thought, and she would overcome her present crotchets and do his bidding as before.

"Neither you nor me," he said. "Hand the box to Elena's steward and tell him the gift originates with Princess Nadezhda Shuiskaya. I understand she helped my wife escape captivity, so letting her take credit for the cosmetics seems like an appropriate reward."

"You're useless." Alexei pinned the fifteen-year-old Yusuf Bey, the new leader of the Mangyt clan, to his seat with a furious gaze. "Worse than useless, because you have yet to learn what you don't know. You haven't the smallest idea how to conduct a major campaign. We aren't stealing sheep this time."

The two of them sat with Ogodai, Ruslan, and the members of the khan's council—Malik Shirin and the heads of the Argyn, Baryn, and Kipchak clans—in the tent set aside for such meetings. As khan Ogodai occupied the central platform; the rest of them sat cross-legged in a circle facing him. In the middle of the circle empty bowls, baskets of fruit, and jugs of koumiss spoke of a meal not long concluded.

"He's right," Kazbek Argyn said. Alexei looked his way, astonished at receiving support from that quarter. Kazbek had never concealed his preference for Ogodai.

But then, Alexei and Ogodai were no longer at odds, at least when it came to defending the horde.

"Listen and learn," Kazbek went on, still speaking to Yusuf. "Arrogant brats don't survive long in battle. Alexei Sultan is twice your age and a seasoned warrior."

"Thank you." Alexei gestured to Ogodai, whose dark brows had creased in a frown. "To clarify, I command my father's men, but my brother the khan controls the operation as a whole." Ogodai's frown eased, and Alexei continued with a nod to Ruslan, seated to his left. "Ruslan Sultan and I brought five hundred warriors. How many have you here?"

"Three hundred from us." Malik Shirin represented the largest and most influential of the five clans.

"Two hundred for the Argyns," Kazbek said. "My son Rafik will lead them."

Baryn and Kipchak each promised a hundred. Yusuf Bey, visibly sulking, admitted to the same. "And four hundred for this camp as a whole, including my personal guard," Ogodai said. "So seventeen hundred altogether, but some must remain to protect the women and children."

"Can we move the camp to a more defensible position?" Alexei leaned forward, drawing an invisible map with his hand as he summoned memories of the traditional winter grazing lands. "Would it help to divide our families among the camps maintained by the tribes?"

"The raiders come from the south." Malik added a long sweeping line to the invisible map. "Most of the clans and tribes hold lands along the line of attack, so we need to consider those families too. We could move them all to the other side of the Sura River, but I don't think it would help, because the raiders have been seen heading in that direction as well. At the moment we have Kazan at our backs and rivers on both sides. And the closer we get to the forest, the harder it is to find enough pasture to graze the herds. This part of the grasslands is nearing exhaustion as it is. That affects both us and the raiders."

"They aren't raiders." Alexei recalled his meeting with the Crimean ambassadors—had it really taken place two months ago? "Not in the usual sense. The rest of the Nogai have united under one leader, but Sheikh-Mamai Bey refuses to surrender his independence. Somehow he managed to get his troops across the Idel, and now he's spreading out across the steppe." He drew another imaginary line marking the course of the Idel River, which the Russians called the Volga. "That's what this is all about."

"Curse him," Ogodai said. "Then we must hit him hard and take him by surprise, before he hears that our forces have increased. Do we know exactly where he camps?"

"I'll send scouts," Malik offered. "I agree that we must hit hard and fast, before they expect us. Time is short, because we have to get the horde to its summer pastures before the lambs and kids arrive."

"I doubt we'll make it," Baryn said. "We should be moving already. But yes, we must take care of the threat first. The animals slow us down and make it more difficult to maneuver."

"You have a larger army now," Alexei noted. "If we can't defeat Sheikh-Mamai on the first attack, I propose starting the migration. If we raid instead of mounting a single offensive, we can afford to assign warriors to defense."

"Yes," Ogodai said. "Once they know we have more men, the advantage of a full-scale attack is lost. But let's mount one before we complicate matters by adding the migration."

Malik picked up his prior line of argument with barely a pause, despite the interruptions. "How to protect those who do not fight? We can't push the camp closer to Kazan, or Safa-Girei Khan and his forces will attack us from behind in the misguided view that we threaten their lands. But from our present position we can use some of our warriors to screen the camp from the invaders while we launch the attack."

"We should consolidate as many of the women and children as possible here, in that case." Kipchak, by temperament a listener rather than a speaker, roused himself to interject this point. "From every clan and tribe."

"That plan will work so long as Safa-Girei stays out of it," Ruslan said. "He's mostly been worried about the Russians recently, but if Sheikh-Mamai encroaches on Kazan's territory, he'll notice fast enough. If your women and children get stuck between the armies, they'll be in worse shape than if you move them all somewhere else."

"We could warn Safa-Girei of Sheikh-Mamai's approach," Alexei said. "But I doubt it would help. He sees *Ata* as an enemy—me too, because I took sides against his uncle. He might grab the chance to steal the women and children instead of protecting them."

"Yes, too big a risk," Kazbek said. "And unnecessary at the moment. Sheikh-Mamai's men have to get past us before they can either attack the camp or encroach on Kazan. With luck, we'll have won or moved on before Safa-Girei even notices. Hand me that pen and paper, will you? This invisible map is good as far as it goes, but it's too vague to plan an actual strategy."

Baryn, who sat closest to the requested supplies, passed them down the line. Kazbek drew two squiggly lines and connected them with a third, then pointed to the squiggles at right and top. "The Idel." He indicated the squiggle to the left.

"And the Sura." An X between left and right marked the camp. "We leave a barrier of a hundred men to guard the women and children. Once we know where to find Sheikh-Mamai, we take the remainder of our forces and launch a lightning attack on his camp. The scouts can give us a better idea of how many warriors we're facing. If the odds are too uneven, we'll either have to request more troops from Bulat Khan or come up with a different plan. But so far the enemy hasn't fielded more warriors than we have, even before Alexei Sultan and his men arrived."

Alexei looked at his half-brother. "We will both fight?"

"Yes," Ogodai said, as Alexei had expected. "But someone needs to lead those who remain." He surveyed the council, as if trying to decide whom he could best spare from the fray.

"How about the arrogant brat?" Kazbek suggested. Yusuf Bey's scowl deepened.

"Perfect." Alexei reached behind Ruslan and Kazbek to smack the sulky boy's shoulder. "Cheer up. When the rest of us were your age, he called us arrogant brats as well." He grinned at Kazbek. "And in my case he was right."

The men laughed. A chorus of "me too" sounded. After a while Ogodai raised a hand. "To be on the safe side, though, since Rafik will lead the Argyn warriors, will you stay behind and advise, Kazbek Bey?"

"I will." Kazbek cuffed Yusuf lightly on the ear. "Shut up and listen, and we'll get along fine."

"Nasan!" Maria cried as Nasan came through the door in response to an urgent summons. "Mother of God, I'm glad to see you. If anyone can figure out what my father has done this time, you can."

Somewhat to Nasan's surprise Maria was alone. Paper and an inkwell lay on the table in front of her, with a quill pen at an angle across the sheet, as if Nasan had caught her in the act of writing. Next to the ink stand stood a small enameled box inlaid with birds and flowers. Nasan could not recall ever seeing anything quite like it.

"I'm writing to Alexei," Maria said when Nasan asked about the paper and ink. "But I'll finish that later. I'm so happy you're here."

"Yes, you said." Nasan crossed the short distance and greeted her sister-in-law, then tapped the box. "Where did this come from?"

"Papa brought it not long before dinner. He wants me to give it to Grand Princess Elena." Maria lowered her voice and stared at Nasan in a way that implied her words carried an extra significance. "To pretend that it comes from Princess Nadezhda Shuiskaya. Nasan, I truly think he has lost his mind!"

"Goodness, yes, who would believe that? Princess Nadezhda can carry her own gifts. But why her, and what is it?"

"Well, that's the thing. I went to open it, and he grabbed my hand away. He says the box contains cosmetics for the eyes, so I'm supposed to urge Grand Princess Elena to swallow it by the spoonful. The only reason I haven't thrown it away already is because I want to show it to you. Your mother says she doesn't know anything about Lithuanian cosmetics, but who knows if Papa told the truth even about that?"

"And why take a cosmetic internally? Can we open the box now?" Nasan thought of her medical books, about conditions affecting the eye and their cures, but she couldn't recall so much as a hint that Grand Princess Elena suffered from any such complaint. "Since you aren't planning to give it to her?"

Maria regarded the box with a doubtful expression. "It's locked. There's a key, but suppose it's not a cosmetic but some kind of poison? Papa acted so strangely, I'd believe him capable of any wicked scheme at this moment."

"Poison." The word struck a chord. "Eyes, cosmetics, poison. What does it do to the eyes?"

Maria frowned, considering. "Brightens them, he said. But Nasan, I don't trust a word that comes out of his mouth."

"Nor should you," Nasan told her. In her mind she saw a drawing on a page: narrow green leaves, black berries the size of blueberries, dark twisted roots. "But most lies contain an element of truth. It's too difficult to construct an entire fabrication without making a mistake that will lead to discovery."

"And the truth here?" Maria reached across the table, missing the inkwell by a finger's width, and clasped Nasan's hand. "Please tell me. I'm ready to burst with fear and anger. What has Papa done?"

"Nothing yet," Nasan said. "And we'll have to open the box and test what's inside to be sure. But there is a cosmetic that widens the pupils. They call it belladonna—beautiful lady. Only you don't ingest it. You infuse it in water and drip one or two drops directly into the eyes. Stupid idea, I think, but some of the harem women do it. My mother knows all about it; she probably just doesn't think of it as Lithuanian."

Maria stared at her, aghast. "What happens if you consume it?"

"You die," Nasan said. "Not always, if you eat a berry or two. They give tiny doses to women in childbirth to ease the pain. Your father wouldn't know that. I'm sure he's never attended a birth in his life. But not in that quantity. If you took a spoonful that size, you'd need divine intervention to last the hour."

"*Bozhe moi.*" Maria gripped Nasan's hand as if it represented her only lifeline. "I'm the daughter of a murderer—and a madman."

"Yes." Nasan returned her clasp with both hands, to show her sympathy. "A would-be murderer, at least. We will check the box, then destroy it. But we must also prevent any other attempts. Let's talk to *Ana*, shall we?"

"She's supervising the cooks." Maria glared at the pretty enamel box. "He planned to use me as his instrument. I'm tempted to feed him the contents myself. Is that a sin?"

"Not unless you follow through," Nasan said. "And I assure you, *Ana* will leave the kitchens for this."

But it was not Sumbeka who took the lead in deciding Koshkin's fate. Bulat Khan listened in growing outrage to the tale reconstructed by his daughter and daughter-in-law, verified through careful experimentation using eye drops derived from the box and a willing maidservant. As Nasan finished, her father slammed his fist against his desk and roared for Jamil.

Few people failed to react with speed when Bulat lost his temper. Within the space of a few breaths the steward stood at the door. "Yes, Khan?"

"The man whose movements you are following," Bulat said. "His name is Fyodor Koshkin. Tell your men to capture him and his son and bring them here. Confine them until I order their release."

"Confine them?" Maria's question came out as a squeak. Only after Jamil acknowledged the order and left did Bulat answer her.

"As a precaution, my dear." His roar had given way to a normal speaking tone. Nasan heard a rare note of approval in his voice. "You did well, the pair of you, to figure out what Koshkin planned and put a stop to it. But we can't take the risk that he will make another attempt as soon as he realizes this one didn't work."

"I understand why you wish to confine *him*." Maria looked and sounded sad. How awful it must feel to have one's last illusions of a parent destroyed in such a way. "But I doubt my brother even wanted to share his lodgings. He had a fit when he heard Papa had fled—well, the whole family did. I can't believe he would aid these nefarious schemes, and he will lose his latest position and perhaps get into greater trouble if he fails to report on time."

A thoughtful expression crossed Bulat's face. "When they arrive, I will speak to him without your father present. He must agree to remain under surveillance: if your father didn't scruple to involve you, why not your brother also? Where is he posted?"

"The Kitaigorod wall," Maria said. "It's a miserable post and he hates it—or so my sister told me the last time she sent a messenger—but he lost his original assignment when Papa fled."

Nasan watched in amusement as her father waved a lordly hand. "Oh, in that case I'll have him reassigned. If he convinces me of his honesty, he can move freely about the estate but not beyond. But if he has fallen prey to your father's madness, he will have more trouble than he can handle whether he shows up on time or not."

Which pretty much put an end to the conversation.

❦

Nasan left her parents' estate before Bulat's men returned with their captives. She wanted to reach home in time to check on Borya, who this morning had appeared on the brink of producing yet another tooth with all the drama his small body reserved for this, and only this, occasion. And she wanted to arrive before Daniil returned from his latest stint in the grand prince's bedchamber. She had almost refused Maria's heartfelt plea to visit her *at once*, but in the end she was glad she went. The potential consequences of Koshkin completing his plans outweighed the needs of a teething baby and even the possible confirmation of her suspicions regarding Grand Princess Elena's pregnancy.

Borya still felt hot when Nasan touched his forehead. After so many false alarms caused by teeth, she hesitated to speak her fears of illness aloud to Zhenya. Why invite the nursemaid to repeat the same reassurances she had already issued a thousand times, especially when they did not reassure? Instead she said, "I have no reason to go out again today. Let me know at once when you see the tooth."

Zhenya barely had a chance to agree before Nasan heard the clatter of horses' hooves that signaled her husband's return. She ran from the nursery and met him as he came through the door at the top of the stairs.

"Such a story I have to tell you!" she cried as she threw herself against his chest and felt his arms close around her.

"And I you." He kissed her, then pulled her toward the sitting room. "Have Sonya supervise the women tonight, and Pashka the men. I want to eat with you."

"Yes." Nasan called her housekeeper and gave the orders. "In here," she told Daniil. "I want to hear every word, but first let me tell you what happened to me today. You won't believe this." And she launched into the story of Koshkin's crazy plan.

"My head's spinning," Daniil admitted when she reached the end. "The best part of the story is your father locking Koshkin up. Otherwise I don't know if I could sleep at night."

"Agreed. I hope he stays under lock and key for the rest of his life, but I suppose that's too much to ask, even of *Ata*." She touched his arm, relishing the sensation of coiled muscle under her hand. "Tomorrow I'll find out from Maria how it went. But what of you? Any more news?"

His eyes warm, he stroked her ear. "You mean can I confirm your suspicions?" He laughed. "The ladies don't discuss such topics with men, you know. But I did sense an inordinate amount of anxiety, like listening to a hive hum. And Prince Ilya stopped by yesterday evening, although his shift doesn't begin until tomorrow. He might have information—from his wife?—because he haunted the royal bedchamber until the little grand prince demanded he stop. I did my best to sound him out, but he evaded every attempt on my part. Which made me more inclined to doubt his good faith but doesn't answer the question of what he *was* doing."

He frowned. "Although there was something. He slipped a folded piece of paper to his wife, and she tucked it into the sleeve of her tunic right away. A note, maybe. I couldn't get close enough to see."

"A note." Nasan pondered, but no explanation presented itself. "Can he write?"

"I wouldn't have said so." Daniil shrugged one shoulder. "I saw no evidence of it during that mission to Staritsa last year. I copied the document, and Koshkin and I signed it as witnesses, but Ilya made an X. So did my cousin Grigory." He flinched at the name, no doubt recalling Grigory's unhappy fate, a public hanging along the Novgorod road. The same fate that Koshkin had escaped by fleeing to Lithuania.

"Hmm," Nasan said. "Was he delivering it for someone else, then? But I doubt Nadezhda reads either, and her husband doesn't need to write to her if she's standing an arm's length in front of him. The grand princess may, I suppose. Read and write, that is. She had a Lithuanian education, despite growing up here."

"But a female education," Daniil noted. "It may not have included reading and writing. Perhaps the packet was something other than a note."

And with that they moved on to happier subjects.

Chapter 10

THE SCOUTS RETURNED THE SAME NIGHT WITH NEWS OF Sheikh-Mamai's whereabouts, and the attackers left at dawn, hoping to inflict as much damage as possible by nightfall. Ogodai and Alexei, flying their individual variations on the winged horse, rode side by side directly behind the vanguard—Alexei at his half-brother's right to reassure the horde that he occupied the position of second-in-command.

In reality the truth was more complicated. Whether Ogodai's grim expression reflected that knowledge or simply the seriousness of their offensive, Alexei chose not to ask. He had already done his best to allay his brother's suspicions. Only time would convince Ogodai of the truth. Until then, a certain amount of jostling between them seemed inevitable, because they were in essence equals. Alexei, older and more experienced, commanded the largest individual force and acted as their father's representative. Ogodai bore the more prestigious title of khan.

Of course, most of Ogodai's beys were older than the khan; Kazbek Argyn had almost as many years under his sash as Ogodai and Alexei put together. But there the charismatic authority based on descent from Genghis outweighed such factors as age and length of command. Here the remedy required Alexei and Ogodai to establish a genuine brotherhood. It would take more than one family meal to do that, although Alexei thought they had made a start. And today's campaign could well prove crucial in firming up or undermining their partnership.

The sun still hung low in the sky when they saw the first smoke from the enemy's hearth fires. Before long the spirit banners, their horse tails drifting in lazy yellow-white curves in the early spring breeze, came into view, partially obscured by the hemispheres of the nomads' tents. Alexei pushed every thought unrelated to the coming battle from his mind.

"They don't expect us," he said to Ogodai, as quietly as possible over the beat of twelve thousand hooves. The camp lay undisturbed, as if the residents still slept. But there must be sentries, so the quiet would not last.

Ogodai must have had the same thought, because he nodded. "I hadn't expected to find them so close. It's good, though, because the horses haven't had a chance to tire. Let's take them, shall we?"

"Yes," Alexei said, but the word had not left his mouth before Ogodai signaled the charge.

The thunder of hooves provoked the banging of drums from the camp. Men poured from the tents, hurriedly pulling on armor and reaching for weapons. But Ogodai's vanguard was already upon them, and the slaughter began.

Borya still had a noticeable warmth the next morning, and he rejected not only the breast but the solid food that Zhenya had introduced a few months earlier. Nasan was studying her child with anxious contemplation, unsure whether the time had come to trust her own instincts (so often proven wrong before), when Maria's voice sounded behind her. She spun on one booted heel and hugged her sister-in-law.

"Are you still worried?" Maria bent and touched Borya's cheek, then his forehead. "He does feel hot. Did he eat something nasty off the floor that's made him sick?"

"I should have thought of that," Nasan admitted. "If Mama-in-law were here, she would tell me reading books has addled my brain. I don't agree. But sometimes I do forget the simplest things, like babies that put everything in their mouths."

"Exactly. Alexander's already starting, but he can't crawl yet or even sit, so he hasn't anything like the reach Borya has." Maria tucked her hand in Nasan's arm. "I'm sure he'll be fine soon. Come and talk with me. Don't you want to hear how Papa reacted to your father rounding him up like a stray sheep?"

"Goat, more like," Nasan said with a wistful glance over her shoulder. *Grandmothers, please let Maria have guessed what's bothering my precious son!* "But yes, let's get some tea and you can tell me the whole."

"He was livid," Maria said once they had settled in Nasan's sitting room. "He's still livid. Especially now that Bulat Khan has decided that Mikhail's an innocent victim and moved him to a much nicer room. Your father intervened to get Mikhail off guard duty and assigned to him while he decides what to do with Papa, so Mikhail worships the ground under *Kaenata's* feet."

She used the Tatar word for father-in-law, Nasan noticed. That was new. Maria's language studies must be progressing apace. Nasan chose not to comment, as it would distract her visitor. "And where did he put your father? Not in a real prison, surely? I don't think there is one on that estate."

"Worse."

"Worse? What could be worse?"

Maria started to laugh. Nasan waited for her to stop, but she seemed incapable. At last she gasped, "Harem."

"Harem?" Nasan burst out laughing as well. However dreadful Koshkin's schemes and however serious their potential consequences, the thought of him locked in a harem chamber was too funny for words. "*Ata* confined your father in the *harem?*"

Maria coughed, caught her breath, and made a visible effort to control herself. "A room for badly behaving concubines, apparently. That's what *Kaenana* told me. I haven't forgiven Papa enough yet to go and see it for myself, but Lyuba ran into the next room yesterday and prattled at him through the grid until he shouted at her to go away. Pretty beastly of him, since she's the only one who missed him when he left. But Mikhail says the main problem is that the room smells like a brothel— his word, and I didn't ask him how he knows what a brothel smells like—and is secure as a royal vault. Not to mention that Papa hates having his plans scotched, however shortsighted and destructive they may be. He's threatening to cast every one of us out of the lineage. He doesn't seem to understand that if he *had* got away with his scheme, there would be no lineage left to cast us out of."

"That must hurt." Nasan's urge to laugh vanished, and she reached for her sister-in-law's hand. "You have every right to be furious with him, but he's still your father."

"Let's say I have a glimmering of what Alexei went through." Maria bit her lip, and Nasan nodded. Her own father had cast off his eldest son at sixteen and not reinstated him until little more than a year ago. Alexei never discussed his exile, except perhaps with Maria, but from time to time Nasan heard an edge of loneliness, even bitterness, in her half-brother's voice.

Then the mischief crept back into Maria's face. "But I do have to give credit where it's due. The thought of Papa imprisoned in a scented harem chamber almost makes up for what I went through when I realized he'd run off. Not the latest—that's unpardonable, and he must have been possessed by demons even to consider such an evil deed—but I owe your father a debt of gratitude for the rest."

"It is hilarious," Nasan agreed. "Now let me tell you what I heard from Daniil last night."

Maria had no sooner left than a royal courier arrived. Nasan, telling herself she should not hover over Borya as if tied by a string, had gone to check on the maids' progress with drying the week's wash and had crossed half the courtyard when a man rode in at full gallop, calling her husband's name. Daniil turned away from the straw target, bristling with arrows after his hour's practice, and went to greet the messenger as he dismounted.

Nasan stopped to watch. She didn't like the look of this. The man's hurried entry meant urgency, and the rider had pushed his lathered horse hard. A military summons? But Daniil was not on active duty at present because of his assignment as a gentleman of the bedchamber, and his most recent four-day shift had ended yesterday evening.

A quick exchange of words, and the courier mounted, riding out at a more reasonable pace. Daniil frowned at the man's departing back. From where she stood, Nasan could see how her husband clenched the centerpiece of his bow, as if reluctant to surrender it. Then he shrugged, snapped the bowstring away from its frame, and walked toward the armory.

Halfway there he spotted her and changed direction. "Who was that?" Nasan asked as he came within earshot. "What did he want?"

"A courier from the Kremlin." He caressed her cheek, a rueful expression in his eyes. "The grand princess has summoned me back into service, starting immediately."

"But you just finished!"

"I know. Prince Ilya Shuisky sent a message announcing a sudden and possibly infectious illness, and the grand prince asked for me as his replacement." He slapped the unstrung bow against his thigh. "It must have been a very sudden illness, since yesterday he gave every evidence of perfect health."

"He's shirking." Nasan deliberately avoided making it a question. "That's what you think."

"Yes. Infuriating man. I'm sure he hates nursemaiding a seven-year-old and a five-year-old, royal princes or not." He reached for her hand. "Walk with me while I put my equipment away and get ready. I can't refuse the summons, whatever I think of Prince Ilya's excuse."

He spoke the truth, so Nasan didn't attempt to dissuade him. "I suppose it's a compliment of sorts that the grand prince asked for you by name," she said, reaching for the one positive element she could see. "You're in royal favor."

He hugged her close. "I'd rather stay with you and Borya, but yes, I suppose it's better for the grand prince to like me than for him to hate me. And what's a few more days, over the course of a lifetime?"

Less than an hour later she kissed him goodbye. "Until Saturday," she said.

"Be safe, my love," he told her. "I'll miss you and Borya every moment I'm gone."

She didn't suspect, then, that those might be the last words she ever heard from him.

♪

Bloodstained and weary but triumphant, Alexei and his brother reached their own camp by sunset. Behind them nomads drove herds of sheep, goats, and—most valuable—horses. Others pulled carts loaded with valuables: jewels, precious fabrics, furs. Once across the great river, Alexei guessed, Sheikh-Mamai's raiders had made a living preying on the merchant caravans that traveled south to Astrakhan and Georgia, north to Kazan and Siberia, and west to Crimea and the Ottoman Turks. A good haul that now enriched Ogodai's khanate and people but would require a steady guard to retain.

At Ogodai's orders, they had left most of the enemy's wives and children in the camp. With their own horde about to get on the move, it seemed like a bad idea to add a large number of extra mouths to feed, especially strangers who would need time to integrate into the existing families. Ruslan had snagged a dark-eyed beauty, now riding in front of his saddle and apparently resigned to her fate. A few other warriors had done the same. Alexei wished them luck. In his experience captives seldom made good bedmates, but there were exceptions. For himself, he rejoiced at having put that stage behind him, although as his absence from Maria lengthened, he acknowledged the power of temptation.

"We didn't lose many men," he said to Ogodai.

His brother turned his head and grinned, more relaxed than Alexei remembered seeing him in years. "No. I wanted to surprise them. I didn't expect to succeed as well as that. We must have killed half his warriors."

"More," Alexei said. "He'll be back, though, looking for revenge. It's your decision—yours and your beys'—but if Kazbek and the arrogant brat have managed to keep your people safe, I'd suggest starting the migration as soon as you can. Tomorrow, even. Keep Sheikh-Mamai guessing where we went."

"Agreed," Ogodai said, somewhat to his brother's amazement. "We'll discuss it at the victory feast. We'll need to find defensible places to stop each night and keep the women, children, and animals surrounded at all times, but staying in one place has become a liability now that Sheikh-Mamai knows where to find us."

"Thank God for the vastness of the steppe." Alexei slapped his brother's arm, not hard. "You grew up well, *ené*. I'm honored to fight with you."

Ogodai's eyes widened, as if he had never expected to hear such words from his older half-brother. Then he laughed. A genuine smile creased his face and lit his dark eyes. "You too, *aby*," he said. "I'm honored to fight with you too."

They broke camp at dawn the next day, heading southwest to the horde's traditional summer grazing lands near the River Don. Timur rode at his father's side, while Ruslan took responsibility for monitoring the warriors they had led from Moscow. After a while Alexei and Ruslan traded places, so that Alexei led and Ruslan kept an eye on Timur. By the time they stopped to eat at noon, the boy visibly drooped after hours in the saddle, and Alexei let him choose whether to continue on horseback or ride in his mother's cart. But it pleased him when Timur elected to stay with the men, and he took his son up on Ajdar so the boy could rest. If trouble reared its head, one of the men could carry Timur to his mother.

Half-listening as Timur's chatter faded into sleep, Alexei experienced a quiet satisfaction. The familiar rhythm of migration—the rolling progress across an ocean of grass, slow but steady and governed by the needs of the grazing herds, the beauty of the steppe in its springtime splendor, the cries of birds, the clean herbal scent of plants trampled under the passing hooves—soothed his restless spirit, confined to city and woodland for the better part of two years. Yesterday's battle might exist in another realm, like the one where the ancestors hunted under the grandmothers' loving eyes.

He missed Maria. He would like to see Baby Alexander, to know that naught threatened his family. At the same time, he relished the weight of Timur's sleeping head against his chest, the knowledge that his son preferred his company even to the joys of traveling in comfort. The boy had a warrior's instincts. Alexei must make the most of the next two years, until custom required him to return his son to the steppe and let Ogodai take over the next stage of Timur's training.

Indeed, at that moment Alexei had but one regret: their journey across the steppe made them harder to reach. If Maria sent him a letter, it might well go astray.

Chapter 11

ON WEDNESDAY, THE THIRD DAY OF APRIL, CATASTROPHE struck in midafternoon, marring a balmy spring day. Nasan, standing in the nursery arguing with Zhenya for what seemed like the ten thousandth time about Baby Borya's feverish irritability, caught the sound of the death knell and raced to the window so that she could distinguish the ringing more clearly. Each set of church bells had a unique sound, and this peal came from the Kremlin, but for whom did it toll?

Her thoughts went first to the grand prince. Just two days ago he'd been healthy enough to demand Daniil's presence, but children could sicken quickly—why else did she fuss so about Borya?—and if Prince Ilya had not lied about his illness, he might have infected the grand prince or his brother even before Ilya himself retired to his bedchamber.

And what of Daniil? She wished her husband present, so she could be certain he was well, then ordered herself to calm down. Daniil seldom fell ill, and it defied belief that he would go from vigorous health to death so fast that no one would have a chance to send for her. Moreover, although he served the grand prince and represented an ancient lineage, he did not live in the palace. Most likely, the bells tolled for a resident, a member of the royal family or the great princely clans.

The slow peal continued, high to low, each note clear and compelling, fading before the next one began, then the twelve sounding together before the rhythm repeated once more.

Prince Yury and Prince Andrei already lay in their tombs, so the bells did not sound for them. Prince Ilya, perhaps? Many of the noble families had joined the Kolychevs outside the inner walls, where they could extend their lands as needed to support families, servants, and animals. But the Shuisky clan ranked so high that it retained its estate within the Kremlin.

Maybe Prince Ilya had infected others of his lineage or taken the sickness from them. Some of the uncles had reached an age when they might not withstand the touch of disease.

It was without question a sin to hope that the death knell tolled for Ilya, but of the possibilities that came to Nasan's mind she liked that one best. "I must find out who died," she told Zhenya. "Don't leave Borya's side."

With a swish of her skirts Nasan went to summon her steward. "Send a man into the streets at once," she ordered when she ran him to earth near the gates. "Find out the source of those bells and for whom they ring."

As if summoned by a spirit, her mother's voice spoke from behind. "For Grand Princess Elena," Sumbeka said. "She died an hour ago. I came to summon you to the funeral. We will gather at the Ascension Cathedral at sunset, but you may as well change your clothes and come with me now."

Nasan spun around. Sumbeka stood there, clad entirely in black, the same clothes she had worn four months ago for Prince Andrei's funeral.

"Grand Princess Elena?" Nasan struggled to push the words through a throat closed by shock. "By all the saints, what happened?"

Did Koshkin find a way to deliver his poison without Maria's help?

Another thought shoved its way into her mind. "And how can they be holding the funeral already? I thought the custom was to wait several days. To let the body lie in state, in the case of royalty."

"I don't know, daughter," Sumbeka said. "But they are. So hurry and change your clothes. We'll try to find out more when we get to the church."

"But Borya," Nasan protested. "He's feverish again."

"Another tooth?" Sumbeka shook her head. "Really, my daughter, must you drive yourself mad every time? I assure you, Borya will do fine here with his nursemaid. I'll take a look at him and instruct her myself, but let's get you dressed first."

Reluctant but resigned, Nasan climbed the stairs and, with her mother's help in place of the maid she lacked the words to summon, donned her mourning dress. She heard Sumbeka leave orders for Borya's nursemaid, then followed her mother down the stairs and into the carriage that had brought Sumbeka here. One question pounded in her head.

Elena dead. How did she die? She was twenty-eight years old and healthy!

And again: *Is Fyodor Koshkin responsible for this?*

The funeral proceeded with the same indecent haste accorded to the corpse of Prince Andrei. Nasan, again bereft of her mother's support but blessed with an adequate substitute in Maria, stood at the front of the ranks of noblewomen and did her best to push aside memories of those other services for her mother-in-law (deeply mourned) and Prince Andrei (savagely murdered). If one counted the nine-day and forty-day memorials, this was her seventh requiem in six months, and she yearned to escape yet another sad and gloomy repetition of the rite.

Worse, she couldn't find Daniil, although she sought him with her eyes among the masses of male courtiers. Normally he stood out because of his height, unusual even in this land of giants, but when she stood on tiptoe she still couldn't catch a glimpse of him. Nor did she see the others who usually served with him in the grand prince's bedchamber. Should they not be at their ruler's side in this moment of grief? Or did another Russian custom she didn't understand operate here? She couldn't use Prince Andrei's funeral as a guide, because he had died stripped of his supporters. For example, at those other funerals the coffin had been uncovered, and at Natalya's mourners had pressed forward to kiss the body before the sextant nailed the lid in place. But Elena's coffin was already sealed, and no one remarked on that—except Maria, when asked, who confirmed that indeed, that was something that normally happened only if a corpse was disfigured or decayed. But Elena had been beautiful in life, and her death had occurred so recently that the stiffness could not yet have left her limbs. A puzzle.

The young grand prince stood at the front, looking so small and scared that she longed to comfort him. His little brother wept with the abandon natural to a five-year-old, while the grand prince shivered but did not sob. Behind them Prince Ivan Telepnev, head bowed, placed a hand on each royal shoulder. The children didn't cling to him, but they didn't pull away either. Nasan could not see Telepnev's expression from her vantage point, but when he had passed her during the procession, he had looked grave, shocked, grief-stricken—the very reactions she would have expected.

She couldn't help but notice how Prince Vasily Shuisky glared at the touching tableau. Prince Dmitry Belsky also, who stood facing Shuisky. Incredibly, the two clans, who seldom agreed on anything from what Daniil had told her, appeared to have found common ground in their opposition to the royal favorite.

For herself, she approved of Telepnev's actions. The boys had lost their father at so young an age that even Grand Prince Ivan must retain only the haziest memories of that time, and now God had taken their mother too. If Telepnev, who had occupied their father's place for most of the last five years, could soften that terrible blow, why begrudge the boys whatever reassurance he could offer?

But Prince Vasily obviously disagreed. Glancing in Shuisky's direction once more to check her own conclusions, Nasan perceived in the shadows a sight that made her bite her tongue. Prince Ilya Shuisky, again hiding behind his uncles, stood with the firm stance of a man who showed not the slightest symptom of illness in the half-light between a pair of pillars decorated with painted saints.

Prince Ilya here and Daniil nowhere to be seen? What does that mean?

She couldn't wait for the service to end.

But as the ritual continued, she caught sight of her husband standing next to his father, dressed in the simple robes of a monastic acolyte. The tall black fox hat concealed Daniil's golden brown hair, causing him to blend in with the surrounding nobles.

She released a long breath of relief. He hadn't stayed away; she had failed to pick him out from the crowd because of his clothing and the dim light in the cathedral. And he was with his father, whose solid bulk seldom failed to convey a sense of competence and calm.

Daniil's face bore a serious expression, as she would expect in this setting. When the service ended, she moved toward him, but the milling men blocked her path. A woman couldn't push her way forward without provoking a scene, and the cathedral had no passages that might lead her past the obstacle the men presented. For a while she waited off to one side, hoping to get closer as the nave cleared. But in the end Daniil's raised hand sent her back to Maria and the other women.

The ceremonial drew to its close. Before midnight Grand Princess Elena lay interred in the traditional resting place of the grand princesses, the Ascension Cathedral in the Kremlin. Nasan, still struggling to understand what had gone wrong, watched the pall bearers place the grand princess's coffin next to the memorial for Sophia, the niece of the last emperor of Constantinople, who would have been Elena's mother-in-law if Sophia had survived long enough.

The thought sparked a memory of Nasan's own mother-in-law, and she brushed away tears. Let the mourners believe she wept for Elena.

Although in truth, Nasan grieved for Elena too. Despite the many calumnies directed at the grand princess and the unrest caused by her determination to counteract the threat she perceived from her brothers-in-law—especially her role in the death of Prince Andrei last year—it didn't seem to Nasan that all the complaints against Elena were justified. Elena had reformed the currency, built the new wall around Moscow, made peace with Lithuania, sent her troops against invaders from the south and east—all in less than five years. Or if not she, then Telepnev acting in her name and that of the grand prince. Did Russia's nobles consider it so bitter a gall to take orders from a woman that they would murder her to rid themselves of her authority?

Nasan longed to discuss these questions with her husband. Daniil's calm common sense, so like his father's, seldom failed to inspire.

No, that was an excuse. She wanted to see him, to hold him, to seek comfort from the stresses of this disturbing day. To talk about Elena and what her death would mean, yes, but also to revel in their love, his touch.

Perhaps he would join them at the house. Surely his duties, already extended beyond his usual shift, would not be further prolonged now that Prince Ilya had recovered?

But Daniil did not return. Instead she received a letter saying that several more days must pass before the palace routine resumed its normal course. In the interim every nobleman assigned to wait on the princes must remain in service.

Nasan crumpled the note into a ball and hurled it at the opposite wall. She had heard enough about loyalty and devotion. She loved her husband, and she wanted him home.

She and their baby needed him too.

The first few days of the migration went well. The weather remained fine, the animals traveled far, eager to graze on the fresh grass after months of diminishing forage. Alexei held his breath as the tail of the Sura River appeared on their right, marking the place closest to Sheikh-Mamai's camp, but that leg of the journey also passed without incident. Another ten days or so, and they would reach the horde's summer pastures. The evidence gathered by the scouts suggested their enemy had retreated across the Idel to lick his wounds.

Alexei didn't believe that and said so.

"No, neither do I," Ogodai said. It was the evening of the third day, and they sat next to each other on the main platform in the khan's tent. Ruslan, the only other descendant of Genghis present, occupied the place at Ogodai's left, opposite Alexei. The usual bowls of mutton stew, baskets of flat bread and fruit, and jugs of koumiss lay in the center. From the edge of the platform to the tent door, the sounds of men feasting filled the room. Timur, under protest, had yielded to his mother's pleas to join her at the women's meal.

"Is he waiting for us to let down our guard?" Alexei asked, referring to Sheikh-Mamai. "Gathering more men?"

"We beat him badly," Ruslan noted. "He will want to avenge his losses, for sure, but his remaining warriors may be much less eager to fight us than he is."

Alexei nodded. Steppe warriors liked to pick their battles, and they would not long serve a leader who led them to defeat— or subjected them even once to a rout. Sheikh-Mamai had come close to the latter. "His personal guard will stay," he said, turning his inchoate musings into words. "The others, less certain. But cross that river twice, even to find replacements? I don't think so. And no one would take an army across the Idel *three* times to punish a small horde like this one. It would be madness."

"Like you, I doubt he crossed it a second time." Ogodai lifted his clay cup. "I'd swear on this koumiss that he retreated south, toward Astrakhan, hoping to recruit the Nogai who live west of the city. If they know the approximate location of our pastures, they can follow the Don north again until they find us. It's a great nuisance, because we will have to mount watch the whole time."

To put it mildly. Alexei didn't want to spend the entire summer when he could be with his wife and young son guarding a nomadic camp against incursions from the south.

He didn't say that. This problem was not of his brother's making, and whining wouldn't solve it. It wouldn't get him home sooner either.

"But *does* he know?" Ruslan asked. "Sheikh-Mamai, I mean. Who would tell him where a particular horde travels on the steppe?"

Ogodai shrugged. "There are always defectors. But we have few of those, and I agree it's unlikely. We can't take the chance, though."

"Of course not," Alexei said. "But the greater likelihood is that he will try to seize your winter grazing lands. Those he has identified. You need to prepare for the possibility that he will have moved in by the time you return. Why waste effort in searching for you when he can wait you out?"

"Damnation." Ogodai smacked his hand against the bolster and added a few choice epithets about Sheikh-Mamai's mother. "You're right. Well, we have half a year to figure that one out. Maybe we can settle closer to Kasimov."

"Not if the Crimean ambassadors told us the truth," Ruslan said. "Sheikh-Mamai has been threatening the Kasimov region as well. The whole line south of the Oka riverbank, as far west as the Don, in fact. And I think he stops there only because he doesn't want to run into the Crimeans, who are out for his blood."

"So are we out for his blood." Ogodai drained the cup of koumiss and set it aside. "If he threatens our grazing rights, that is. The man's a menace. Why didn't he stay on the other side of the Volga where he belongs?"

That question had no answer, and Ogodai probably didn't expect one. "Right," Alexei said as he reached for a bowl of stew. "He could have made everyone's life easier."

"But here we are." Ruslan took a piece of bread from the nearest basket. "I can imagine worse fates than a summer on the steppe. Tell me about that doe-eyed beauty who lives next to Alexei's Guzel. What's her name, and is she likely to respond if I issue an invitation?"

"What happened to the doe-eyed beauty you captured?" Alexei wasted no time in pointing out that Guzel was no longer his. "She looked amenable enough when I saw her."

Ruslan groaned. "So she did. But turns out she's anything but. Stole a dagger from behind my back and nearly took out my eye before I grabbed it from her. So I let her go. Can't spend the rest of my life worrying about ambushes and poisons."

The men nearby burst out laughing, teasing Ruslan without mercy. After a while, Alexei joined in. Ruslan might not enjoy being the butt of the joke, but the humor defused the tension caused by the possibility of Sheikh-Mamai's vengeance quite wonderfully.

*

"As I have told you a dozen times, I did *not* cause the death of Grand Princess Elena." Koshkin spit out the words, one by one, but his interrogator failed to indicate by so much as the flick of an eyebrow that he placed the slightest weight on Koshkin's repeated denials. "How could I, Khan, when you have kept me immured in this ..." At a loss for words, he waved a hand at the tiled and painted chamber, so feminine in its fabric, coloring, and scents that he couldn't stand to look at it. That his ingrate of an eldest son had won his freedom in a matter of hours and now sat at Bulat Khan's side watching the khan's interrogation twisted the knife in ways that Koshkin considered heartless, if not outright cruel.

"This room for three days," he finished. A lame ending, but the best he could manage under the circumstances. Fury roiled in his gut, curdling the meal he had eaten not an hour or so before. He forced his hands open. Bulat would no doubt read clenched fists as evidence of guilt, and Tatar khans tended to act first and worry about the justice of their reactions later. The khan had already proven more intimidating than Koshkin liked to admit, even to himself.

"The question is what you did before my men brought you in." Bulat's implacable tone did not lessen Koshkin's discomfort. "We watched you after you left my house the first time, but you had who knows how long before that to work your mischief, and no surveillance is perfect. A man who would implicate his son and daughter in treachery would stop at nothing to achieve his ends. I don't trust you."

He spoke the last four words with ponderous clarity, raising Koshkin's hackles another notch.

"I have no access to the court." Koshkin mimicked Bulat's tone and saw his adversary's eyes narrow. *Take that, Khan! Two can play this game.* "I asked my daughter to take Elena a gift, and she agreed. Why do you assume I had ill intent toward the grand princess? Because I gave her cosmetics? The idea's absurd!"

Bulat exchanged glances with Mikhail, who blushed and hung his head.

What's that about?

No one enlightened him. But another searching look at Mikhail's abashed face told Koshkin the answer. His son had probably spilled everything he knew about Koshkin's hatred for Elena.

"Those cosmetics turned out to contain a deadly poison," Bulat said in the same biting tone. "What would have happened to your daughter if she had delivered the box as you requested? What would happen to your son after you forced him to harbor you? Innocence wouldn't save them. Have you no care for your own offspring? For my clan, now linked to yours? You disgust me, Koshkin."

It was worse than Koshkin had thought possible. No wonder Mikhail blushed and cringed like a whipped puppy in his father's sight.

Maria had betrayed him. Maria and her brother both. They had talked to Bulat. They had revealed his plans to the enemy, leaving his grand scheme unrealized. Koshkin's rage threatened to explode within him, but he couldn't release it yet. He remained Bulat's prisoner, which meant that Bulat held him in the palm of his meaty hand.

"Poison or not, women use it in Lithuania." He snarled. "As a cosmetic for the eyes. Elena would have come to no harm."

"Do you take me for an idiot?" Bulat snarled in return. He did it better, which stoked Koshkin's simmering anger into raw fury. "They use it in the harem too, but they don't *swallow* it. And why should we believe you gave your entire supply to Maria? That you hate Grand Princess Elena is common knowledge."

Was it? Koshkin found that unlikely. He had told no one but his children and his son-in-law.

And his faithless wife. Every one of them a traitor.

His heart burned with the effort of containing his rage. "I do not," he blustered. "A few unwise words, said in the wrong quarters. I served the grand prince like anyone else until that scoundrel Prince Ilya tricked me into fleeing Moscow."

"More lies." Bulat scowled at the pink flower tiles on the wall with such intensity Koshkin expected to hear them crack at any moment. "You'd sell your own grandmother into slavery to save your miserable hide. You fled Moscow for Staritsa, then abandoned Prince Andrei in turn—for where, Lithuania? I've seen weasels with more loyalty than you."

"I admit nothing," Koshkin said, returning scowl for scowl. "You can't prove I intended harm to the grand princess, because I didn't. I returned to Moscow to visit my family, ungrateful bastards that they are."

Bulat rose and smacked him across the face with the full force of an arm accustomed to wielding a battle ax. "I don't need to prove it," he said in a tone so menacing that Koshkin couldn't control his instinctive need to cower. "You are not in Lithuania now. If I order your execution, believe that my men will carry it out, no questions asked. And I *will* get to the bottom of this, with or without your help." He shook a fist at the walls. "You can rot here for the rest of your days. I won't shed a tear. Maybe I'll withhold your food to hurry the process along. That seems to be the style among the Muscovite royal family these days."

While Koshkin stared at him, again robbed of speech, Bulat slapped a hand on Mikhail's shoulder. "Come, son," he said. "Let's leave your father to consider his options. He hasn't many. He can talk or he can stay in this room he hates for the rest of his life—which won't be long if I get tired of listening to him."

Leaving Koshkin sputtering, Bulat strode from the room. Mikhail sent his father one semi-apologetic glance before following the khan out.

Chapter 12

LESS THAN A WEEK AFTER GRAND PRINCESS ELENA'S funeral Maria rode into Nasan's courtyard, surrounded by half a dozen members of Bulat's personal guard. Nasan heard the clatter and ran for the door to the outside, reaching it in time to see her sister-in-law slide from the back of her lovely white mare and toss the reins to the nearest warrior. The man and his companions led the horse toward the stables. Maria, her outer robe crushed in both hands, raced up the stairs and grabbed Nasan by the elbow, almost pushing her into the house.

"What is it?" Once inside Nasan dug in her heels and refused to budge. "What's happened?"

"In here." Maria waved at the entrance to the sitting room. "Please?"

Nasan frowned but complied. Something had upset her sister-in-law; that much was clear. But what?

She repeated the question as soon as she closed the door behind them. Maria dropped onto the window seat in a swirl of silk, pulling Nasan with her. "Prince Vasily Shuisky has assumed full control of the government," she said as Nasan settled beside her. "He and his brethren have begun to move against their clan enemies. The Belskys have chosen to back them, it seems—or at least not to oppose the Shuiskys' grab for power. They're exacting retribution for past slights, because Grand Princess Elena is no longer alive to protect her favorites. They've already arrested Prince Ivan Telepnev and thrown him in the same cell where he and Grand Princess Elena confined her uncle Mikhail until his death. And they've forced his sister into a convent, stripping the grand prince and his brother of the two remaining people most familiar to them."

Nasan struggled to keep up. "It's started then," she said. "A war among the most powerful clans. Shuisky and Belsky against Cheliadnin for the moment, but once they defeat their common enemy, they will turn against each other. Exactly what the old grand prince tried so hard to prevent."

"Yes," Maria said. "But it gets worse. *Kaenata* received word today. Rumors that Prince Vasily himself murdered the grand princess. He hated her, you know, more even than Papa did. He resented her favoring Prince Telepnev over himself and his kin."

"Do you think that's true: that he murdered her? People spread the most scandalous stories at moments like these." Nasan shook her head, not in denial so much as disbelief.

Maria shrugged. "I don't know. It's true that she was young and, as far as anyone knows, healthy. For her to die so suddenly of unknown causes does seem suspicious, and if anyone benefits from her death, the Shuisky clan seems to be doing so. They're an older princely house than Moscow, and they have long resented serving a family they consider less prestigious than themselves. But the real problem is that Elena's death removes the last barrier against chaos, because there are lots of older houses, yet they agreed among themselves that the princes of Moscow should take precedence. Without an adult grand prince, a grand princess, or even an uncle to occupy the center, the rival factions—the Belsky clan in particular, as you say—will challenge the Shuisky clan's right to rule on behalf of young Grand Prince Ivan. There's even talk that the grand prince and his brother may die next. If that happens, there will be no one left who can unite the clans until the leaders get together and select a new ruler themselves."

"That's bad." Nasan didn't like to think how bad. "If the nobles are fighting one another, they can't defend the land against incursions from abroad. Russia will be back where it was five years ago, vulnerable to invasion from all sides: Lithuania, Poland, Crimea, Kazan. Does Prince Vasily care so much about increasing his power that he would risk the realm for his own gain?"

"He already has," Maria said. "So yes. He's even taken over Prince Andrei's quarters in the Kremlin and added them to his clan's estate. Trying to make himself look more royal, I suppose. None of that proves he murdered Elena, of course, although his behavior is suspect and so is her death. If we can, we should try to find out what happened. But there's more." She patted Nasan's hand. "Be brave."

"Brave? Why brave?" *Do I want to hear the answer?*

"The Shuiskys didn't stop with arresting Telepnev and forcing his sister into a convent. They want to destroy the power of the entire Cheliadnin clan and its supporters. They've ordered the ladies-in-waiting confined in convents as well—except for Princess Nadezhda, of course, because she's one of them. Solomonida and her daughter have been sent to the New Maiden's Convent. Not tonsured yet, but that may follow." She stopped, putting a hand over her mouth as if to hold back the words that must come next.

Nasan had to ask, although she dreaded the answer. "And Daniil?"

"Yes," Maria said. "Daniil has been arrested too. All the gentlemen of the bedchamber who supported Telepnev, in fact—again excluding Ilya Shuisky."

Nasan burst into tears. Maria hugged her, murmuring, "I'm so sorry, I'm so sorry." Nasan clung to her, sobbing, incapable of speech. Short of losing her baby, this news was the worst she could imagine. In the Kremlin arrest too often meant a death sentence, as the recent funeral of Prince Andrei demonstrated. Would she ever see her beloved husband again?

When the tears eased, she pulled away. Maria regarded her with eyes warm with sympathy, but as soon as she saw that Nasan had recovered even a little of her composure, she said, "We have to get you and the baby away from here. *Kaenata* is sending carts, so order Sonya to muster every servant you have to pack any item that can be reasonably declared to belong to you or your father, including basic clothes and weapons for Daniil. Make sure she tells the staff they'll be working at your parents' house until your father secures Daniil's release."

"The Shuisky family would confiscate our property?" Nasan's head reeled with the suddenness with which disaster had struck. "Yes, I suppose they would. Very well, let me summon Zhenya and have her get Borya ready. And give Sonya her orders. Tell your men to saddle Sorkhokhtani and bring her out with your Kumai. I will change as quickly as I can."

As she rose from the window seat, she caressed the patterned cushion with her hand. The room had been hers for such a short time, and now she must leave it. The Shuisky clan would take her house and her lands while she returned to her parents' home. She could already hear the rumble of cartwheels approaching the gate.

But no loss compared with the tragedy that had befallen Daniil.

⁘

The weather for once favored Ogodai's horde. After ten— or was it twelve? Alexei had lost count—solid days of warm breezes and intermittent clouds that shaded but did not rain, the riverbank of the Don became visible on the horizon.

"Almost there," Alexei told his son, again riding at his side. "See those trees? We'll stop not far from them, before we reach the hills."

Excited, Timur rose in his stirrups as if he could draw closer by extending his own height. Alexei reached to steady him, laughing at the boy's eagerness. "By nightfall," he said. "We'll camp on our own grazing lands this evening."

The snap of a bowstring startled him. The arrow flew past his nose and buried itself in Timur's mail. The boy cried out and tumbled back onto his saddle, then continued to fall. Alexei grabbed him around the waist and hauled him off the horse with one mighty pull, settling Timur in front of him while reaching for the pony's reins with his free hand.

"Attack!" he yelled in his best battleground roar, but his men were already reacting. He called to the nearest rider and, when the warrior came close enough, handed him Timur. "Take him to his mother at once. Tell her to summon the shaman. And not to pull out that arrow until she knows what damage it's done." He patted the whimpering boy's cheek. "You'll be fine, son. Just a scratch. You're blooded now."

Timur nodded. Alexei watched him swallow, control his wobbling chin, take a single sobbing breath. "Brave lad," he said, wishing he believed his own assurances. But the mail had done its job, he thought, so unless the arrow carried poison or infection set in, Timur should indeed recover.

The moment he saw his son safely away, Alexei shouted for his men. He found them with Ruslan, preparing to charge the enemy.

Ogodai rode up with a force of a few hundred. "I left the others to guard the women and children and the animals," he said in response to Alexei's querying eyebrow. "Let's go. If this is Sheikh-Mamai again, I want not the slightest hint that he can get away with taking *us* by surprise."

Alexei didn't argue. He'd planned to urge the same course himself. Instead he kneed his horse into motion, gesturing his men forward with an upraised arm. They fell into place behind his standard. "Capture one or two if you can," he told Ruslan. "Pass it down the line."

This time Ogodai was the one raising the eyebrow. "To be sure it *is* Sheikh-Mamai," Alexei said. "One of those men shot Timur. I'm in no mood for mercy, but I want to know whether we face one enemy or two. How would Sheikh-Mamai track us here without our noticing him?"

"Timur, shot?" Ogodai asked. "Will he recover?"

"I think so. He made an easy target, but that's no excuse. He's obviously a child." Alexei paused. "It may be time to send him back to Moscow," he added after a moment. "If I can do so without endangering him or us."

"His mother won't like that," Ogodai noted. "But I understand. Let's capture one or two of the enemy as you suggest and see what we're facing, then decide."

They rode south in near-silence, side by side, chasing the raiders. Before long the familiar circle of white felt tents appeared ahead of them. At Ogodai's signal the warriors formed a long line, three or four abreast, and encircled the camp in the same way that Tatars encircled animals marked for the hunt.

Their quarry fought fiercely, but with relatively small numbers of men they couldn't withstand the combined forces of Alexei and his brother. It soon became clear that these opponents couldn't be more than stragglers from Sheikh-Mamai's horde, if that, and Ogodai ordered them subdued but not killed. As the sound of clashing weapons and singing bows died to a whisper, two of Alexei's warriors hauled a protesting

Tatar whose fine robe and velvet cap indicated that he might lead this camp and forced him to his knees before the khan.

Ogodai paced before him, projecting what Alexei recognized as an excellent imitation of their father in a rage. "You attacked my horde. Why, when we were heading to our own grazing lands? We did you no injury, and only a fool would take on so many armed men for plunder." He stopped in front of the cowering leader, now face down in the dirt, crossed his arms and stood legs apart, glowering.

Not bad, ené. Alexei did not grin, which would undercut the effect of Ogodai's performance, but he silently applauded his younger brother's air of authority.

"Answer me!" Ogodai roared.

The leader, who couldn't be much older than twenty— another arrogant brat, Alexei decided—pushed himself onto his knees but didn't look at Ogodai. "We need the land for our herds. The forces of Sheikh-Mamai Bey press on us, and we have lost many cattle."

"Hmm," Ogodai said. "What's your name?"

"Azamat Bey." Ogodai's change of tone seemed to reassure the young man, judging from the slight lift in his shoulders, but he kept his eyes fixed on the ground.

"I am Ogodai Khan." Ogodai gestured at Alexei. "My older brother, Alexei Sultan. Will you join forces with us? Sheikh-Mamai is our enemy too. He attempted to take our winter pastures and could try again. Fight for me, and you may share our summer grazing lands. We have many warriors to protect what belongs to us."

Azamat Bey rocked back onto his heels, astonishment visible on his face. "You would ally with us?"

"Why not?" Alexei said. He hadn't anticipated this move, but he understood the logic of it. "The more fighters we have to oppose Sheikh-Mamai, the better our chances of success."

He drew his brows together, mimicking his younger brother's stern frown. "But remember, we have three or four times as many men as you. One hint of treachery, and you will rue that day." His mind filled with the image of Timur, carried tight-lipped away, the arrow still protruding from his shoulder. "And you'd better hope that my eldest son suffers no permanent injury, or I'll have the head of the man who shot him."

The young leader's shoulders slumped once more. "Agreed," he said in a small voice.

"A good day's work," Ogodai told Alexei as they rode back to their own camp. "Thank you for your support with the bey. Will he keep his word, do you think?"

Alexei shrugged one shoulder. "If he has any sense. Hard to tell if he does. We'll watch him. Right now I'm more concerned about Timur."

"Yes." Ogodai kicked his mount into a gallop. "Let's go find out how he's doing."

Koshkin paced the ridiculous flower-strewn chamber, kicking hassocks and cushions as he passed. It had become his daily dose of activity, the only release for his spleen. As he walked, he muttered an endless stream of invective, each curse more elaborate and inventive than the last. Most of them he aimed at Bulat's head, but he spared a few for his unsatisfactory children, who like the khan seemed perfectly content to leave their loving father in captivity to rot.

At least Bulat Khan hadn't carried through on his threat of execution. Most likely he had intended to intimidate his prey, and it had worked. But Koshkin had yet to devise a scheme that would get him out of his scented confinement. The men, burly warriors all, who delivered his food twice a day pretended not to speak or understand Russian. His eldest daughter refused to visit him. His son had appeared just once, in the thrall of Bulat Khan. If his four middle children had expressed the slightest concern for their father's whereabouts, Bulat had not chosen to relay the news to Koshkin.

Even so, he sensed that something had changed since yesterday morning. Although locked away in the center of the house, Koshkin had heard the rumble of carts and the rapid chatter of voices in that language he did not understand. A baby's cry sounding at midnight, answered by the cry of a second infant. The Kolychev girl's clear voice, his daughter's exquisite soprano, both sounding at times when the Kolychev girl, at least, should have departed for her own home. But never Daniil Kolychev's rich baritone. Alterations in patterns created opportunities for a skillful mind to exploit. Koshkin had danced to the piping of others for too long. The time had come for him to chart his own destiny once more.

Which meant he needed to begin by deploying his sole asset. Lyuba chattered nonstop. She visited him often—more often than he desired, in truth. And although as a good father he had hesitated to involve her in his plans (not least because he placed no confidence in her discretion), needs must. Let her find him a key, and he would free himself without laying any blame at her door. Then he could figure out how to use Grand Princess Elena's death to his own advantage.

Because due to a twist of fate, this time he was innocent. Thanks to Maria's meddling, whoever killed Grand Princess Elena hadn't done so with his belladonna.

⚘

As Alexei approached Guzel's tent, the sound of rhythmic chanting and shaking beads reassured him that his former lover had done as he bade her and summoned the shaman to tend to their son. So when he ducked his head under the lintel, he was more than a little surprised to find no healer present. The cover above the smoke hole had been removed, permitting some light to enter and the fragrant steam of the hearth fire to escape; the tent smelled of sage and incense; he had distinctly heard the shiver as a shell-encrusted drum hit the ground. But none of the people inside the tent wore the distinctive robes or face-shielding plaits of the shaman, who appeared to include shapeshifting or invisibility among her many skills. He said a silent prayer against the evil spirits such abilities might invoke.

Guzel sprang to her feet as Alexei stepped over her threshold, his brother right behind him. Beyond her he saw the Russian nursemaid bent over a pale-faced Timur, lying flat on his back under a pile of felt coverings. The arrow no longer protruded from his left shoulder. Ogodai's twins were nowhere in sight— another surprise, given the presence of their nurse.

"How does Timur?" Alexei asked the raging harpy hissing in front of him. After his past interactions with Guzel, he hadn't expected her to greet him with open arms, but the expression on her face suggested that she stood two steps shy of murdering him, as if he'd shot their son himself.

"Fine," she snapped. "No thanks to you."

"I sent him to you," Alexei reminded her, his voice sharp. "What does that mean, fine? Did you remove the arrow? I asked you to wait."

"Grusha did." Guzel pointed at the nursemaid. "She dosed him and bound the wound, said the spells for healing and smudged the tent. Unless evil spirits attack, he will recover." She glared at him again. "It's more than you did for him."

"Stop it," he said. "I told you to send for the shaman before you did anything. Why didn't you?"

"Because Grusha knows what she's doing," Guzel said. "She learned medical skills from her former mistress. See for yourself."

Alexei crossed the tent, pushing past the mother of his child, who yielded reluctantly at best, and crouching at his son's side. He reached out a hand to rub the boy's cheek, and Timur's eyelids fluttered.

"My warrior," Alexei said. A smile curved Timur's mouth, and pink flushed under his father's hand.

"He looks better than I would have expected." Ogodai spoke from behind Alexei's right shoulder. "Good job, lad. You'll be a khan yet." Timur's smile widened, and for a moment his eyelids parted, but he didn't speak.

Alexei checked the wound and found it clean and neatly dressed. The mail and Timur's silk shirt had done their work, and the arrow had not further torn the boy's flesh on removal. God willing, he would heal quickly and completely.

"You did well," Alexei told Grusha. "I will reward you for this."

"And I," Ogodai added. Alexei heard his brother's feet retreating to the far side of the tent, toward the door. A quiet exchange between Ogodai and Guzel followed, but Alexei, distracted, made no attempt to listen in. From Grusha, kneeling close by, he caught the distinctive aroma of sage.

Sage. The herb the shaman used to cleanse the air of illness and infection. Guzel had mentioned that Grusha said the spells for healing and smudged the tent. And he remembered hearing the beat of a drum. But how did Grusha know the spells if she was not a shaman? And if she *was* a shaman, why hadn't she said so? No one in the camp—except perhaps the shaman herself—would object to her exercising such skills if she possessed them.

He had yet to find an answer when Grusha interrupted his thoughts. "Prince Timur will recover, Sultan," she said. "In full, I think. I rubbed the arrow with a cloth and found no dirt or poison. I have covered the wound with a spider's web so it will heal faster and dabbed it with mint and vinegar against infection, so we have reason to hope for the best. We'll know for sure in a day or two."

Alexei stood. "Good," he said. "Watch over him while he heals. I'll ask my sister-in-law to appoint someone else to look after the twins while you care for my son. Once he regains his strength, we can decide whether to send him home to Moscow."

"You wouldn't," Guzel cried. "So soon? When will I see him again?"

He turned toward her. The beauty that had drawn him a decade ago had faded, and anger distorted the sweet face he had loved. Yet recalling their time together, her gentle nature (not much in evidence since his return), her tender care for their child, and his own regret for too much time spent apart from his son, he grieved to inflict his next words on her. But he saw no alternative, since he doubted she would agree to live in Maria's shadow in Moscow and he couldn't imagine walking out on his son once more.

She faced him, hands clenched at her sides, the rage so endemic since his arrival visible in her stance, her expression. But beneath the anger he saw grief, an emotion he knew too well. The knowledge that he had, after all, abandoned her as well as their son softened his voice as he took one of her clenched hands in both of his. "If it will keep him safe, then I must. But if I do, I'll bring him to see you again soon."

She pulled her hand away and showed him her back. "You won't. You care nothing about me and my needs. You made that clear when you left. And again when you kept Timur with you in Moscow without even asking me."

Hearing the tears in her voice, he wrapped his arms around her. She stiffened, but he stepped closer, encircling her. "I know you miss him," he said. "I miss him too, when he's with you. I'm sorry we ended up like this. I swear, I bear you no ill will."

For a moment she stood rigid in his hold, but as he was about to release her, she turned and buried her face in his shoulder. Alexei wiped her wet cheeks with his hand until she pulled away. Nostalgia tugged at his heart. Although he'd never experienced with her the deeply satisfying partnership he now enjoyed with Maria, for a long time they'd been comfortable together. And they had produced Timur, who would always be a bond between them. "We can do better than this," he said. Guzel nodded, although her tension didn't ease.

Alexei let go of her and walked to the door. When he reached it, he twisted his head, looking past Guzel to Grusha. "Send a message as soon as he awakes."

"Yes, Sultan," the Russian said. Then he left, Ogodai again close behind him.

Chapter 13

NASAN, DRESSED IN THE BOYS' CLOTHES SHE WORE TO practice swordsmanship and archery with her husband, stood at the entrance to the bare cell that the Miracles Monastery offered in place of her father-in-law's beautiful study and bed-chamber. She waited in silence, as commanded, while Nikolai's mentor conferred with him. An intense discussion with Elder Gennady had won her a brief meeting with her father-in-law, but only on the condition that he agree to receive an unknown Tatar youth.

Unknown to Elder Gennady and the monks, that is. Nikolai, she hoped, would recognize the name she had given from his first encounter with the Golden Lynx four years ago. Short of an all-out assault on the Kremlin Nikolai represented her best hope of discovering Daniil's whereabouts and pleading for his release.

"I've not seen him before," Gennady said. "A Tatar boy, too young for a beard, calls himself Girei."

From the doorway Nasan watched her father-in-law rub his own bushy beard, which spread out across the simple cross and black robe that he wore. Even from that vantage point she saw his blue eyes twinkle as he looked her up and down. "A bold lad, to come alone and unannounced," Nikolai said. "But

I remember him well. A friend of my son's, as I recall. Please allow him to enter."

Elder Gennady departed, favoring Nasan with a stern frown as he passed her. When he turned the corner, she slid into the room, leaving the door ajar so that no one could suspect Nikolai of keeping secrets, and hugged her father-in-law. He looked happy, despite the stark surroundings—more at peace than Nasan had seen him since his wife's last illness. She remarked on it as she took the seat he indicated.

"A simple life," he said. "It suits me well. But what brings you here, Girei?" The slight emphasis he placed on the last word revealed that he understood she served some purpose beyond the duty to visit an honored family member.

"Have you heard what's happened at the palace?" she asked, keeping her voice as low as possible without allowing it to become a hissing whisper. "The arrest of Prince Telepnev and his supporters, the Shuisky clan's assumption of power with the tacit consent of the Belskys? They released Prince Dmitry Belsky's brother, I'm told—the one the grand princess kept imprisoned for years." Not more than a day had passed since Maria's unannounced arrival had upended Nasan's world. The news of the Shuiskys' coup might not yet have reached the cloister, despite its proximity to the royal living quarters.

"I have not." His hands tightened, and the serenity she'd noticed on her arrival noticeably decreased. She regretted being the cause of his distress.

Quickly she filled him in, ending with the news of Daniil's captivity. He followed her with his usual swift comprehension, interrupting with only the occasional question and anticipating her conclusion as she approached her final sentences. "And the thing is," she said, "that without the grand princess to hold court, my contacts among the women are limited, and those most likely to help have also been sent away. So with your son"—her voice broke, and Nikolai clasped her hand in his—"imprisoned and my brothers somewhere on the steppe, there is only my father to make inquiries. He wields great power, of course, but he labors under certain constraints because of his long friendship with Telepnev. I hoped your friends and family might have their own sources of information. If we could at least find out what the Shuiskys have done with Daniil …" She shuddered, unable to finish the sentence. Daniil locked up was bad enough, but fears of him beaten or starved woke her shivering in the night.

Nikolai patted her hand in a fatherly manner and gazed at the icons in the corner, his brows drawn together in a frown. "I've disturbed your peace," she said as the silence lengthened. "I apologize. Should I go?"

He jerked his head toward her. "Don't apologize. You did right to bring me this news. But I must investigate the paths open to me. I am new here and no longer my own master." His mouth quirked in what Nasan read as self-mockery. "A situation I sought that now burdens me. Can Girei return tomorrow?"

"I think so." She took a deep breath. Her next words would not improve his state of mind. "Borya and I are living with my parents. The government has confiscated your town estate, except for the items we managed to remove before they came. The villages remain in the family, but not under Daniil's control."

He groaned. "What did I ever do to Vasily Shuisky to deserve this?"

An unanswerable question. "So my time is also not entirely my own," she said. "But if not tomorrow, then certainly the next day."

"Let's say the next day, then. Tomorrow I will learn what I can, including whether I have the right to pursue my connections in the world. Monks intercede, do they not? But I have not yet joined that august company." He rose and kissed her right cheek, then her left. "Go with God, my child, and may He preserve my son from harm. And thank you again for sharing the news of my family's troubles with me."

Nasan returned his embrace, resisting the urge to throw herself against his burly frame and sob in a way no Tatar boy would do, then left, blinking back her tears.

Yet the visit comforted her. Nikolai would find a way to help, of that she felt certain. And she trusted him to succeed.

One more supporter on her side. In these days of crisis the love of her family—and of Daniil's father—was all she had.

"Come, Lyuba. Wouldn't you like a hug from Papa?" Koshkin put on his most coaxing face, infused his tone with the warmth needed to appeal to a bored and lonely seven-year-old. "You come to talk to me every day; you're such a good girl. But if you can find the key and open the door, we could play tag or throw a ball. That would be fun."

The tousled head dimly visible through the grille work nodded. "But where to look, Papa?"

A puzzle, that. Did the servants leave the key in plain sight? He hoped they did, or his plan would fail, and he was getting desperate.

But Bulat's steward did not send the same person every day with food. There was a chance. "Look near the door, sweetie," he said. "It's a pretty big key. Maybe it hangs on a nail? Make sure no one sees you, though. Some people here want to keep you away from Papa, and that's wrong."

A rustling sounded, and the tousled head disappeared from the other side of the grille. He heard light footsteps in the hallway. A day had passed since he developed this plan, and by a great stroke of luck Lyuba had arrived in the early afternoon, when the household was generally quiet—perhaps even asleep. But suppose the key hung out of the child's reach? His steady monitoring had revealed no sentries on duty, which suggested that Bulat relied overmuch on the security of the harem room and his captive's unwillingness to test the boundaries of his imprisonment. But there could be other obstacles, including an elderly guard invisible to Koshkin's gaze.

Tension tightened his stomach. "Are you there, kitten?" He strove to keep his voice calm, warm. "Do you see anything?"

"Yes," she whispered. "I'm reaching now."

More rustling, followed by a whoosh, a gasp, and feet hitting the floor. Rapid footsteps, racing down the hallway in the wrong direction.

Has she run away?

He had time to move from wondering to panic to a state close to despair before the rapid footsteps returned, this time heading his way. Another jump, and he heard a distinct clang of metal hitting the floor.

"Did you get it, Lyuba?" He tried to keep his voice steady, despite the excitement that clenched his insides into knots.

She didn't answer, but he heard metal touching metal, then a click as the key turned. The door swung open, and she dashed toward him. "I did it," she cried as he swept her into a hug. "It was so high that I couldn't reach it at first. But then I remembered Timur's play sword, and I used it to knock the key down. Aren't you pleased, Papa? Can we play tag now?"

Relief made him weak. It had worked. A long shot, but it had worked. God was on his side once more. He sent a silent prayer of thanks to the heavens, kissed his youngest daughter's cheek, and set her down in the corner farthest from the door. "In a moment, kitten. You've done wonderfully, and I'm so proud of you. Papa has just one task to perform first. Wait here, and I'll be right back." As she stared at him with wide green eyes, he strode at top speed across the room, stepped through, and locked the door behind him.

"Papa!" Lyuba howled. As he checked for sentries and found none, then walked at a swift but steady pace away from the room that Bulat had designated as a prison, Koshkin could hear his daughter pounding her fists against the door—kicking it, even. The sounds of her hurt and disbelief stopped him in his tracks for the space of a heartbeat. Then he moved faster, sliding through one harem chamber after another as he sought a path to the outside. He needed to escape before someone heard the girl's cries and came to investigate.

As he crouched in a doorway near the outer gate, he spared a thought for Lyuba. He was a beast, he knew, for exploiting a child in that way. But she'd given him his opportunity, and he would make it up to her later. She needed a father able to defend her interests, not one incarcerated at Bulat's pleasure for a crime he hadn't had the opportunity to commit.

The arrival of a carter driving a wagon half-filled with felt cloths and oak barrels gave Koshkin the means of escape he needed. While the carter argued with Bulat's steward, Koshkin sneaked to the back of the wagon and made a place for himself amid the felts. The possibility that the steward intended to buy the felts accelerated his heart and turned his muscles taut as bowstrings, but fortune continued to favor him. While Koshkin peered from his hideaway, servants removed several of the barrels from the wagon, replacing them with baskets and a money bag. The carter moved to the front, snapped the reins, and issued a command to the horses. Soon the wagon was underway. Koshkin discovered that he could breathe once more.

While the carter maneuvered among the narrow streets, Koshkin pulled the money bag under his pile of felts, untied it, and transferred two large handfuls of coins to the pouch he always kept hidden beneath his robes. He returned the bag to its prior location and eased his way from under the felts. A quick glance revealed the carter staring straight ahead, oblivious to the existence of a passenger.

Koshkin debated: enjoy the ride or complete his escape? The wagon slowed for a turn, and he grabbed the chance to slide off unnoticed. Although he could put greater distance between himself and Bulat in the cart, the risk of staying seemed too great. When the guards found him missing, someone might recall and chase the wagon. Or the carter might catch him with stolen coin. Koshkin darted into the nearest alley and considered his next move.

An hour later he had collected several sets of spare clothes and a hooded cloak from his son Mikhail's lodgings, as well as other supplies and additional coins, one of which he handed to the landlady—an old crone if he'd ever seen one—to persuade her to forget this and his previous visits.

"Haven't seen a thing, have I?" The crone bit the coin, looked at it, and produced a gap-toothed smile. "That young man you stayed with done with the room?"

"Seems so," Koshkin told her. "He's found other lodgings." And so he had, the bastard—with Bulat. *Take that, son!*

While the crone slid the coin into a pouch at her waist, he left for the destination he should have picked in the first place instead of trusting his miserable excuse for a family: the Church. Specifically he sought the whereabouts of Father Spiridon, the family chaplain the Koshkin clan had supported for so many years.

Spiridon was a good man, one who remembered past benefactors. As a priest he had probably been allowed to keep his home even when Grand Princess Elena and her misbegotten favorite confiscated Koshkin's estate. And if Koshkin told the full story of his mistreatment at the hands of Bulat and others, no doubt Spiridon would agree to give him a bed.

Once he had a base of operations, he could start discreet inquiries. Because it seemed likely that someone had killed Grand Princess Elena, and that person, thanks to Maria and her interfering in-laws, was not Koshkin. As a result, he had no sin weighing down his conscience and no crime to conceal. And if he could identify the guilty party, he trusted his ability to turn that information against the culprit and his clan. He needed only to convince those responsible for the murder that the alternative to meeting his demands would be exposure of their crime, with all the civil and religious penalties that entailed.

Koshkin's escape against the odds meant that he had again found the right path. Now he had to walk it without flinching until he reached his goal.

Nasan returned from the monastery and went to change her clothes. Although she much preferred living in her own house with Daniil, one advantage of again sharing a home with her mother was that no one raised an eyebrow at seeing her dressed as a boy. A small—no, tiny—boon to offset the mammoth disaster of her husband's arrest.

Once changed, she went to check on Borya, whose budding fever had yet either to abate or yield a tooth. It had never taken so long before, reinvigorating her fears of illness, as usual lurking in the back of her mind waiting to pounce.

The baby's forehead still felt warm to the touch, hotter indeed than yesterday. She ordered Zhenya to prepare a concoction of willow bark, very weak because of the child's age, and overruled any objections. "If his tooth pains him, it will help with that too," Nasan said in the authoritative tone she had learned from her mother. In situations like this one, it worked best. "I'll return right after dinner to check on him."

But as she left the nursery, Maria ran toward her. "Is Lyuba in there? Have you seen her?"

"She's not." Nasan caught her sister-in-law's arm. "Slow down. You sound quite frantic. I went to visit Papa-in-law in the Kremlin, to tell him about Daniil's arrest and the loss of the estate. Lyuba wanted to come with me, riding her pony, but I said no. I haven't seen her since I returned, but I went straight to my room, then came here."

"She didn't meet Father Job for her lesson. You know how she loves to study." Maria twisted her hands together. "And when I went looking in the obvious places—her own room, the stables, the sewing room, the kitchens, that little parlor where she and Timur like to play, here in the nursery—I couldn't find her. So I asked the servants, and no one could remember seeing her since the morning service."

"But what do you fear? She's a sensible girl, despite her age. Where could she go to get herself in trouble?" Nasan leafed through memories in her head. Her father's study? No, Lyuba had a healthy respect for Bulat, as did the entire household. *Ana*'s sitting room then? The prayer hall? But what there would draw the attention of a Christian child? Besides, someone would have discovered her during the noontime prayers.

"The orchard?" she asked. "The garden?" A seven-year-old girl could get herself in trouble climbing trees or falling into ponds.

Grandmothers, protect her!

Nasan had developed a deep affection for her small sister-in-law, whose active mind and energy made them kindred spirits. "The kennels? The attic?"

"I've asked Jamil to search those places," Maria said. "I'm probably panicking for no reason. There are lots of places she could be, petting puppies or making mud pies in the kitchen garden. But it's unlike her to run off without telling a soul."

"Let's look around then. If Timur were here, I'd assume they'd decided to play hide and seek, but alone? Maybe she went to the attic, and one of the maids has her." Nasan caught Maria's hand and tugged.

"If Timur were here, they'd be making such a racket we would have no trouble finding them." Maria tugged Nasan in the other direction. "I've already been that way."

"So they would," Nasan said. "Lead on, then. She must be somewhere, and Jamil's searchers will find her."

But Jamil's searchers could not. They reported back in midafternoon, when Nasan again stood in the nursery assessing her sleeping baby. The willow bark had done its work, and his fever had lessened. Zhenya reported that he had fed too, so Nasan decided that she could safely leave him for a while and join the search for her missing sister-in-law.

By now she shared Maria's alarm. It seemed inconceivable that one little girl could vanish from sight without a single member of this populous household seeing her go. Had someone taken the child against her will?

It was not until suppertime that the servant charged with delivering food twice a day to the harem prison discovered Lyuba curled in a ball in a corner of the room and her father gone. As he reported, the child had cried herself to sleep, or so it appeared from the tear marks that made two long lines against her cheek. Her hair was even more tousled than usual, and when he delivered her to Sumbeka's sitting room, where Maria and Nasan had gathered to talk over ideas on where to look next, Lyuba was so distraught her words barely made sense.

"Hush, hush, child," Sumbeka said. "Take a deep breath. Release it. Again. Where is your father, and how did you come to be locked up there and him missing?"

Lyuba took the required breaths, but in such long sobbing gasps that the women could see that control remained a long way out of her reach.

Maria pulled the child onto her lap, tugged a cloth from the sewing basket lying on a nearby table, and wiped her sister's cheeks.

"Good girl," she said, although she must know that Lyuba's presence in the harem room meant she had done something far from good. "Calm down and tell us. Where is Papa?"

"Don't know," Lyuba said with another sob.

"How did you get locked in then?" Maria smoothed the tousled hair. "Even if you made a mistake, things will go better for you if you tell us what happened."

Lyuba rubbed her eyes with both fists. "Papa did it."

"What!" Sumbeka, Nasan, and Maria said at once.

Lyuba took a big gulp of air. "He told me to get the key and open the door. So I did. But then he went out and locked it. He said he'd come back, but he didn't. I kicked ever so hard and screamed. Only nobody heard me."

"But why did you let him out?" Nasan said, incredulous. A week's effort, undone by a seven-year-old with a key. *Ata* would be furious, and rightfully so. Someone would answer for this: if not Lyuba, then whoever left the key within reach.

But then, who would guess Koshkin would exploit his own child in such a way?

"He's my Papa." Lyuba made this pronouncement as if the answer were the most obvious thing in the world—and Nasan supposed it was. "He said I had to, so I did."

Sumbeka, uncharacteristically silent until this point, spoke. "I understand, child. You must do what your father tells you. But what he told you to do this time was a very bad thing. Did you not know that Bulat Khan had shut him in the room to keep him safe?"

Lyuba's face crumpled once more, and she buried her head in Maria's shoulder, sobbing. "He told me he loved me," she blurted out. "That he wanted a hug. I didn't mean to do wrong."

"Please don't punish her," Maria said. "I'm sure he did exactly as she says. And being our father's daughter is punishment enough." She patted Lyuba's hair once more. "Darling, I'm sorry, but Papa will say anything if he thinks it will get him what he wants at a given moment. The only person he loves is himself. It took me years to learn that, and Mikhail too. Now you're learning it as well."

Lyuba sobbed harder, if that was possible. Nasan glanced at her mother, then at the weeping child. The disillusionment in Maria's voice seemed, right then, like the saddest thing she'd ever heard.

But every word Maria spoke was true, and thanks to Lyuba's misguided attempt to obey her father, they now had not only an angry Bulat to appease but Koshkin on the loose, planning who knew what.

A sick baby, an escaped prisoner, a captive husband: could this day get any worse?

Chapter 14

THE CAMP, ENLARGED WITH THE ADDITION OF AZAMAT Bey plus his people and herds, spread a good distance along the bank of the Don and into the grasslands to the east. Alexei, standing at the door to his own tent, couldn't see where it ended. Between him and the horizon a second horde of women had gathered, chattering as they shepherded lambs, kids, and foals to their mothers before moving in to gather the remaining milk. The combination of human and animal sounds created a cacophony equal to that of a battle.

The women not involved in the milking had their hands full as well—making cheese, rolling felt, brewing koumiss, cooking and baking flat breads. Although quieter, they were no less busy.

Give me a sword and a bow any day.

The thought brought Timur to mind. Would his son recover fully, avoid infection, regain the full use of his arm? Would his spirit break under its first taste of war? And what of the trip to Moscow—how likely was it that Timur would not do better here, under his father's eye, than on a long journey across the steppe? The boy might even hear the wrong message if sent away: that one could and should shirk one's responsibilities.

Despite what he'd said to Guzel, at that moment Alexei accepted that he must keep their son here, and not only for her comfort.

But he should write to Moscow. His father—and, more important, Maria—would want to know about their attack on Sheikh-Mamai, the attempted raid by Azamat Bey, and Timur's injury. With the horde settled on its traditional summer pastures, Alexei could spare a few men to convey letters to his family. He stepped across his threshold and took paper, pen, and ink from the saddlebags his servant had left next to the latticework of the tent.

After completing his self-appointed task, Alexei rolled the paper and returned it to the saddlebag where he had found it, then went in search of his brother.

He found Ogodai in his chief wife's home. Grusha's absence while she nursed Timur had not resolved the conflict between Firuza and her husband, so far as Alexei could see. When he walked in, husband and wife faced each other, arms crossed and eyes locked. The twins were not present.

"I *went* to Guzel's tent. Grusha wasn't there. She stopped by in the morning, then went about her business. I know they're lying to me," Firuza was saying as Alexei came in.

Should he retreat? Share his own suspicions about where Grusha spent her time? Was this argument even *about* Grusha, really?

Since retreat seemed pointless when he stood in Ogodai's direct line of sight, Alexei stopped and cleared his throat. Neither his brother nor his sister-in-law paid the least attention.

"Yes, I understand," Ogodai said. "Then challenge her, follow her, do whatever you want. It bothers you, I see that. But wherever Grusha goes, she's not with me. I like her well enough, but I don't desire her and never have. Although if you don't stop fussing at me, I may pick one of the other women to amuse me. What's the point in staying true if you're going to hurl accusations at my head every other day?"

Their pose reminded Alexei of his occasional clashes with Maria, a thought that brought a flash of nostalgia that he immediately suppressed as absurd. Missing her passion was one thing, but missing their quarrels? He must be besotted.

"Should I come back later?" he asked, pitching his voice at a level where they couldn't fail to hear him, acknowledging their warlike pose without taking sides. "I don't want to interrupt your discussion."

Firuza burst into tears and retreated behind a screen that closed off one section of the tent. Ogodai emitted an exasperated sigh and uncrossed his arms long enough to pick up a tied scroll that lay on a nearby chest and toss it across the room. "Here," he said. "It's for you." Alexei caught it midflight. "From your wife."

Ogodai waved a second scroll. "This one came from *Ata*, addressed to us both." His strained expression relaxed into a sardonic grin. "I'm guessing you want that one first. The joys of matrimony being enhanced by absence, and all."

"I heard that!" Firuza said from behind the screen.

"Thank you." Alexei twisted off the yellow ribbon, broke the seal, and scanned the contents, feeling his own eyebrows rise as he read. The contents drove Grusha and his brother's marital troubles straight out of his mind. "By the Prophet (on whom be peace)," he said when he reached the end. "Did *Ata* tell you what's going on in Moscow? Elena's death, Telepnev's fall, our brother-in-law's arrest? And Koshkin! I know he's my father-in-law, but I swear I should have throttled him when I had the chance."

"Yes, he told me." Ogodai tossed the second scroll. "See for yourself. Firuza and I were discussing it when you came in."

Alexei nodded, choosing to let the lie stand.

Right. You were engaged in a civil discussion about events in Moscow. Apparently they didn't realize how much he'd overheard.

But clearing that up could wait. The news from Russia was more important. "I have letters to go out when the couriers leave," Alexei said. "I'll write another once we decide on a response."

"And will you send Timur with them?" Firuza reemerged from behind her screen. Before he could answer, she drew her brows together as if considering whether to say more, then added, "His mother begged me to intervene, to ask you to let him stay with her, but I can't say I agree. It *is* dangerous here so long as we must fear retaliation from Sheikh-Mamai."

"From what *Ata* and Maria write, things aren't much better in Moscow," Alexei said. "I did tell Guzel I might send Timur home, but I don't see how I can. If Sheikh-Mamai is threatening the steppe to the north, as the Crimean envoys have insisted he does, Timur would be in greater danger on the move than here, where I can watch over him. And although I want to keep him safe, I don't like the idea of teaching him that one should run from a fight. The part that troubles me is not being able to look after my wife and my second son."

"*Ata* will protect them. Still, I understand." Ogodai paused, then said with what Alexei read as studied indifference, "If you wish to rejoin them, we can probably manage here now that the migration's done."

"A noble offer." Alexei strove to match his brother's tone. "But I agreed to this assignment, and I will complete it. Unless you're saying you have no use for me."

Did Ogodai still resent him, despite everything? He might, although Alexei had gone out of his way not to challenge the khan's rule or even to suggest he would consider challenging it.

"You know I'm not." Ogodai's eyes widened in shock, and Alexei experienced a spurt of satisfaction that his brother hadn't even imagined such an interpretation for his words. "Without you and your men," Ogodai went on, "we couldn't have launched that raid on Sheikh-Mamai." The shock vanished in a grin, genuine this time. "Although I think we might have stood our ground against Azamat."

"Another overconfident stripling," Alexei agreed. "You roared at him magnificently. *Ata* would have cheered at the sight. I almost did myself, but I wanted Azamat cowed as much as you did."

"You'll stay, then?"

"Yes," Alexei told him. "So will Timur. Some solution will present itself, no doubt. But I rejoice if my presence here has improved your opinion of me." He slapped his brother's shoulder, allowing his own grin to surface. "Besides, think of the fit *Ata* would have if I showed up in Moscow and announced that I'd left you to fend for yourself while I came to *his* rescue."

"He'd disown you all over again, most like." Ogodai gestured to the door. "Very well. I appreciate your sacrifice. Let's go ponder our options, shall we?"

Alexei followed his brother out, glad to leave the strained atmosphere of the tent behind him. But he did make a mental note to follow up on his suspicions of Grusha and the shaman. Clearly, Ogodai and his wife could use a little help, whether they realized it or not.

Bulat roared until Nasan put both hands over her ears. "*Ata*, please. I know you're angry, and I don't blame you one bit, but you're terrifying the household," she told him.

"That child should be beaten." His growl probably traveled to the nursery, where the women had left Lyuba still sobbing her heart out. "Why didn't you keep an eye on her?"

"Her *father* should be beaten," Sumbeka snapped. "The child only obeyed his orders. And she's distraught as it is. She won't forget this day for a long time, if she ever does. I'm sure she learned her lesson."

Bulat grumbled, but obedience to a father was a sacred obligation on the steppe. "Very well," he said at last, although his voice still sounded as though the concession pained him. "I agree. The child acted as she should. And we'll recapture Koshkin, I'm sure. But when we do, keep her away from him."

"Of course." Maria bowed. "And forgive us, please. I in particular am at fault here. I should have supervised her visits more closely. It never occurred to me that Papa would try to subvert her—or that she could free him if he did. The key should be moved as well, if you bring Papa back here."

"Yes, that was ill done." Bulat had not lost his resemblance to an angry bear in the middle of a thunderstorm, but he had reduced his growl to a more normal speaking voice. He raised it again to shout for Jamil.

Nasan exchanged glances with her mother and sister-in-law, and as one they withdrew. Jamil raced passed them as they reached Sumbeka's sitting room, and they could hear shouting.

But nothing worse, and after a while Jamil's footsteps sounded once more. In response to a nod from her mother, Nasan peeked out the door and pronounced Jamil unharmed but heading for the outside. To hunt for Koshkin, the women assumed.

Hours later the steward returned. Maria had gone to the nursery to check on her baby and her sister, but Nasan followed her mother to Bulat's study, taking care to stay a good distance behind. As chief wife Sumbeka insisted on her right to stay informed on matters to do with her household, and Bulat rarely gainsaid her, but Nasan was not sure that his tolerance would extend to a daughter. Best to avoid drawing attention to herself.

Bulat sent them a sideways glare when they entered but did not deny them entrance. Jamil stood in the middle of the floor, wringing his hands. Sumbeka moved to the sofa near the window, and Nasan sat next to her. Mikhail Koshkin already occupied a small covered bench near Bulat's desk.

"You didn't find him anywhere?" Bulat barked at the steward, who looked, if anything, even more distressed than he had when they first walked in.

"We did not, Khan," Jamil admitted. "We checked the house where Koshkin stayed with his son, and the landlady said he had stopped by. He gave up the lodgings and left with whatever possessions he could carry, but he didn't tell her where he planned to go."

"Devil take him," Mikhail burst out. "First he forces himself on me, then he causes a firestorm of mischief and would have done worse if not stopped. Was that not bad enough? Must he steal my things and surrender my room as well?"

"You will stay here," Bulat said. "Jamil, send a man to collect his belongings." The steward acknowledged the order with a dip of his head.

"Thank you." But Mikhail continued to grumble at his father under his breath.

"There was a carter here today," Jamil volunteered. "We questioned him closely, but he says he saw no one except me and our servants. Insists he took no passenger, and I think he tells the truth, because he seemed quite indignant at the thought."

"Could Koshkin have slipped out while the men were loading the cart?" Bulat demanded.

"He must have slipped out, Khan," Jamil said in what passed for a reasonable voice, although its tremor suggested continuing anxiety. "Either then or at some other time. He could even have sneaked into the cart when our backs were turned, but if he did, he either paid off the carter or escaped without being seen. But my men searched every nearby tavern and shop, both here and around his lodgings, and found no sign of him."

"Any ideas, son?" This query Bulat directed at Mikhail. "Does your father have a favorite place to drink, gamble, whatever?"

"He's in hiding, Khan," Mikhail said. "I know of no such place, but I doubt he would visit it in any event, for fear someone would recognize him."

"We'll keep watch, Khan," Jamil said. "Sooner or later we will find him."

"Like the weasel he is, he's gone to ground," Bulat concluded. "Has he left the city, then?" But no one could answer him.

Wrapped in the hooded cloak, too warm for an April after-noon, Koshkin hid out in the chapel of his old estate, waiting for Father Spiridon to arrive. When the priest at last appeared, Koshkin still lurked in the shadows, fearful that some of the faithful would recognize him—or at least wonder at his pres-ence. But few members of the household chose to attend the service, and except for Spiridon and his family, the two or three that Koshkin saw struck no chord of recognition in his brain.

What had happened to his people when the government confiscated his estate? After receiving not so much as a curious glance from those in attendance, Koshkin relaxed. Even so, he remained concealed and quiet until the prayers ended. Only when the tiny congregation had departed, together with the priest's wife and children, and he was alone with Spiridon did Koshkin dare step forward and lower his hood.

The priest leaped backward as if an unclean spirit had materialized before his face. An elderly man with a beard almost as white as his vestments, he had acquired a look of anxiety that Koshkin didn't remember from their interactions a year ago.

"Lord." Spiridon clutched at his cross, which dangled right over his heart. "Where have you been these many months? We heard such rumors. And the grand prince's troops, speaking of treason and captivity. We thought you quite lost."

"Lies," Koshkin said. "I would not betray the grand prince." Although he had. "An enemy sought to bring me down—and for the most evil of reasons: lust for my beautiful bride." Better, for there he spoke only the truth. "I need your help, lest I fall into his hands before I have a chance to clear my name."

"An enemy." Spiridon repeated the phrase as if unable to comprehend its meaning. "And out of lust for your lady, who was arrested and held for some weeks. A great sin indeed. But you can't shelter here, Lord. Prince Ilya Shuisky has taken over your estate and sent your people to distant lands owned by his clan. Except for me and mine, those who remain serve him."

"What?" Koshkin tore off his hooded cloak, threw it to the boards that lined the church floor, and stamped on it. The only alternative was to howl his outrage to the world, not the best choice when he stood on hostile ground. Mikhail had mentioned the grant of the family estate to Shuisky, but not this latest outrage. "My enemy has grabbed my servants for himself? And what of the house? Does he live here?"

"No," Spiridon said. "Only his people. That is, they live in the town, as most servants do, but they work here during the day."

Koshkin picked up the cloak, shook it free of dirt, and wrapped it once more around his shoulders, then took Spiridon by the arm. "Father, I have nowhere else to go. The Tatars have turned my eldest and youngest daughters against me, as well as my son Mikhail. The rest of the family lives too far outside Moscow, and it's imperative that I remain here until I've restored my fortunes. You served me for many years. Can you not shelter me in your own home for a short time while I right the wrong committed against me by the basest of men? Is that not what Mother Church expects of her priests? I promise I won't trouble you more than necessary, and I can pay for my keep."

Doubt warred with fear on Father Spiridon's kindly face, but in the end responsibility won out. "Very well," he said. "Come with me."

Chapter 15

"YOU AGAIN?" ELDER GENNADY LOOKED ANYTHING BUT welcoming, and Nasan bit her tongue to prevent a snappy retort that could only undermine her mission here. It had cost her enough to don her boys' clothes and leave her still fretful and feverish infant at home in the nursery.

"Lord Nikolai asked me to return today," she said in her most pacific tone. "Otherwise I wouldn't bother you."

"But that's the problem." Gennady glared at her as if she were an intrusive insect intent on diving into his soup. "You distract him from his studies, pull him back toward the world when he should separate himself. That he asked you to visit him again does not excuse you for reminding him of what he willingly left behind."

How to handle such truculence? Did the elder honestly believe that Nikolai would not be distracted by knowing that his son faced death and he could do nothing to save him because of a choice that he himself had made?

"It's important." She held out her hands in a pleading gesture. "He may have information that will save a life. His *son's* life. Is that not a noble cause?"

"Hmm." Gennady's scowl did not ease, but he turned to speak to the icons in the corner. "To save an earthly life or to pursue salvation: which is the nobler cause?" He snapped his head back to face Nasan. "Are you Christian, boy?"

"Yes," Nasan said. She bowed to the icons, which she had already greeted on entering the room as was the custom, and crossed herself. The elder's eyebrows moved farther apart, if by only a fraction. "Lord Nikolai wishes to pursue salvation, and you wish the same for him. I understand that. I wish to save a life in the present, although salvation is also vital." She hated to beg, but she saw few other options. Nikolai might not have the information she sought, but her father's inquiries had so far yielded poor fruit. And this grumpy old monk stood between her and finding out. "A few moments, please. I swear I will not distract Lord Nikolai from his studies for long. He did ask to see me."

"Oh, very well." Gennady, still visibly displeased, lurched to his feet. "I suppose you will stand there all day distracting *me* if I refuse. But don't try this again."

"Thank you, honored elder." Nasan saw no reason to promise, as she had every intention of returning if the situation warranted it. But she got the point. She would need a very, very pressing reason to get past her father-in-law's mentor a third time.

Nikolai proved far more welcoming, although the pleasure in his face also provoked comment from the irascible elder. "I thought you more serious than this, Nikolai Borisovich," Gennady said sternly. "Otherwise I would not have accepted you as my acolyte."

"Forgive me," Nikolai responded, sounding less than contrite. "I am willing—indeed, eager—to put court life behind me. But the fate of my son does concern me. I doubt that I can overcome that entirely, and I am not sure that I wish to."

The quiet certainty in his tone had its effect. "I have told this boy Girei not to return," Gennady grumbled as he withdrew. "So say what you have to say and dismiss him. If the world remains always with you, how can you place yourself with complete trust in the hands of God?"

"I'm making life difficult for you, Papa-in-law," Nasan murmured when the elder had disappeared down the hallway. "I apologize. But *Ata* has uncovered no information as to Daniil's whereabouts except to confirm that he doesn't lie in the Kremlin. He believes that the Shuiskys may have sent my husband to a noble estate, perhaps even their own. Compared to the others arrested, Daniil has done nothing but fulfill his oaths of loyalty to the grand prince and to Telepnev. *Ata* can't discover why they wish to imprison him in the first place. The grand prince likes my husband, more than he likes Prince Ilya and his uncle."

"To clear the slate," Nikolai said. "To make a point, if you prefer, so no one will question who won and who lost. The grand prince's likes and dislikes have no relevance here, because he's too young to enforce them. Does he not love Telepnev, who has served in his father's stead these five years? Does he not love his nanny? Of course he does. More even than Daniil, Grand Prince Ivan will suffer for this change of power. I only hope worse does not happen to him. Shuisky is ambitious but no fool. He knows that cubs grow into wolves one day and bite the hands that tore their families from them. He may take steps to ensure that this cub doesn't get that chance."

Nasan shivered. As much as she yearned to see Daniil home safe, her father-in-law spoke the truth. "Yes, poor child. He has lost everyone who cared for him except his little brother, who can neither hear nor speak." She paused to honor the grand prince's loss, but the passage of time and the memory of

Gennady's grumbling soon forced her into speech. "But what of my husband? Did you learn anything of his captivity? *Do* the Shuiskys hold him? That would make it difficult to rescue him."

His blue eyes flashed with something that could be anger, and he tapped the table beside him as if unaware of what he did. "It seems not."

Nasan waited, her natural impatience pushing her to prod, to urge, to drag the information out of him if he didn't respond now, this moment. How could he delay, when he knew how desperate she was for answers?

She thought she would explode like one of those muskets Daniil hated so much before Nikolai at last gripped her hand. "With Gennady's permission I left the monastery yesterday. It seemed futile to approach the court, so I went to Maria's uncle Mikhail, who has somehow managed to keep himself above the fray. He told me that my son has been confined to the Monastery of St. Daniil the Stylite, an hour's ride south of the city, across the Moscow River. Apparently Vasily Shuisky found the similarity of names and disparity of personalities amusing. My Daniil is indeed as far from a hermit as a man can be, but I fear that the 'joke' nonetheless leaves me cold."

He paused long enough for her to frown as she struggled to absorb what he'd said, then added, "Daniil is not alone, from what I heard. His cousin Roman is imprisoned at the monastery as well, with several other gentlemen of the bedchamber recommended by Telepnev. Five or six young men altogether."

"We must get them out." Nasan leaned forward so she could keep her voice low. "What does that mean, confinement in a monastery? Is Daniil under guard?"

"Almost certainly." Nikolai hesitated, as if he didn't want to add to her distress.

"I'm upset already," she told him.

His grip tightened. "Understood. Well, the truth is that I don't know exactly what kind of confinement he faces. I have heard of men weighed down with fetters and thrown into pits." A small cry escaped Nasan, and she covered her mouth with her free hand lest the elder arrive to investigate.

"Peace, child," Nikolai said. "Don't forget that my abominable nephew Semyon faced so few restrictions that he managed to escape within a few months. For Daniil—locks and guards, probably. Perhaps not more—fortunately for them, they are among the least important of those taken. I assume that's why the Shuiskys didn't shut them up in a Kremlin tower. And I do know that St. Daniil's has fallen on hard times of late. It may be possible to free them. But then what? You can't bring a group of escaped prisoners to Moscow."

He made a good point. She could not, and would not want to. "I'll have to work that out," she said. "You're right."

The heavy tread of Elder Gennady's feet sounded outside the door. Nasan pulled her hand from Nikolai's, stood, and bowed. She hoped he understood that she would have preferred to hug him but couldn't, with his mentor so close. "I owe you an enormous debt," she said, as compensation for the embrace she must not dare. "I will leave you to your contemplation. Thank you for agreeing to receive me." She spoke those last two sentences at a higher volume, aiming them at the listening ears on the other side of the door.

"My dear Girei." Nikolai's eyes twinkled once more. "If you succeed in your appointed task, it is I who will owe you an enormous debt."

For the first time since she arrived, Nasan felt her tension ease. "I promise you, Lord. My kinsmen and I will find a way."

❦

Alexei had not forgotten his decision to learn more about what took Grusha away from her duties, if only because the knowledge might help his brother and sister-in-law settle their differences. So when he next visited Timur in his mother's tent, found the boy sitting up and cheerfully consuming a large bowl of mutton stew, and had had a chance to admire his son's bandage, he took a moment to ask Guzel about Grusha's whereabouts. "I thought Firuza released her from nursemaiding so she could care for Timur," he said by way of explanation. "Have you seen her today?"

"She stopped by this morning and redressed the wound." Guzel gestured at their son. "*Mashallah*, he's doing much better. Then she said she had a task to perform for the khan, so I told her we would be fine while she completed it."

Alexei studied her through narrowed eyes. At least she wasn't snapping at him any longer; his apology seemed to have borne fruit. But these lies about his brother annoyed him, and Guzel's refusal to meet his gaze suggested that she *was* lying, independently of his own suspicions of where Grusha went and for what purpose.

As usual, he decided to tackle the issue head on. "You should stop that, you know," he said. "I have no idea why Grusha's keeping secrets, but the pair of you are causing trouble between my brother and his wife. I don't believe she's performing errands for the khan. I think she's practicing with the shaman. Unless you also want to convince me that spirits chanted our son back to health. Why won't either of you admit it?"

Guzel's dark eyes, wide and vulnerable, met his. Her mouth dropped open, and she gasped. A flash of triumph warmed him. He would get the truth from her now.

Then she pressed her lips together in a stubborn line and shook her head. "I gave her my word. I can't say. You must ask her yourself."

He glared at her, but he had known her for a long time. If she'd promised not to talk, she would not, no matter whom her silence hurt.

"I will," he said after a while. "You can bet on that." He didn't care if his tone sounded grudging. But when he saw the worried expression on his son's face, he chucked the boy under the chin. "It's all right, Timur. No one's in trouble— not Grusha and certainly not your *ana*. I'll be back in a bit, and we'll play chess, shall we? I'm sure your uncle has a board and men."

Timur agreed, and Alexei went off in search of Grusha.

Along the way he ran into Malik Shirin and Ruslan, walking side by side and deep in discussion of equipment and fodder. He joined them, adding to the details Ruslan provided about the supplies they and their men had brought from Moscow. But the whole time he kept an eye open for the drab figure of the Russian nursemaid. Her dishonesty and carelessness for the needs of others irritated him, and he was determined to put a stop to her behavior before she caused any more damage.

Ogodai and Firuza might not appreciate his interference. They might even find something else to fight about. But at least he could prevent them from falling out over this phantom. They ruled together, so not only their marriage but the horde itself would suffer if they continued not to get along.

If he hadn't been watching, he'd never have noticed her. The pale brown of Grusha's dress, an effect heightened by her anemic coloring and lack of decoration, allowed her to blend into the dry landscape of the steppe. He suspected that much of the time she kept to the shadows as well, but for a few crucial moments she had to cross the sunlit grassland before ducking into a tent that stood apart from the rest.

"Who lives there?" he asked Malik, pointing to the lone tent.

"The shaman," Malik said. "Have you forgotten?"

"Just checking," Alexei told him. "Come with me, both of you. We're going to pay her a visit. Is it the same one you had before?" He remembered that old crone well.

"The same," Malik confirmed. "Not the one who fled when Bahadur Bey died, but her replacement. Why do you want to visit her? Your son's not taken a turn for the worse, I hope."

"Timur? No, he's fine. Not quite blooming with health, but by this time tomorrow I'll have to tie him to his bed to keep him from racing around like a yearling colt." Malik and Ruslan laughed at that, and Alexei gestured at the tent once more. "We're going to solve a mystery. Unless I have added two and two and made six, I suppose."

He ignored their eager questions as he strode toward the tent. Naturally, they followed. Who could resist the lure he'd set out? The whole situation seemed so absurd that he did wonder if he stood on the brink of making an utter fool of himself, in which case his friends would tease him for weeks. But even then, he'd know more than he had managed to discover so far.

When he threw the shaman's door open without warning, however, Alexei knew that he'd guessed right.

Grusha, sitting at the hearth fire, leaped to her feet. The drum she'd been beating when the three men burst in fell to the floor, its tinkling shells sounding the same musical chord Alexei had heard the day his son was injured. Her eyes wide with terror, she stared at them, wordless. She couldn't have looked more frightened if they'd charged in with swords drawn. What on earth was wrong with the girl?

The shaman, in contrast, rose smoothly to standing. She had tied the plaits that so often obscured her features at the nape of her neck, and her unlined face revealed her to be somewhere in early middle age, not the ancient Alexei had thought her. She bowed her head, pressed her palms together, and said, "Tulpar Sultan. And Shirin Bey. Your companion I have not met, but the spirits tell me he is Ruslan Sultan. Another Crimean. How may I serve you? Your mission must be urgent for you to break down my door."

Alexei didn't bother to correct her use of his former name. Nor did he challenge her assertion that the spirits, not camp gossip, had led her to identify Ruslan. "Our apologies, wise one," he said instead, acknowledging her bow with a dip of his head. "I wished to surprise your student. She has concealed her visits here in ways that cause trouble for her and for others, and I can't imagine why. Since she lies whenever anyone asks her, I wanted to catch her in the act."

The shaman gestured at Grusha. "Sit, child." When Grusha crumpled into a boneless mass near the fire and hugged her drum to her chest, the shaman extended her sweeping arm to encompass the three men. "You too. I will answer your questions."

When they were settled, the shaman spoke, her voice as rich and sonorous as Alexei remembered. "She came to me some months ago, describing encounters with a spirit and asking if I would teach her. She has a son, as you know, and she wishes a better future for him than to live as a slave. For herself as well. I tested her and discovered that she has indeed been chosen to serve the other world. She has a fine memory for spells and considerable knowledge of healing. But she yields too easily to the demands of those who wield power over her, as you can see from her fear that Firuza Khatun would refuse to release her from the role of nursemaid. A shaman's life demands discipline and conviction. To see if she had the persistence she would need, I told her that since she insisted on keeping secrets, I forbade her to tell anyone about her training until I gave her leave, no matter the consequences.

Your presence here assures me that she has done well. If it has caused problems for others, I regret that, but all will be revealed before her initiation ceremony, which will take place at the next full moon. I will insist on her making a full confession before she begins the rite. That Grusha can fulfill her vow even when it makes her life difficult is more important than a silly spat between a couple who should have already developed the skills to solve such problems on their own."

Alexei stared at her, speechless in the face of her calm conviction that her own purpose justified the trouble she'd caused.

But he had his answer, and while he knew better than to argue with a wise woman, he also saw no reason to keep the secret she shared with Grusha.

He rose, touched his hand to his heart, and said, "Thank you for your explanation." Without another word he left, Malik and Ruslan at his heels.

"Is that what you were expecting?" Ruslan asked once the lone tent lay behind them.

"More or less," Alexei said. "Not the ridiculous secrecy oath, but there had to be some reason the girl was willing to put up with my sister-in-law's fury rather than confess to something no one would care about if she told the truth, and that's as good an explanation as any."

"So what comes next?" Malik said.

"I talk to my brother, of course." Alexei slapped his friends' shoulders. "You two can skip that part if you like."

He grinned at their relieved faces. "I wanted someone who could confirm what I saw in the shaman's hut, but I doubt that will be necessary. She didn't hesitate to explain what was going on, so if Ogodai asks, she can tell him too."

♪

"You're joking." Ogodai, discovered leading his horse from the corral, stopped and stared open-mouthed at his brother. "What an absurd piece of nonsense. And this is what has Firuza after my blood? That wretched nursemaid's inability to issue a simple statement in her own defense?"

Alexei whistled for Ajdar and, when the horse responded, mounted bareback. A trick he hadn't performed since he last lived on the steppe. It pleased him that he hadn't lost the skill. "I'll ride with you."

Ogodai mounted, and they headed for the far edge of the camp, where their father's men had pitched their tents.

"From what Nasan told me in Moscow, Grusha's been a slave most of her life," Alexei said. "It's not surprising she finds it hard to believe she can express a wish and have people take it seriously. Nor is it hard to believe she wants a better future for her son and a more secure situation for herself. A shaman's life can be difficult, but if she's good at it, she'll never want for food and shelter."

"True." Ogodai frowned at the horizon. "I could have done without the vow of secrecy, but my big problem is how to convince Firuza. I don't suppose you have any ideas."

It sounded like an almost-question. Alexei wondered how much to read into it. Did his brother really want advice?

He decided to take a risk. He was eight years older than Ogodai, and he'd learned a few things from his year with Maria—not the easiest bride, however much he loved her. "When my wife was with child, she often reacted far more strongly to perceived slights than she does at other times," he said, choosing each word with care. "She worried that I would find her unattractive, even though I assured her I didn't. Perhaps if you spend more time with Firuza, including at night, she will feel reassured. Rules are important, but sometimes bending them will serve you better than rigid compliance." He recalled something else Nasan had said, relayed by Maria. "If we settle this business with Sheikh-Mamai's horde, that will help too, as it will relieve her fears that she will lose you in battle."

When Ogodai nodded slowly without speaking, Alexei added, "And if that fails, she will learn the truth in a few weeks."

"I suppose," Ogodai said, the frown still creasing his brows. "It troubles me that she doesn't trust me, though."

"I suspect she does, in a way. Otherwise she wouldn't say a word." Alexei laughed softly, remembering. "Maria once decided I wanted to divorce her and marry someone else. All because I swore I could have made a better alliance than with that appalling father of hers. She didn't tell me for months. I couldn't figure out what I'd done wrong. Women!"

Ogodai laughed too, echoing the sentiment. "Yes, women! As if anyone couldn't find a better ally than Fyodor Koshkin." He extended a hand. "Thank you, *aby*."

"Think nothing of it." Alexei clasped the hand, then released it. "Glad I could help. And now, please excuse me. I promised my son a game of chess. Do you have a board somewhere?"

Chapter 16

"DOES PRINCE ILYA SPEND A LOT OF TIME HERE?" KOSHKIN, sprawled on a bench after a plain but tasty meal served by Father Spiridon's wife and daughters, enjoyed the pleasantly full sensation in his belly and the swish of home-brewed ale against his tongue.

"He does not." Spiridon had dismissed his sons after the meal, a boon that Koshkin appreciated, since the lads jabbered faster than the best Turkmen racehorse. Intelligent boys, no doubt—and he admitted to a flash of longing for the cheerful presence of his own younger sons—but their presence could only complicate today's discussion.

"When Prince Ilya took control of the estate a year ago," the priest went on, "he stopped by a few days after you left to review the servants. He ordered the better-looking young women and those capable of bearing arms to his uncle's estate in the Kremlin, then dispatched the others to the family lands in Shuya. He sent us a few men and older women to replace them, but not enough."

"He had designs on the girls' virtue, I suspect." Koshkin wrinkled his nose in distaste. "The man's a boor. Too bad you couldn't prevent him."

"So I thought, Lord. I did protest, but he paid me no heed. An ungodly man, I fear."

"So he is. I'm sure you did your best." Koshkin decided to let the topic go. He had more important things on his mind than the virtue of maids who, if they had objected in the first place, had lost their battle twelve months past. "You've not seen him since then? He doesn't live here, you said."

"He stayed here twice around the time when the grand princess died." Spiridon raised his own lacquered goblet and took a long draught. "An evening near the end of March, then the nights before and after her funeral. I've not had a sight of him since."

That was odd. An evening not long before the grand princess died, then two nights surrounding her death. As if Ilya had something to hide. From his regular household, if no one else.

Well, he had a wife. "Did he bring a woman with him?"

"No." Spiridon shook his head. "But he had a visitor the first night. A man in a long dark robe, with a flat hat like those the foreigners wear."

"Old, young?" The thrill of discovery ran through Koshkin's veins. His instinct for the telling detail sent prickles of anticipation down his arms. A break in the pattern, followed by a death—and the man he most wanted to implicate in a crime at the center of it. Again he sensed that he had found the correct path, that his fortune would soon change—and for the better.

"Of middle years, I would say." Spiridon rubbed his beard as if drawing the memory from it. "He had the look of a royal physician. Or a scholar. An apothecary, even, but they too come from the German lands."

"An apothecary." Koshkin allowed his satisfaction to flow into his voice.

An apothecary from the German lands. Who might have furnished Shuisky with belladonna of his own—or something yet more deadly.

He was moving too fast, letting satisfaction and hope push him beyond the boundaries of what he knew. But what, failing some nefarious scheme, could drive Prince Ilya Shuisky, that complacent lover of creature comforts, to spend three days at an abandoned estate without even maidservants to occupy his nights—never mind entertain a German who, doctor or not, could not possibly equal him in rank?

"Where in the house did he stay?" Koshkin asked.

Spiridon hesitated, visibly drawing into himself rather than answer the question.

"Spit it out, man!" Koshkin urged. "I won't blame you. In my quarters, I gather?" Spiridon nodded.

"Yes, of course he did, the bastard." Koshkin straightened on his seat and set the goblet aside. "It's the most comfortable area of the house. Tonight I'm going in there. You still have the key, I assume?"

Spiridon did not answer in words. He walked to the collection of icons in the corner of the room, reached behind the most distant of the group, and pulled out a metal key the length of his hand. He held it out to Koshkin, who took it with a cry of relief.

"But please, Lord," Spiridon said. "If anyone catches you, don't tell them where you got it. I do have a family to support."

"You won't regret it." Koshkin slapped his shoulder. "When I come back into my own, I will reward you."

"Then I wish you great success, Lord. Whatever it is you seek." Spiridon still looked doubtful, but Koshkin ignored him. A mystery, a key, and access to his own home. His plans were coming to fruition at last.

❀

This time, after Nasan had returned from the Miracles Monastery and changed her clothes, she discovered that Borya's tooth had made its appearance. With his fever gone, the baby had again reverted to his usual cheerful self, and she spent a good hour cooing over and playing with him before hunger and stimulation made him fretful. She waved goodbye as Zhenya carried him off to feed and laughed when he waved back. Then, reassured for the first time in a week (about her son, if not Daniil), she went to share what she'd learned with her mother.

She found Sumbeka, as expected, in her sitting room. Maria sat beside her, Baby Alexander at her feet, gurgling as he rolled from one pillow to the next. Sumbeka clutched a scroll of paper to her chest. Maria had another spread out against an inlaid table and was poring over it.

"Timur was injured," Maria said as Nasan came through the door. "In a raid. Alexei says he's recovering nicely. And Grusha healed him! He's convinced she isn't involved with your brother but has been taking lessons from the shaman. For some reason the silly girl won't admit it, though, so Firuza still suspects her. Is that not absurd? Alexei has promised to find out the truth, but after the news we sent and what with worrying about Timur and the possibility of attack, he hasn't had time. Hadn't, I mean, when he wrote this."

"Wait. Slow down!" Nasan reached for the scroll her mother held and skimmed it as fast as she dared. "How can I keep up? And I have so much to tell you too. I'm glad Timur's not badly hurt. About Grusha as well, if *aby* is right. But who is this Azamat Bey? I never heard of him."

"No, nor have I," Sumbeka told her. "But Alexei says he's a young man—twenty, at most. He must have been a child when we last made the migration. And perhaps his horde lived somewhere else then. Ogodai writes of pressure exerted by this fiend Sheikh-Mamai."

She gestured for the scroll, and Nasan handed it back. "Sit, daughter. You can read it later. Everyone is well—or will soon be well. That's the most important thing. Tell us what happened with your father-in-law. Did he find out where Daniil is being held?"

"He did." Nasan sat as ordered. "At a monastery dedicated to St. Daniil the Stylite. My husband's patron saint. Papa-in-law says it lies within an hour's ride south of the river, and that the Shuisky clan thought it amusing to imprison my husband in a place associated with his own name day." She shuddered. The callous cruelty of that "joke" underlined everything that worried her about Daniil's arrest. "Four or five other young men, including his cousin Roman, are captives there as well."

She glanced at Maria. "The information came from your uncle Mikhail. We're grateful to him."

"He has no love for the Shuiskys." Maria released her own paper—the letter from her husband, Nasan assumed. The thought intensified her distress, so she set it aside. Maria's husband was in danger too, in a different way. "And I know of the monastery, although I've never visited it. It has a special significance for the grand princes of Moscow. Their ancestor founded it. Another Daniil."

It didn't comfort Nasan to hear that her husband lay imprisoned in a monastery founded by the grand prince's ancestors, although she could hope that his patron saint would stand him in good stead. Better still if Daniil received support from his own ancestors. But at least he had her devotion and her parents' good will to see him through.

"What choices have we?" she asked Sumbeka. "We must get Daniil out. And his companions. They're no more guilty than he is, and they would suffer even more if he escaped and they didn't, although Papa-in-law was right to remind me that we can't bring them back to Moscow if we arrange their escape. Can we visit this monastery?"

Sumbeka rose to her feet, dropped the scroll on a side table, and held out her hands. "Come, both of you. I suggest we start by conferring with my husband. I'm sure he has plans underway. This disrespect for his son-in-law has angered him greatly."

They found Bulat pacing his study, a handful of his personal guard trailing him like ducklings behind their mother. It was a funny image, but Nasan's spirits remained in the depths. She reminded herself that she knew more about her husband's whereabouts than she had this morning, but the reassurance had little effect.

Bulat stopped his pacing to hear what they had to say. A lordly wave of one hand sent the guardsmen to cluster on a sofa to his right. The women sat in a row opposite him, and he took his favorite chair behind the desk. "An odd place to hold captives," he said when Nasan finished her tale. Sumbeka had already shared the news sent by Alexei and Ogodai before yielding to her daughter. "I've passed by that monastery many a time. It's deserted. A church, a cemetery, a few rundown buildings."

"Yes, this grand prince's grandfather moved the monks to a less hazardous location," Maria said. "Too many raiders come up from the south. But I think hermits still live there. Those who seek to perform their spiritual feats in isolation want to avoid the temptations of the richer cloisters."

"Fewer monks mean fewer people who might object to or even notice the captives' presence," Nasan said. "I would like to scout it out, see if there are guards or any signs Daniil and the others are there. Is that possible?"

Bulat gestured at the guardsmen. "I could send warriors. Not enough to alarm anyone, just to report back on what they find."

Nasan bit her tongue as an idea popped into her head. It would take careful presentation to her father, but it might serve the purpose better than his proposal. "Suppose Maria and I were to go as pilgrims? With an escort, of course, but we could draw them from the Kolychev soldiers. If we're all Christians, we can make the excuse more believable." She hesitated, then added in a rush, "I think we should dress as boys."

"Boys!" Maria said. "I can't dress as a boy. It's not proper."

"But it will protect you," Nasan told her. "We could pretend to be brother and sister, if you insist. Husband and wife, no, because I look too young as a boy."

"Why not go as sisters?" Maria asked. Her face crumpled in what appeared to be genuine distress. She'd traveled a long way from the conventional Russian girl of two years ago thanks to Sumbeka's tutelage, but moments like this one revealed that the restrictions placed on her since birth still held her in their grip.

Sumbeka answered her. "Nasan is right. It's safer for you to go dressed as boys. If the monastery has become a prison, you must take every precaution. I will agree only if you take at least a dozen men."

Her delightful smile crept out. "I think you must go, Maria. You are certainly capable of riding for an hour, and I feel certain that you know how a pilgrim should behave. My daughter, in contrast ..." She let the phrase trail off, and Nasan felt herself blush. But she didn't argue. Her one experience of Christian pilgrimage, begun under her mother-in-law's guidance, had soon veered off along a quite different path.

"I will permit it," Bulat said. "If I pick the escort myself. And if you go armed. Your point about the Kolychev warriors is a good one, daughter. Not only do they belong to the Christian faith, but their incentive to find their lord outweighs even that of our own men. As for you, *kilen*"—he dipped his head to Maria in a rare gesture of respect—"we will not force you to betray your conscience, but you would do us a great favor if you could set your most praiseworthy scruples aside and accompany my madcap of a daughter. Will you agree to that?"

Nasan forced her jaw not to drop. That her autocratic father, of all people, could manage such a speech had until now lain outside the bounds of her imagination.

Why, he can display tact when he wants. No wonder he is a great leader as well as a renowned general!

So it didn't surprise her when Maria bowed her head and pressed her palms together. "Of course, *Kaenata*," she murmured.

The sun set with excruciating slowness, leaving Koshkin itching with impatience by the time the last red-gold ray slid beneath the horizon and the mauve of twilight deepened to black. Before night could render the courtyard impassable, he left Father Spiridon's home through the back door and circled the walls with an outstretched hand marking his way. His hooded cloak again served him well, but he had supplemented its coverage with dark trousers and robe, another involuntary gift from his eldest son.

As he reached the end of Spiridon's wall, he marked the location of the main house. He didn't dare carry a light of his own, but the entryway at the top of the stairs boasted a single lantern. Two more marked the gates to the outside, and a fourth lit the stables. So long as he kept his distance from them, he could cross his own courtyard on memory and reflected light. He set off as quickly as he dared, hurrying from plank to plank. His felt boots concealed the noise of his passage, and the cloak turned him into a scurrying figure almost invisible in the near-blackness. Even so, he was glad when his reaching hand connected with the sanded wood of the outer stairs. Ahead of him lay storerooms: a quicker entry but guaranteed to give him a longer journey in total darkness.

He hesitated. *Up or in?* He could mount at least three-quarters of the staircase before the lantern at the top threatened to undo his attempt at concealment. And the key that dangled at his waist had been fashioned for that lock. It should work on the storerooms too, but he couldn't be certain and hesitated to take the risk. Yet if the gate guards saw him, they would raise the alarm, and his efforts would come to naught.

A quick survey of the premises revealed no guards. If they in fact manned the gates, they would focus their attention on those without, paying little heed to those within the walls unless he shouted at them. The house itself lay dark. According to Father Spiridon, the few servants sent by Prince Ilya had retreated to their huts in the city. Only the maids once slept in the house, and Ilya had removed them to his own home or sent them elsewhere.

Climb or don't climb?

He put one booted foot on the lowest step, then the other. Staying as close to the wall as he could, he edged his way up the stairs.

As he approached the top, the circle of light from the lantern forced him to hug the banister. From the farthest corner of the platform he surveyed the door. Perhaps he should have taken the risk of making his way through the house, or even retrace his steps with that in mind. But whatever he did, he couldn't stand here and dither. Fear compressed his insides. He had arrived at the point of greatest danger.

What to do? He could blow out the flame, but that might draw the very attention he wished to avoid. As fast as he dared, he grabbed the ring that held the lantern and moved it to the far edge of the platform. It gave off enough light that he could pull the key Spiridon had given him from its hiding place within his cloak, maneuver it into the lock, and turn it. In a time that could not have taken more than the length of a breath but felt like eons, Koshkin twisted the key. The door opened under his hand, and he stepped through.

He remembered the lantern, out of place on the wooden platform. Even at the risk of being seen, he must not set the house on fire. He bent almost double, grabbed the iron ring once more, and returned the lantern to its hook. He shut the door and locked it for good measure, then leaned back against it and filled his lungs for the first time since leaving Spiridon's home. He returned the key to its hiding place in his cloak and walked through the rooms, ears pricked like a cat's to hear the smallest sounds of a human presence.

Only his long acquaintance with the house and the short distance he had to travel made it possible to find his own bedchamber. By the time he got there, nerves had him sweating under the long cloak, but he had concluded that the house was deserted. Once inside his own room he cracked the shutters. The moon had risen, yielding enough light to see that his belongings remained largely untouched. A gauze veil draped across the bed evoked memories of sandalwood and jasmine, and he buried his face in it, the sensation of Roxelana's warm, silken skin bringing him close to tears.

Enough. His path forward required him to succeed in reestablishing his fortunes. The mission that had brought him here tonight.

He had a lineage to protect, a standing to reclaim. Regrets and nostalgia could wait. He turned to the chests that lined the walls, unsure what he sought or even whether anything remained to find. If Ilya had a secret, why hide it here? Yet instinct told him that the meeting with the man who might be a royal physician or apothecary was not innocent. Its timing alone indicated as much. And if Ilya had committed a crime, why *not* leave the evidence where his family lacked the means to discover it? Especially when, if anyone did fall over it, Ilya could attribute the substance to Koshkin, the former owner of the estate. A villain like Ilya would not hesitate to blame his own sins on others!

The moonlight revealed a candle and tinderbox. He closed the shutters once more and hung his cloak in a way that barred any light from escaping, then struck a flame and watched the wick catch fire. He secured the candle on its stick and set to work.

Anger drove his hands through the piles of clothing that lined the chests. He would return soon to take his property back. But for the moment he left the clothes in place, searching for something that was not his and should not be present.

He had almost decided to give up the task as fruitless when his hand clasped a round container not much bigger than his palm. He pulled it out and held it up to the candlelight. He didn't recall ever seeing it before. It didn't belong to Roxelana, who in any event had kept most of her possessions in her own chamber. And it certainly did not belong to him.

He tugged at the top of the container, but it stuck fast. Better not to examine the contents right then. Sufficient for the moment to know that the container, whatever it held, belonged to someone other than himself or his wife. He would take it back to the priest's house, where he could examine it at his leisure.

Koshkin reclaimed his cloak, then tucked the container in the hidden pocket next to the key. Candlestick in hand, he wrapped the cloak around himself and followed the route the servants used down to the storeroom on the lowest level of the house. The key turned after all. Before he opened the door, he blew out the candle and set it to one side.

If anyone noticed, they would think a servant had been careless. But even if they suspected an intruder, what did it matter? He already had what he'd come for.

Or so he hoped.

*

Back in the bedchamber that Spiridon and his wife had vacated for the use of their guest, Koshkin lit a full set of candles, then used the tip of his eating knife to pry the top off his find—a round metal box, quite plain, nothing like the decorated chest in which he had placed the belladonna. Inside lay a packet of folded paper that, when opened, revealed a fair quantity of dried leaves, spiky like those of the pine trees so common in the northern woods. Sprinkled among the dried leaves were seeds. Dull brown with a light green collar not unlike that of an acorn, they did not resemble seeds from a pine cone.

He frowned at the packet. Dried leaves that might be pine, seeds he didn't recognize. Definitely a discovery, but of what?

Still puzzling, he closed up the paper, replaced the lid, slipped the box back inside his cloak, rinsed the eating knife well, and prepared for bed.

Tomorrow he would make inquiries.

Chapter 17

THE NEXT MORNING NASAN AND MARIA SET OFF FOR THE Monastery of St. Daniil the Stylite. For the occasion Nasan's father had given both his daughters-in-law new sets of men's clothes, designed to make them look like a pair of noble brothers—just old enough, at fifteen, to have started their military service. That way no one would remark on their lack of beards.

"I feel so exposed," Maria complained. Mounted on her beautiful white mare, Kumai, she flicked the skirt of her long coat as if in illustration.

"One more layer, and you would roast by the time we reached the monastery." Nasan regarded her without sympathy. "How can you be exposed? A hat to cover your hair, a collar high enough to conceal it, a robe down to your calves, trousers underneath, and boots! The only difference between what you're wearing now and your usual riding dress is a hand's breadth of fabric at the bottom of the robe and no veil flying from the tip of your hat."

Nasan herself would gladly have stripped off half the layers and ridden in trousers and shirt. On a sunny day in the third week of April nothing seemed more appealing than a mad gallop across the steppe. Or even this pathetic excuse for the same, if they ever reached the open country beyond the city walls.

She knew better than to suggest such an idea. Maria would have a fit, and so would *Ata* if he heard of it. But with her bow slung from her left hip and her quiver dangling from her right shoulder, the heavy robe with its collar pressing on her cheeks and the quilted hat with its turned-back, embroidered velvet brim, she felt like a partridge ready for the oven. The cross ostentatiously dangling from her neck made her think of the tags the butchers used in the market, but it was essential to their story, so she wouldn't take it off.

At least it was April, not June, never mind August. A memory of laughing at Daniil as he recounted tales of summertime battles shocked her back into the present and today's goal. What small discomfort would she not happily endure to bring him home to her once more?

She kicked Sorkhokhtani into motion. "Isn't it fun for once to ride without people judging you for your clothes or your behavior?" she asked Maria. "Once we get beyond the city walls, we can expect to find a breeze coming off the river. No one will imagine that we are not what we seem. It's the beauty of being a noblewoman. Men don't expect to see us outside the confines of the home, so they don't. See us, that is."

Maria pulled a face that suggested she didn't believe this for a moment. "It's easy for *you* to say. Just because you love dressing like a man doesn't mean I have to." Yet she released the reins, and fleet Kumai soon trotted at Sorkhokhtani's side.

Nasan made no further attempt to press her point. Maria could sulk as much as she wanted about the strip of fabric missing from the bottom of her robes and the Russian man's hat she wore instead of her usual pointed cap. Sulking or not, she hadn't turned back. Surely she would soon recognize the pleasures of riding this way, with the breeze cooling her face and the road opening before her. For sure, Kumai appreciated the chance to stretch her legs, to trot and canter with the other horses, especially Sorkhokhtani. The two mares had formed a bond, as horses often did.

When they'd left Moscow behind them and traveled about halfway to their destination—Nasan's estimate—through the glories of wildflower-strewn fields, she ventured to introduce another topic. Time to test whether the beauties of springtime had pulled Maria out of her crotchets.

"You should take the lead, don't you think?" Nasan asked. "After the captain of the guard explains what we're doing there. You're so obviously Russian."

"I agree," Maria said, no longer grumbling. "Your Russian's good, but it doesn't quite sound native. The fewer questions asked, the more likely we are to learn what we want to know without arousing suspicions. And even though you're Christian, if the monastery is abandoned as they say, how could you have a reason to visit it?"

"What will you tell them, then, when they ask what brings us here?" Nasan cooed to her horse, whose high spirits got the better of her at times. She sensed Sorkhokhtani's urge to gallop—shared it, in fact.

Maria touched her cross, as if seeking inspiration. "I thought about it last night. I checked the *Menaion*, and this is the day devoted to St. Savva. So I'll say that my grandfather took the tonsure at the monastery under the name Savva, and every year my family comes to say prayers over his grave."

"Oh, that's inspired. I love it." Nasan clapped her hands. "I wonder if there was a monk Savva. Is it a common name?"

"Pretty common." Maria giggled. "But we can just pick the best-looking grave and pray over it. Even if the graves are marked—and if the monastery is abandoned, they may not be—it's not likely that anyone there can read. Unless there's an ancient who can swear the monastery never harbored a Savva, who will know?"

Nasan laughed too. "You're right. Oh, I can't wait to give it a try."

⚘

"It does look deserted," Nasan said as they approached the structure that the captain of their escort had identified as their destination. Ahead of them gently rolling fields and copses of trees surrounded a picketed fence no higher than the horses' knees. Many of its pickets leaned lopsidedly in one direction or the other, and holes marked spots where hands, perhaps eager for firewood, had tugged the stakes loose from their supporting logs. Some of the logs had rotted and collapsed.

Within the fence a wooden church still stood. Beyond it Nasan glimpsed the cemetery where they would pray over Maria's imaginary ancestor before rambling in a casual stroll about the rest of the complex. If you could call a few decrepit cabins and a collection of small cells, only a few of which gave any signs of habitation, a complex.

"Dismal, isn't it?" Maria said, echoing Nasan's thoughts. "Would they really confine someone here? It looks as if Daniil could escape with a good whoosh of his breath."

"I wonder." As the captain neared the church, a few skeletal monks in moth-eaten homespun robes of a dull, dispiriting brown emerged from the less dilapidated cells. Nasan shuddered at the sight of them. "I feel as if I should offer them our food. They're wasting away."

"We can try, but I doubt they'll take it. Conquering hunger is part of their spiritual mission." Maria wrinkled her nose. "So is refusing to bathe or change clothes."

As they came within speaking distance, Nasan heard the captain giving the story they had settled on. One of the monks extended a skinny arm in the direction of the cemetery, and Nasan, with Maria at her side, directed her mare toward the church.

Exhilaration filled her. They had made it this far. The monks had accepted their story. Soon she would discover whether her husband was detained here. She addressed a quick, silent prayer to God. Then a more ancient plea forced itself into her thoughts.

Grandmothers, save him! Bring him back to my side, alive and whole!

The spring breeze tugged a stray wisp of hair against her cheek, and she smiled as she tucked it back into place. The spirits had answered.

"This one," Maria announced. Nasan, peering forward, saw that the grave was better tended than most and marked with one of the few wooden crosses that did not lean in rather alarming fashion to either left or right. From the elaborate script that decorated the triangular slats encasing the cross like a wooden hat, the grave might even belong to a monk named Savva.

"Good choice," she murmured. Maria cast her a shy glance of appreciation, then moved into a cycle of memorial prayers. Nasan stood to one side, echoing her sentiments and imitating her gestures to the best of her ability.

Many of the prayers evoked the nine-day and forty-day commemorations for their mother-in-law, still much missed six months after her death. Inwardly Nasan redirected her prayers to Natalya. Could she look down and see what had happened to her son? Now that she lived with the angels, could she intercede on his behalf?

When Maria decided they had expressed sufficient devotion, she led the way out of the cemetery. Saddened by the reminder of Natalya's firm but loving presence and racked with fear for her husband, Nasan found it difficult to appreciate the beauty of a sun-filled day in the country. Yet it was lovely to be outside the city, its foul odors and closed vistas for the moment only a memory.

The two women, trailed by their escort, strolled around the monastery grounds, ostensibly looking for a place where they could share a meal before their return. The hermits paid them little heed, waving away the offer of bread as Maria had predicted they would and intervening only once, when they strayed too close to one of the decrepit cells.

Until, that is, they reached the edge of the compound. One storeroom lay apart from the rest. Although not noticeably better constructed, it boasted a door with an iron hasp and barred with a sturdy beam. Two of the hermits scurried in front of them and urged them to go no farther.

"The hospital," the younger of the two said. "One of the brothers fell ill last week. We can't risk exposing others to the contagion."

About to offer them the benefit of her medical knowledge, Nasan stopped herself mid-word. First, she didn't believe that she looked at a hospital or that any patient lay inside. Second, she had learned from Father Job that holy men such as these placed their trust in God to heal or not as His Divine Will decreed. And third, near the far corner she glimpsed the best-fed man she had seen since their arrival—dressed like the hermits, true, but Nasan had spent too many years around warriors not to recognize both the musculature and the stance of a man-at-arms. Moreover, the captain of the Kolychev guard had engaged the improbable hermit in conversation. He didn't need help from Maria and Nasan, especially since the hermit/warrior might fall silent, rather than opening up, if too many strangers surrounded him.

So she mustered a small bow and placed her hand on Maria's arm. "Let's withdraw, brother. We've trespassed on the holy monks' hospitality long enough. I propose we take our noon meal in that field we passed on the way here."

Before long, the members of their party had returned to the Moscow road. Once the dilapidated monastery buildings passed from view, the riders stopped in the first copse they found that contained a stream and grass for the horses. The escort spread cloths and distributed baskets of food, and the captain accepted Nasan's invitation to eat with her and Maria.

"I saw you talking to that monk who looked like a fighter." Nasan picked up a slice of rye bread topped with homemade cheese but waited to bite into it until she finished her question. "What did you discover?"

"Ah, Tsarevna." The captain sent her an approving smile. "Trust you to figure that one out. I too would swear that 'monk' was no holier than I, probably much less. And I'd take an oath that he's engaged in the same occupation as I am, as well. What he does there, I can't tell. But I doubt he serves any sacred purpose."

"Does he guard my husband and his fellow captives, do you think?"

"It wasn't a hospital," Maria put in. "That *I* would swear. Only a madhouse would bar its patients in."

"Agreed," the captain said. "Whether Lord Daniil and the others are confined there, of course I don't know. But if our young men are at the monastery at all, then I would look for them first behind the only barred door I saw. There is nowhere else they could be, unless the church has a crypt."

"Yes, I thought the same, and so I will tell my father. When we complete our plans, his men can start their search with the storeroom." Nasan bit viciously into her bread and cheese. Imagining Daniil's suffering made her furious.

"*His* men?" Maria asked. "Not the Kolychev men who accompanied us today? What have you in mind?"

Nasan looked at her, anger yielding to incredulity. Could Maria really not guess?

But then, Maria had not grown up in a nomadic horde as Nasan had. "A Tatar raid," she said.

The words sparked an image in her mind, and the answer to her ongoing dilemma as to where to take Daniil once they rescued him presented itself in a blaze of clarity.

"And I will accompany them," she added. "With Borya and his nursemaid. Assuming *Ata* agrees, that is. From here, once we free my husband, he and I can ride straight for the steppe. Those imprisoned with him can accompany us if they like. They too cannot return to Moscow."

The only problem would be if Daniil refused to abandon his oath to the grand prince even now.

Well, not the only problem. Maria produced one argument after another as they rode back to Moscow. The steppe was not a safe place for a baby. Daniil would become an outcast. A young woman couldn't take part in a Tatar raid (an absurdity wilted by a tart reminder that Nasan had already done so, more than once). Nasan would miss her parents and her sister-in-law (true), as well as the creature comforts of the city (also true but immaterial under the circumstances). Borya and Alexander would not grow up together (a genuine loss, but not an outcome she would risk Daniil's life to secure).

Nasan struggled to maintain the semblance of patience as she fended off one objection after another. Her sister-in-law had her heart in the right place; it wouldn't do to yell at her. If only Daniil's situation were less dire!

At last the obvious answer occurred to her. "If my husband and I go to live in Ogodai's horde, Alexei can return to you and Alexander."

"If your father permits." Maria sounded doubtful, as if Bulat's autocratic façade rendered him incapable of kindness.

"Again, assuming *Ata* permits," Nasan said. "This whole plan requires his permission and his assistance. But I think he will agree. He insisted on sending Alexei only because at the time Daniil was assigned to attend the grand prince, and now he's not. My husband even told *Ata* he would go, if he had the opportunity. As Ogodai's sworn brother Daniil is the perfect person to manage his warriors. He'll enjoy it, too, although he may need to recover before Alexei can return."

Maria gasped, as if the reality of Nasan's words had not sunk in until then. "You would do that for me?"

"Well, naturally." Nasan patted her sister-in-law's hand where it rested on the reins. "You would do the same for me, would you not?"

"I would," Maria said. From that moment on not another protest over the plan crossed her lips.

Only a few streets from the urban estate occupied by Bulat and Sumbeka, Nasan caught sight of a small man in a hooded cloak. Something about the way he moved, scuttling like a furtive animal, struck a chord of recognition. "Isn't that your father?" she asked Maria in a near-whisper.

Maria's eyes widened like a cat's in the dark. "It is."

Nasan beckoned to the captain. "Arrest that man." She pointed at Koshkin's back. "The one with the hood. He's the one who escaped before. Bring him to Bulat Khan's estate as quick as you can."

The captain nodded. A muttered order to the closest guards, and two soldiers swooped on their prey before Koshkin noticed them.

"Neat," Nasan said as the two guards tied Koshkin's hands behind his back and slung him facedown in front of the smaller one's saddle. The man swung into place behind their captive, and the entire party proceeded at a slower pace. "Well done!"

Koshkin, swearing like a trooper in a tavern, appeared not to agree. But when they reached Bulat's estate, the khan expressed more delight than Nasan would have believed possible.

"Come." Bulat gestured at his daughter and daughter-in-law. "You can change your dress later. Let's discover where our reluctant guest has been, shall we?" Without waiting for an answer, he ordered the guards to convey Koshkin to his study. "And fetch the khatun. She won't want to miss this."

The men, Russians all, stared blankly in response to this last. "Tsaritsa Sumbeka," Nasan said, guessing at the reason for their bemused expressions. "*Khatun* means *tsaritsa*." The youngest among the guards ran to obey the order while the captain and a handful of others dragged their prisoner to the study.

Within the house Nasan felt no qualms about pulling off her heat-retaining hat and stripping the knee-length robe from her body, already perspiring from the ride. With shirt, trousers, vest, and broad sash, she considered herself adequately covered, although it didn't escape her notice that Maria shed nothing but the hat.

Nasan struggled to control her impatience. For sure, she accepted the need to recover Koshkin and had ordered his capture to prevent whatever insane scheme he might have devised since his flight. But what she wanted most was to pour out to her parents her news about the warrior monk and the renovated, locked storeroom she and Maria had discovered at the Monastery of St. Daniil—as well as the solution she had found not only to their problem but to Maria and Alexei's. None of that did she dare broach in Koshkin's hearing.

By the time she crossed the threshold of Bulat's study, the captain had already tugged the hooded cloak from a protesting Koshkin and was twisting it in his hands.

"Search him," the captain said. The words hadn't left his mouth before he produced a sigh of satisfaction. From sa stitched pocket inside the cloak he pulled an iron key and a small, circular metal box. Koshkin's expletives increased.

Bulat crossed the room and cuffed him, hard. "Shut up, before I have you thrown back into the harem chamber. And don't think you'll play games with your little daughter again. I've made sure there are no keys within reach, and I'll forbid her to go anywhere near you. You should be ashamed of yourself, taking advantage of a seven-year-old. Why should she bear the blame for your misdeeds?"

Koshkin had enough sense not to respond. Nasan reached out a hand to the captain. "Give me the box. It looks important. And what does the key open? Not this, obviously."

"It looks like our house key," Maria offered. Koshkin glared but did not answer.

Sumbeka arrived while Nasan was still turning the metal container in her hand, debating on the best way to pry it open without disturbing whatever lay inside. Bulat took it from her and twisted the lid, revealing the contents. He handed it back. Cautious as a rabbit amid a wolf pack, Nasan touched the folded paper inside.

Folded paper. A packet, like the one Daniil had seen Prince Ilya Shuisky give his wife, which Daniil thought was a note. A thrill of excitement ran through Nasan like lightning through a forest, sparking small fires as it passed.

Have we found something important at last?

And Koshkin. Always at the center of trouble.

Maria voiced the thought Nasan hadn't yet had a chance to articulate. "Oh, Papa, what have you done now?"

Bulat prodded Koshkin in the ribs. "Answer her."

Sumbeka pressed closer to Nasan. She took the box and with the tip of a small knife turned back the paper, revealing spiky leaves mixed with dried seeds.

Nasan stared in horror.

"Recognize it?" Sumbeka asked, her tone like steel.

"Of course," Nasan said. Sumbeka placed a finger across her daughter's lips, and Nasan nodded to show she understood. Sumbeka withdrew her finger, and Nasan glanced at Koshkin, who had yet to speak.

"Well, I wish you'd tell me," he said in a pettish voice that seemed quite inappropriate to the danger in which he stood. "Prince Ilya Shuisky left it in my bedchamber. I was trying to find out what he wanted with a bunch of dried pine needles when you and your thugs grabbed me."

Bulat snarled at him. "You'll have to do better than that."

An odd sensation gripped Nasan's insides. In the four years she had been aware of Koshkin's existence she had not once felt the need to defend him. But the pettishness, combined with his total lack of concern, suggested a conclusion that she would have previously considered impossible.

"I think he's telling the truth for once," she said, no less surprised at hearing the words drop from her lips than those who turned their heads to stare at her. "But you had the belladonna, and now we catch you with this. Do you honestly not know what it is?"

"Something dangerous, I assume. Otherwise why would Prince Ilya hide it at my estate?" Koshkin shrugged, and Nasan longed to slap him. "But no, I've never seen it before. My chaplain says Ilya had a meeting with a German doctor. A few nights before the grand princess died."

He glanced at his daughter. "What about you? Am I the only ignoramus here?"

"I too would say dried pine needles," Maria admitted. "But the seeds are not pine seeds. And I trust Father Spiridon. We can check with him."

"Do," Koshkin said with another elaborate shrug. "Meanwhile, maybe the scholars can tell the rest of us what it is."

"No. You're better off not knowing—for the moment, at least." Nasan looked at her parents. "Can we put him somewhere safe while we check his testimony with the priest? And I have news you should hear. We can include Maria, but I need more than a hunch that her father may be innocent to risk discussing what I suspect in front of him."

"Good idea." Bulat gestured at Koshkin, then the door, addressing the Kolychev captain. "Lock him in the harem room again. Jamil can show you how to get there if you need directions." He bent over Koshkin, grabbed his prisoner by the chin, and glared into his eyes. "And you, remember what I said. No escape attempts. *Especially* none that involve your daughter. I should beat you to a pulp for the way you used her before. But I swear on my father's ancestors that your next ploy will be your last. We'll let you go when we solve the mystery of this container and its contents, and not one moment before. Understood?"

Koshkin muttered imprecations under his breath. Bulat's fingers moved to Koshkin's throat, and the pressure visibly increased, until Koshkin let out a muffled yawp and yielded. Bulat released him. The red marks left by his hand stood out against Koshkin's neck, but nobody said a word as the guardsmen hauled their prisoner out the door.

Only when all signs of Koshkin's involuntary departure had faded did Maria ask, "So what is it? Not pine, obviously."

Sumbeka nodded to Nasan. "Tell her, daughter. She's earned the right to know what mess her father has gotten himself into this time."

"Yew leaves." Nasan picked up the knife her mother had used and pressed the paper into place, then restored the lid. "And seeds. Extremely toxic when dried. But there are several reasons why I think your father has no idea what's in the box. First, the German doctor. Yew grows to the south and west, but I don't think it does well this far north. Whether he or Prince Ilya came up with this scheme, they would need a supplier. And Prince Ilya still has connections in the Kremlin, the only place where he could expect to find a German doctor, whereas your father wouldn't dare approach any of the court physicians."

"Because they would turn him in," Maria said bitterly. "Yes, that's one reason."

"The second is this packet," Nasan went on. "My husband saw Prince Ilya give his wife just such a packet not long before Grand Princess Elena died. He told me about it the last time I saw him." Her voice caught, and Sumbeka gave her a quick hug. "Daniil thought it was a note, but we weren't sure Princess Natalya could read, and he had some evidence that Prince Ilya can't write."

Oh, beloved, are you still alive? Will I ever see you again?

Nasan took a deep breath and composed herself. "But there's one more thing I find it difficult to believe that Koshkin would know." She glanced at her mother. "I'm almost certain that Grand Princess Elena was with child. I can't be sure, because I didn't examine her. But she had that glow of happiness that women acquire in the fifth or sixth month, and when she stepped on her robe as she turned, so that the fabric grew taut, I could see a rounding in her belly."

"Ah." Sumbeka dropped onto the nearest bench. "Yes, that's vital."

"Why?" Maria touched the top of the box, as if probing its secret. "What does it ... oh, Mother of God." She stopped mid-sentence and dropped onto the bench next to Sumbeka. "Poor Elena."

"Yes," Nasan said. "You've guessed it. The most common use of yew, other than in making bows and cabinets and the like, is to end an unwanted pregnancy. Like the one a widow would have four years after her husband's death. And the most common side-effect, because the toxicity varies and can't be easily judged, is death."

Sumbeka picked up the circular container and handed it to Bulat. "Put it in a strongbox, husband. It's far too dangerous to leave lying around."

Chapter 18

KOSHKIN STORMED AROUND HIS PRISON, KICKING PILLOWS against the wall and mouthing every bad word he knew. By what vicious twist of fate, the machinations of which evil demon, had the damnable Kolychev girl caught sight of him as he was leaving his—yes, *his,* despite the theft of his property by that equally damnable Ilya!—home. And with the cursed box concealed in his cloak, because he'd been heading to the hut of the old witch who lived by the city wall in the hope that she could identify the contents if he paid her enough. Now here he was, again thrown into this jasmine-scented hellhole, his chance to restore his fortunes thwarted once more. And no gullible child to help him escape this time. Instead, outside the door stood a pair of bulky guards bearing curved sabers of ominous sharpness and scowls that suggested they would welcome the opportunity to use their weapons on him.

At least the Kolychev girl had shown signs of accepting his story. And Spiridon would no doubt confirm it, being an honest man and a priest.

He grabbed one of the kicked pillows, dropped it back on the bench where he'd found it, and slumped onto the seat.

No doubt he'd get out of this perfumed prison someday, but would he have lost his opportunity by then?

"We need to ensure that Shuisky's men don't move my husband, or that we can track them if they do." While Nasan waited with her family to hear whether Father Spiridon would confirm or deny Koshkin's story about how and where he had secured the yew poison, she took the opportunity to fill in her parents about the situation at the Monastery of St. Daniil. "I don't think we did anything to arouse the suspicions of the hermits or the man who looked like a warrior. We retreated right away when the monks told us not to approach the renovated storeroom, and the captain"—she indicated the leader of the Kolychevs' guards with an upturned palm—"says he didn't even ask the warrior monk questions, just examined the storeroom while chatting about the weather. So there should be no reason for those at the monastery to worry about our visit. Still, I'd hate to come this far only to discover that Daniil was within reach and we looked the other way while the Shuisky clan transferred him to a more secure prison."

"A good point." Bulat addressed his next words to the captain. "Russian, Tatar—it makes no difference for this task so long as you pick good scouts capable of deflecting attention from themselves. And of putting up a fight if necessary. Consult with the leader of my forces, and select a dozen men with the right abilities. Get to the monastery as soon as you can, but unobserved. Don't take your eyes off the monks, keep me informed, but act only if you see preparations to move my son-in-law. Then do what you must to secure his release and that of his companions, take them as far south as you can get, and send me word at this estate without delay."

"I will lead them, Khan, if you please. This is my lord at risk." The captain stood and, when Bulat accepted his offer, left.

"I must tell Lord Nikolai too," Nasan said. "But not yet. Elder Gennady left no doubt that he expects me to stay away from the cloister in future. I must be able to vow that I come only to say farewell. The sooner the better, I think, as the longer my husband remains in captivity, the more he will weaken." She couldn't bear to mention the possibility of his death. It would be bad luck, like invoking the Evil Eye. "But once we free him, assuming we can, we should leave for the steppe right away. So if we want to confirm that the dried yew caused the grand princess's death, we need to find out more about her symptoms so we can link them to the poison."

"And with Prince Ilya and his wife," Sumbeka added. "Apologies, *kilen*, but I would prefer corroboration of your father's word."

"Father Spiridon will provide that." Maria left the implied comment about her father's trustworthiness unanswered. She must know better than anyone how often truth came second to the prospects of immediate advancement in Koshkin's fertile brain. "He's a godly man. Too much so to lie to protect Papa. But how do we find out more about whether yew killed the grand princess? We can't ask Princess Nadezhda. She's guilty of murder, deliberate or not, if Nasan's deductions are correct."

"It has to be a lady-in-waiting, the closer the better, one in attendance that day," Nasan said. "My husband was in the palace but not in the grand princess's chambers, obviously. And we have to resolve this question before we rescue him, for the reasons I just gave."

"Who else, then?" Sumbeka asked.

Silence fell, then Maria and Nasan said together, "Solomonida!"

"She was sent away, you told me." Sumbeka held out her hand for the small box that contained the yew and, when Bulat gave it to her, turned it absently as if doing so would reveal its secrets. "To a convent, like the children's nanny and many of the other ladies. I don't think we should force Daniil to remain in captivity while we hunt Solomonida down."

"We won't have to." Maria's voice shivered with excitement. "They sent her to the New Maiden's Convent, which is just outside Moscow, no farther than we rode today. And this time we can go dressed as women, all three together with an escort. They won't admit us if we arrive in men's clothes." She wrinkled her nose at Nasan, as if challenging her to argue otherwise.

Nasan let the challenge pass. Maria spoke the truth. "Even I know that much," she said instead. "Will they let us see her, though? Will it not cause talk?"

"I think that if *Kaenana* comes with us, they will." Maria giggled softly. "She has a way about her. No nun would dare refuse."

"Solomonida is my neighbor," Nasan mused. "Or was, until the current crisis. We can say that we come to offer solace."

"And her daughter is Lyuba's best friend," Maria added. "We can bring her with us. Lyuba, I mean. Best to leave no chance that she will get bored and seek out Papa."

"Bringing Lyuba is a good idea," Sumbeka agreed. "And not only to keep her away from your father. Arriving with a child should undercut any fears among the nuns that we have an ulterior motive. Very well, let us set out tomorrow morning."

Morning brought drizzle and a cool breeze, but by the time the women were ready to leave, the gray skies yielded in places to patches of blue and a peekaboo sun. Nasan, glad of the breeze and the cooler temperature, waited with poorly concealed impatience for Maria and Lyuba to mount their horses. Sumbeka, regal and serene on her chestnut mare, didn't reveal her feelings by so much as the flicker of an eyebrow. Not for the first time, Nasan admired her mother's phenomenal control.

One day, perhaps, I will do as well.

But that day must wait, she knew, for less fraught circumstances. Daniil's rescue, if such a thing was even possible, depended on a successful outcome for today's trip.

Or did it? Could she not leave the mystery of Grand Princess Elena's passing to others, take her son and her father's men, and storm the suspiciously well-kept storeroom watched over by the suspiciously well-fed monk? If they found Daniil, their questions were answered, and they need only flee south before the Shuisky government learned what had happened.

But if they did *not* find Daniil, then ... then matters became far more complicated. Information about Prince Ilya's role in the grand princess's death, if Solomonida had any such, could become a basis for negotiations.

Not Nasan's method of choice. She always preferred the straightforward approach. But the only goal that mattered was to secure Daniil's freedom. So the convent came first.

The ride passed in pleasant conversation, despite the tension that kept Nasan constantly on guard. Before long, white stucco walls appeared on the horizon. Within, the usual profusion of gold crosses and cupolas signaled the religious intent of the complex. But the solid walls, slotted with openings for archers and topped with machicolations edged in the shape of birds in flight, conveyed a far more menacing impression. Nasan recognized those shapes; they marked the walls of the Kremlin, too. She noticed them whenever she left home.

"Why, it looks like a fortress!" she cried. Even the positioning, just east of the curving Moscow River, affirmed the convent's defensive purpose.

"It is a fortress," Maria said as if one encountered a convent acting as a fortress every day. "There's a whole ring of them around the city—especially to the south, to block raids from Crimea. That's why it's surprising that the Monastery of St. Daniil has been left to fall into such decay."

In a short while they reached the north entrance. Sumbeka rode forward, requesting admission, which the nun at the gate granted to the women but not to their escort.

"Wait for us," Sumbeka ordered. "The horses will do well enough in that field. But don't go far. We'll return as soon as possible."

And with assurances from the leader of the escort ringing in their ears, the three women rode through the open gates.

Once inside, a silent figure in a long black robe, a matching scarf covering her head and a candle in her hand, led the way to the abbess's quarters. Another Elena, renowned for her piety and transferred from the Convent of the Veil in Suzdal a decade ago, not long after the grand princess's husband founded the New Maiden's Convent to commemorate his victory over the Lithuanians, which had included his capture of the western fortress of Smolensk. So much Maria had shared during the journey here. Nasan, trailing behind the silent nun, wondered what made a woman decide to abandon earthly pleasures and even the delights of a husband and children to dedicate herself to God. No answers occurred to her, but she freely admitted that her failure to understand might have more to do with her own sinfulness than the demands and rewards of the monastic life.

As expected, Sumbeka charmed the abbess from the moment the three of them entered the room. A slender, even gaunt, figure of medium height—meaning that she stood at least half a head taller than Nasan, although Maria could look her in the eye—Abbess Elena radiated goodness and calm. Nasan thought of her as a spiritual counterpart to Sumbeka, and indeed the two women, although physically distinct, did display a similar serenity and style. Even Sumbeka's regal air had its counterpart in the abbess's brisk practicality.

"I trust you will permit us to greet our neighbor and friend," Sumbeka said after disposing of the preliminary courtesies. "I have brought my daughter and daughter-in-law, as well as my daughter-in-law's sister, who has a deep affection for Solomonida's Anna. It can't be easy for a child, even one so obedient and eager to please as Anna, to live among the holy sisters."

Her delightful smile broke out. "Or, no doubt, easy for the holy sisters either." Lyuba opened her mouth at that, but Nasan assumed the atmosphere of the convent intimidated the child, because she shut it again without speaking.

The abbess allowed her lips to curve in response. "Small girls do have their own needs. And unlike the convents of the western lands we don't normally take in children. I will permit the visit, so long as it ends by the Sixth Hour. Solomonida has refused our invitations to join our order, so I see no reason to forbid contact between her and those from outside the cloister." Her smile faded as her brows drew together. "I prefer not to rule a place of detention, but it seems I have little choice."

"We must leave before the Sixth Hour in any event," Sumbeka assured her. "I have an escort kicking its heels outside your gates. A short conversation will suffice."

"Very well." Elena rang a small bell, and the silent nun returned. "Show them to Lady Solomonida's chambers," the abbess said. "And return for them before the midday service."

"Thank you." Sumbeka placed her palms together, fingers extended, and bowed over them. Nasan and Maria, who had not essayed a single word since entering the room, copied her gesture before falling into place as she left the room.

❦

"Oh, how lovely to see you!" Solomonida leaped to her feet and dashed toward them, arms outstretched as if she meant to hug the three of them at once.

Anna, crouched in a corner with her dolls, turned her head listlessly at the sound of the opening door, then let out a yell of delight. "Lyuba!" She darted around her mother and ran to greet her friend. They met halfway across the plainly furnished room, laughing, dancing, hugging, and crying at the same time. "Can you stay?" Anna asked. "Mama, please say she can stay. It's so lonely here."

"I know, darling," Solomonida told her. "And I wish Lyuba could stay." She glanced at Sumbeka, then Nasan and Maria. "How wonderful if you could all stay, or we could leave. But I fear that's not so."

"Alas, no," Sumbeka said. "The abbess has given us until the midday service, and then we must go. But we have some very important questions to ask, and if you can answer them, it may help us secure your release."

Solomonida tugged them toward the far side of the room. Nasan followed, biting her tongue and urging her insides to calm. So much hinged on Solomonida's answers. Daniil's future perhaps.

Anna and Lyuba had returned to the dolls, engaged in a voluble conversation about their long days apart and what had happened to them since they last met. Lyuba's doll told of Papa's confinement and escape, the trouble she had been in as a result. Anna's oohed and aahed, then counteracted that tale of woe with one of her own—hours spent on her knees, dull food, and people who never stopped saying "hush." Lyuba's doll conceded that Anna's doll might have suffered more. "At least I get to do lessons and run in the garden," Lyuba said with a sigh. "I miss you, Anna."

The two girls moved on to a happier game, and Nasan turned her attention to Solomonida. Maria and Sumbeka regarded her expectantly; she guessed they wanted her to take the lead, since her grasp of what poisons could do to a human body far outweighed theirs.

She leaned forward and kept her voice low. "We came to ask what you saw the day the grand princess died. Her symptoms, in particular. We have information that suggests she didn't die a natural death."

"No," Solomonida said with a shudder. "She couldn't have. I saw no signs of illness, and I attended her day and night in those last few days. Nor had she accrued enough years that she might die without warning—a bad heart or an apoplexy, say."

Her lips tightened. "Forgive me, I can't share everything I know."

"We have guessed that she was with child," Nasan said.

Solomonida gasped and put her hand over her mouth. "Yes, she was. She had become quite desperate."

"To rid herself of it?" Maria asked in a soft voice.

"That would be a great sin," Solomonida said, shock visible in her face. "No, to bear it in secret and find a home for it. Princess Nadezhda had promised to help her."

"She did, I think. Help her, I mean." Nasan tried to keep her voice level. Did Solomonida truly believe that Grand Princess Elena would risk leaving living evidence of her indiscretion, when at the best of times she and her two sons clung to the throne like drowning men to a raft? "Can you tell us, then, when Elena sickened and how?"

"It was about this time of the day." Solomonida spoke ruminatively, staring at a nearby candle as if summoning the memory. "She complained of thirst, and Princess Nadezhda brought her a tisane, but soon Elena turned pale and clutched her stomach, began to sweat. The cramps worsened until she lost the child. It's dreadful, I know, but we rejoiced for her, that she was relieved of her burden. We understood her symptoms as signs of the miscarriage underway. For a while she rallied, and we thought all would be well. But then her pallor returned—even stronger, turning her skin ashen. The sweat and the cramps came back too. Princess Nadezhda offered more of the tisane, and she drank it, but this time it did no good. She complained of visions, then slipped into a state beyond sleep, as deep as death. Only when she stopped breathing did we realize she had died."

She covered her face with her hands, weeping. "The worst afternoon of my life. She was so vibrant one moment, and the next—gone. Please, let's talk of something else. In the middle of the night I wake and still see her, eyes gazing blankly at the ceiling, her beautiful face bruised, almost blue."

"So that's why they sealed the coffin," Maria said. "Because someone would have questioned the discoloration of her face. I wondered. Poor thing."

"Yes," Solomonida said between sobs.

Nasan moved to embrace her. Solomonida shook in her hold, and without releasing the hug, Nasan turned her head to address her mother. "Have we anything to give her? A cup of wine, perhaps?"

"Not here," Solomonida said bitterly. "Here we have only small beer, except at communion."

"We should have brought some," Nasan said. "I didn't think what a shock it would be for you to relive that nightmare. Forgive me, please."

"Did I tell you what you wanted to hear?" Solomonida's teeth still chattered.

"You did. I know now what killed the grand princess, who administered the poison, and, most important, how it was done. Thank you." Nasan smoothed loose hair from the side of Solomonida's headdress as if her friend were no older than Lyuba and Anna. Her mother had often done the same for her, but could a familiar touch bring comfort in a situation so dire?

Sumbeka spoke for them all. "We're in your debt, my dear. We'll find a way to use the information you've given us to release you and your daughter from this place. But for now let's talk of other things until the good sister comes to chase us out." She touched Solomonida's hand. "Your daughter, for example. She must be a great comfort to you."

"She is," Solomonida said. "Although spending so much time indoors depresses her, and she's suffered from some passing illness. A rash, fever—perhaps not even a real sickness, as it was gone this morning. Nothing serious. And what of your infants, Nasan and Maria?"

The conversation turned to baby stories until the black-clad nun arrived to escort them to the gate.

⚜

"You're free to go." The harsh tones spoken from an open door jerked Koshkin to his feet.

He stared at Bulat, not troubling to conceal the hatred in his eyes. "That's all very well, isn't it? Now that you've robbed me of my only chance to reclaim my position."

"These?" Bulat, contempt visible on his face, held up the circular box and Koshkin's key, then tossed him the key and held out the box.

Koshkin grabbed them both. "What is it? Aren't you going to tell me what that meddlesome daughter of yours discovered?"

"Should I?" Bulat's sneer left no doubt who was khan and who a mere functionary. Then, unexpectedly, he laughed. "Fool or not, you have guts. Well, why not? Come with me and I'll tell you the whole. I suppose I owe you something for foiling your plans, whatever they were."

Bemused, Koshkin followed Bulat to the airy room where the guards had dragged him that day.

"Sit." Bulat waved at one of the covered benches that lined every room Koshkin had seen in the house. When Koshkin obeyed, the khan gestured to a slim man who might be the steward. The man poured red liquid into chased goblets and handed one to Koshkin, the other to Bulat. Then he left the room, although Koshkin noted that a pair of warriors remained at the entryway, spears crossed. An experimental sip revealed the liquid to be good red wine. A surprise, in this Muslim household.

Bulat leaned back, his goblet untouched. "In brief, the situation is as follows," he said. "Despite your arrant stupidity with the belladonna, this time you gave us a valuable clue. That box contains the dried leaves and seeds of a yew tree. They grow south and west of here—in Crimea and Lithuania—not in Russia itself. Every part of the yew tree is poison, and taken in sufficient quantities it brings death. Your priest confirmed your story, so although we have yet to identify the German, we're reasonably certain that Prince Ilya Shuisky gave the yew to his wife and told her to brew it into a tea and give it to the grand princess." His beetling brows drew together. "It's him you want, is it not?"

Koshkin took a long drink, set the goblet aside, rubbed his hands together. The warmth that filled him came more from satisfaction than the wine. "He betrayed me. I want to see him, even more than Elena and Telepnev, suffer for what he did to me. I don't grieve their downfall, but yes, it's Ilya I want. He lied to urge me into flight, used my wife against her will, drove her apart from me. Give me an opening to avenge myself on him, and I'll forget any ill will I bear you for this captivity."

Bulat studied him with the same intent expression he might use to assess the flight of an arrow. "Perhaps fortunately for you, perhaps not, I have a bone to pick with the Shuisky clan myself at the moment. They must learn that I will not tolerate their mistreatment of my son-in-law. So I have no objections to causing some trouble for them. Suppose I arrange a meeting for you with Prince Vasily Shuisky? Do you suspect him, too, of murdering the grand princess?"

A meeting with Prince Vasily, Ilya's senior uncle and the head of the government. *Perfect.* Koshkin shrugged. "I don't know. I doubt it. But he benefited. I want him to hear that I can expose his nephew and make life difficult for him if he doesn't give me what I want. His clan enemies would love to hear the news of Ilya's crimes."

Bulat's intense gaze did not abate. "Use your opportunity well, then," he said in a contemplative tone. "If you lay out your evidence clearly, no doubt you can win back your place at court. But I suggest you watch your step from now on, because no doubt Prince Ilya—and his uncle Vasily too—will take the first chance they see to stick a knife into you."

Win back his birthright, restore his clan, enjoy the power he'd craved for so long. Perhaps even reclaim his wife. Koshkin's chest swelled at the thought.

And he already knew the approach he would take. He'd planned the whole thing. What else could he do from the confines of Bulat's perfumed cell but scheme?

"Thank you," he said. "That will suit me excellently."

"Good." Bulat gestured at the door. "You may stay with your son Mikhail until then. I don't recommend returning to your own estate. Not so long as it officially belongs to Prince Ilya."

Koshkin hesitated. How he would love never to see this blasted house again!

Still, the offer was generous, and one Bulat had no need to make. The khan was right, too, about the undoubted desire among the Shuiskys to rid themselves in the crudest manner possible of anyone who sought to bring them to account for their crimes. And Koshkin still had to complete his preparations to ensure that so unhappy a fate did not put a permanent end to his schemes to advance his lineage. A few days spent glowering at his traitorous son and avoiding his equally traitorous daughter were a small price to pay for survival.

"Thank you," he said again, hoping that the sound of his gritting teeth did not reach Bulat's ears. "I accept your hospitality, and I appreciate your assistance."

Chapter 19

"WHAT'S THAT?" OGODAI POINTED AT A DUST CLOUD IN the distance. The early summer sun was already drying the grasslands, and the cloud could signal anything from a stampeding flock to an invading army.

Alexei strained to see. The cloud grew larger as it came closer. "Whoever or whatever it is, it's traveling fast." He tapped his son—recovered enough after another week's rest to ride, if not for long—on the head. "Off with you, Timur. Your mother will have my hide if I let any further harm come to you. Once your uncle and I find out what we're facing, I'll send for you—assuming it's safe. For now, stay with the other boys."

He used the same tone of command he employed with his warriors, knowing that Timur would obey. The boy ducked his head and left. His arrow wound, thanks be to the Almighty, had left no permanent injury that Alexei could detect, but it had instilled a certain caution. A good thing, on the whole.

"Let's ride out and meet them." Ogodai called to the warriors within earshot, and they clustered around him. Ruslan took the position on the khan's left, Alexei as always on his right, and the three of them led the way at a walk.

Alexei swung his bow case into position and checked the placement of his quiver. He saw the others do the same. By the time trouble arrived, it was usually too late to reach for a weapon. He'd learned that from his father before he reached Timur's age. The thought reminded him of how much less sheltered his childhood—still more his youth—had been than his son's.

The cloud dissipated as the riders drew closer, revealing half a dozen bedraggled men, mostly of middle age, wearing long Tatar-style robes and turbans that ranged from askew to tattered. The camels moved with a strong, even gait. Healthy beasts, but their panting and the green spittle around their mouths indicated that their riders had pushed them hard.

"Merchants," Alexei said.

"Merchants?" Ruslan echoed. "Where are their goods?"

He was right. No spare animals, no pack camels, no saddlebags even. "They can't be warriors," Alexei pointed out. "No armor."

"And no women or children," Ogodai added. "So not a traveling family. Or slave traders, for that matter, since no one is trailing them. Such a small group, men but not dressed as warriors, does suggest merchants. Their lack of both goods and escort tells me they ran into thieves on the steppe and made a run for it. Let's offer them a meal and hear their story."

Alexei beckoned one of his swiftest riders forward. When the man reached his side, he jerked his chin at the approaching merchants. "Find out who they are. If they seem peaceable, invite them to join us. If not, ride like the demons of hell are at your back. We'll surround you." To his brother he added, "We should keep moving forward. Bakir's a good man. I don't want to lose him to a stray arrow."

Ogodai answered by kicking his horse into motion, and the others kept pace with him.

The arrival of a mounted warrior in their midst cast the visitors into a state of confusion. Several of those riding near the back wheeled their camels—or tried to, as the hard-ridden beasts were having none of it—to escape not just Bakir but the approaching trio of leaders and their men. But no one drew a weapon, and Alexei's concern for Bakir's safety evaporated.

Bakir drew to a stop next to the man in front. What appeared to be a rapid exchange took place. Before Alexei and the others came within hearing range, the six newcomers fell into line behind Bakir, who led them toward Ogodai.

"Khan, this is Wali," Bakir said. "He and his companions were traveling with a caravan across the steppe from Astrakhan when they were attacked from the northeast. Only the six of them escaped. The others were captured or killed, their goods confiscated."

"Dine with us," Ogodai told the newcomers. "You're welcome to stay until you recover enough to continue your journey. We wish to hear more about those who attacked you. They may be our enemies as well." He introduced Alexei, then Ruslan, by name and title, then commended Bakir and sent him back to his place. The massed warriors parted, allowing the merchants and their camels through, then closed up behind them to escort them back to the camp.

"I think we must visit Princess Nadezhda." Sumbeka walked into the nursery, where Nasan and Maria were playing with the babies, and made her announcement in a decisive tone. "I'm concerned about Solomonida and Anna, and I'm tired of waiting for the men to solve things. They've had the crucial information for two weeks, and what have they done? Poor Daniil will have wasted into one of those hermits you describe by the time they make their move, and I'm sure they have even less incentive to worry about a woman and her child, especially when Solomonida and Anna are in a safe place."

Nasan pointed to Lyuba, huddled in a corner and coughing. "Lyuba has a fever. I think she caught something from Anna, because Solomonida described the same symptoms. I'm worried about the babies."

Borya, sitting in front of her, opened his mouth—revealing a fine set of eight pearly teeth—and cooed with delight. As he reached for the rattle she held, he overbalanced, and the coo changed to a howl. Alexander howled in sympathy, but Maria tickled him, and soon both infants were laughing.

"Yes, I can see they're in terrible danger." Sumbeka laughed too. "Let's save our sympathy for Lyuba, shall we?" She spoke to Zhenya, the nursemaid. "The illness my daughter describes lasted no more than a few days. It was so mild that the child's mother wondered if it was even a real sickness. But I'm sure Lyuba would be happier in bed, with someone to look after her. And it's probably best if she doesn't play with my grandsons until she feels better, although the way these things work, it may be already too late. Watch them carefully and let us know if you see any change."

"Of course, Tsaritsa." Zhenya bowed. "I always do. If you will excuse me for a moment, I'll fetch Alina to care for our Lyuba." Receiving a nod of permission, she departed.

"As soon as she returns, we will go." Sumbeka held up a hand. "Yes, I heard you the first time. But Borya is not sick now, and neither is Alexander. And if they do get sick, you will want to hover over them, whether that will help them or not."

Nasan started to protest, but her mother cut her off before she could finish her first word. "Don't misunderstand me. I too have had infants, and I too have hovered. I will no doubt hover over these two as well. But that makes it even more important that we take care of the visit before that moment comes."

"I thought we decided not to approach Princess Nadezhda," Maria said. "Because to do so would be tantamount to accusing her of murder."

"I don't intend to bring up the grand princess's death," Sumbeka explained. "For one thing, we don't know that Nadezhda intended to kill her. I would guess the opposite, because Nadezhda loved Elena. Think how the death torments Solomonida, who bears no responsibility for it. If Nadezhda gave Elena the tisane to help her rid herself of the child, or out of some other desire to help, how much worse must she feel? I'm sure Nadezhda can imagine it might somehow have contributed to Elena's symptoms. I have never found Nadezhda to be slow, and she has few illusions about that abominable husband of hers."

"Do you think Prince Ilya misled her?" Nasan asked. "His clan benefited more than any other from the grand princess's death, and he took care to absent himself from the court right when it happened. He lied about being sick; I saw him in the cathedral during Elena's funeral, hiding behind his uncles, and he looked perfectly well. And what took him there if he wanted everyone to believe him ill, I can't begin to guess. To gloat, perhaps, at his own success in getting rid of her. Or he may have thought people would believe he could recover so fast." She punched a nearby pillow, eliciting another yell from Borya, and hastened to comfort the child. "His fake illness is the only reason Daniil was on duty that day. If that wicked man was responsible for my husband's arrest, I will kill him with my bare hands and enjoy doing it."

"I think they would have arrested Daniil anyway," Maria said. "Because of his support for Telepnev. But Prince Ilya is a swine of the first order, and if he not only murdered the grand princess but manipulated his wife into administering the poison, he deserves to die." She glanced at Sumbeka. "If we're not going to ask Nadezhda about the grand princess, what reason do we give for our visit?"

"We want to see how she fares—and I do want to see that. We will express sympathy if needed, and we'll ask her to intercede for Solomonida. Anna's welfare is at stake, and I think Solomonida's as well. She will pine away from loneliness in that miserable cell—or yield to the pressure and join the nuns even though that's not what she wants."

"And what of her sister," Nasan said, "left alone in the house with a dying father? Solomonida's captivity can't be good for Darya either, because it adds to her burdens and forces her to worry about her sister and her niece at the same time she fears for her father."

"Exactly," Sumbeka said in approving tones. "Not even the most addled Russian boyar can imagine that Solomonida poses a threat to the welfare of the realm, so it's time for Nadezhda to plead for her release. If we're right, her husband most definitely owes her a favor."

Zhenya returned with a younger servant, a pretty girl with a kind face, light brown eyes and hair, and the single long braid of an unmarried woman dangling over her left shoulder. Sumbeka greeted them with a brisk nod. "Good, you're back. Alina, help Lyuba reach her chamber and stay there to look after her. She's not feeling well."

She beckoned to Nasan and Maria. "Come, daughters. We have an errand of mercy to perform."

Dinner coincided with the arrival of messengers from Moscow. Alexei read with pleasure his wife's assurances that she and Alexander were well, her declarations of love, her shock at the news of Timur's injury, her intense desire that he return. Other news evoked comment: his sister's plan to free her husband and bring him to the steppe, which would allow Alexei to go home, and the incredible story of Koshkin's recapture, the deadly poison he'd found, and the insane but successful murder attempt by Koshkin's worst enemy.

"Our sister is astonishing," Alexei told Ogodai and Ruslan. The bedraggled merchants were still in their borrowed tent, presumably washing and changing their tattered robes for those sent as a gift by the khan. It was not every day that merchants sat down to dinner with descendants of Genghis.

"What has Nasan Khanim done now?" Ruslan asked. Alexei heard trepidation in his friend's tone.

Ogodai grinned. "You mean besides proposing a Tatar raid on a Russian monastery and solving yet another medical mystery? Yew leaves! However did she guess?"

"Good question," Alexei said. "Although *Ana* seems to have recognized them too, from what Maria writes. But it was Nasan, of course, who verified the symptoms. It's a good thing that girl's on our side."

"She'd be dangerous otherwise," Ogodai agreed. "And speaking of danger, here are our guests. I hope they've begun to recover from the attack against them."

He addressed the leader, Wali. "Did you find pasture for the camels?"

Wali, now resplendent in scarlet silk, bowed almost double and assured him that they had. Voluble thanks poured from his mouth. His five companions, no less illustriously clad, copied both words and gesture. Alexei had to suppress a smile, lest they take his amusement as an insult. The six of them looked like nothing so much as a set of puppets he'd seen at a stall set up on the ice last winter in Moscow.

For the occasion, because he wished to learn more about the merchants and the attack on them, Ogodai invited Wali to sit opposite him on the khan's platform. Again Alexei took his place on his brother's right, Ruslan on Ogodai's left, so that the four of them formed a square. Malik Shirin ushered the other five merchants to a place of honor with himself and the resident beys, including Azamat of the neighboring horde. The rest of the warriors formed lines based on their status within the camp, juniors against the outer wall, those of higher standing in rows behind the beys. The women had chosen not to attend—in part because of their honor, which required them not to associate with strangers at a feast, but also as a matter of practicality. Looking around, Alexei couldn't imagine where even one more body might fit. The servants were hard put to serve the meal without stumbling over a diner here or a misplaced dish there.

Ogodai didn't go straight for the information he wanted. Alexei, who knew the steppe code of courtesies as well as anyone, would have been amazed if his brother had. The four of them explored backgrounds and shared stories, traded compliments and assurances of their respect for one another until the main part of the meal gave way to dried fruit and koumiss. Only then did Ogodai broach the subject of the raid that had stripped Wali of his goods and most of his companions.

"Tell us about the attack on your group," Ogodai began. "Did you recognize the leader? Any of the banners?"

Wali shook his head. "I hadn't seen them before, Khan. They fell on us the afternoon of the first day after we left Astrakhan. Killed our escort, robbed us of our goods and our animals, and captured almost twenty of our men. The six of us escaped only because we were ahead of the others—except for the escort, which turned back to face the threat."

"You didn't fight?" Ruslan asked.

"We had no weapons. Only the escort was armed. We thought of trying to rescue the captives, but the raiders outmatched us in weaponry and skill. Once they killed our defenders, we decided our best chance was to ride as fast as possible, which we did." Wali looked embarrassed at this admission.

"What other choice did you have?" Alexei spoke to that embarrassment. "It wouldn't save your comrades for you too to be killed or captured."

"Thank you, Sultan," the merchant said. "Can you help us, Khan?"

"We could send scouts." Ogodai spoke not to Wali but to Alexei. "What do you think? Would that be worthwhile?"

Alexei considered the question. "Yes," he said after a pause. "For our own sake as well as Wali's, we need to find out what's going on. If it is Sheikh-Mamai who attacked them, he poses a danger to us as well. To anyone crossing the steppe, in fact. If it's not Sheikh-Mamai but a rogue horde of brigands, at least Wali and his men can warn other merchants to beware." He turned his attention to Wali. "Where do you hail from?"

"Caffa," the man said.

"Then you have a long journey still." Alexei acknowledged this point by drawing his finger across the cloth in front of him, which still bore a cup and bowl, to trace the route from the Don to the tip of the Crimean Peninsula. "But if we're to send scouts, we need you to tell them where to look. Better yet, show them, if one of your men can stay behind."

Wali glanced over his shoulder at his five fellow merchants, each of whom appeared to be following the conversation among the leaders. "They have families in Caffa," he said, a doubtful note in his voice.

"But we'll allow you to stay with us until you recover," Ogodai pointed out. "We can supply additional camels and provisions for the journey. Even another escort, if you wish, after we defeat our enemy. Between our horde and Azamat's we control much of the territory you must cross. From here it's a straight journey down the Don, then around the small sea until you reach the passageway to Crimea. That must be worth something to you."

"I agree." The voice came from the far end of the five, the youngest of the merchants—a man not more than twenty, Alexei guessed. "I have no wife or children as yet. I will remain to help the scouts find their way. If we don't stop these bandits, we can neither return to trade nor rescue our friends."

"And you are?" Ogodai asked.

"Zahid, Khan. And proud to be of service." The young man rose and bowed.

"Welcome." Ogodai returned the bow with a dip of his head. "And thank you."

Princess Nadezhda received Sumbeka, Nasan, and Maria in the same sitting room where they had gone, almost a year ago, on another mission of mercy. Then the three women, plus Solomonida, had wanted to help Maria's stepmother, now living in Lithuania but at that time a prisoner of the Shuisky clan.

Who would have thought, then, that in a matter of months the Shuisky clan would have succeeded in making a grab for power the likes of which would put a Tatar court to shame? That they would dare assassinate a grand princess they disliked, eliminate her favorite and his supporters, isolate Russia's young ruler and his brother from those not under their own control?

And greater danger lay ahead, among those who would oppose the Shuiskys' rule. If the wholeness of the kingdom could be compared to the flat circle that formed a shaman's drum, Nasan sensed it fracturing before her eyes.

Today's errand was easier in some ways than that visit a year ago and more difficult in others. Nadezhda and Solomonida were friends, yet that friendship had not sufficed to keep Solomonida and Anna out of the convent. Because Nadezhda did not care to save them, or because she lacked sufficient influence with her husband? Neither possibility boded well for today's endeavor. But they must try.

The princess greeted them with a distracted air. To Nasan's critical eye, strain distorted Nadezhda's pretty face. Black hair curled from under a headdress somewhat askew, as if the wearer had slapped it on at the last moment without taking time to conceal her tresses completely. The dark circles under her eyes spoke of sleepless nights. Yet her voice, as she welcomed them, was steady.

She offered refreshments, which Sumbeka refused on behalf of the three of them. "We won't keep you long," she said by way of explanation. "I'm sure you have many tasks to occupy you. We've come to plead for your friend Solomonida and her daughter, who have spent the last month in a convent against their will. We visited them a couple of weeks ago, and we could see the location is not good for the child. She appeared ill when we saw her. Nor does it benefit Solomonida—still less her sister, who must care for their father alone."

She produced her most charming smile. "I asked my husband to intervene with Prince Vasily Shuisky, and he promised to do so. But the skies will fall before the two of them turn from their affairs of state long enough to consider the needs of one woman and her child. Hence I throw myself and my daughters on your mercy."

"Ah, it grieves me to hear that." Nadezhda clutched her hands together and blinked. Nasan saw the hint of tears in the princess's eyes. "This last month has been so horrible." Her voice trembled, and she wiped the tears away. "My dearest

Elena gone, and the tisane I gave her quite ineffective, despite my husband's promises that it could only do her good in her condition." Nasan exchanged glances with her mother and Maria, but no one spoke. "And the other ladies-in-waiting sent away, even my friends."

Do I believe her?

Nasan wasn't sure. Nadezhda looked and sounded sincere. Yet it would be foolish to ignore the reality that if the Shuisky clan profited from Elena's death, then so did Nadezhda. However much Nadezhda hated her husband, she couldn't be oblivious to the advantages of his ridding Russia of Elena and Telepnev. So long as the Shuiskys held power, Ilya's crime would lead to his advancement, and that could only benefit his wife and his sons.

Nadezhda, appearing not to notice her listeners' reaction, continued. "And what of those poor children—the grand prince and his brother? Stripped of father, mother, nurse, and the gentlemen of the chamber most familiar to them. Surrounded by my husband and his relatives, most of them near strangers to the boys." Her tears turned to sobs, and Maria, who sat closest, hugged her and murmured soothing words.

"They wanted to force Solomonida to accept the tonsure," Nadezhda said after a while. "I managed to prevent that. At the time I didn't dare plead with my husband and his uncle to spare her entirely—indeed, I was too preoccupied with my own distress to make the effort. That shames me, because so many good men and women have suffered much more than I have, and I didn't do everything I could to alleviate their pain."

She reached for Nasan's hand and said, "Including your husband, my dear. I was sorry to hear about his arrest. I couldn't plead for him either, but I would have if I'd had the slightest hope Ilya would listen."

"Thank you for that," Nasan said. "It's been very difficult for me too. But if you prevented the men from forcing Solomonida to become a nun as they did the princes' nanny, that is already a great deal."

Whatever doubts plagued her, Nasan meant every word. If Nadezhda truly didn't know what she'd done, her situation was tragic. If she suspected that her husband had tricked her into causing the death of her beloved princess, she would feel worse.

"Still, a month has passed since their banishment," Nasan went on. "Perhaps your husband's uncle will listen to you now. You might plead on Sheremetev's behalf rather than his daughter's. I'm sure he needs constant care, and even with help from the servants how much can one woman do?"

"I will try that," Nadezhda promised. "You will visit me again? Without Elena, without Solomonida, without a woman to preside over the boyars' daughters and wives, it has become so quiet here I can't stand it." She produced a watery chuckle. "I even miss your stepmother, Maria. Have you had any word from her since she reached Lithuania?"

"None at all," Maria said with a fine disregard for the truth. "I hope she's well."

About to remind her that they *had* heard, Nasan shut her mouth. Maria was right: her father's return to Moscow must be concealed, especially from the Shuisky clan, despite Princess Nadezhda's many kindnesses. "I too," she said instead. "That story she told us the last time we saw her broke my heart."

"Yes," Sumbeka said. "It always amazes me, the depths that lie inside, unspoken. To see such a creature in a new light reminds me of how quickly I judge, and at times how wrongly." She rose and pressed her cheek against Princess Nadezhda's pale one. "We have troubled you enough for one day. Thank you for receiving us in the midst of your grief, and thank you for agreeing to help our mutual friend Solomonida. For sure, you will see us again. And if loneliness threatens to swallow you, please come and visit us. We live not so far away."

A brief round of farewells, and they were on horseback once more, heading home.

Chapter 20

"IT CAN'T BE ANOTHER TOOTH." NASAN POINTED AT HER son, who lay sweating and fretful in his cradle. A pink rash covered his body, as if an artist had dipped a brush into a pot of rose-colored paint and flicked it, sending dots everywhere. Some overlapped, but most remained separate. "Fevers, yes, but he never had a rash before. It looks like the measles."

"Do you think he caught it from Lyuba?" Maria asked. "She didn't have a rash, just fever and a cough. Either way, she's back to her usual bouncing self."

That was true. So true that Nasan had welcomed Lyuba's departure for her lessons a few moments ago. Even when the child tried to speak in a whisper or move quietly, the result was loud enough to send Borya in his current state into wails of discomfort. Now they had several hours, until the noon meal, to settle him.

"That doesn't mean a baby will do as well." Nasan bent to touch her son's forehead for the twentieth—fiftieth?—time since entering the room. Zhenya, already scolded for not having sounded the alarm quickly enough, sighed in her corner and reached out a hand, as if to stop her mistress from worrying. Nasan ignored her.

Sumbeka swept into the room. "What's going on?" she demanded, startling Borya into another outburst. "Is he ill?"

"Yes, *Ana.*" Nasan indicated the rash with one hand. "And he has another fever. Maria thinks he may have caught whatever Lyuba got from Anna."

"Well, if he did, he will recover soon enough." Sumbeka's voice was more sympathetic than her words. "Leave him with Zhenya for now, daughter, and come with me. My husband has news of yours."

"He does?" Nasan clapped her hands together, and Borya wailed louder. Zhenya left her corner and picked him up, murmuring a soothing lullaby.

"Give him the willow bark potion," Nasan said. "It will help the fever, whatever its cause. I'll be back as soon as possible."

"Yes, Tsarevna." Zhenya rocked Borya in her arms. "The moment I have him calmed and back in his cradle, I will make it."

"I'll make it," Maria offered. "You keep him quiet. Or give him to me, and I'll sing to him."

Zhenya handed her the child. "Yes, sing to him, Tsarevna. That always soothes him."

"You see, daughter? They have matters well under control." Sumbeka caught Nasan by the arm and ushered her toward the door. "We're going no farther than your father's study. One of them will come running if Borya needs you. And early as it is, you'll have the rest of the day to watch over him."

Nasan complied, but she couldn't resist a backward glance over her shoulder. Maria gave her a warm smile and made a swift shooing motion with her hand. With a sigh, Nasan followed her mother out.

They found Bulat, as promised, in his study. The man who had led the Kolychev guards the day Nasan and Maria made their journey to the Monastery of St. Daniil sat, fully armed, on the same sofa he had occupied when they returned that day.

"He has news?" Nasan asked as she crossed the threshold behind her mother.

"Tell them," Bulat said.

"Yes, Khan." The captain stood at the women's entrance and waited for them to sit before resuming his own place on the sofa. "Tsarevna, we're almost certain that your husband and the others arrested with him are being kept in the storehouse we saw, the one the monks tried to chase us away from. We've watched that well-fed one go in and out since the day we arrived. Sometimes he brings food—not much and not often. Last night, when he came after dark, I sent the smallest and swiftest of your father's scouts down the side of the building to overhear. The lad couldn't swear, but he thought he heard men's voices—two or three, one of which resembled Lord Daniil's. Very weak, he said. Not surprising, if he and his companions have been starving for the better part of a month. We must move soon if we are to save them."

"What can we do, *Ata*?" Nasan leaped to her feet at the news, her worries over Borya's illness swamped by this new disaster. "We must rescue them!"

"Can you appeal to those in power?" Sumbeka grasped Nasan's hand and pulled her down again. "To take them without authorization places our men, our daughter and grandson, and even the captives themselves at risk if caught."

Bulat gave a quick shake of his head. "The Shuisky clan is still consolidating its power. I have argued with Prince Vasily since I first heard of Daniil's arrest, but to no avail. Nikolai Kolychev has entered the monastery, so he no longer poses a threat to them. They don't dare touch me, because I have sons to avenge me—sons outside their reach. Nor do they dare refuse me. Instead they hem and haw, then do nothing. I succeeded in arranging the meeting for Koshkin, but only after I told them Koshkin has sworn to make the information about Prince Ilya's guilt public if the Shuiskys don't negotiate with him. Even so, they haven't met with him yet. Releasing Daniil offers them no such benefit. Quite the reverse, because they see him, correctly, as a staunch supporter of those they have deposed or murdered. Moreover, I have lost patience with them. To attack my son-in-law in this way shows their disrespect for me. I've put up with their nonsense long enough."

He regarded Nasan with a frown of such intensity that she shivered in her scarlet slippers before she understood that he didn't even see her. The men of the Shuisky clan were the target of his rage.

"Prepare yourself, daughter," he said. "We move tonight. We've already waited too long to rescue your husband. We have nothing to gain from further delay—and much to lose if his fragile hold on life weakens still more."

"Tonight?" Nasan, back in the nursery with her mother and sister-in-law, paced from wall to door and back, wringing her hands. She must look like a keening woman, but she couldn't stop herself. The alternative was to punch something, and that would upset the babies once more. "I want to save my husband—you can't imagine how much—but how can I go anywhere tonight? How can Borya, when he's not well?"

"It is a problem," Sumbeka agreed. "But if Daniil has suffered as much as the captain believes, we can't expect him to ride as far as Ogodai's horde. Zhenya can take Borya in a cart, with a man to drive it, while you ride with a spare horse in case Daniil is stronger than the scouts think. Or Zhenya can stay here with Borya and join you later, while you travel with the driver. Either way, you will need at least two carts—one for you and Daniil and a second for any other captives you rescue. And extra riding gear, in case any of them are strong enough to mount a horse."

"I won't leave my baby behind!"

"Then take him with you," Sumbeka said. "But with or without Borya you have to head south once you free your husband and his companions. Otherwise, we must first find a way to hide them here in Moscow, then engineer a second escape. And the first will be next to impossible. Even your father can't refuse a direct demand from the grand prince to search his house. You know as well as I do that Vasily Shuisky will issue such a demand in Ivan's name if he gets even a hint of Daniil's presence here."

Glancing at Maria, Nasan saw her sister-in-law biting her lip, as if she either didn't know what to say or had decided not to protest.

Nasan understood. She didn't know what to say herself. How could she place her son at risk to rescue her husband? But then, how could she chance her husband's life to nurse her son through an illness that could well be minor, the outcome of which only God could predict?

If I cause the death of either of them, I will bear that burden the rest of my life.

"Suppose Borya worsens on the road?" she asked. "Or in the house, and I'm not here?"

Sumbeka hugged her. "It's a terrible choice, my darling, and only you can make it. Know that whatever you choose, we will support you."

An assurance that comforted Nasan not one bit.

⁂

"I thought I told you not to come back." Elder Gennady looked, if possible, less welcoming than before.

"You did." Nasan, dressed in her boys' clothes, again stood in the doorway of the monk's cell at the Miracles Monastery. "I came to say farewell. To lessen Lord Nikolai's distractions, not add to them."

"You said that the last time. Much good it did. And you promised to leave him alone." Gennady waved a book at her, a small one bound in plain leather. A prayer book, perhaps.

"My family has called me home. I have news for Lord Nikolai, and I must deliver it in person. It will hearten him, I swear," Nasan pleaded. Bad enough that she had decided that preserving Daniil's life must take precedence over the health of their precious infant. How could she leave the city without letting her father-in-law know that the Tatars planned to rescue his son? She held out an icon of the Sainted Miriam, its jewel-encrusted gold cover glinting in the faint light that straggled through the mica window. "And I brought this icon depicting the Mother of God as a gift for the monastery, to thank you for your assistance, today and the other times."

"Oh, very well," Gennady said with a sigh. The same words he'd used on her previous visit, although more resigned than grumpy this time. "You know the way. But be quick about it." He took the icon from her and propped it in a corner. "I will commend your gift to the abbot. It is most beautiful. The holy father will be pleased."

Nasan bowed from the waist. "Thank you, honored elder." She left before he could change his mind. As she reached the door, she glanced over her shoulder and saw him caressing the icon cover. For once, he looked almost pleasant. She made a silent vow to thank Maria for suggesting the gift.

At the door to Nikolai's cell she stopped and cleared her throat.

"Enter," he said. When she poked her head around the door, he gave her a big smile. "Girei! I didn't expect to see you again." More conspiratorially he added, "Elder Gennady told me he had banned you from the premises."

She slid through the door, closed it behind her, and hugged him. This time she didn't care if people suspected the worst. She would be gone before they had a chance to draw the wrong conclusions. "He did. I vowed this would be the last time—and I fear it must be, Papa-in-law."

Intercepting his glance at the closed door, she said, "What I have to say is most secret. My father's men think they have found Daniil and the others at the monastery as you told us, and their captors are not treating them well. *Ata* has decided to free them tonight. Borya and I will meet them south of the city"—she saw no need to mention that she intended to take part in the raid—"and we will travel as fast as possible to my brother's horde. If we succeed, I'll find a way to let you know. A message that your package has been delivered, perhaps."

"It's good you came today," Nikolai told her. "I too have made a decision: to take my initial vows and retire to the monastery at Ferapontovo. The one you visited during your journey north two years ago. I have the elder's approval." Another smile, this one mischievous, creased his face. "He believes, I think, that I will not fully concentrate on my studies until I abandon the lure of Moscow." He touched her cheek. "This is an extraordinary thing that you and your father do for my son and his cousin. I have no words to express my gratitude. I will pray for your success, even though it means that Daniil and Roman must leave Russia."

"There's nothing left for them here," she said sadly. "The Shuisky clan will not soon forgive them for supporting Telepnev, whereas my brother will welcome them. But I thank you for your prayers, and I wish you contentment in your new life as a monk. As for gratitude, there is no need. Daniil is my beloved husband."

Her sorrow evaporated for an instant in a mischievous impulse of her own. "My father regards the arrest as a personal insult. I would not be any member of the Shuisky clan who dares cross *Ata*'s path from now on."

"A formidable enemy, indeed," Nikolai said. "I wish you Godspeed, my daughter, and I look forward to receiving that message about the package. Address it to Brother Nikon. And send it to Ferapontovo, as I leave tomorrow."

"And I this afternoon." She stood and hugged him once more. "I'll miss you, Papa-in-law. Do take good care of yourself. I hope we meet again someday."

"And you, my child. I chose well when I married Daniil to you." The warmth of his expression stayed with her for a long time after she slipped out the door, leaving it ajar.

She didn't tell Elder Gennady she was leaving. Let him find out in due course.

♪

By the time Nasan reached her mother's house, preparations for her departure were well underway. The cart that would carry Borya and his nurse south—big enough to hold Daniil if he was too weakened by his captivity to ride—stood loaded in the courtyard. She saw a second cart nearby, its long shafts resting on the ground.

The rooms inside were a-bustle: women packing and gathering supplies, men honing weapons and saddling horses. Nasan, still in her boys' clothes, sought out her mother and sister-in-law and found them in the nursery. A quick check of Borya revealed a baby still covered in pink rash and fretful but no worse than he had been this morning. Zhenya and Maria must have dosed him with willow bark, because his forehead seemed cooler and Nasan saw little evidence of sweating. She said a silent prayer to the grandmothers that he suffered from nothing more serious than the infection that had laid Lyuba and Anna low for three days.

"Oh, there you are, Nasan," Maria said. "Did you get in to see Papa Nikolai?"

"I did." Nasan gave them a quick summary of her visit. "What's been happening here?"

"Borya seems the same," Sumbeka said. "But it's been no more than a few hours. Since his fever hasn't worsened, I think if you keep dosing him with willow bark and keep him as quiet as possible, he will recover soon. I'll come with you, if you like."

Nasan embraced her. "I love you, *Ana*, but you must stay here. Suppose Alexander is next? Since Zhenya is coming with me, he will need you as well as Maria and Alina to look after him." She surveyed the room to see how Alexander was faring. "Where's Lyuba?"

"Solomonida stopped by," Maria said. "She and Anna didn't stay long, since they came only to say thank you. And they took Lyuba away with them. She'll be back in the morning, but it means she won't see things she must not talk about."

"So Princess Nadezhda succeeded!" About to clap her hands, Nasan remembered the effect on Borya the last time and stopped. "Oh, I'm so glad. Give Solomonida my good wishes when you see her again. I will miss Lyuba, though. Do tell her we'll meet again, as soon as I can arrange it. I don't want her to think I abandoned her." She felt her lip tremble. "I will miss the two of you even more. You must come to celebrate Borya's birthday."

Sumbeka patted her cheek. "We'd have to travel with you today," she said with a watery chuckle. "It's not three weeks away, silly child. If we'd thought of it, we could have celebrated before you left, but as it is we have barely time to get some food into you before you go."

"And Borya's not well enough for a party," Nasan said past the lump in her throat.

"His name day, though," Maria said. "On the twenty-fourth of July. We might manage that. Or Alexander's birthday. *His* name day is too soon."

"We'll work out something," Sumbeka promised, her voice unsteady. "First let's rescue your husband and see the three of you safe in Ogodai's horde and Alexei back here where he belongs. Then we'll find a way to be together once more." Another hug reassured Nasan of her mother's love, but she couldn't fail to notice that the cheek pressed against hers was damp.

But then, weren't tears rushing down her face and Maria's, too?

"Come." Sumbeka tugged both young women toward the door. "Let's get you fed and Zhenya and Borya settled. I hope the men knew not to unsaddle your horse."

Chapter 21

"LOOK, *ATA*, BAKIR. THE SCOUTS. AND ZAHID." TIMUR stood in his stirrups. "I think someone is chasing them."

"Off with you," Alexei said. "Let Ruslan know." He pointed at an angle to their left, back the way they'd come. "Ride as fast as you can, ask for his help, then find your uncle and tell him too. Do whatever Ogodai says. Understood?"

Timur saluted hand over heart like any warrior receiving an order and galloped in the direction Alexei had indicated. Once convinced that his son would remain out of danger but be happy at having a useful task to perform, Alexei turned his attention to the group heading at top speed toward the horde. Steadying Ajdar with his knees, he pulled his bow from its case and nocked an arrow to the string, then released the animal to walk toward the advancing riders. He itched to move faster, because the situation didn't look good, but until Ruslan and his men arrived, an all-out attack by one person would do more harm than good.

Timur performed his task well, though, because Alexei and his horse had crossed less than a quarter of the distance that separated him from the scouts when a full hundred mounted warriors raced past him on both sides. Right away he loosened his grip on his own steed. Ajdar loved to race with other horses, and it took only one muttered *chu* to get him from walk to gallop. They caught up with Ruslan and his riders just as the lines split to surround the scouts—and if necessary their pursuers—from both sides, aiming to encircle the enemy. As those in the front reached the meeting point at the far side of the circle, a cry went up: "Sheikh-Mamai!"

Alexei stood. Long years of practice enabled him to balance despite the speed of the moving horse, and he thought he saw riders fleeing the circle even as the two lines sought to close them in. He dropped onto his saddle once more.

The banner definitely belonged to Sheikh-Mamai. Alexei's forces and Ogodai's must have seen several dozen of those sets of concentric circles embroidered in black on a yellow background when they raided Sheikh-Mamai's camp. It wasn't the kind of thing one forgot. But what did it mean? A full-scale attack, a handful of renegades, a small foray that had spotted and pursued the scouts?

By the time he reached the vanguard, he could see that the cry of "Sheikh-Mamai," although accurate, was premature. Not the main army, by any means, but a small scouting party from the other side.

He called to the warriors in the lead to abandon the chase and, when they returned, to escort Ogodai's scouts, with Bakir and Zahid, back to the camp. "We're in it now," he said to Ruslan as they headed for the tents clearly visible on the horizon. "Sheikh-Mamai knows where to find us. I hope the scouts discovered where to find him."

"Yes." Ruslan scowled at the not-so-distant tents. "From here on, it's a fight to the death. Let's hope we can surprise him before he surprises us."

*

The late afternoon sun still lit the sky when Nasan, mounted, took her place next to the cart holding Zhenya and the baby, driven by one of Bulat's men. A spare horse, large enough to carry Daniil, was tied behind the cart, where it ambled in blissful satisfaction as soon as the party passed the city walls and the beast could alternate between an easy walk and mouthfuls of grass snatched from the edges of the path. A contingent of 150 men, each with an extra mount or two, surrounded them—armed warriors who would accompany the party to Ogodai's horde both to protect the travelers from marauding bandits and to prevent any attempt by the Shuisky forces to recapture Daniil and his fellow prisoners.

Nasan could only hope that those in power in the Kremlin would not soon discover their captives' escape. She trusted Sorkhokhtani and the ambling horse to cover sufficient ground to put a healthy distance between her family and the Shuiskys' soldiers, but a cart couldn't move at much more than a trot. Which meant that if Daniil could not ride, it would be difficult to ensure his safety if the news reached Moscow before they had traveled at least a few days' journey into the steppe.

An hour or so later, they passed the Monastery of St. Daniil and kept going. The sun had sunk almost to the horizon by the time they stopped. Nasan rested her horse and went to check on Borya, who had relaxed into sleep. Was it just the dim light, or did his high color appear to be fading?

She didn't ask, because Zhenya could see no better than she could. Instead, she commended the nursemaid, collected her horse, and remounted. Leaving a fifth of the escort behind to guard the carriage, she took her place among the warriors. She couldn't wait to see her husband, whatever his condition.

Besides, you never knew when an extra archer would come in handy.

❦

By the time the monastery church again appeared ahead of them, its cupolas were no more than dull moonlit gleams against the night sky. Shivering at the sight—a reaction that had nothing to do with the cooling breeze and everything to do with fear of what she might find—Nasan pulled her bow from its case. Near the back of the advancing escort, she had no intention of forcing herself into the lead. Her father, her husband, and every warrior present would unite in deploring any such attempt on her part. But she had enough experience, from her childhood on the steppe and the summer she'd spent in the northern woods, to predict that such a fluid situation as a rescue attempt could expose her or Daniil to dangers that no one had anticipated. It seemed best to prepare herself for defense—even for offense, if circumstances required it.

For that reason, too, she rejected the suggestion from the Tatar officer leading her father's troops that she remain behind. "I'll stay out of your way," she told him. "I nurse no ambitions for glory. But to wait alone places me at greater risk than accompanying you. And it places you at greater risk, too, if you must spare men to protect me. I can defend myself if need be, but I yield responsibility for the attack to you."

Grudgingly he accepted this argument. Most likely, he had heard more than a few rumors about the khan's daughter and her exploits. It surprised Nasan that he had even bothered to challenge her. Most of her father's men knew better than to make the attempt.

They moved the horses at an almost silent walk through the rickety fence and into the courtyard. Nasan remained in the rear. After they circled the outskirts of the monastery, a place so quiet she assumed the monks must be resting before rising again to pray, they found the scouts waiting motionless on the far side. The storehouse that the scouts had identified as holding prisoners stood before them, also unlit and emitting no noise. The monk who looked like a warrior was nowhere to be seen. To all intents and purposes, the storehouse appeared deserted.

Was Daniil ever here? Have they moved him? Killed him?

Nasan pressed a hand to her mouth, forcing the words to remain unspoken. The Kolychev guards captain regarded her with a frown, perhaps because he couldn't imagine what she was doing there. She didn't ask. To break this silence was clearly not a good idea.

The man next to her passed her the reins of the spare horse they had brought in the hope that Daniil would be able to mount and ride alone. Nasan acknowledged the transfer with a nod; the horse, like her own, patiently cropped grass. Another warrior, appointed as her defender, stopped beside her, holding the reins of two more horses in case the raid freed others besides Daniil. As the rest of the men spread out, some encircling the monks' cells, others directing their energies to the storehouse, she prevented Sorkhokhtani and the new horse from joining them. With the woods at her back she concentrated on controlling her breathing. *In, out, in, out.* The exercise didn't calm her so much as harness her emotions for the possibility of action to come, but the steady rhythm sufficed to reassure the horses.

From the far end of the grass lane that separated the cells from the church she saw a raised sword gleam in the moonlight. The silent dark exploded in hoofbeats and Tatar howls. While she forced her two mounts into stillness with the power of knees and hands, the crash of an ax against wood, the clash of weaponry, the hiss of a thrown torch turned the horrors of a Tatar raid from threat into reality. Monks poured out of the cells, many without their hoods. The well-fed one ran straight toward her, and she dispatched him with a single arrow to the chest. Smoke stung her eyes, the odor of ash defining each inhalation of breath. The burning huts lit the night, but the images that passed before her were creatures of nightmare, black shapes against the flames, swords rising and falling. She couldn't see whether those felled by the blades were monks or Shuisky troops posing as monks. She suspected the attackers couldn't tell either.

A roar signaled the moment when the ax blades broke through the wood. Nasan released her grip on the horses enough to let them move toward the storehouse, its door now open to the elements.

Tension gripped her. The breathing exercise no longer worked. Her mare moved restlessly under her, and she struggled to keep her grip on the reins of the sidling gelding. The smoke and flames spooked both horses.

Is Daniil alive? Is he injured? Can he ride?

Two men came out—one carried between a pair of Russian soldiers. The other, Daniil's cousin Roman, clutched at the arm of a third. She urged Sorkhokhtani forward, only to stop when she realized that the man carried by the soldiers was too short for Daniil, his hair too dark even in the dim light cast by the moon.

Where is he? Not dead, grandmothers! Please not dead!

A tall figure staggered through the storehouse door. A warrior supported the figure on either side. With the light at their backs, Nasan couldn't swear that she had identified those at the sides of the trio. One had the shape of the Kolychev captain; the other could be any of his men.

But she recognized the person in the middle. Daniil, far too thin and unsteady on his feet but moving, if not exactly under his own power. Issuing a steady stream of reassurances to the spooked horses, she advanced toward him. It took every bit of control she had not to leap from the saddle and throw herself at him. The moment of greatest danger still lay ahead.

But the touch of her hand on his cheek, the brush of her lips across his mouth as she leaned sideways in the saddle, and the "my husband" she murmured into his ear marked the sweetest moment she had ever experienced.

"Wife of mine," he whispered. "You came for me."

He was alive. Not well, but alive and conscious. He knew who she was, that she had rescued him. Things could be worse.

Even so, his condition shocked her. Despite the efforts of his two helpers, Daniil could not sit straight on the gelding provided for him. Seeing him tumble into his assistants' outstretched arms, Nasan dismounted and handed Sorkhokhtani's reins to the nearest of her father's men. "Take her. She's done wonderfully, as always, but she has traveled a long way today. I won't burden her with a pair of riders. Walk her slowly into the night and watch for pursuit or response. We'll catch up with you soon. Take the other released captives with you. There were only three?"

He raised a hand in salute, then engaged in a brief exchange with the Kolychev captain before answering her question. "Only these three survived, Khanim. The men found two bodies."

Nasan shuddered, incapable of speech. How close she had come to losing her beloved Daniil!

Thank the Almighty that *Ata* had decided to launch the raid tonight. And that she had not delayed out of anxiety over their son, who might already be on the mend.

She turned to adjust the stirrups of the other horse. The sounds of battle were fading, the screams of monks abating. The abandoned monastery lacked the usual peasant villages, and the site lay far enough from Moscow that unless additional guards lay hidden somewhere in the vicinity, the Tatars should be well away by the time anyone in the city realized what had happened and had a chance to react.

"Torch the storehouse before you leave," she told the Kolychev captain. "Best if those in the palace imagine that all their prisoners died in the raid. And what of the monks? Will they keep quiet?"

"Your father's orders, Tsarevna," the man said. "No survivors." He sounded grim, and Nasan—thinking of Nikolai, his goodness and patience—thought she understood. To kill men sworn to God's service was a great sin, no matter the reason.

But the captain added, "No way to tell which were genuine holy men. If any were. Most likely, they all served as guards. For sure, not one among them slipped my young lord so much as a crumb the whole time I watched them. They deserve what happened to them."

She had misread his grim tone then. The captain approved of her father's orders; he didn't question them.

Nasan mounted the gelding and extended a hand toward her husband. "Help him up." With a mighty heave the Kolychev captain and his colleague—whom Nasan now recognized, although his name was playing hide-and-seek at the back of her mind—half-lifted and half-shoved Daniil onto the saddle behind her. His arms closed around her waist from behind. "Hold on," she said. "And let me know if you start to slip."

He pressed his lips against her neck in reply. With as much care as she could manage, Nasan turned the unfamiliar gelding and walked him toward the fence.

When she reached it, she discovered that a milling horde of warriors had preceded her. Daniil's cousin clung to the waist of the man who had waited beside her during the height of the raid. Watching him, she remembered Roman at her wedding, laughing and joking, teasing and toasting Daniil, who'd responded in kind. And now look at them, unable to ride unassisted, barely able to stand.

What villains these Shuiskys are!

The third captive had fared even worse: the largest of the Russians supported the man, who appeared semiconscious at best, in front of him. She stood quietly to one side, desperate to talk with Daniil, find out how he was, but afraid to drain his strength still further. His body formed a bulwark against her back, his face pressed into her shoulder, his arms circled her waist.

Grandmothers, keep him in the saddle!

For in truth, if he did slip, she doubted she could catch or stop him. But so far he remained upright, if one could call it that, by clinging to her.

He so seldom showed weakness. If she could be certain of his recovery, she might even enjoy being the stronger partner for once.

The warriors soon reorganized themselves, the freed prisoners and those assisting them in the center and the leaders of the escort and the scouts at the head. With the mission accomplished, the group, enlarged by the addition of the scouts, resumed its noiseless passage. After a while, they overtook the man leading Sorkhokhtani, who greeted Nasan with a whinny before blending in among the other mounts and their riders. The scent of smoke dissipated as they left the monastery behind them, and the soft green aroma of grass took its place. The moon stayed high and the sky clear. Nasan, blessing their good fortune, moved in a dreamlike state toward a destination that seemed both distant and unreal.

Somehow, Daniil managed to stay on the horse until they reached the cart. Then he again fell into the arms of the Kolychev captain and one of his men. Nasan threw the gelding's reins to the man leading Sorkhokhtani, slid to the ground, and ran after the two men carrying Daniil. As she reached the cart, she remembered Borya and his nurse. "Careful," she told the men. "Our son is inside, with the woman who cares for him. Let me go first, to warn her."

They nodded, and Nasan scrambled under the covering that hid the bed of the cart from passersby. Zhenya sat up, rubbing her eyes. "How's Borya?" Nasan whispered.

Zhenya guided her mistress's hand to the child's forehead. It felt cool to the touch. "He's all right?" Nasan heard the catch in her voice and chided herself. Stupid to think, even for a single, half-formed instant, that she couldn't have both her husband and her child.

"Yes, Tsarevna," Zhenya said softly. "He is not yet completely recovered, but I think it was the same illness that Lady Lyuba caught, despite the rash. Not the full measles but that other kind that comes and goes. Another day or two and he will be quite restored."

Nasan turned her palm and brushed it down her baby's cheek, warm and silky under her touch. She bent closer to catch his smooth, steady exhalation. Zhenya was right.

"And the young lord?" Zhenya asked.

"We found him. And two of those imprisoned with him. The others had already died. One of the three may not survive, but my husband and his cousin will recover, I think." Nasan edged toward the opening. Her hand touched a pile of blankets on her right. "Is this the bed you prepared for him? He's much weakened by his ordeal. We'll have to look after him well."

When Zhenya whispered agreement, Nasan poked her head through the covering and beckoned the men to bring Daniil forward. "Here." She indicated the pile she had identified. "And thank you. Put the other two men in the second cart." She moved aside to let the men enter with their burden and watched them lay Daniil on his back. Inside the cart, without the benefit of moonlight, she couldn't see well enough to judge the extent of his injuries, if any. That must wait for morning.

As the men withdrew, she caught the Kolychev captain's sleeve. "Do you return to Moscow or ride south with us?"

The man shook his head, not in negation but as if he had yet to absorb his change of circumstances. "Nothing for me in Moscow now, Tsarevna. I'll see if your husband and brother have a use for a fighting man when we reach the horde."

"No question of that," Nasan told him. "We always need good warriors like you. Lord Nikolai and I are in your debt. Lord Daniil too. Tell the leader of the escort to rest the horses and the men. We must be on our way before dawn."

He acknowledged the order and left. Nasan pulled off her hat and her boots, then went to lie beside her husband. She heard the baby babbling, Zhenya settling into sleep, Daniil's exhausted breathing. She curled up next to him, her hand caressing ribs that should be less prominent, cheeks unnaturally hollow. She murmured endearments in Russian and Tatar.

Despite the hours of riding and fighting, the swing of her emotions from fear to joy and back, the relief of having Daniil at her side, she could not sleep. The anxiety that had racked her since the moment she heard of her husband's arrest rolled over her in waves, as if she felt safe to experience it only now that danger, although still present, had receded from that terrible island where she hadn't known whether he clung to life or had died in isolation and despair.

The dreams, when they came, brought shrieking demons from the depths to pull and tug at her restless body. Only the arrival of the light and the sensation of the moving cart, despite the aches and pains caused by yesterday's exertions, provided some relief.

Chapter 22

DANIIL SLEPT LONG INTO THE MORNING. THE RESCUE PARTY had left Moscow well behind by the time the first sight of him in the light sent Nasan into a spiral of shock that did not soon abate. She had expected, from the presence of those prominent ribs, that he would look thinner than before, but this gaunt shape with its matted hair and beard, its wrists and ankles rubbed raw with fetters now removed, its filthy clothing and dirt-covered face that nonetheless revealed layers of bruises under the grime bore little resemblance to her handsome husband. How could any government treat its prisoners so poorly, never mind a man who had shown unswerving loyalty to its cause?

The mere sight of him in his present condition broke her heart, yet she suspected that the removal of his clothing would reveal still greater injury.

"We must find a way to clean him," she told Zhenya in a low voice. Daniil slept like the dead, but he clearly needed every moment of slumber he could command if he was to heal. She didn't want to risk waking him. "What I wouldn't give for my mother's bathing room!"

"And food." Zhenya signaled their driver to stop the cart. "Very light at first. I made some broth while we were waiting yesterday. I'll fetch it if you watch Borya for me."

"Yes, broth is good. Ask after the other men we rescued while you're out." Nasan sat Borya on the rug in front of her, where she could play and babble with him (quietly) while restraining any attempts to grab at his father. The baby seemed much recovered today, although less rambunctious than usual. "Tell the men to feed them broth as well. Sips at first, but frequent. And perhaps some slices of good bread. Again, just small pieces until their stomachs readjust."

Borya reached for Daniil, and she caught the baby's hand. "*Ata* is resting, darling. We must let him sleep so he can wake up and play with you soon. Where is your lion?"

"Aslan," Borya said. It was his first word after *Ada* and *Ama*—the closest he had yet managed to the Tatar *Ata* and *Ana*—and with him not yet one year old, Nasan was secretly very proud of him.

"Yes, *aslan*." She repeated the Tatar word for lion to encourage him. "Where is Aslan? Can you find him?" From where she sat, she could reach the lion with an outstretched hand if need be. "Is he on the chest?"

But "chest" was not yet in Borya's vocabulary. She turned the baby so he faced the chest. "Chest," she said. "Do you see Aslan on the chest?"

With a delighted chuckle Borya rolled onto all fours and crawled toward the chest, then pulled himself into a standing position and grabbed for the stuffed toy. The grab overbalanced him, and he sat down with a whump, lion in hand. He opened his mouth to scream, but Nasan intervened. "Oh, clever Borya. You found your lion!" And just like that, he was all smiles again.

She caught the lion by the tail and pulled it slowly toward her. "Come, Borya. Follow the lion." He crawled to sit between her stretched-out legs once more. She caught him in her arms and hugged him, then settled him and the lion in her lap. "Let's tell Aslan a story, shall we?"

By the time Daniil stirred, Zhenya had returned with the broth and reclaimed the baby. She had also persuaded some of the guards to heat a basin of warm water and procure a second empty basin, a set of soft cloths, and—miracle of miracles—a pair of scissors and a comb. "You'll have to ask one of the men to shave him, Tsarevna," she said as she handed these over. "But at least you can trim his beard and his hair." She tapped the driver on the shoulder, and the cart resumed its slow progress south.

"And the other men?" Nasan asked.

"The weaker one died overnight, but the other—your husband's cousin, the Russian captain said—is sipping broth. He looks no better than our young lord, yet he lives."

"Understood. We must care for them both, then." Seeing Daniil open his eyes, Nasan dipped a cloth in the water and with great gentleness drew it down his cheek. She repeated the motion across his forehead and down the other cheek. Next came his chin and the tangle of beard, but as she turned to squeeze out the cloth in the empty basin and checked to see if she could rinse it without turning the rest of the water into a muddy disaster, he groaned and tried to raise himself on his elbows.

She dropped the cloth and helped him sit up. He leaned forward to kiss her, almost toppling them both. Borya escaped Zhenya's grasp and hurtled toward him at a rapid crawl, calling "*Ada, Ada.*"

"*Gospodi.*" Daniil regarded his son with astonishment. "Look at him go, and in a moving cart at that. He has more energy than I do at the moment. I'm weak as a kitten. And he can talk!"

"A few words, anyway." Nasan laughed. "Mama, Papa, lion. But he can say those in two languages, if interchangeably and not quite correctly. He's working on Zhenya, but it comes out as Za-za. And you, poor darling, need food and a good rest. Can you manage some broth?"

"I must look like the devil himself. What happened back there?" He took the small bowl of broth from her hand.

"Slowly," she said. "If you drink too much too fast, it will come right back up. We need to teach your stomach to hold food again." He nodded and sipped while she regaled him with the story of his rescue—not the details, because he still seemed ready to collapse, but the gist.

"And we're heading south now?" He frowned, as if he found the news hard to take in. "Leaving Russia? Roman and me both?"

"We have to—for the present, at least." She took the empty bowl and set it aside to refill in a short while. "The Shuisky clan confiscated your estate, and your father has decided to take his vows and move to Ferapontovo. That should keep him safe, but it means there's nothing there for us. If we return, they will throw you back into jail. Or worse, since we helped you escape. Roman can decide later whether to join us on the steppe or head for Lithuania, but he has to pick one or the other. He can't go home."

"Yes, I see." He plucked at the blanket that covered his legs. Nasan could tell that he wasn't happy with the outcome, but what other option had they?

"I would have liked to speak to Papa," he said after a pause. "What you did was amazing—and your father, too. He never fails to surprise me. But I would still have liked a chance to say goodbye."

"I know, dearest." She clasped his restless hand. "I too wish that had been possible. But you can write your papa a letter.

Alexei will take it back to Moscow, and I'll ask him to find a man who can deliver it to Ferapontovo. I know it's not the same as talking to your father face to face, but it will reassure him to know you're safe and give you a chance to say what you want him to hear."

"You're very good to put up with me, crotchety thing that I am. You've done wonderfully." He held out an arm, as if to hug her, then drew it back and looked at it askance. "Lord, I'm fit for the dung heap. Hand me that towel and the basin, and let's see if I can't make myself somewhat more suitable to share the bed of a beautiful woman. Are those scissors?"

Joy at having him here to complain filled her. "First things first, my love," she said. "We need to get you clean, change your clothes, comb that mop on your head, and feed you well. But oh, it's so good to have you here with me."

"You came for me," he said. "That astonishes me most of all."

She kissed him, not caring about the dirt. "Well, of course. For a while there, I thought I had lost you forever. And that was a prospect I could not abide!"

"Won't you come in? It's pouring." Nasan peered through the opening at the back of the cart. It was morning, several days after her rescue of Daniil, and they had traveled far enough into the steppe that they could safely stop and raise tents for the escort rather than plow on while blinded by sheets of rain. Her husband, stripped to the skin, stood with one hand on the side of the cart, balancing himself under the downpour. With Zhenya inside and no other women in the camp, he saw no reason for modesty. Or so he'd told Nasan the first time she protested.

"It's the only way I'm going to get clean on this trip," he said. "Hand me that soap, will you? When I'm done, my captain has promised to make me look less like Daniil the Stylite himself. The saints must have grown beards to their knees sitting on those pillars for forty years at a stretch."

"Are you sure you can walk?" From Nasan's vantage point Daniil's nakedness (a sight that normally provoked far different sensations in her) revealed the full extent of the abuse inflicted on him. It would be a miracle if he had survived without cracked ribs. For sure, he must have endured more than one beating to carry such an extraordinary collection of bruises.

Next to her, Borya had pulled himself to standing by hanging onto the rim of the cart. He stared at his father and babbled, as if he too wanted to play in the drenching rain. Every so often he said "*Ada*" and shuffled his feet, propelling himself to one side or the other. Once or twice he let go of the rim without, Nasan thought, noticing that he stood by himself. He was so near to walking she could feel it. Would today be the day?

Daniil smiled at him. "Stay away from Shuiskys, little man," he told the baby. "And you won't need to stand out here in the rain like Papa." To Nasan he added, "Don't coddle me, wife of mine. I won't get stronger lying on my back. Besides, the tent's close enough that I could fall forward and hit it with my head." He handed her the soap. "Give me the blanket I dirtied. I'll wrap it around myself and be on my way. And hand over the scissors and the comb. Next time you see me, I expect to look like a human being again. Even the blanket should be clean by the time I return, although wet as the Volga."

"You're mad," Nasan said, resigned to the inevitability of his going. "Won't you even put on a pair of trousers?"

"They'd be soaked through before I got there." He leaned forward and kissed her, then patted Borya on the head. "This fine lad will keep you occupied, and I'll be back to pester you before he takes his next nap. You want me to recover, don't you? Our real reunion hasn't started yet."

She wrinkled her nose at his lascivious grin. "I'll be here, with towels to dry you off and a set of clean clothes. Zhenya's made fish soup and bread, too. We'll keep it hot for you."

"That's what I'm talking about," he said, laughing. "Keeping it hot. You do that. But why fish? Is it a fast day?"

"I have no idea." Nasan tried to count backward, then forward, in her head and gave it up as not worth the effort. Secretly pleased that Daniil could imagine desiring her, she nonetheless left his teasing comment unanswered. He didn't need encouragement to exert himself in that way. "It will be good for you as you recover your appetite. Not like that fatty meat the men love."

"Mama hen," he said, but the affectionate note in his voice reassured her that he didn't mind her fussing. "I promise, I'll be good. The blanket, please."

She handed him the covering that had topped the bed when the men first brought him in, which did indeed look as if someone had dragged it across the steppe between a pair of horses, and watched him wrap it around his waist and stagger toward the tent shared by the two captains and their highest-ranking aides.

Daniil's cousin Roman should have been there too, but as soon as he could rise from his bed, he'd overruled everyone's protests and announced he would head for Kiev. Twenty or so of the Kolychev warriors elected to go with him, although the captain and the fighters who had served Nikolai and Daniil the longest remained.

Nasan understood Roman's decision to leave. Hard enough to lose his lands without also having to adjust to a change of language, religion, and custom. Yet his departure only underlined the sacrifice made by the Russians who stayed.

Daniil had reached the tent. When he stepped over the threshold, turning to wave as he went in, Nasan sighed.

"Hopeless," she said to Zhenya, who had positioned herself at the opposite end of the cart, near the driver, throughout this performance. "He'll either cure or kill himself, but what can one do?"

"Indeed," Zhenya said. "But he's right, Tsarevna. You want to keep him safe, but he's a warrior—and a good one. You're lucky to have such a man."

"I am. And it's true: I'd hate it if he sat around and pined. Although he could be a bit less determined." Nasan tucked an arm around Borya's waist. "Come, Borya. *Ata* went to talk with the men. Let's find Aslan, shall we? I think Zhenya has him."

"Aslan," Borya said. "Za-za." He flopped down and crawled across the layers of felt mats toward his nursemaid, who picked up the stuffed lion and held it out for him to see. Convivial noises—men joking and laughing—sounded from outside the cart as Nasan followed the baby along the cart bed.

When Daniil returned an indeterminate time later, her jaw dropped. It was like looking at a stranger. An incredibly handsome if rather gaunt stranger. The captain had shaved Daniil's beard and mustache completely off, and his tawny hair, clipped short to remove the tangles, had a natural wave that she found most appealing.

"I know," he said in response to her stare. "He's turned me into a damned Pole. But there was no other way, or so he told me. Too much dirt and too many clumps."

"I love it." Nasan scrambled to her feet and ran to hug him. Against her cheek, his felt warm and smooth. "Won't you consider keeping it? Men in the horde don't have so much facial hair, as a rule. You'll blend right in." She jumped back as the wrap-around blanket, cleaner but every bit as wet as the Volga, threatened to soak her robe.

His shoulders shook with laughter. "Seems like a risky proposition, letting someone with a sharp knife near my jaw every day, but if it makes you happy, my love, I will consider it. And now, maybe I should take those clothes and the soup, in that order? I don't want to shock poor Zhenya into hysterics."

Zhenya faced the front of the cart. Nasan dropped the soaked blanket as close to the door as possible—there was no way to dry it until the rain stopped—and handed Daniil a large soft cloth made of cotton. When he was dry, she traded the cloth for a pile of clothes. He dressed quickly in shirt and trousers, pulled on a pair of felt boots that lay near the chest that had held the clothes, and went to sit beside his son. "You can look now, Zhenya," he said.

Borya pulled himself up, clinging to his father's shirt, until he was standing. He teetered on unsteady feet, but he managed to release one hand. "Aslan," he said.

Was he ready? One way to find out. Nasan picked up the lion and knelt not more than a foot in front of the baby. "Here, Borya. Come get him."

"You think he can walk?" Daniil said.

"We'll see." Nasan waved the lion. "Here, Borya. Come to *Ana*, and you can have Aslan."

And as the adults watched, the baby let go and tottered three steps before falling forward into Nasan's arms. "Borya, you're walking," she cried as she hugged him. "Clever baby!" She nuzzled his cheek, turned him around to face Daniil, and handed the child the lion. "Take Aslan to *Ata*."

Daniil held his arms out wide. "You can do it, Borya. Bring me the lion." And while his parents and nursemaid watched in awe, Borya repeated the miracle.

"Za-za." The baby dropped his lion at his father's feet. "*Ada. Ama. Aslan.*"

Daniil hugged him too, then picked up the lion. "What does Aslan say?" The baby produced a very creditable roar. "Wonderful. Good lad."

Daniil held out his hand to Nasan. She sat beside him, and Zhenya ladled soup into bowls and placed them in front of both adults, whisking Borya and the lion away with practiced skill.

"Now I know I'm home," Daniil said. "Even if home is a cart on the steppe."

"Yes," Nasan told him. "Tomorrow we will travel again, but wherever you and Borya are is my home."

"So tell me what I missed during my arrest. How was my father when you saw him, and what has been going on at court?"

"That will take the rest of the journey," she said. "I'd better get started. But brace yourself. Epic tales sound tame next to this saga, and I swear every word is true."

⚘

Alexei, Ogodai, and Ruslan were walking through the camp discussing strategy when they noticed a commotion near the women's tent. They strode toward the noise, pushed through the doorway, and stopped as soon as they had crossed the threshold.

Ahead of them Firuza stood tall on her platform, an expression close to shock on her face. Guzel, at Firuza's right, supported her with a discreet arm around her waist. Timur perched at the edge of the platform, his eyes sparkling with curiosity and excitement.

The figure that faced them wore a fringed ankle-length robe made from tanned animal skins and a fur hat with a pointed tip. Light brown plaits no wider than Alexei's little finger dangled in front of the woman's face, and in one hand she held a circular drum—a covered hoop about as wide as his forearm, with a frame perhaps three fingers deep. A pale membrane made from animal skins covered the front of the drum, painted with lines representing the four cardinal directions and meeting at the World Center, the source of harmony. Dozens of small shells decorated drum and robe, shivering and tinkling each time the woman moved, and assorted implements—a brass mirror, a bone spoon, a whisk, a flat paddle for beating the drum— dangled from loops stitched to the hide. To one side Alexei saw the horde's usual shaman, similarly attired. He couldn't see her face either, but he recognized the figure and the stance.

Recalling their last conversation, he realized this must be the promised confession. Three weeks had passed, and Grusha—he guessed, for who else could the second woman be?—had come to fulfill her teacher's command that she tell Firuza the truth about her absences, her selection by the spirits, her desire to train, and her vow of secrecy.

So indeed it proved. The woman bowed. "Great Khatun," she said, her voice clear and strong as Alexei had never heard it. "My teacher"—she indicated the shaman with a sweep of the drum—"commands me to offer you an apology for the distress my cowardice has caused you. Earlier this year, while I was watching your children, a spirit captured me. I didn't dare tell you. The experience terrified me, and I sought out the shaman. She told me to approach you, to ask openly for permission to study with her, but when I refused out of fear, she commanded me to keep silence, no matter what happened, until she herself allowed me to speak. That is where I went, those many times you questioned me, when I left the children with Guzel and told you the khan had summoned me. It was not true. I beg for your forgiveness and ask that you"—another sweeping gesture encompassed the entire tent—"and all those here attend my initiation as your new, junior shaman. It will take place three days from now, at the full moon."

The change in her astonished Alexei. Admittedly they had neither a long nor a close acquaintance, but he would never have guessed she could speak with such power. The mouse had become a tigress.

Firuza gave a strangled sound. She sought Ogodai with her eyes and, when he circled Grusha and joined her on the platform, threw herself into his arms. Over her head he spoke to Grusha, who had not risen from her bow.

"We forgive you," he said. Alexei heard tension in his brother's voice, but Ogodai continued to project the image of a khan, in control of his people and his lands. "Ask the members of the horde for whatever you need. And we will attend your ceremony." He dipped his head at Grusha, who had straightened as soon as he forgave her. "And now, leave us. I wish to be alone with my wife."

Alexei exchanged glances with Ruslan. Without a word the two of them ducked out of the tent and moved to one side to avoid the women who streamed past them.

"Come on," Alexei said. "Let's call for the horses, ride out to the edge of the camp, and send a servant to find us some koumiss. We seem to have brought one mess to a successful conclusion at last, but we still have a war to plan when my brother returns to earth."

Chapter 23

"I AM HONORED THAT YOU HAVE AGREED TO RECEIVE ME, Prince Vasily Vasilyevich." Koshkin bowed to the new ruler of Russia—in effect if not by law—and hoped that his distaste for the man in front of him didn't show. At sixty Prince Vasily was a massive figure with gray hair and pale blue eyes, but he still bore a disturbing resemblance to his nephew, the detested Prince Ilya. "Permit me to congratulate you on your recent nuptials. The daughter of Tsarevich Peter. How you have risen in the world!"

The glower that last comment provoked from Prince Vasily gave Koshkin pause. He hadn't meant to sound sarcastic, but his underlying resentment over his mistreatment at Shuisky hands had slipped into his speech. He must take more care from now on.

Although sarcasm would be hard to resist. Lounging in a chair that bore a distinct resemblance to a throne, wearing robes fit for a tsar, married to the cousin of Grand Prince Ivan himself, receiving his supplicants in the Faceted Palace as if he were royalty, Prince Vasily gave every evidence of placing himself above the Lord's anointed. Nor had Shuisky hesitated to keep Koshkin waiting six weeks for his promised interview.

"What do you want, Koshkin?" Vasily glared from under beetling brows. "I could have you executed as a traitor, given your flight in support of Prince Andrei of Staritsa. Some rumors even place you in Lithuania—evidence of disloyalty on its own, if you travel there without authorization. My respect for Bulat Khan goes only so far."

"Yes, Prince. I know that." Koshkin bowed again for good effect, although he felt anything but humble. "My gratitude to you and to Bulat Khan runs deep. But given what I have discovered about your nephew, I think you may prefer to hear me out. Prince Ilya, I fear, has served his family ill, although no doubt he sought to advance his lineage, as every man does. And there are other witnesses to his crime besides myself."

Prince Vasily's glare vanished in obvious astonishment. "Are you mad? You pushed Bulat Khan to urge this interview on me so that you could slander my nephew?"

"It is not slander, Prince. I have definite proof that Ilya murdered the grand princess, an offense even more heinous than fleeing to avoid the possibility of arrest, which is the worst charge that you can justifiably lodge against me. I see that he concealed his crime from you—indeed, how could he have confessed when doing so would implicate you as well?—so this news must come as a great shock."

Roaring, Prince Vasily struggled to his feet and lunged for Koshkin, who dodged to one side of the fake throne. He had asked to hold this interview in private, and rather to his surprise Prince Vasily had agreed (had Bulat Khan hinted at the need for discretion?). As a result, the room contained no tall-hatted pikemen who might intervene to save him from Shuisky.

"Hear me out." Koshkin extended a pleading hand. "I have no wish to make this information public. What I want is the return of my estate and the restoration of my former position at court. My sons' positions as well. I always served you well, and I will continue to do so."

"That remains to be seen." Grumbling, Shuisky resumed his seat. "I make no promises. Talk."

Good. He was getting somewhere. Koshkin had no idea whether Prince Vasily had in fact known in advance of his nephew's treasonous plans against the throne, but his anger seemed genuine. Most likely he told the truth, and Koshkin would gladly proclaim Vasily's innocence if doing so furthered his own goals. What mattered were the ends, not the means.

"Prince Ilya purchased a poison from a foreigner, perhaps one of the royal physicians," he said. "We have not identified the man. It consisted of the dried leaves and seeds of a tree known as yew, not found in the Russian lands but available to the west and south of us. Bulat Khan and his family recognized it." Good to remind Vasily that others besides Koshkin himself knew of Ilya Shuisky's perfidy.

He decided not to mention the possibility of pregnancy and abortion. He had only the Tatars' word for that, and the charge struck him as even more inflammatory than allegations of murder. "Ilya told his wife to brew it into a tea and administer it to the grand princess, with the result that Elena died. I have a portion of the poison here." He pulled the small packet from his cloak and held it out to Shuisky. "You can verify its nature and what I have said. But make no mistake. I have sent the rest of the poison, as well as a complete record of what I tell you here and a list of the witnesses, to a safe location, where it will remain unopened for as long as I continue in good health. Should anything happen to me …"

He left the sentence unfinished. Whatever Shuisky's faults, Koshkin had never considered the prince stupid. Koshkin had in fact dispatched such a record to Jan Radziwill in Lithuania, with a request to keep it sealed until a member of the Koshkin family required it. And for safety's sake, he had left another with his cousin Kobylin, with similar but more explicit instructions.

Shuisky had listened to this laying out of information with steadily mounting anger, but as Koshkin reached the end, Shuisky rubbed his ample beard and frowned, more in contemplation than in rage. "And my nephew? What do you demand that I do with him?"

Koshkin managed an elaborate shrug. "I care about restoring the standing of my own lineage, not about debasing yours. I would characterize your nephew as dangerous, but I won't speak out against him unless you force my hand—or he does. His fate is and should be for you to decide."

Shuisky grimaced and grumbled, but as Koshkin had calculated, he had little choice but to buy Koshkin's silence. An accusation against his nephew would rebound on him— whether Vasily had ordered the death or not—and his rapid ascent to near-royal power would crash under a combined assault from envious boyars and princes furious at his willingness to profit at their expense.

"Very well," Shuisky said at last. "I will restore your rank as junior boyar and your generalship. You may reclaim your estate from my nephew Ilya. I will tell him you have my authorization. But I'm warning you, Koshkin: give me one good excuse to doubt you, and I'll string you up myself—and Ilya with you."

Koshkin bowed low, although joy filled his chest with the lightness of air, bearing him on a cloud of satisfaction he hadn't experienced for years. "Your generosity overwhelms me, Prince," he said. "I promise you won't regret this decision."

"Get out of here, Koshkin," Shuisky said. "And I repeat, tread carefully."

*

Ogodai and Alexei lost no time in putting the camp on a war footing once more. The most skilled female warriors of the combined camps escorted their fellow women and children, including a grumbling Timur, to the river bank, where they would defend the families from whatever dangers might threaten them. Firuza accompanied them, lamenting the pregnancy that prevented her from joining the female guards.

Alexei, watching them depart, had a bright mental image of his younger sister. "How Nasan would love to join them!" he said to Ogodai, mounted to his left. As soon as they saw the women and children on their way, they planned to hold a strategy session with the beys and Ruslan.

"Yes, too bad she's not here," Ogodai replied. "Her big chance to become a warrior heroine, and she's missing it. She'll be livid when she hears."

"Maybe." Alexei thought of the last letter from their sister. "But not if she's launching raids on monasteries and solving mysteries in her spare time. You think she succeeded in freeing Daniil?"

"We'll know soon," Ogodai said. "If she did, they should arrive any day."

His words proved prophetic. Before everyone invited to the strategy session had time to settle into place, they poured out of the tent once more in response to the noise of approaching troops. Alexei stopped in midstride, shaking his head in surprise at the sight of a clean-shaven young man on a bay horse, accompanied by two hundred or so warriors bearing the banners of Bulat Khan and the Russian St. Nicholas, as well as a lone cart and what at first glance seemed to be a boy on a sorrel mare that Alexei recognized as Sorkhokhtani. The "boy," obviously Nasan, threw one leg over her saddle with a typical steppe flourish and sprang to the ground, then raced to greet him.

"*Aby*," she cried as she embraced him. "It's so good to see you. Oh, Maria will be delighted to have you home!" He had no chance to respond before she ran to hug Ogodai.

The clean-shaven man whom Alexei now recognized as Daniil dismounted with more caution than his wife. Thinner than Alexei remembered, Daniil came to join them with less than his usual catlike fluidity of movement, but his grip when they clasped hands was strong and his smile warm. The bear hug he exchanged with Ogodai caused Daniil to wince but not withdraw. From these details Alexei concluded that Daniil's captors had treated him ill but that he was on the way to recovery.

The cart rolled to a stop, and a young woman emerged from the back carrying a toddler who could only be Borya. Nasan went to collect the baby and present him to his uncles, only to stop midway. "But where is Firuza? The women?"

Ogodai pointed in the direction of the Don. "We sent them away, *sengel*. The camp's on the brink of war. You and Borya and your nurse should join them. They can't be far ahead of you; they left"—he stopped to judge the position of the sun—"about an hour ago, I'd guess."

"I can stay and fight," Nasan said, as Alexei had guessed she would.

"They need you there," Ogodai told her with admirable aplomb. "Firuza can't join them because of her condition, so they're one archer short."

"Oh, very well." Nasan, still holding Borya, stood on tiptoe to kiss her husband. He caught her round the waist to steady her. She soon dropped back onto her heels and held out the child to Ogodai. "But bless your nephew before I go. You haven't even greeted him. And don't endanger my husband, if you please. I just finished patching him together from the last time."

Daniil glanced at the sky, as if seeking divine intervention. It didn't take much imagination to guess how little he appreciated this special pleading. But he didn't complain, perhaps because he too could hear the note of anxiety in his wife's voice.

Ogodai grinned at his sworn brother. "I'll wrap him in sheep's wool and felt," he promised.

"The hell you will," Daniil muttered. But Nasan laughed, handed her son to the nurse, hugged the three of them once more, remounted, and consented to follow the path of the departing women and children.

Ogodai sent a half-dozen of the Kolychev warriors to see her and the cart safely to their destination, with orders to remain at the women's camp to aid in its defense if need be.

At least, that was what he said. Alexei strongly suspected that his younger brother wanted a guarantee that their sister would not sneak back to join them at the worst possible moment. A decision he applauded, since he wouldn't put that possibility past her for the length of time it took him to draw a single breath.

From the relieved expression on Daniil's face, he guessed that Nasan's husband saw things the same way.

With Nasan successfully diverted, the leaders settled in to make plans. Alexei, surveying the room, counted fourteen heads in addition to his own: Ogodai, Ruslan, Daniil, Ogodai's five clan leaders supplemented by Rafik Argyn, and Azamat Bey with his four-member council.

For simplicity's sake, Ogodai had abandoned his khan's platform and taken the center-north seat in a large circle that spread around the entire interior of the tent. It didn't escape Alexei's notice that Yusuf, the young Mangyt bey whom he and his brother so distrusted, occupied the least prestigious position at center-south, right in front of the door. Kazbek sat cross-legged next to his reluctant student, "to keep an iron hand on his shoulder," in Kazbek's own words.

Yusuf Bey would soon exchange this unwanted tutor for another, though. Kazbek intended to assist in the planning, then to supervise the warriors charged with guarding the women and children near the Don. The other leaders would take direct or indirect part in the attack—even Yusuf Bey, under strict oversight by warriors with more experience. Alexei could only hope that Kazbek's lessons would stick.

The glower on Yusuf's face underlined his dissatisfaction with these plans, but no one paid much attention to him. Alexei promptly forgot about the fractious young bey and concentrated on the discussion among those with opinions worth hearing.

"We can't surprise them this time," Ogodai said. "Sheikh-Mamai has gathered a larger force, we have to assume with the intent of avenging the defeat we dealt him before. And since his scouts chased ours almost to the doorway of this tent, he knows where to attack. We must move out and meet him on a ground of our choosing with the largest number of men our combined hordes can provide."

"Agreed," Kazbek said. "And as soon as possible. Thanks to Azamat Bey and your honored father, in the person of Daniil Nikolaevich, we have a good four hundred more fighters than we did before. At this point delay is misguided. We risk a surprise attack on *our* camp if we don't move soon. What advantages have we?"

"Knowledge of the terrain," Azamat said. Alexei signaled his agreement with a nod. His initial unfavorable assessment of their young ally had undergone revision upward in the course of this campaign: although inexperienced, Azamat lacked the arrogance that prevented Yusuf from accepting and learning from his own mistakes.

"My people have spent summers here since our great-grandfathers lay in their cradles, if not longer," Azamat went on. "Yours too. Sheikh-Mamai hails from beyond the Great Mother River."

"I suggest we follow the northern tributary," Malik Shirin said. "Keep the river at our backs, ensuring we have water for both the horses and ourselves and preventing any attack from the rear."

"Good idea." Alexei tested his memories of the northern tributary, placing it in reference to Sheikh-Mamai's camp. The merchants had reported being attacked from the northeast, and indeed the camp was in that direction, but the scouts had discovered that it lay much closer to the Don River than expected. "If we move quickly, we can draw him away from this camp."

"And if we spread out along the tributary, we may surround him." Ogodai bent forward to address his brother-in-law. "You've kept quiet, Daniil. Ideas? Suggestions?"

"It's not my terrain." Daniil sipped from a cup of the ever-present koumiss, grimaced at the taste, and set the cup aside. "How do our troops compare to the enemy's in terms of size and strength?"

Ruslan answered the question. "When we fought them before, the size of our camp about equaled theirs. Perhaps we had a small advantage. As Kazbek noted, we have a larger force now, but so does Sheikh-Mamai. So at best we can hope that our two sides are still roughly equal. We can also assume the same level of ferocity. Our one weakness is that we have families—sent away but still vulnerable. Sheikh-Mamai's horde has secreted all but the fighters in some location we have yet to discover."

"Then we should indeed move as soon as we have a plan," Daniil said. "Today. Tomorrow at the latest. Before they find out where you sent the women and children."

"Agreed," Ogodai said. "Malik Shirin's suggestion pleases me, and Daniil Nikolaevich and Kazbek Argyn are correct about the timing. Azamat Bey is also right: our knowledge of the terrain gives us the advantage we need, despite our obligation to protect this camp and our families. Malik, you take Yusuf Bey and the combined Shirin and Mangyt forces and head up the tributary to a point beyond Sheikh-Mamai's camp. Leave as soon as we conclude this meeting. You will support our left flank, led by Alexei Sultan and Ruslan Sultan."

He glared at the Mangyt bey. "Malik is in charge. If I hear so much as a whisper that you disobeyed or argued with him, I'll not only kick you off my council but exile you from my horde and our combined ancestors. Understood?"

When Yusuf mumbled agreement, Ogodai went on. "Azamat, you and Rafik Argyn take the section closest to the Don. You support the right flank, which Daniil and I will lead. Your men and Malik's together must extend across the middle, so that you can fall in behind the flanks as we move forward. At first light we form a pincer and attack from three sides at once. Questions?"

There were no questions. Before the sun reached its zenith, the warriors rode out.

However good the strategy, it was unrealistic to expect it to work exactly as planned. The initial step went well—Alexei silently commended the discipline with which Ogodai's troops spread out along the small tributary, then slowly formed the shape of an unstrung bow, the two ends advancing more or less evenly toward the enemy's camp. As commanded, he and Ruslan led the pincer to the left. Ogodai and Daniil mirrored them on the right.

For what seemed like a long time—unless the perception reflected no more than the warped expectations created by the knowledge of battle to come—the rolling grasslands lay undisturbed ahead of them. But as the sun reached its zenith, a circle of tents fronted by spirit banners became visible.

With a flash of unease Alexei noted the color of the horsetails that dangled from the spirit banners: black, for war. The enemy anticipated their arrival. How would that change their prospects for success?

At the center of the camp stood the bright yellow banners he remembered from their last attack: Sheikh-Mamai's standard. Another sign of potential trouble: in a camp at peace the standards would not be clustered in such a way, as if to mark the leader's location.

"Are they expecting us?" Alexei asked.

"Looks like it." Ruslan turned to warn the troops. "Has your brother seen them?"

"Hard to say. He's approaching from a different angle." Alexei tapped the nearest rider with his whip. "Alert the khan. The enemy may be waiting for us."

The messenger rode off. Alexei saw him reach Ogodai. A brief exchange, and the rider headed back their way. As he came within hailing distance, a volley of arrows launched from the camp.

"Shields up," Alexei yelled. "Shoot at will!"

All around him the snap of bowstrings mingled with the thud of arrows hitting shields. The warning came too late for the messenger, who fell forward over his saddle. Ruslan grabbed for his reins, and the man gasped, "Khan says faster." He slid from the saddle and lay still. The arrow protruding from his back left no doubt as to the reason. Or to his fate.

Ruslan relayed the order, and their pincer broke into a gallop. To his right Alexei saw Ogodai's pincer galloping with them. Risking a glance over his shoulder, he noticed that the warriors in the middle, who should be moving forward as well, stood dithering in the field, their backs still close to the water. Rafik Argyn and Malik Shirin were shouting at them with no obvious effect.

"Take charge," Alexei told Ruslan. "I'm going to rally the center."

"God preserve you," Ruslan said. His raised arm signaled to the warriors that they should follow him.

"And you." Alexei peeled off from the left pincer and wheeled Ajdar in the direction of the milling troops. As he reached them, he saw Daniil Kolychev galloping toward him and concluded that Ogodai had recognized the problem as well.

"You take that side," he shouted to Daniil. "I'll handle this one." Daniil raised a hand in agreement and honed in on Azamat Bey, chivvying the bey's mounted riders into a ragged advance.

Ahead of them the pincers halted under withering fire. The leaders didn't retreat, but the screams of men and horses filled the air, and falling bodies left gaps in the lines. Alexei had no difficulty imagining the fear and confusion, the agony of watching friends die. Without reinforcements the lines would break, turning defeat from a possibility into reality. He needed to bring the reserve force up. Now.

"What are you waiting for?" he demanded of Yusuf Bey. "Can't you see what's happening? Didn't you hear Malik ordering the horses into position? Get moving, you dolt, before you lose us the battle!"

"He told me not to go anywhere," Yusuf said in a sulky voice. "It was bad enough with Kazbek. Now Shirin's giving me orders, and he's no older than you. Thinks I haven't the brains of a sheep."

Alexei cuffed him so hard on the ear that his hat fell off. "Nor do you. Indulging in childish pets in the middle of a war? Stay here and mope if you like. I'm taking control of your troops." He raised his voice to a battleground roar and directed it at the milling warriors. "Men, with me. Ride as if your lives depend on it, because they do. And those of your wives and children too. Do you want them to be dragged off in chains, weeping over your dead bodies?"

The standard bearer who never left Alexei's side waved his banner. The scarlet winged horse rippled in the wind. "For the khan!" Alexei shouted. "Go!"

The answering roar came from five hundred throats. "For the khan!" The riders took off like bullets from a musket, and Ajdar shot after them. Glancing over his shoulder once more, Alexei saw Rafik Argyn galloping at Daniil's side, Azamat close behind them. Malik Shirin, near the middle of the rush, moved up fast and soon rode at Alexei's right. Yusuf plodded along in the rear.

No matter. With help from Daniil, Malik, Rafik, and Azamat, Alexei had rallied the troops. His brother and Ruslan would get the backup they deserved. Ogodai could deal with Yusuf later.

The arrival of the missing center turned the tide. In the heat of battle Alexei couldn't take time to check who lived and who died, but his heart warmed at the sight of Ogodai and Ruslan riding side by side toward the camp, their surviving warriors forming a solid mass at their backs. Malik and Rafik passed him, Azamat a horse length or two behind them and the rest of their forces streaming in his wake.

Alexei nodded to Daniil, who directed his horse right, toward Ogodai. The slightest tug on the reins sent Ajdar racing left to catch up with Ruslan. Then they were amid the tents, heading for the standards clustered at the center, where they expected to find Sheikh-Mamai and his personal guard.

Alexei's sword rose and fell, defending his horse and himself. When he had a clear line of sight, arrows flew from his nimble fingers. The heady furor of battle invigorated him. He thought of nothing beyond the next target, the next opening, the ultimate goal. In the close quarters of the camp, among makeshift paths filled with enemies, Ajdar of necessity slowed his pace. Reaching Ruslan and Alexei's own men became more difficult. But his winged horse banners still flew free amid his father's nine horsetails, so he knew that at least some part of his force survived.

The enemy's clustered yellow standards were toppling, one by one, as Ogodai's warriors forced their way to the middle of the camp. The last one fell as Alexei slashed his way past another contingent of defenders and reached the main tent. Daniil broke through at almost the same moment. Alexei rode to join him. Shields raised, they turned as one to survey the situation.

As tended to happen on the steppe, Sheikh-Mamai's supporters were deserting him as their defeat became more likely. Quite a few had already dropped their weapons. Some continued to fight and were cut down, but even as Alexei and Daniil watched, many more either fled or fell to their knees and begged to switch sides.

"Almost done," Alexei told Daniil while scanning the mob of screaming warriors. He could still see the banners, but they lay beyond Sheikh-Mamai's fallen standards. The enemy's tent concealed Alexei's own men from view. Yusuf was nowhere in sight, although Alexei caught a glimpse of Ogodai, leading a mop-up charge composed mostly of Shirin warriors with a spattering of Mangyts led by Rafik Argyn. The Mangyts' enthusiastic response to the khan's commands suggested that they enjoyed their reprieve from the yoke of their juvenile bey. A large gathering of Azamat's forces closed in from the opposite side.

"Ogodai's better at this than I expected," Daniil said. "I always knew he had fighting skills, but he was such a good second-in-command to your father. I never thought he would grow into a khan as strong as this." He gave Alexei a rueful smile. "Goes to show you, doesn't it? He'll be Bulat one day."

"Now there's a terrifying thought." Alexei returned the smile. "One Bulat in the family is more than enough. But you're right. I never gave Ogodai credit either. I saw him as my little brother, the favored one. We could join him, but since he seems to have matters under control, let's oversee those bent on surrendering, shall we? Better that they not get the chance to change their minds and attack from behind."

"Heaven forfend," Daniil said. "Your brother looks set to win the battle. Let's not lose him the war. Although it seems strange not to be in the thick of the fight."

"Oh, there are enough troublemakers on this battlefield to keep every leader occupied," Alexei assured him. "That lot over there, for example, were on Sheikh-Mamai's side when we arrived. Now they look like they're arguing over what to do. Let's convince them that switching sides will benefit them. We needn't mention that it will benefit us too."

"Lead the way." Daniil tipped his shield in the direction of the group Alexei had indicated.

Alexei laughed and urged his horse into motion. "My pleasure."

The mood in the camp that night was bittersweet. Due in part to the enemy's strength but even more to the delay in the center's advance, casualties in the pincers had been heavy. One loss that few mourned was Yusuf Bey, killed by stragglers precisely because he had lagged so far behind the rest of the army that no one was around to protect him. But since by general acclaim his tribe chose almost at once to elect Azamat, a fellow Mangyt, to take Yusuf's place, Ogodai's horde could only benefit from the change.

But Ogodai, Ruslan, Malik, Azamat, Rafik, and many of Alexei's closest warriors had survived. Most of the merchants' captives also returned unharmed, if worn down by the rough treatment they had receivd as slaves. The khan summoned the imam, who prayed for the fallen, then oversaw the burial of as many as possible before the sun set. Only then did the warriors collect the women and children—a reunion that brought more wails of sorrow and shouts of joy—before returning to their own camp.

Yet despite the pervasive atmosphere of grief, fine weather on a long midsummer evening, the satisfaction of having routed a dangerous enemy, and relief among those who had returned combined to create a feast that surpassed any Alexei could remember. The members of the horde set up spits here and there about the camp, piled food nearby, organized games and singing in which men and women mingled—sometimes participating side by side, more often with one group watching the other. Shrieking children dashed amid the crowd, followed by the camp's dogs and chased by harried parents who hauled them back from the flames in the nick of time. Alexei himself grabbed Timur more than once. Nasan, he noted, had tied a long silk sash about her son's waist so that he could toddle unharmed. Borya staggered hither and yon, arms outstretched to catch whatever the bigger boys were throwing, seldom managing more than a few steps before tumbling to the grass and resolutely struggling to his feet once more, until his father swung the child up onto his shoulders, where Borya clung to his hair.

Alexei was considering joining them when Ruslan came over, twisting his hands in a gesture that indicated discomfort, a grim expression on his face. "What's troubling you?" Alexei asked. "The casualties among our men? We lost too many good warriors today. That idiot Yusuf. If the enemy hadn't killed him, I'd have been tempted to do him in myself."

"That, of course," Ruslan said. "But I also have news I suspect you don't want to hear. I've decided to stay here, on the steppe, rather than return to Moscow. I miss the grasslands, and your brother promises to find me a wife. I can't marry in Russia unless I convert, but here I can live a full life. Daniil and I will work together, managing the khan's troops."

It was an unexpected blow but not an incomprehensible one. Ruslan spoke the truth, and the yearning to remain on the steppe was one that Alexei shared. Only his love for Maria and the knowledge that his father needed his help, whether Bulat admitted that inconvenient truth or not, pulled Alexei in the direction of Moscow.

"I understand," he said. "Ogodai's lucky to have you fighting on his side. I hope he appreciates that." A memory struck him, and he grinned. "But watch out for the doe-eyed beauties. I don't want to have to explain to Timur that one of them sent you to join your ancestors."

"Don't remind me." Ruslan groaned but returned the smile. "And you keep an eye on that stripling of yours. He'll be yearning for doe-eyed beauties soon enough."

"So he will," Alexei said. "I'm sending him back here for fostering when he turns twelve, so I'll count on you to steer him straight."

Laughing, Ruslan raised a hand and left. Alexei watched him until he disappeared among the crowd. It felt like the end of an era—a marker of how far he had traveled since the early days of his exile.

He was still digesting the news when Ogodai, waving what looked like a rib bone, appeared. "We did it!" he announced by way of greeting. "It's too bad Sheikh-Mamai ran off before the end, the bastard, but the men who surrendered insist he's desperate to cross the Volga. I've scouts heading out tomorrow morning to verify that they're telling the truth. But I doubt he'll trouble us again."

"So do I," Alexei said. "After two such routs no one will follow him if he tries. Your grazing lands should be safe now." He punched his brother playfully in the shoulder. "You can always send for me if they aren't."

"You're welcome to stay." Ogodai studied the bone as if not sure whether to continue, then added, "We couldn't have done it without you. Especially that final battle. The lines were about to break when you and Daniil rallied the men. Sheikh-Mamai would have overwhelmed us."

He dropped the bone, which a dog swiped the moment it hit the ground, rubbed his hand on the side of his trousers, and held it out. "Thank you."

Alexei regarded him with narrowed eyes, then bypassed the extended hand and hugged him. "We're brothers," he said. "Let's try not to forget that in the future."

Ogodai slapped him on the back as he withdrew. "I agree. For starters, I'll show you where to find the best meat on the steppe." He grinned. "The rate everyone else is stuffing themselves, you'll go hungry if you stand and watch."

"Lead the way." Alexei returned the slap. "Then let's go and find out how many people our little sister shot today. I wouldn't be surprised if she outdid us both."

Ogodai's roar of laughter pierced even the surrounding din. "I'd be surprised if she didn't!"

Chapter 24

Moscow, July 1538

ALEXEI FOLLOWED THE SOUND OF HIS WIFE'S SINGING—
not the lullaby she'd been crooning the last time he returned
from campaign but the kind of playful song that mothers use
to teach colors and sounds to their infants. Timur walked at
his side, then dashed ahead, running toward Sumbeka's sitting
room. By the time Alexei caught up, cries of welcome had sent
the singing to the land of memory. Standing in the doorway, he
saw first Maria and Alexander—sitting up on his own—then
Sumbeka and Lyuba, on the floor next to her nephew. Bulat sat
to one side, regarding his family with magisterial calm.

Timur, as usual, took the lead. "*Babai*, *Äbi*, Auntie,
everyone—we've arrived." He pulled at the collar of his shirt.
"And I'm a warrior. I have a scar!" Lyuba gasped and ran to
hug Alexei, then Timur.

Maria jumped to her feet and scooped Alexander off the
floor. Alexei caught her around the waist as she said, "You're
safe, both of you. Oh, you can't imagine how delighted I am
to see you!"

"And I you, my darling." He kissed her. When he looked up
again, Timur was showing an admiring Lyuba his scar.

"He's recovered?" Maria asked. "He seems well enough."

"Completely," Alexei assured her. "He has sufficient energy for ten boys. And he's proud as an eagle to have that scar to display." When she laughed, he took Alexander from her arms and lifted him to shoulder height. "Look at this fine fellow, sitting up by himself." He nuzzled the child's cheek. "Is he crawling yet?"

"Almost. He scoots on his bottom and wriggles on his tummy, but he hasn't quite figured out how to straighten his arms. Did you see Nasan and Daniil? Borya?" She moved aside so that Sumbeka and Bulat could come forward—once they had paid proper respect to Timur's scar, of course. The boy was already showing Lyuba how he'd received the injury in the first place, with appropriate groans and gestures.

Alexei withheld his answer long enough to greet his stepmother and his father. "I'm glad to see you both," he told them. "I have much news. But to answer Maria's question, yes, Nasan and Daniil reached the horde safely. Daniil, although not restored to his full strength, distinguished himself in the battle against Sheikh-Mamai. Nasan enjoyed guarding the women and children, although in fact Sheikh-Mamai never had a chance to threaten them. And Borya, who I'm sure is even more important than his parents"—he sent his wife a teasing smile—"is not only walking but talking, if you consider a dozen or so mangled words talking."

"Well, what else would they be?" Sumbeka demanded. "Wait till it's your child saying '*Ata*,' and you won't be so picky."

"I remember," Alexei said, laughing. "I know, it's a wonderful thing. Ogodai and Firuza send their love. Daniil and Nasan also. And Ruslan sends his respects. He decided to stay with the horde."

"And Sheikh-Mamai?" Bulat asked in the gruff voice that his son had learned concealed some softer sentiment that Bulat didn't wish to acknowledge.

"Defeated." Alexei spoke to that hidden concern. "He escaped, but I doubt he'll be back anytime soon. Word has it that he's fled across the Volga with his personal guard. No one else would follow him. We even captured his standards. A large number of his warriors have switched their service to Ogodai, who looks to be well on his way to building a good-sized khanate. And we secured the grazing grounds, both winter and summer, as well as establishing an alliance with the neighboring bey."

"You and Ogodai are getting along better, then?" Maria asked.

He caressed her cheek. "Yes. We're brothers again, and not only in name. I missed you and Alexander, but I was glad to return to the steppe for a while and more than glad to make peace with Ogodai."

She tipped her head to one side. "And Guzel?"

What was she imagining? He stroked her face once more. "You can ask Timur. She was angry when I arrived, angry when he was wounded while with me, and angry when I left with him. In the interim she exchanged perhaps a dozen civil words with me. But I didn't try to overcome her anger either. I didn't want to see her, only to give Timur an opportunity to spend time with his mother."

She nodded. "I understand."

He leaned forward and whispered in her ear, "I've been gone a long time, *kaderle*. Can we not be alone?" In response to her murmured "I'd love that," he placed Alexander on the floor, where the baby scooted toward Lyuba and Timur. Alexei clasped his wife's hand in his and took a few steps toward the door.

Bulat's voice sounded behind him. "Welcome home, son. You did well. I'm proud of you."

Astonished, Alexei turned. He couldn't remember the last compliment he'd received from his father, let alone a beaming smile like the one Bulat bestowed on him now.

When he didn't respond, Bulat raised both eyebrows. "Moscow *is* your home, is it not? Where will the Russian branch of our lineage go, if not through you and Alexander?"

Alexei's answering smile gave way to rueful laughter. Who but Bulat would present this evidence of his eldest son's full restoration to the family in a manner suggesting that only an idiot would not have seen such a momentous announcement coming?

"Thank you, *Ata*." He squeezed Maria's fingers, and she squeezed his in return. "Indeed, Moscow is my home, and this is my family. I'm glad to be back. With all of you."

❦

Koshkin strolled the courtyard of his restored estate, Father Spiridon at his side. "Ah, home," he told the priest. "You have no idea how sweet the sight. I thought I would never see this place—or for a while, this land—again."

"The structure seems sound, despite its months of neglect." The priest indicated a door jamb, a lock, a cornice in need of repair. "A few jobs for the returned carpenters, but naught they can't fix, and quickly."

"Agreed." Koshkin jerked his chin in the direction of a middle-aged man whose ample girth indicated that the staff in Shuya had not deprived him of food. "The steward will take care of it. It's good to see my servants restored, as well as the property. Prince Vasily made a huge fuss before he yielded, but he did in the end yield handsomely."

"It pleases me to have a congregation again," the priest said.

"And what of the maids Ilya forced into service? Have you spoken with them?" Koshkin stopped in the middle of the courtyard, planted his feet against the stones, and swiveled his head from side to side, reveling in the sight that met his eyes.

His lands, his estate, his people, his court position—each small piece of evidence confirmed that his exile had ended at last.

Father Spiridon's kindly face creased in a frown. "Some resisted, without much success. One or two bore children they didn't want, and at least one of those abandoned her babe at the nearest convent. Most yielded to his demands as the best they could expect. A great sinner, Prince Ilya. That he indulges his lusts is bad; that he corrupts others means that his fate will not be a happy one on the Day of Dreadful Judgment. Or before, now that his uncle has confined him to that cell in a Kremlin tower on trumped-up charges of dishonest dealings."

"They aren't trumped-up," Koshkin said with a bitterness he couldn't conceal, although hearing about Prince Ilya's detention had been a pleasant surprise. Ilya had embarrassed his uncle and been punished, not for having caused Grand Princess Elena's death but for getting caught in a crime the exposure of which threatened his clan. "Ilya Shuisky couldn't deal honestly if he tried. I hope he stays locked up. The thought of him roaming around with vengeance on his mind keeps me up at night."

"A truly wicked man." Father Spiridon hesitated before asking, "Will our lady rejoin us, now that you have returned home?"

Koshkin shuddered at the question. Even the sweetness of revenge could not render the subject of his marriage less painful. "I don't know," he told the priest in a voice brusquer than he intended. "When I saw her in Vilnius, she claimed to be happier there than she ever was in Moscow. I believe she had in mind the restrictions placed on boyar wives rather than her marriage."

"Will you divorce her if she doesn't return?" Father Spiridon gripped the staff he carried as if he hated to ask that question. "It's not a sin if the Church grants you permission, but that seldom happens."

Divorce her? I should, if I can no longer have her. If I don't want her.

But the truth was that he did want her despite everything she'd said, everything she'd done, even her implicit threat of using the deadly nightshade on him. He couldn't bear to shut the door on hope.

"Perhaps someday," he said, meaning never. "I've no need to remarry, though. Seven children are enough. And she may yet change her mind. I dare not travel to Vilnius at present. But if the right diplomatic mission comes along, we'll see."

Spiridon leaped at the change of subject. "Your children, what of them? Lady Maria's back with her husband, and Lady Varvara still has your younger sons in Murom. Have the older boys regained their rank at court?"

"Not at court. Bulat Khan has requested that Mikhail remain in his service. And at his house." Koshkin grimaced. He hadn't forgiven Bulat for his own arrest and confinement in the harem—or Mikhail for taking the khan's side over his own father's—but he did owe Bulat a debt for his ultimate assistance, which had made Koshkin's attainment of his goals possible. "Foma seems happy enough with his posting to Murom, where he can alleviate the burdens of military life at Varvara's house."

He didn't mention Maria's ongoing refusal to speak with her father or allow her sister Lyuba any contact with him. Or that Mikhail, too, kept his distance, heedless of the risk Koshkin had taken on his family's behalf. "Mikhail will come back to this house in due course," he said instead. "Until he does, service under Bulat will do him good. Let him learn how a real autocrat behaves. I need to ensure that Prince Vasily Shuisky doesn't forget how much he owes me. It will be easier to do that without a host of distractions in the house."

One of the kidnapped maids appeared, weeping, at the periphery of his vision. Koshkin touched the priest's arm. "A parishioner in need, Father."

Spiridon excused himself and set off across the courtyard. As soon as he separated from Koshkin, the girl darted toward the priest, dropped to one knee, and kissed his hand. Father Spiridon patted her head and said words Koshkin could not hear, then urged her to her feet and escorted her toward the family chapel.

Koshkin watched them go, again relishing the reality of his return.

Life was good. He had done what he set out to do almost five years ago. His descendants would remember his name with awe, due to the advancement he had secured for their clan. And he had a new set of plans in the works.

Yes, Shuiskys beware. Koshkin's ascent had just begun.

Nasan stood at the door of her new home and recalled the day—was it only four years ago?—when she had pleaded with the grandmothers to let her father marry her to a nomadic chieftain. How she had longed for a white felt tent facing south and a life on the steppe, where no one expected women to sit in cloistered rooms plunging their embroidery needles into harmless fabrics with no greater concern on their minds than the shape of a leaf or the arrival of their next child. How she had yearned for a place where she could practice her swordsmanship and her archery, ride from dawn to dusk, win a reputation as a heroine of renown. How she had wanted to imitate the women of the epic tales, defend her honor and her man, mother a race of heroes.

Daniil came up behind her and wrapped his arms around her waist. She leaned against him, treasuring the warmth of his hold and the staccato sounds of her son's attempts at speech. Outside, the lowing of the herds mingled with the rumble of an approaching storm, but the felt over their heads, extending to cover the smoke hole in the absence of a hearth fire, would keep out the wind and the rain. She had her tent and more: a husband she loved, an adorable son to carry on their line, and perhaps someday a daughter to raise as a heroine in her own right.

"Happy?" Daniil said into her neck.

She pressed closer to his chest, then turned to face him. "Happy," she said. "Happy doesn't begin to capture what I feel. And what of you? Do you miss Russia?"

"Not so long as I have you, wife of mine." He took her hand and led her toward the center of the tent, where Borya played with his nursemaid and his lion. As he pulled her down beside him, he added, "And to think there was a time when I didn't want to marry you."

Nasan laughed and kissed him. "Nor I you, husband. But the grandmothers knew best. They always do."

Thus my family transmitted its tales to me. Thus have I written them down, so that my children will know that they descend from a line of warriors and that Father Sky and Mother Earth, under different names, continue to guide them along the road between birth and death and await them in the hereafter.

I, Lyuba—short for Lyubov, which means Love—noblewoman of the Russian lands, wife and sister to Tatar khans and sultans, call on you to retell the legends for each new generation, embroidering them as needed to impart their essence to your listeners. For the heritage we cherish as our past lays the stepping stones for our future.

Historical Note

LET'S BE CLEAR. NO ONE KNOWS WHAT KILLED ELENA Glinskaya. But even in 1538 the sudden death of a woman aged somewhere between twenty-eight and thirty, outside of childbirth, aroused comment. Many people at the time assumed poison, as they did in reference to any unexplained death. I took that idea and ran with it. Fyodor Koshkin and Ilya Shuisky are both fictional characters, but their families and motivations are real.

When archeologists exhumed Elena in 2001, she had high levels of mercury in her bones. Mercury was an ingredient in cosmetics at the time, although the scientists ruled out that explanation for her death. Because of the ambiguity, I chose other poisons, known before 1600 but impossible to trace given the technology of the day.

The allegations of Elena's affair with Telepnev are also just that, rumors based on the reality that her husband was married for twenty years without issue, then another four before his first son, later known as Ivan the Terrible, was born. These rumors also circulated at the time, including in the lands bordering Russia.

It is best not to take such allegations too seriously: women in power, from Queen Cleopatra and Empress Wu of China to Hillary Clinton and Angela Merkel, have often endured attacks on their looks, demeanor, or morals. Elena Glinskaya was no exception to this rule. And although often described by historians as young and handsome, Telepnev first appears in the service records in 1505, suggesting that he could not have been born later than 1490 (fifteen was the normal age of entering government service at that time, but we have no guarantee that the earliest mention of his name marks his initial assignment). That would make him at least eighteen to twenty years older than Elena, or in his forties by the time her husband died—none of which either precludes or predetermines the possibility of romance.

The pregnancy, however, is a complete fabrication. In an age without reliable birth control it seems likely that any affair would sooner or later lead to pregnancy in a healthy young woman who had already borne two sons, and while I was researching poisons that might have been available in that time and place, I discovered that yew leaves were used as an abortifacient and often led to death in the event of an overdose. Princess Nadezhda was in the right place at the right time and with the right motivation to unwittingly cause a tragedy. Means, motive, and opportunity may not always solve a crime outside the realm of detective fiction, but they certainly aid in the creation of one. And so this story was born.

On a more mundane level, the deaths of Prince Andrei of Staritsa and Grand Princess Elena receive such brief treatment in the Muscovite annals that we have little more to go on than the day and time of their deaths and a notation as to where they were interred. As a result, we have no definite information about their funerals, except for one notation in a 1550s chronicle that Elena was buried on the same day that she died—highly unusual for a grand princess at the time, although "on the same day" is itself not always as unambiguous a description as one might expect. In Andrei's case, because he died in prison, we don't even know if he had a proper state funeral with the nobility in attendance; that he does here is based on the needs of the present book. Otherwise, the information about royal funerals, such as that they took place at night, comes from Grigory Kotoshikhin, a seventeenth-century clerk who fled to Sweden and left a description of Russia in his own time. How much of the ceremonial Kotoshikhin describes was already in use in the 1530s is anyone's guess.

The Monastery of St. Daniil the Stylite—now the headquarters of the Russian Orthodox Church and the patriarchal residence, its bells restored from Harvard University in 2008—was in fact deserted in 1538 for the reasons Maria indicates. It came back into use in 1560, when Grand Prince Ivan, by then crowned as tsar and thirty years old, revived it. Whether it was ever used as a prison, I don't know, but imprisoning noblemen in monasteries was far from unheard-of in the sixteenth century. Again, Daniil's presence there fits the needs of this story better than the next most likely alternative: his captivity at a noble estate, where Nasan would encounter much greater difficulty in freeing him even with the assistance of her father's troops.

For those encountering Nasan, Daniil, and their extended family for the first time, a note on the Tatar words sprinkled throughout the book. Here most of them express relationships, which Tatars even today often use in preference to names (the custom, now largely confined to older women, of showing respect by avoiding a husband's name is an extension of this practice). The terms given here—*ata* (father), *ana* (mother), *aby* (uncle or older brother), *ené* (younger brother), *sengel* (younger sister, with the "ng" as in song), *apa* (aunt or older sister), *babai* (grandfather), *äbi* (grandmother), *kilen* (daughter-in-law), *kaenata* (father-in-law), and *kaenana* (mother-in-law)—may not be exactly those common in the sixteenth century, but they are close. Alexei should call his stepmother *uti ana*, rather than mother, but that seemed to introduce an unnecessary complication. The correct address in Russian, even in the 1530s, for a khan's daughter or daughter-in-law was *tsarevna*, just as *khan* was translated as *tsar*, *khatun* as *tsaritsa*, and *sultan* as *tsarevich*.

Last, let me say a few words about Lithuania, the portrayal of which in this book may surprise my readers. In the modern West people do not generally think of Lithuania or Poland as hotbeds of humanist culture or even as states of significant size and political importance.

Both preconceptions are wrong. In the 1530s Poland-Lithuania, united under the Jagiellonian dynasty although not yet a single political entity, was huge, encompassing much of modern-day Belarus and Ukraine. It was also culturally and diplomatically tied to many of the other Eurasian states: Hungary, the Holy Roman Empire, Italy, Spain, France, and the Ottoman Empire—as well as Muscovy. Polish and Lithuanian students attended Italian universities. King and Grand Duke Sigismund I "the Old" married Bona Sforza, a relative of the Borgia family (and equally suspected of using poisons against her enemies), in 1517. He imported Italian architects and rebuilt Cracow and Vilnius according to modified Italian styles. By the middle of the sixteenth century Poland-Lithuania could lay claim to a reputation for limited monarchy, a functioning legislature (albeit one confined to the nobility), religious tolerance—including of its Jewish community—and an acquaintance with Renaissance culture that Muscovy could not match, despite Russia's own influx of Italian architects and technicians. The Protestant Reformation also made headway in Poland and its allied states, especially Lithuania and Livonia—the former bailiwick of the Order of Teutonic Knights, which fell under Lithuanian, then Polish, control at this time.

Although the Radziwill clan was prominent in Poland-Lithuania and did include a member called Jan, for this book I borrowed only his name. And although I did make an effort not to contradict known details in the lives of Bona Sforza and her son Sigismund Augustus, who co-ruled as grand duke of Lithuania and king of Poland with his father in these years, his putative relationship with Roxelana/Juliana is, of course, fiction.

NASAN'S FAMILY

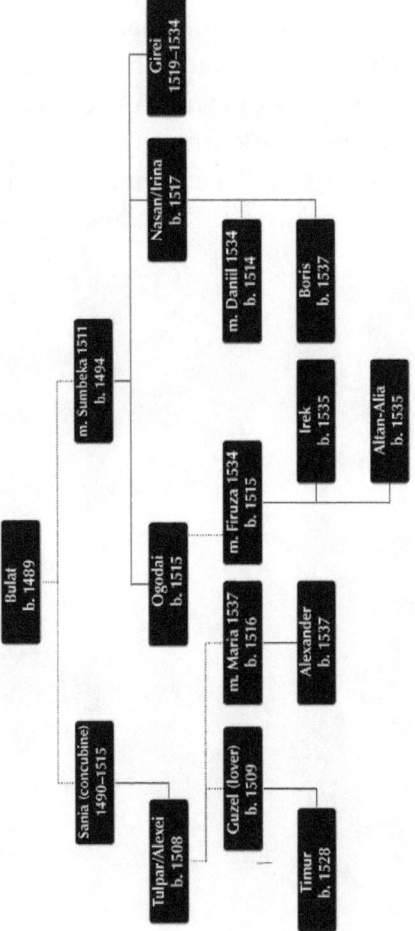

Bulat
b. 1489

Sania (concubine)
1490–1515

m. Sumbeka 1511
b. 1494

Tulpar/Alexei
b. 1508

Ogodai
b. 1515

Nasan/Irina
b. 1517

Girei
1519–1534

Guzel (lover)
b. 1509

m. Maria 1537
b. 1516

m. Firuza 1534
b. 1515

m. Daniil 1534
b. 1514

Timur
b. 1528

Alexander
b. 1537

Irek
b. 1535

Altan-Alia
b. 1535

Boris
b. 1537

Dotted lines indicate marriages and romantic relationships; solid lines indicate parent/child links.
Most couples had additional children who died before birth or in infancy; Bulat also has wives and concubines not listed by name.

KOLYCHEV CLAN

SELECTED MEMBERS OF THE HOUSE OF MOSCOW, 1440–1537

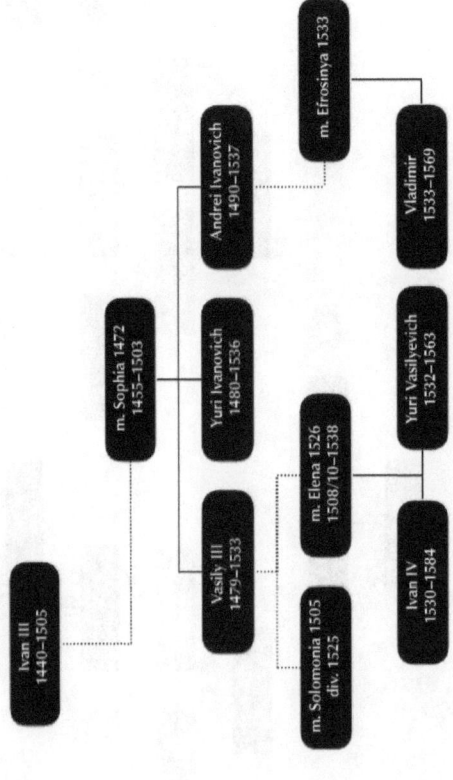

Acknowledgments

HERE I TIP MY HAT TO MY INVALUABLE WRITERS' GROUP, now in its tenth year, and to the members of Five Directions Press for their encouragement and support. As I have said before, I can't imagine writing a novel without them. And while I extend my gratitude to the many fine scholars whose works I consulted—and in particular to Ann Kleimola, who sent helpful comments on an earlier draft, as she has on the four previous books in this series—let me state yet again that none of them is any way responsible for the fictional use I have made of their findings.

To my husband and son—and, of course, the cats, who purred encouragingly at all the right moments—words cannot express my gratitude.

Last, to those who read the earlier books, my thanks. I hope you have enjoyed these journeys through the world of Ivan the Terrible's childhood and that you consider *The Shattered Drum* a worthy ending to the series.

The Author

AS A CHILD, C. P. LESLEY THOUGHT EVERYONE MADE UP stories while falling asleep. It never occurred to her that anyone would pay her for them, and for a long time, she was right—no one would. But after years of producing horrible prose, reading books about novel writing, and pestering hapless fellow writers and friends to read her drafts, some of the advice stuck, and she finished *The Not Exactly Scarlet Pimpernel*, then *The Golden Lynx* and its sequels: *The Winged Horse*, *The Swan Princess*, *The Vermilion Bird*, and *The Shattered Drum*.

She is currently working on Songs of Steppe & Forest, a series featuring characters from the Legends series who never had the space to tell their stories. The first, *Song of the Siren*, follows Roxelana (renamed Juliana) as she struggles with the consequences of her journey west, the marriage she has abandoned, and the events of the years between this book and the time we meet her again in 1541.

When not thinking up new ways to torture her characters, Lesley edits other people's manuscripts, reads voraciously, maintains her website, and practices classical ballet—an interest reflected in *Desert Flower* and *Kingdom of the Shades* (Tarkei Chronicles 1 and 2). She also hosts New Books in Historical Fiction, a channel in the New Books Network. You can find out more about her and her books at www.cplesley.com.

FORTHCOMING IN 2019

Song of the Siren

SONGS OF STEPPE & FOREST 1

Wawel Castle, Poland, December 1541

"LADY JULIANA WILL LIVE," A MALE VOICE SAID. "NOT AS she did before, of course. I doubt the young king will have much use for her now, despite her charms. It's too bad about the scarring. She was a beautiful woman." The cool, dispassionate tone contradicted any hint of concern implied by his words.

Was? She *was* a beautiful woman? I lay flat on my back, too weak and dispirited to demand that he explain what he meant. I tried to force my eyelids open, but I hadn't the strength even for that. Trapped in a nightmare world, I huddled, shivering, waiting for the ogre to appear at the door. I pushed and twisted, but my arms weighed heavy as granite on the bed and my feet stuck to the floor.

The doctor's callous verdict echoed in my head. Too bad about the scarring? She *was* a beautiful woman?

Tragedy bared its teeth, sucked me into its vortex. Without my face I was nothing. I had no purpose, no means of survival, no self. I existed to mirror the desires of men, to fulfill their passions while expressing none of my own. My beauty was the only currency I possessed. If I could not use it to draw men to me, I would starve. What point, then, in living?

Tears slid from the corners of my eyes, wetting the linen beneath my head. I lacked the power to wipe them away. "Oh, look," another voice said. My maidservant, Hanna. "She's crying. Do you think she heard you, Doctor?" A soft cloth touched my cheeks.

"Perhaps." The doctor still sounded indifferent, as if discussing my case at some society of physicians. If I had the energy, I would slap him. "I see no sign that she's awake, but I've had other patients report things I said under similar conditions. Smallpox causes extreme exhaustion. She may be able to hear but not respond. Just in case, you should talk to her, reassure her, like this."

Garlic-inflected breath passed my nose, and I guessed he had bent closer to examine me. "You will recover, Lady Juliana," he said, and this time I heard actual kindness in his voice. "The worst is over."

But I knew he was wrong. The worst lurked somewhere down the road of a bleak future, waiting to pounce when I was least prepared to resist.

http://www.fivedirectionspress.com/song-of-the-siren

PRAISE FOR LEGENDS OF THE FIVE DIRECTIONS

"*The Vermilion Bird* vividly envisions the culture clash between Russians and Tatars in the sixteenth century. Fans of historical fiction will enjoy this glimpse into a seldom explored corner of history, while fans of romance will delight in the unlikely love that blooms between a bluff Tatar prince and his scheming Russian bride—who is also the stepdaughter of his former lover."

—Linnea Hartsuyker, author of *The Half-Drowned King*

"Lyrical and compelling, *The Swan Princess* draws the reader into the world of sixteenth-century Russia, a world unfamiliar to many readers, which becomes vividly real in the hands of this master storyteller. The characters of Nasan, Daniil, and the others leap off the page. Perhaps most intriguing is the portrayal of the clash between the two vibrant but alien cultures of the Russians and the Tatars—frequently at war, occasionally bound by an uneasy and watchful peace."

—Ann Swinfen, author of *Voyage to Muscovy*

"An action and suspense-infused historical adventure that kept me turning the pages right to the end. The characters are so well-drawn, the historical facts so cleverly woven into the narrative, time and place so brilliantly evoked, I felt I was experiencing sixteenth-century Russia firsthand."

—Liza Perrat, author of the Bone Angel Trilogy

"Rich with cultural exotica and imaginative re-creation. We're swept backwards five centuries to an Eastern Europe of leather armor and Ottoman daggers, wrestling matches and horse races, a hooded eagle on a shoulder, a sheep's head on a platter. If you're suffering from Regency romance fatigue, *The Winged Horse* is the perfect antidote."

—Michael Schmicker, author of *The Witch of Napoli*

"Swiftly paced, with compelling characters and vivid scenes evoking distant Muscovy, *The Golden Lynx* is a find for lovers of historical fiction."

—*Russian Life*

If you enjoyed this book, please consider leaving a review at your favorite online bookseller and/or on GoodReads.

Five Directions Press publishes fiction, often but not exclusively devoted to exploring the rich tapestry of women's lives in many times and places—some real, some fantastical. For more information, see www.fivedirectionspress.com.

This book was typeset using Garamond, a body font dating from the early days of printing, with headings in Tangerine, chosen for its Arabic lines, evocative of Tatar script. The ornaments come from Type Embellishments One LET.

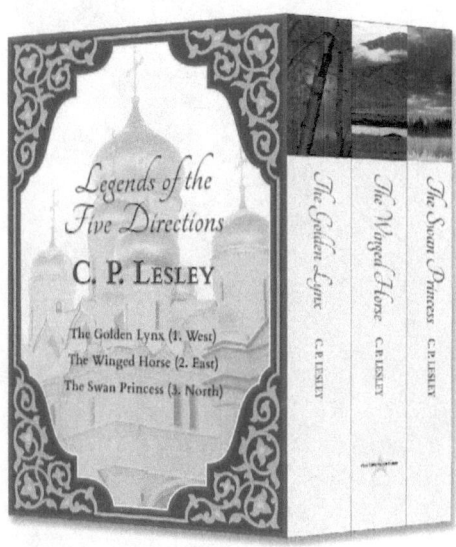

WHO IS THE GOLDEN LYNX?

This question drives the first book in Legends of the Five Directions, a series that will sweep you to the distant world of sixteenth-century Russia, amid the descendants of Genghis Khan and courts that could teach the Borgias a thing or two about political ambition, assassination, and chicanery. Follow Nasan and her kinsfolk as they struggle for power, honor, identity, and love across the steppe and through the vast forests of the Russian North.

"A richly depicted, exciting adventure set amongst the Tatars of 16th-century Central Russia. Fans of historical romance will find this a delight."
—Yangsze Choo, author of the acclaimed novel *The Ghost Bride*

http://www.fivedirectionspress.com/boxsets

The Falcon Soars
Falcon Trilogy 3

After causing the death of her lover and bringing the wrath of the IRA down on her family, Peppa Mueller is determined to redeem herself, even if it means suppressing her falcon totem. But past enemies are looking for her.

Her promising neurosurgery career is interrupted by an assassination attempt. Then the one friend she's always counted on is called away on an emergency mission to Tibet. Convinced the mission will fail without her medical knowledge, Peppa jeopardizes her career and upcoming marriage to join him.

In the wilds of the Himalayas, Peppa will find out that out that unless you make peace with your past, there is no future.

"Unpredictable, intelligent, and imaginative, this story soars into the unknown. Climb on and enjoy the flight of your life."

—JJ Marsh, author of the Beatrice Stubbs series

http://www.fivedirectionspress.com/falcon-soars